PRAISE FOR *Thunder of Time*

"A fast-paced thriller."
—*Rocky Mountain News*

"Enough toothsome confrontations and century-hopping to please both dinosaur and time-travel aficionados."
—*Booklist*

PRAISE FOR *Footprints of Thunder*

"A classic end-of-the-world novel in the tradition of *Lucifer's Hammer*—an utterly original vision of the apocalypse."
—*Douglas Preston,*
New York Times **bestselling author of** *Blasphemy*

"Riveting, nonstop action."
—*Booklist*

"*Footprints of Thunder* kept me up past dawn, red-eyed and riveted. A true roller coaster of a read."
—*Lincoln Child,*
New York Times **bestselling author of** *Deep Storm*

ALSO BY JAMES F. DAVID

Footprints of Thunder
Fragments
Ship of the Damned
Before the Cradle Falls
Judgment Day
*The Book of Summer**

*Forthcoming

THUNDER OF
TIME

James F. David

A TOM DOHERTY ASSOCIATES BOOK
NEW YORK

This is a work of fiction. All of the characters, organizations, and events portrayed in this novel are either products of the author's imagination or are used fictitiously.

THUNDER OF TIME

Copyright © 2006 by James F. David

A Tor Book
Published by Tom Doherty Associates, LLC
175 Fifth Avenue
New York, NY 10010

www.tor.com

Tor® is a registered trademark of Tom Doherty Associates, LLC.

ISBN-13: 978-0-7653-4684-1
ISBN-10: 0-7653-4684-2

First Edition: April 2006
First Mass Market Edition: January 2008

Printed in the United States of America

0 9 8 7 6 5 4 3 2 1

Footprints of Thunder was my first novel, and has proved to be the most popular. To many of my readers, dinosaurs are simply irresistible. I admit to sharing that feeling, so it was a joy to revisit the world created in *Footprints of Thunder,* where dinosaurs from the Cretaceous past and modern humans came face-to-face.

Thanks to Gale for being my first reader, the worst job in the world, and to Bethany, Katie, Abby, and Drew, for early reading and helpful feedback. For most of you, science fiction would not be your first choice in genres but you are stuck with me and this is what I write. I'll try to do more books like *Before the Cradle Falls* in the future.

This book is dedicated to all of those readers who asked, "Just what is it that they discovered on the moon?" Now you can know.

Both the novelist and the physicist are seeking truth—for the novelist, truth in the world of the mind and the heart; for the physicist, truth in the world of force and mass. In seeking truth, both the novelist and the physicist invent. Both kinds of invention are important; both ultimately must be tested against experiment.

—Alan Lightman, in *The Future of Spacetime*
    by Stephen Hawking, Kip Thorne, Igor Novikov,
    Timothy Ferris, and Alan Lightman

DRAMATIS PERSONAE

Alaska/Fox Valley Environmental Research Station

VALERIE CONROY—Materials control assistant, Fox Valley Environmental Research Station.

JENNIFER DEWITT—Assembly specialist, Fox Valley Environmental Research Station.

TORU KAWABATA—Director, Fox Valley Environmental Research Station.

LATOYA MONTANA—Chemical engineer, Fox Valley Environmental Research Station.

PHAT NYANG—Program and system analyst, Fox Valley Environmental Research Station.

EILENE STROMKI—Sled dog racer and Elizabeth Hawthorne's guide.

VINCE WALTERS—Assistant Director, Fox Valley Environmental Research Station.

MARISSA WELLING—Physical chemist, Fox Valley Environmental Research Station.

LAWRENCE WHITEY—Engineer, Fox Valley Environmental Research Station.

MARGARET WINGLET (WINGS)—Executive assistant, Fox Valley Environmental Research Station.

Washington, D.C.

JOEL BASS—Secretary of State, former U.N. ambassador, former governor of California.

WILLAMINA (WILLA) BROWN—Vice President, former Ohio State University professor of economics.

MASON CLARK—Chief of Staff for President Pearl.

JOHN FLANNERY—Chairman of the Joint Chiefs of Staff, general, army, former Green Beret and tank commander.

ELIZABETH HAWTHORNE—Former White House Chief of Staff, defense lobbyist for Grayson, Weinert, and Goldfarb.

MARLIESS KRUPP—Director, Homeland Security, former deputy director of the FBI, attorney general of Idaho.

COURTNEY (COURT) LEFAVRE—Counsel to the president.

CAROLINE MAUCK—Director of the CIA, former ambassador to England, and former U.S. Attorney General under the Pasternak administration.

JARED PEARL—President, former governor of Florida.

HONOR PERKINS—Secretary of Defense, general, former candidate for president.

BILL RAWLINS—Partner at Grayson, Weinert, and Goldfarb, specializing in defense lobbying.

Yucatan Team

MITCH HOPE—Dinosaur ranger, temporarily assigned to the Office of Security Science.

JOSE IBARRA—Dinosaur ranger, former neighbor of Mariel Weatherby, temporarily assigned to the Office of Security Science.

CARROLLEE CHEN-SLATER-PUGLISI—Special investigator, Office of Security Science, married to Emmett.

ROBERT RIPMAN—Dinosaur hunter, guide, poacher, childhood friend of John Roberts.

JOHN ROBERTS—Field investigator, Office of Security Science, childhood friend of Robert Ripman.

NIKKI RYDEN—Friend of Kenny Randall, civilian specialist, Office of Security Science.

MARION WAYNE—Senior dinosaur ranger, temporarily assigned to the Office of Security Science.

Moon Team

REGINA (REGGIE) BATES—Associate Director, Office of Security Science, physician, astrophysicist.

NICK PAULSON—Director, Office of Security Science.

ROSA PEREZ—Experimental air and spacecraft navigator and pilot, assigned to Area 51, Groom Lake, Nevada.

EMMETT PUGLISI—Field investigator, astrophysicist, cocreator of the Randall-Puglisi time quilt model, married to Carrollee.

JONATHAN SMITH—Aurora pilot, operating out of Area 51, Groom Lake, Nevada.

PHIL YAMAMOTO—Senior programming specialist, Office of Security Science.

Eco-terrorists

WINIFRED (CHIPMUNK) JOHNSON—Defender of the environment, shares the temple of her body with the soul of a chipmunk.

RAMONA (STAR) KOSLOWSKI—Environmental activist, tree sitter, follower of Vince Walters.

Space Station

NEV RHYAKOV—Cosmonaut, fond of American rock-and-roll oldies.

Russian Special Forces

ANATOLE (ANDY) BARANOV—Captain, Spetsnaz (Russian Special Forces), Weapons Recovery Unit.

LEONID (LEO) IVANOV—Senior sergeant, Spetsnaz, scout, Weapons Recovery Unit.

IVAN MORTIKOV—Security systems specialist, Spetsnaz, Weapons Recovery Unit.

KARL PETROV—Sergeant, Spetsnaz, Weapons Recovery
  Unit.
ALEKSANDER PROSOL—Spetsnaz, Weapons Recovery Unit.
BORIS SMIRNOV—Spetsnaz, Weapons Recovery Unit.

DRAMATIS PERSONAE

THUNDER OF
TIME

PROLOGUE

How did you sleep this week?"

"The same."

"Still having the nightmares about dinosaurs?"

"Of course."

"Which one?"

"All of them?"

"Why do you insist on starting like this?"

"Because it's a waste of time."

"Yet, you keep coming back?"

"I can't stop picking my nose either."

She did not think it was as funny as he did.

"Fine. I dreamed the one about the friend I lost when Portland was taken. I can see the city but it's like . . . like it's a ghost. You can see right through it. It was like that just before they bombed it. My friends and I were out of town when it happened, and when we headed back to Portland it wasn't there anymore. We never did find our homes again. In fact, all we found in the Portland quilt was a lot of trouble. That's where I met my first dinosaur. But we never found Portland. It had just disappeared! Except, every once in a while we could see it shimmering in the distance like a mirage. The city was coming and going, like it was trying to get back from wherever it went. Portland is like that in my dream. I can see people in the city, standing in the streets; men, women, and children, and they're trying to get out but they can't. There is some kind of invisible barrier stopping them.

My friend is there in the front, pounding his fists on the barrier, begging me to help him, but every time I reach out for him, my hand passes right through him like he's made of smoke. All of the people are like that, like they are ghosts."

"Why do you call them ghosts?"

"I didn't say they were ghosts, I said they were like ghosts."

"Ghosts are the spirits of the dead."

"What's your point?"

"Did you do the homework I assigned you?"

"I left high school behind ten years ago. Actually, it left me—gone like everything and everyone in Portland and fifty cities around the world. Believe it or not, I still have the last homework assignment Mr. Landers ever assigned. It's an essay on my biggest personal challenge and how I overcame it. I've been thinking of rewriting it."

He laughed. She waited for him to stop, that annoying blank look on her face.

"Yes, I did what you asked. I knew all of it anyway."

"What did you find?"

Exasperated, he sighed. She would not give up until he recited.

"Scientists call what happened to the planet a 'time quilt.' Nuclear testing back in the fifties and sixties caused it. When they started testing hydrogen fusion bombs, the megatonnage was enough to create tiny black holes. The black holes created ripples in the fabric of time that radiated into the past and future. Wherever the ripples intersected, things and people dropped through holes in time. That explains why history records bizarre events like people suddenly vanishing, frogs mysteriously falling out of the sky and even explains spontaneous human combustion."

He stopped, looking directly at her.

"Did you know that all of this was discovered by a college kid? He based his theory on the work of Zorastrus, an ancient prophet."

"Tell me the rest," she said patiently.

"Eventually all of the little ripples converged to make a

few super waves and when these intersected it created a huge temporal rift and our time and the Cretaceous period collided. That's why dinosaurs are grazing on golf courses and decimating the elk herds."

"What else did you find?"

He hated her when she was like this. A plump woman, gray hair tied in a tight bun, wearing a pinstriped business suit, she looked like a high school teacher. With bookshelves lining two of her walls, her office felt like the school library—not that he had spent much time there.

"No one knows for sure what happened to the people who disappeared. Most scientists think they were displaced into the future."

"Where they are alive, right?"

"Some think so."

"Some?"

"All right, most think so. But they're not sure about the people in Portland because that was where the president decided to try and fix the whole mess by detonating a hundred warheads. It didn't work."

"It stopped further time disruption."

He did not say anything. He sensed where she was going with this and he did not want to go there.

"You said there were people inside Portland with your friend. Did you recognize any of them?"

"No."

"None of them?"

"I said, 'no.' "

"Were your friend's parents there?"

"Maybe. Sometimes in my dream I can see his dad's church. There are people in front of it. They might be his parents."

"You don't recognize anyone else?"

"No."

"Your father isn't there?"

"No," he said too quickly.

Now she waited. She used silence as a weapon; a battering ram that knocked down his resistance. He held out, letting minutes pass.

"Close your eyes," she said finally. "I'm going to guide you through your dream. Maybe I can help you identify some of the people you are seeing."

"Forget it. I don't believe in hypnosis."

"We've done this before, and you know it is not hypnosis." He gave in.

"You don't have to guide me. The son-of-a-bitch is there."

"Who?"

"My father! That's what you were fishing for."

"And he's asking for you to help him?"

"No. He's the only one not asking me for help. All of them—my friend, strangers, my friend's parents—everyone is asking me to save them. They want me to get them back from wherever it is they ended up. Believe me, wherever they are, they don't want to be there."

"But not your father?"

"No."

"He likes it there when no one else does?"

"No. He wants to get back, too!"

"But he is the only one not asking for help. Why do you think that is?"

"I don't know, but last night I dreamed about the one-eyed tyrannosaur again. That dream scares the shit out of me. In the dream, he has both of his eyes and he has me and a friend trapped under a log. His huge jaws are snapping at us."

"We've talked about that dream. You weren't under that log, your friends were. You had left them. They put an arrow in its eye and got away."

"I didn't leave them! We were separated! I would have helped them if I had known what was happening. Those two were helpless without me and I'm not the kind of guy who abandons a buddy in trouble."

He was half out of his chair. Now he settled back, realizing he was nearly shouting. Her face was as impassive as ever.

"Let's finish with the other dream first," she said.

"You know, we never discussed my dream about the little old lady and her pet dinosaur," he said, his breathing returning to normal. "She fed it sugar from her apartment window and turned it into a pet."

"You saw that re-created in a television movie. It happened at the edge of the New York time quilt, not in Portland, and you've never been to New York."

"But in my dream I killed her pet dinosaur."

"Her iguanodon was killed by members of a street gang, not you."

"Not in my dream. I shoot it right between the eyes and then she comes hobbling across the meadow, crying, and lies down next to the iguanodon and dies of a broken heart. Shouldn't we talk about that dream?"

Now she drew the silence weapon again. He looked at her book titles. *Complete Works of Anna Freud, Love and Guilt, Postmodern Therapies in the New World*. She was still using the weapon. He looked past her and out the window. An apatosaur strolled by, ignoring the occupants of the building. He got up and walked to the large window that made up one wall of her office. She rotated in her chair, watching him. The window looked out into the Portland Preserve, which was supervised by the National Park Service and their dinosaur rangers. A half dozen apatosaurs grazed the perimeter near the fence line. With no predators in the preserve, the apatosaurs had grown careless; none were keeping watch.

"This is why I picked you," he said. "If I have to be in a city, I don't want to be any deeper than this."

"That's flattering."

He had not offended her and he ignored the remark.

"Why isn't your father asking for help?" she probed again.

He stared into the meadow but now he was seeing the dream.

"When I was nine, I played Little League baseball. My dad was a big baseball fan. I was small for my age then, and not very good. When they had to let me play, they always stuck me in right field—little kids can't hit to right. My dad liked to stand behind the plate, coaching me, telling me to 'knock it out of the park.' I remember my last time at bat. I swung at the first two balls and missed. Then Dad said, 'Wait for a good one.' I let the next one go. It was right down the middle. As I walked away from the plate he said, 'You'll never be worth nuthin.' I never played again."

Now he went back to his chair, slumping, settling deep into the soft leather.

"In the dream, my father isn't asking for help because he thinks there's nothing I can do to help him. He thinks I'm worthless."

There was silence again, but it wasn't a weapon this time. It was medicine.

"So you went your own way," she suggested.

"I'm very good at what I do."

"You're a killer."

He smiled, then shrugged.

"Yes, but I'm very good at it. Dad would be proud."

1 · NORTH QUILT

While there are those who would play politics even in this time of unprecedented crisis, my decision to seal the break in time with a nuclear detonation on American soil was the only viable option. While we cannot bring back the family and friends we have lost, or send the dinosaurs back to their own time, we have stopped the time disruption once and for all.

—*Scot McIntyre, President of the United States*

WESTERN ALASKA, OCTOBER,
TEN YEARS AFTER THE TIME QUILT

"Hike!" Eilene Stromki shouted to her dogs, urging the team on.

There was little need to shout, no need to crack a whip. Her huskies lived to run, winning the Iditarod two of the last three years since it had been resumed. Sixteen miles out from her ranch, they were climbing a six percent grade. The dogs were laboring, breaths deep but steady, each dog steaming like a locomotive. Eilene knew her dogs like family; their personalities, their likes and dislikes, what spooked them and what motivated each.

Kamiak ran in the lead, a position he was bred for. Another lead dog, Max, was back at her compound and was almost as good as Kamiak, but there wasn't another dog in Alaska with Kamiak's nose for the trail. Bacardi and Tecumsah ran second in line as swing dogs, both strong and quick to answer to Eilene's commands to "Gee!" and "Haw!," turning the sled right and left. Wemme and Roscoe ran next in line, perfectly matched in strength, stamina, and heart.

Blacky and Nellie were mid team, followed by Draco and Monty, good natured, steady and strong. Lindy and Wanda came last, running as wheel dogs just in front of the sled. It would be Lindy's last Iditarod. Reliable, and a peacemaker in the pack, she had run seven races with Eilene, and she would retire her reluctantly. Like a grand dame reaching middle age, Lindy clung to her youth, even as the trail aged her prematurely. Sensing her retirement, Lindy pushed herself hard, never holding the others back. The team would sense no weakness in Lindy's last run.

"Hike, Kamiak!" Eilene shouted, encouraging her powerful lead dog to keep a steady pace.

Eilene's teams seldom won sprints, but the Iditarod was 1,100 miles of treacherous terrain and fickle weather. Victory went to the strongest, not the swiftest. With legs as powerful as pistons, a broad chest, and the heart of a champion, Kamiak was the key to Eilene's victories. With a blaze of white on his chest, the wolf-gray husky punched through the thin frozen crust to firm footing underneath. The lead dog had to be the strongest to set the pace and break the trail. The swing dogs, Bacardi and Tecumsah, did a share of the plowing, each pair in the rest of the team finding the way easier than the one ahead. Only Kamiak at the lead had no one to compact the snow for him. Eyes busy, the lead dog picked the best footing for the rest as they raced over nearly hidden trails and across frozen lakes. With a preternatural feel for the trail, Kamiak deftly skirted loose snow, polished ice, and crumbling ledges, and he did this in thick fog and howling blizzards.

The day was mild; comfortable. At fifteen degrees, slight southerly wind, and thin overcast, Eilene wore only goggles, the hood of her parka thrown back, enjoying the crisp feel of the wind on her permanently weathered face. She loved the silence of the trail, the few forest sounds masked by the constant whooshing of the wind past her ears and the steady thumping rhythm of paws. She'd heard that marathon runners entered a psychological zone somewhere between the sixth and tenth mile, oblivious to their surroundings, totally within themselves, as if running in an alternate dimension, a dimension of one. Sled dog racing was the opposite; the quiet isolation teased the senses into opening wide, like the iris in total darkness, blossoming to its fullest to catch every stray photon. Eilene was more alive on the trail, more aware of nature's nuances, every scent, sight, and sound. After a long trail run, Eilene came back to civilization more than what she had been when she left.

"Gee," Eilene called, signaling a turn.

Kamiak, who knew the trail, had already started into the right turn before the command. As they came to the turn, Eilene leaned into it, then dropped briefly to the ground, holding on to the handlebars, dragging the sled around to complete the turn. Three quick running steps and she was back on, the team straining to bring the sled back to running speed.

Eilene was using her racing sled today. Built out of lightweight wood, the sled carried most of the required gear: axe, sleeping bag, snowshoes, spare booties for the dogs, food for both her and the dogs, spare boots and clothes for her, and a rifle. The rifle wasn't required under the rules, but Eilene began carrying one after a moose had gotten into her team, killing two of her best dogs.

Another mile and she slowed the team to a walk. The dogs, with their tongues lolling and legs still strong, were ready to run on command. They crested a small ridge, then started down a gentle slope. Eilene gently applied the brake to keep the sled from sliding into her dogs. The crest was rocky, but as they came down the slope the soil improved and the forest thickened with old growth firs. Three months a year there was a hiking trail here, now buried under a month's snow. The trail led to a small lake, loaded with trout. It would be a snow meadow by now, the surface frozen a foot thick, covered in a deep blanket of snow.

There was a fork in the trail now and Kamiak automatically veered right. They hadn't taken the left fork since the government stole more of the land and fenced it off. Now it was restricted, with no hunting, fishing, or sledding. Eilene had run the perimeter many times, curious about what went on inside, but there was little to see. The base was built in a small valley known locally as Fox Valley, named by the trappers who had worked the area up until the last section of fence went up, cutting them off from their livelihood. Eilene resented being cut off from land she had hunted and fished since childhood, but the fence worked two ways. It kept her out, but it kept the government people in.

The lake was just ahead, a bright white oval ringed by ancient protecting forest giants. Coming through the last of the trees, Eilene let Kamiak lead them into the center where she stopped the team and set the brake. As one, the dog team lay down to rest, panting to control their body temperature. Their thick fur protected them from the cold of the snow.

While the dogs rested, Eilene would check their condition, examining each paw, each limb, chest, and muzzle, looking for wounds, wear, or bruising. She also noted how long it took them to recover, an indicator of their physical condition. Sled dogs were as finely conditioned as Olympic athletes, and the dogs would soon be up and prancing, anxious to resume the run.

Unzipping the sled bag, Eilene dug out "honeyballs" and tossed the snacks to the dogs. Sled dogs could burn up to ten thousand calories a day and the baseball-sized honeyballs were loaded with the fuel and nutrients the dogs needed. Made from beef, powdered eggs, brewer's yeast, vegetable oil, multivitamins, and honey, they were relished by the dogs. Tossing the last honeyball to Lindy, Eilene leaned against the sled munching on honeyball crumbs, enjoying the feel of the bright sun on her weathered face.

Suddenly there was a peal of thunder, followed by a bright flash and a warm blast of air. The dogs yelped in surprise, jumping to their feet and jerking the sled. Eilene stumbled and fell, confused. The blast of heat told her that the lightning had struck nearby.

Getting to her feet Eilene searched the sky for the storm. Being at the center of the lake gave her a 360-degree view and there was nothing but thin overcast. Eilene could still feel the warmth from the lightning strike and briefly worried that it had started a forest fire. Then through the trees to the east she saw a ribbon of bright green—not the forest green of the north woods, but bright variegated greens. With a splat, a large mass of snow dropped from a fir bordering the lake. With her finely tuned senses, Eilene heard the forest begin to play the symphony of spring; the steady drip, drip, plop sounds of the spring thaw. Her dogs were standing, ears pointed, listening to the sounds of spring in winter.

"Let's go take a look, Kamiak," Eilene called, releasing the brake. "Hike," she shouted, the dogs straining against their harnesses, breaking the sled free. Guiding the team toward the peculiar colors in the forest, she kept the dogs to a walk, letting Kamiak pick his way through the trees. Eilene was amazed by what she saw. She knew these woods; a long march of trees, interrupted only by the occasional lake, natural meadow, or forest road. The closest logging was six miles south. Yet, now the forest ended abruptly and at its edge was vegetation like she had only seen in movies. Most of the foliage was knee high, but there were taller shrubs and, in the distance, towering palms. Instead of needles, leaves were broad, flat, and glossy and a riot of green.

Calling for a stop, Eilene left the sled in the trees, her team alert, curious, sniffing the unfamiliar. Humid heat washed her, flowing through the trees, past her team to dissipate in the vastness of the north. Stopping at the edge of the forest she stared dumbstruck.

Eilene wasn't a traveler, if you didn't count the long sled races, and she rarely left Alaska. She had never been farther south than Seattle and no farther east than Calgary, so she had never experienced tropical vegetation. She looked at it now with the same childish wonder of Dorothy, stepping from her fallen house into Munchkinland. A fern at the edge of the clearing tilted toward Eilene, its tip barely over the crude line that marked the beginning of the harsh conditions of a northern coniferous forest, as if to taste this new environment. Eilene kicked the fern, the only plant she could identify. It was real, giving way as she tapped it back and forth.

"Kamiak," Eilene said, loud enough for her team to hear. "I heard about these but I never saw one except on TV."

The heat of the jungle warmed the forest and Eilene unzipped her parka. Taking two steps into the vegetation, she sniffed air flavored with foreign perfumes and the stink of rot. Every nuance of the jungle smelled as fresh to her as a baby's first tastes of food. Behind her, more sensitive noses were busy with canine curiosity. With even less experience than Eilene, the dogs could not tell harmless plants from predator animals and missed the olfactory warning.

"It's a time quilt," Eilene announced, talking to the dogs. "They got something like this down where Portland used to be, except I heard most of the original plants are dead now. Damn foolish city folks turned it into a park."

Suddenly, thirty yards away, a head appeared in the chest-high foliage, stared right at Eilene, then dropped down again. The head was triangular, earless, the skin reptilian green. Cursing her stupidity, Eilene remembered that the Portland time quilt hadn't just brought plants to the future. Eilene hurried back to the team.

"Trouble coming, Kamiak," Eilene announced.

Sensing her fear, the team paced and whined in their harnesses, anxious for action, flight or fight. The trees were raining now, the snow melting at a dangerous pace. As the water dripped from higher boughs to lower, the burden on the limbs increased, the lower boughs bending, threatening to break. Under a steady shower, Eilene pulled Kamiak around 180 degrees and started back the way they had come. The runners cut deep into the wet snow now and Eilene ran behind the sled, pushing to help get the sled up to speed. Risking a look behind, she saw the dinosaur standing at the edge of the forest, head down, sniffing the snow. Then its head came up and it sniffed the air. It stood on two feet, counterbalanced with a long tail. It had two long arms ending in clawed hands, its head carried on a long neck. When it finished sniffing the air it looked at Eilene and her team retreating through the woods, then at the snow again. Then it raised its head, let out a screech as sharp and as penetrating as a chainsaw hitting a tree spike. A few seconds' later two more of the creatures came out of the jungle foliage, heads down, sniffing the snow.

"Hike, Kamiak, hike!" Eilene shouted.

Risking another look back, she could see all three of the creatures had their heads up now, pointed at Eilene. Then the first creature, slightly bigger than the other two, raised its head and bugled long and loud. Then all three charged into the woods. Quickly, Eilene estimated the speed of the predators—she wouldn't make it across the lake.

"Haw! Kamiak, haw!" Eilene shouted.

At Eilene's command, Kamiak executed a sharp turn, and like a train of Conestoga wagons circling to repel an attack, the dogs came around. The dogs barked and yelped, snapping at each other in confusion. Eilene threw the sled to its side, and then dug in her sled bag for her rifle. With the rifle in one hand, Eilene commanded her dogs to lie down and drew her knife, running along the line of dogs, cutting them free. Then she threw herself behind the sled, slapping the rifle on the side, taking aim down the open sights.

Eilene and her team were near the middle of the lake, the surface slushy from the jungle heat. The heat was dissipating quickly; however, the ice surface was still protected by two feet of wet, insulating snow.

The attacking dinosaurs came out of the woods, a surreal spectacle of long-extinct predators, emerging from a winter wonderland forest, their three-toed feet digging deep into the snow for traction with six-inch serrated claws. Driven by hunting lust, they came on, oblivious to the unfamiliar surface or the rapidly falling temperature.

The dinosaurs spread out as they came. Lining up her sights on the chest of the big dinosaur in the lead, Eilene's finger tightened on the trigger. She took her time, making sure of the shot. She only carried six rounds. Then the dinosaur slipped, wobbled, and went down, skidding through the mush on the surface. Her target now lost in a spray of snow, she turned to the left, finding this dinosaur swinging wide as if to circle and come in behind. Her dogs were all up now, barking and posturing. Then with the bravery of youth, reckless Tecumsah charged the dinosaur Eilene was taking aim on, Roscoe and Wemme right behind. Eilene fired over the heads of her attacking dogs, the report of the rifle triggering a new level of aggressiveness in the dogs, their knife-sharp barks echoing off a distant ridge. The slug hit behind the dinosaur's right shoulder. The beast stumbled, slipped, and skidded, spraying pink snow. Tecumsah, Roscoe, and Wemme charged the wounded predator. There was no time to confirm the kill.

A flanking dinosaur came from behind Eilene's right shoulder. She pulled the bolt back, ejecting the spent shell, and then shoved the bolt forward and down, setting another round in the chamber. Turning, she saw the dinosaur behind her leap. The dinosaur jumped with power evolved for bigger prey. The dinosaur flew at her, clawed feet extended. She fired from the hip, the bullet burying in the belly of the beast. The expanding lead slug tore through soft tissues, ripping open vital organs, but nothing could stop the physics of the attack. Reflexively, Eilene turned, curling into a fetal position. As she cringed, a gray blur flew over her head, crashing into the onrushing dinosaur.

Still trailing the remnant of his harness, Kamiak flew at the dinosaur. The dinosaur twisted in midair at the threat. That motion saved Eilene's life, as claws as sharp as surgical instruments missed her by inches. The dinosaur landed next to her, its tail driving her into the wet snow. Kamiak was at its throat and the dinosaur ignored Eilene, fending off Kamiak. Two more dogs came over the sled, indistinguishable blurs joining the fight.

Dodging the flailing tail, Eilene searched for her rifle, buried somewhere in the slushy surface of the snow. But with each whip of the powerful tail the gun was driven deeper. Now Bacardi and Lindy jumped the sled, joining the fight. The dinosaur struggled to its feet, Kamiak hanging from its neck. With a swipe of its clawed hands, it knocked Kamiak free. The dog tumbled across the snow, then rolled to his feet, three long bloody gashes in his gray side. Kamiak staggered a few steps and then collapsed. With two more quick swipes, Draco and Wanda were tossed aside, landing with a splash of blood.

Gut-shot, the dinosaur stood, staggering in a circle, blood pumping from a hole in its midsection. There was a gash on its neck, streaming more blood. Barcardi and Lindy were circling, just out of the reach of its long arms, keeping the dinosaur's attention. The dogs only had to stay out of the dinosaur's reach to win the fight. The dinosaur was slowly bleeding to death.

Behind her, Eilene heard another fight erupt as her remaining dogs took on the big dinosaur, quickly losing the fight. Like Custer surrounded by his faithful men, Eilene watched her side slowly lose the battle. With a final painful yelp, the fight behind her was over, the big dinosaur coming around to help mop up the rest of her dogs.

Circling around the sled, the beast came on slowly, as wary of its footing as of the circling dogs. Bacardi and Lindy parted, letting the big dinosaur through. The beast went directly to its mate, sniffing at its wounds. The gut-shot dinosaur snapped at the big one but did not bite. A deep whimper emanated from the big dinosaur. Then it hissed at Eilene. Pulling her knife, Eilene backed away, inching around the sled and the little protection it afforded. If the dogs could draw the dinosaurs away from the sled, she could dig for the rifle. But Bacardi and Lindy were no match for two dinosaurs, even if one was wounded.

Blacky, Nellie, Draco, Monty, Wanda, and Kamiak were all dead or dying. Risking a look, she saw Tecumsah, Roscoe, and Wemme savaging the body of the first dinosaur she had shot. The beast was still moving, but lying on its side, ineffectually swiping at the dogs. Putting her fingers in her mouth, she whistled for the rest of the team. Tecumsah, Roscoe, and Wemme came running. Her whistle surprised the remaining dinosaurs and both heads snapped around to look at her, then at the oncoming dogs.

Bacardi didn't wait for reinforcements; darting inside the reach of the big dinosaur, he snapped at a leg, then leaped back. Bacardi was too slow. With a jabbing swipe, Barcardi was impaled in the neck, his head nearly severed as the dinosaur finished the sweep. With a triumphant roar, the dinosaur bellowed at Lindy, challenging the canine. Growling, wise Lindy held her distance, dancing out of reach.

Now Tecumsah, Roscoe, and Wemme arrived, jaws bloody, snapping at the wounded dinosaur from behind. The dinosaur turned to face the dogs, but the capacity for whipcrack turns was being lost with each drop of blood. As the dinosaur turned, Tecumsah charged inside its reach, taking a piece of one leg. Weak, pain clouding its judgment, the dinosaur jabbed at Tecumsah who dodged the strike, and then clamped his jaws behind the dinosaur's claws. With a screech the dinosaur jerked free, half lifting Tecumsah off the ground before a clawed finger was torn from its hand. Off balance, the beast staggered backward, tail flailing, slapping the sled into Eilene who tumbled back, skidding across the surface of the lake. The wounded dinosaur went down, Roscoe and Wemme charging. Violently shaking the trophy finger, Tecumsah dropped it, going for another piece of the fallen dinosaur.

With their backs to the big dinosaur, the dogs did not see it turn away from Lindy, enraged by the screams of its wounded mate. Lindy charged when it turned, the big dinosaur sensing the attack and snapping back around like a bent limb suddenly released. Four claws caught the leaping dog in the head, her skull crushed from the blow, her eyes, nose, ears skinned from her head. Then the dinosaur turned toward its beleaguered mate. Eilene shouted a warning, but the dogs could not hear over their blood lust.

With two quick steps, the dinosaur was within reach, swiping at Wemme, catching the husky in the side, knocking him off the wounded dinosaur. Wemme landed, rolled, yelping in pain, a cry so pitiful it would echo in Eilene's mind forever. Wemme's cry saved Roscoe, who dodged the next blow. Brave, reckless, Tecumsah attacked the big dinosaur, ripping a hunk from its calf, and then darting aside. But the big dinosaur was not gut-shot, its throat had not been torn open, and it was strong and quick. It caught Tecumsah with a back swipe that ripped his haunch, sending Tecumsah tumbling across the snow.

Seeing a chance, Eilene got up and ran for the fallen dinosaur, now struggling to roll over and get to its feet. Eilene buried the eight-inch blade in its neck, sawing furiously. Reflexively, the dinosaur raised its clawed foot, swiping at Eilene who jumped back, falling into the snow. With the knife in its throat, the beast could only whimper now, trying to dislodge the weapon. Turning, the big dinosaur saw its mate take its last gurgling breaths, lying in a bed of pink snow. Now it looked at the bloody mound where Tecumsah, Roscoe, and Wemme had finished off the first dinosaur Eilene had shot, and then back at the dinosaur with Eilene's knife in its mate's neck. Then it whimpered: a sad mournful sound. When the whimper died, the animal was silent. The big dinosaur was alone in an environment beyond its experience, as foreign to the beast as the surface of Mars would be to Eilene. However, it did not retreat to the deepness of the forest where it had the advantage. Instead, it raised its head, staring at Eilene, not with the hunting eyes she had seen before, but with malevolence.

Weaponless, Eilene backed away, the dinosaur studying her moves, judging her as an adversary. Slogging through wet snow, Eilene looked as helpless as she was. The big dinosaur was smart, calculating. Then, without warning—no hiss, no screech, no call—the dinosaur leaped over the sled, landing ten feet away, eyes fixed on Eilene, who continued to back across the lake. The dinosaur took a step toward Eilene when Roscoe ran to a position between Eilene and the dinosaur. The dinosaur paused, studying the dog. Now Tecumsah circled the beast, taking position next to Roscoe. Tecumsah was bleeding, his left haunch and tail soaked in blood.

Like most sled dogs, Eilene's were a mixed breed of malamute, Siberian husky, and wolf. The dogs were bred for stamina, not aggressiveness, but the dinosaurs had awakened a gene that brought out the wolf in her dogs. Eilene's heart cheered for her brave dogs, but two dogs were no match for the dinosaur.

The dinosaur's eyes were busy, studying the dogs and Eilene, assessing the threat, planning the attack. Then there was movement to the beast's left, and its head cocked. Eilene looked to see Kamiak coming through the snow, fur matted with black blood. He came in an arc, leaving a trail of bloody pawprints in the snow, red polka dots marking the path from where he had been thrown, to Eilene. Then Kamiak pushed between Tecumsah and Roscoe, taking a position a half body ahead of the other dogs. Once again Kamiak was in the lead.

With the return of the heart of the team, the dogs had new courage and it welled up in Eilene too.

"Go back to where you came from, or you'll end up dead just like the others!" Eilene shouted.

The dinosaur's head cocked sideways but it held its ground, replying with a defiant scream that crossed the roar of a lion with the shriek of an eagle. The dogs responded with guttural growls, heads low to the ground. Then the dinosaur lowered its head, eyes locked on Kamiak. With a bark Kamiak charged and with a hunting instinct called from their genetic memories, Roscoe and Tecumsah ran left and right, circling the dinosaur. The dinosaur took a swipe at Kamiak, but the dog's attack was a feint, the badly wounded dog skidding to a stop, prehistoric claws slicing air. Now Tecumsah darted in from behind; the dinosaur turned to fend off the new attack. As he did, Roscoe attacked. Taking turns, watching for openings, the dogs circled, wolflike, patient. Eilene ran for the rifle.

Circling wide, she briefly distracted the dinosaur, letting Kamiak draw first blood, ripping open the calf of the dinosaur and escaping the murderous blow aimed at his head. Tecumsah struck next, then Roscoe, each timing the attack and getting out safely. The wounds were mere nicks but they were accumulating, slowly weakening the beast, slowing its response.

Eilene reached the far side of the sled, and dug. Her knife

was still in the neck of the dinosaur so she dug with her hands. The melted snow had refrozen, and her nails broke, her fingers dripped blood. Jumping up, she threw herself over the sled, fishing her axe out of the sled bag. Chopping frantically, she broke the ice up, then threw handfuls to the side—there was the butt of the gun. Now she chopped along the length of the rifle. On the other side of the sled the dogs continued to circle, attack, run, feint. Kamiak was the slowest, feigning attacks to protect the other dogs. Tecumsah was reckless, taking the most chances, doing the most damage. Working as a pack, the dogs were holding their own, but the nips and bites were annoying, not debilitating.

With a quickness and power the dogs could not match, the dinosaur leaped over the attacking Tecumsah, landing outside the circling dogs. With a sweep of its tail it knocked the legs out from under Tecumsah, who tumbled through a spray of snow. With another leap, the dinosaur attacked Roscoe, claws cutting deep into his side. Roscoe was swept up, the dinosaur clamping down on the dog's neck. There was a yelp, and the sharp crack of vertebrae breaking. With a shake of its head, Roscoe was thrown into the snow.

Eilene chopped the last of the ice from the barrel, took it in both hands, then braced her feet and pulled. The rifle came free, Eilene falling back, gun in her hands. Working the bolt, she loaded a new round, then turned and rested the rifle on the sled. Kamiak and Tecumsah attacked as one now, Kamiak from the front, Tecumsah behind. Aiming high, Eilene fired just as the dinosaur spun, ignoring Kamiak, swiping at Tecumsah. The young male sled dog was struck on the shoulder, thrown across the lake, silently skidding into a drift. Only Kamiak was left now.

The bullet found prehistoric flesh, disappearing deep into the green hide. The dinosaur grunted, but did not go down. Turning back, it tried to catch Kamiak inside its reach, but the wily sled dog was already bounding back. Eilene fired again, hitting the dinosaur in the lower left haunch. This time it yelped, spun, and tried to leap at Eilene, but its wounded leg failed and it came down short, head slapping the snow.

Eilene loaded another round—only two left. Eyes on Eilene, the dinosaur quickly got to its feet. Eilene fired point-blank into its chest. At the impact the beast rocked but made no sound. Eilene worked her last bullet into the chamber. Gathering itself, the dinosaur flexed its legs, ready to leap again. Eilene held her ground, rifle ready. She had only one round left—where to put it? The head was swaying and too small a target. Then Kamiak attacked, leaping at the dinosaur, coming inside its reach, tearing at the wounded side and then darting out. Coming out of its squat, the beast swiped ineffectually at the dog, then turned toward Eilene who backed up a step, rifle ready. The dinosaur stepped closer, the sled still between it and Eilene. Then it took another step and another, stopping just short of the sled. Blood was streaming from the three bullet wounds and a dozen other nicks and bites. Reaching for the sled, the dinosaur started to push it aside, then wobbled and fell forward, its long neck flopping across the sled, its eyes closed.

Eilene held her position, the head barely an arm's length from her. Kamiak charged in, tearing off a piece of flesh. The beast opened its eyes then, still filled with hate. Suddenly it opened its mouth and screeched that metal-tearing sound that tested Eilene's nerve. Before it ended its defiant roar, Eilene stepped forward and jammed her rifle in its mouth.

"Eat this!" Eilene said and pulled the trigger.

The back of the dinosaur's head blew out, the jaws clamping on the rifle. Eilene tried pulling the gun out but it was held firm in a death grip. She left it. She had no bullets anyway. Kamiak came to stand next to her, both dog and mistress watching the dinosaur for signs of life. When a leg twitched, Kamiak attacked it, shredding the muscle. While Kamiak worked over the carcass, Eilene checked her other dogs. All were dead, two of them in pieces. She checked Tecumsah last. His eyes were open, as lifeless as the glass eyes in a taxidermist's drawer.

Kamiak came back now, slowly, limping, spent. Plopping down by Eilene, he settled into the snow, lying on his good side, his gray fur matted and black with blood. Eilene checked the wounds. He needed stitches.

"I won't lose you too, Kamiak!" Eilene vowed.

With one leg against the shoulder of the dinosaur, Eilene freed her sled from under the fallen dinosaur, and then emptied her sled bag. Wrapping Kamiak in bandages, she gently eased him inside the bag, leaving only his head exposed. Next she put on her snowshoes, cut the harness short, and rigged it to loop over her shoulders. Then she pulled her sled toward home.

"This wasn't supposed to happen anymore, Kamiak," Eilene muttered. "They told us it was safe again. Someone's got to do something or none of us will ever be safe."

Behind her, zipped snug in the sled bag, Kamiak whimpered agreement.

2 • LOST WORLD

The time quilting was a result of a one-time convergence of forces unleashed as a result of an incomplete understanding of the quantum universe. With current controls on nuclear testing, another such convergence would be impossible.

—*Arnold Gogh, Ph.D., National Science Foundation*

SASKATCHEWAN, CANADA, OCTOBER

Emmett Puglisi hung from the open door of the helicopter, his face contorted by the powerful headwind. His head half frozen, he continued to lean into the wind, the biting cold distracting him from his churning stomach. Emmett didn't get airsick easily, but the pitching of the low-flying helicopter had stirred the remains of his breakfast to a bubbling soup with a head of foam. The foam he could taste. He swallowed hard, sending a peristaltic wave back at the rising vomit.

"Sit down, Em," his wife shouted.

Carrollee Chen-Slater-Puglisi sat behind him, securely buckled into her seat. Carrollee wore bright-white coveralls, with white earmuffs. Her lipstick and eye shadow were pale, but her cheeks rosy—most of the glow natural.

Emmett unhooked the safety cable, and then returned to sit by his wife. The crewman slid the door closed, then leaned against it, took off his gloves, retrieved a pair of fingernail clippers and went to work on his nails.

"Sticking your head into the wind like a Labrador retriever is just creating wind resistance and slowing us down," Carrollee said, her breath visible in the now chilly cabin.

"We should be just about there," Emmett said, ignoring his wife's jabs and his churning stomach.

"Relax, Em, if it happened again, it's not going anywhere."

"That's the problem," Emmett said.

The flight took twenty more minutes and twice Carrollee had to pull Emmett back to his seat. The crewman had finished with his nails and was working a crossword puzzle. He stirred, listening to the earphones built into his helmet. Then he put his gloves back on and signaled Emmett and Carrollee to come to the hatch.

"Pilot says we're coming up on it now," the crewman shouted.

Attaching safety lines to the belts they wore, the crewman slid the door open, letting Carrollee and Emmett lean out, looking ahead. They were flying over a frosty landscape, devoid of vegetation except for a few random trees. The heavy snows hadn't set in yet; a dusting sprinkled the tundra. Leaning out as far as they dared, the Puglisis looked ahead and could see the variegated green of the quilt. As they came closer they could see the vegetation was lush, contrasting sharply with the late fall tundra.

Now they were over the quilt. Emmett and Carrollee looked straight down, the vegetation a blur. They flew on, the landscape below as featureless as the tundra they had passed over.

"Pilot says to look ahead," the crewman said.

Emmett looked to see a herd of animals—hundreds of them. They were on the move, heading south.

"Pilot wants to know how close you want to get?"

"Keep clear, we don't want to spook them."

Emmett took the camera that hung from his neck, steadying himself. He swayed dangerously until Carrollee and the crewman each put a hand on him. His third shot satisfied him.

"Ask the pilot to put us down south of the herd," Emmett said. "We'll let them come to us."

Emmett and Carrollee returned to their seats. Emmett put on his glasses, and then pulled his computer from his pack and downloaded the image. The identification program worked valiantly but finally could only manage to generate a list of probabilities: Indricotherium, .373; Macrauchenia, .223; Deinotherium, .181; Moeritherium, .046.

"This is useless. Without some way to scale the animals, the program can't tell whether those animals are fifteen-ton indricotheres or sixty-centimeter moeritheres—sort of midget elephants."

"Those weren't midgets," Carrollee said.

"No matter what they are, they aren't from the Cretaceous."

"Don't go all end-of-the-world on me. Wait until we see them up close."

The pilot landed, and the Puglisis hopped out, pulling on packs. It was noticeably warmer at ground level but still cool enough for parkas. Carrollee's parka was the same bright white of her coveralls. Emmett's was camouflage. They took packs and wore headsets to stay in touch with the helicopter. Emmett replaced his glasses with prescription goggles. When he worked in the field he wore them, the strap keeping them on his head.

The crewman with the freshly trimmed nails sat in the hatch, legs dangling, working the crossword puzzle. He looked up and tapped his helmet and then pointed to Emmett and Carrollee. They understood and turned on their headsets.

"Read me now?" the crewman asked.

"Yes," they both replied, cutting into each other's transmissions.

"We'll leave the light on," he said as they walked off.

They headed east, climbing a small hill. Halfway to the top, their headsets crackled to life.

"Doctors Puglisi?" the crewman called.

"We're here," Emmett replied.

"What's a publican?"

"What?" Emmett said, slightly out of breath.

"A publican. I need a three-letter word for 'publican's offering.' "

"Ale," Carrollee said. "A publican is a British bartender."

"Thanks," the crewman said.

"We're not here to help you with puzzles," Emmett said, irritated.

"Of course not," the crewman said. "But you've got to check in by radio every few minutes anyway."

Carrollee shrugged, smiled, and walked on. Soon they were warm enough to remove the parkas and they paused, tying them to their packs.

"Doctors, you there?" came the crewman's voice again.

"What is it?" Emmett asked.

"What do you call Peruvian currency? It's four letters."

Emmett sighed.

"Don't know," Carrollee said.

"First letter's an I as in indigo," the crewman said.

"Inti," Emmett said, putting on his pack and resuming the hike. "I-N-T-I."

"Gotcha."

They reached the crest, dropping the packs and resting. The landscape before them was rolling and lush. There were a few distant trees. Carrollee, a botanist, squatted, studying the growth.

"It's not Cretaceous, Em. This is grass. Grass doesn't appear until the Eocene at the earliest but everything was pretty much tropical rainforest then and this is too evolved for that. Probably Miocene."

"I thought so."

"Any point in staying, Em?"

"Might as well identify the animals. It will help date the quilt. With better data I can refine the model, and maybe get some idea of what is happening."

"Doctors?" the familiar voice called. "I need the name of a custard filled pastry that has eight letters. Starts and ends with an N."

"Napoleon," Emmett and Carrollee said at the same time.

"Like the emperor?"

"Yes," Emmett said.

Carrollee began sampling the vegetation, pulling up different grasses that Emmett could not tell apart. Emmett set up his computer and cleared his camera's memory. Then he took out a couple of energy bars and tossed one to Carrollee who dropped it in a pocket and continued bagging samples. Emmett was at the highest point on the hill and looked north, using his binoculars. As usual, he clicked the binoculars against his goggles before he remembered to lift them out of the way. He could see a dust cloud. Given the lush surroundings, the herd had to be made up of large heavy animals.

"Doctors?" came the airman's voice again. "What do you call an Olympic sword? Ends with an E."

"Sabre," Emmett said.

"Four letters," the crewman said.

Emmett could see the leading edge of the herd now, cresting a small rise.

"It's on the tip of my tongue," Carrollee said.

"I can see them," Emmett said.

Carrollee joined Emmett.

"The calves look as big as elephants," Carrollee said.

The herd came down the small valley below the Puglisis. Emmett and Carrollee sat in the grass, just their heads showing. A light breeze rustled the grass around them.

"We're upwind, Em," Carrollee said.

"It doesn't matter. They won't recognize the scent as a threat."

The herd was close enough now for Emmett to get a good picture and after he fed it through the recognition program it

came back Indricotherium, .789. However, the animal pictured on the screen differed. The computer showed the animals as thick necked, with deerlike ears, back legs that were
heavier than the front, and a thick barrel chest. Its nose
drooped off its snout. The animals in the valley carried their
weight evenly on symmetrical legs, and the neck and chest
were trimmer, making the neck look longer and more flexible. The ears were more like small elephant ears and the
nose was longer, like a short elephant trunk. The artist's conception was close on the color, a light tan, the skin hairless,
however, the real nose had several black rings.

"Look at the size of the one in front," Carrollee said.

The leader was broad chested, the head on the long neck
towered nearly four meters.

"That will be the matriarch. She must weigh thirty tons,"
Emmett whispered.

They quieted now as the herd spread out below them.
They could see tails now, long and tufted with dark fur.
There were calves too, ranging in size from small cars to
moving vans. Another breeze swept past them and suddenly
the matriarch's snout lifted in the air. Then she snorted, and
bellowed, a deep honk that rumbled across the valley.

"What was that?" the crewman radioed.

The matriarch turned to face the Puglisis, who now
ducked into the grass.

"I thought you said they wouldn't pay any attention to
us, Em?"

"They shouldn't. We're no threat."

"Doctors, do you need help?" the crewman repeated.

"We're okay," Emmett said.

"Don't speak so soon," Carrollee said. "Take a look."

The pack was reorganizing now, the calves hurrying inside the perimeter of the herd, the smallest actually walking
under their mothers. Other adult indricotheres were moving
out from the herd, positioning themselves between the females with calves and where Emmett and Carrollee hid.

"This doesn't make sense," Emmett said.

"Give me your computer, Em," Carrollee said, grabbing it.

She typed furiously and then turned the computer back to Emmett. At the top he read: "What predators are contemporary with Indricotherium?" In response was: "Smilodon; Hyaenodons; Amphicyonids; Entelodonts; Phorusrhacos."

"What are these?" Carrollee asked.

"Well, sabre-toothed cats, hyenas, bear-dogs, carnivorous pigs, and terror birds. But you didn't screen for region. If these are indricotheres, then you're on the wrong continent for sabre-toothed cats and terror birds."

"And the others?"

"I don't think you would find bear-dogs—"

"Em, that still leaves the flesh-eating pigs and prehistoric hyenas."

"They couldn't take down an indricothere."

"But they could a calf or maybe one of the sick or old."

Emmett looked back to the herd, which had resumed" its travel, the calves protected by the outlying pickets. Then they heard a snuffling sound behind them. As of one mind, they slowly rose, looking over the tops of the grass. They could see the rough backs of several animals, each as big as a hippopotamus.

"Oh no," Emmett said. "Entelodonts."

"The pig things?"

"Yes."

Carrollee squatted, reached into her pack and pulled out a .45 caliber automatic.

"Where did you get that?" Emmett asked, surprised.

"I borrowed it from our crossword playing friend."

With that cue, Emmett triggered his radio.

"We could use some help here."

"Problem, doctors?"

"We're trapped between predators and the herd."

"We're on our way," the crewman radioed back.

"Let's move, Carrollee."

Their two choices were bad and worse. Stay and face the carnivorous entelodonts sniffing down their trail or inch closer to the indricothere herd. Emmett and Carrollee chose the herd. While the matriarch led the herd down the valley,

the pickets walked parallel. With its head high, the closest
picket spotted the Puglisis hurrying through the grass. It
trumpeted a warning, then started forward, swinging its
head menacingly. Carrollee and Emmett dropped to one
knee. The indricothere stopped, trumpeting another warning. Behind it another was coming with long ponderous
steps.

"We have to find just the right distance between the indricothere and the entelodonts, the balance point where we
won't trigger an attack from the indricothere but close
enough so the entelodonts don't dare get closer."

"That's the plan?" Carrollee asked, dubious.

"It's the best I could do on short notice," Emmett said.

Now they looked back; the entelodonts were still coming
through the grass. There did not seem to be as many.

"Oh no," Carrollee said, turning slowly.

Another entelodont was now between them and the indricothere. The indricothere studied the scene, deciding the entelodonts weren't hunting the herd, and then angled away,
keeping an eye on the entelodonts and their prey. The next
picket in line mimicked the move.

"So much for the balance point theory," Carrollee said.

"Okay, you come up with a plan."

"Got it right here," Carrollee said, lifting the gun.

Standing, the Puglisis could see the entelodonts clearly
now and they were nightmarish: pig shaped, but bigger than
a cow, with crocodile-shaped snouts and curved fangs protruding from the top jaw. They were coming on, nose down,
sniffing. As if she had fired a gun every day of her life, Carrollee turned toward the entelodont behind them and shot it.
The kick of the .45 caught Carrollee by surprise, the gun flying from her hand. The report of the pistol echoed across the
valley, entelodonts and indricotheres freezing, but only
briefly. Then the stampede began. Tons of indricothere flesh
began to move, the earth vibrating under the merciless
pounding.

Carrollee dove into the grass, looking for the gun. To Emmett's surprise, the love of his life had managed to put a .45 caliber slug into the entelodont. The entelodont was turning in circles, gnawing at its shoulder. The other two were pacing back and forth, confused.

Having found her gun, Carrollee pulled Emmett into a run. They ran toward the stampeding indricotheres, which were quickly moving away. The entelodonts now had their courage back and approached their wounded comrade. Snapping and snarling, the wounded entelodont drove his mates away, and then charged after Emmett and Carrollee. The entelodonts were fast, closing quickly. Carrollee pointed behind her and fired again, missing. This time the predators only flinched, and then came on.

With the sound of pounding hooves closing quickly, the Puglisis turned to take their stand. Carrollee fired again and again, but her initial marksmanship had been luck. With time for only one more shot, and multiple attackers, Carrollee took aim at the center entelodont—bleeding from a shoulder wound—and fired. Suddenly the ground seemed to erupt, little geysers of earth spraying the onrushing entelodonts. Then they heard the thump of the helicopter over the pounding of their own hearts. From the open door of the helicopter, the crewman was firing a machine gun. Brass casings rained down as round after round were fed into the breech. The entelodonts pulled up, hooves tearing at the earth as they tried to avoid the hail of lead spraying the ground between the entelodonts and the Puglisis. The attack was halted, the entelodonts retreating.

"Shall we have pork for dinner?" the crewman radioed.

"Just scare them off if you can," Emmett said.

Resuming fire, he stitched lines back and forth, dividing the group, and then driving the entelodonts off. The helicopter landed and Emmett and Carrollee climbed inside. The crewman closed the door, and then sat down, pulling out his crossword puzzle book.

"Épée," Carrollee said suddenly.

"What?" Emmett asked.

"An Olympic sword. It's an épée."

"That fits," the crewman said. "It's all coming together."

"No, it's all coming apart," Emmett said. "And I don't know why."

3 ▪ NICK PAULSON

I could explain, but could you understand? Is it not said that the sins of the father will be visited on the sons? I say that the sins of the sons will also be visited on the fathers.

—*Zorastrus, Prophet of Babylon*

WASHINGTON, D.C.

Nick should have been awed by the size of the indricotheres, but all he could see was another disturbing data point. The images brought back by the Puglisis were displayed on the wall screen of the conference room. A gray and rumpled Phil Yamamoto sat at the computer that controlled the playback. Phil's nose nearly touched the screen, as he ignored the wall-sized projection. Phil was a small man with a thick head of hair, graying on the sides. His face was round, his skin wrinkled, heavy bags below brown eyes bright with intelligence.

"Not seen these before," Phil said. "Want a close up?"

"No, Phil, let it play."

"I could clean it up for you."

"No."

Phil and the digital world were as one, and when he spoke binary, digits obeyed his command. His preternatural skill with computers was the reason Nick had talked Phil into retiring from the Air Force. Nick was the first director of the new federal agency whose mission was to protect the country from the kind of disaster that had put the Cretaceous period and the modern era on a collision course, costing the country nearly twenty percent of its population. To accomplish his mission, Nick needed the best and brightest, even if they came wrapped in wrinkled clothes and wore ragged athletic shoes.

Nick studied the images projected on the wall. There was little doubt about the accuracy of the Puglisis' identification. Indricotheres were the largest mammals ever to walk the planet and evolved during the Oligocene, twenty-five or thirty million years after the Cretaceous.

"Use Emmett's estimate of the period and load it into the model, Phil."

"Already done. And before you ask, the Alaska and Mississippi data are in there too. I'm still waiting on a good identification on that California quilt—Cisnero and Ling are near blows over dating that one. The only species they had previously identified was half digested by an amphibious predator the size of a blue whale. It's all over the PresNet. Real nasty stuff. Name calling too. Ling called Cisnero an 'obsequious quisling.' I had to look those words up."

Phil enjoyed gossip as much as he did breaking into secure Web sites.

"It's coming up now," Phil said.

Then on the wall, a jungle appeared and a second later the view was plunged into the jungle, racing faster and faster, leaves pushed aside as if the camera had been fired from a cannon. Reaching inhuman speeds the image suddenly broke into a clearing, coming to an abrupt stop in front of a Tyrannosaurus rex. The beast bent, mouth opening, but instead of the roar of a T-rex, Nick heard the theme from *The Twilight Zone*. Nick sighed.

"Well, it's a better intro than the raptor stuttering like Porky Pig," Nick said.

"Ra-ra-ra-raptor is a classic," Phil said.

The Randall/Puglisi model appeared. The model was named after Kenny Randall, who had developed the original, and for Emmett Puglisi, who had improved it to the point that it predicted the quilt found on the moon. A dozen of the

Earth's best minds had proposed modifications to the model
in the decade since the planet had been time quilted, but only
a few had improved its accuracy. However, the new rash of
time quilts forced them to reexamine everything.

The original graphic representation of the Randall equations used rings resembling ripples on a pond. The rings began as drops in space/time representing explosive events
with a magnitude of approximately ten megatons. As each
ring expanded, new rings appeared inside some rings or in
other locations. New rings traveling behind old rings expanded faster, catching and merging with the rings ahead of
them. Rings also overlapped and where rings of sufficient
strength crossed, dates would appear. The dates coincided
with previously unexplained, but documented, phenomena
such as a great salt water flood in the Arabian desert in 1413,
burned ducks falling from the sky in 1973, and a soldier
transported instantly from the Philippines to Mexico City in
1593. Kenny Randall had used these events to build his original model with great success. As with all theories, however,
there were anomalies that did not fit the model. These had
not been important after President McIntyre had attempted
to use a "nuclear fix" to reverse the time quilting, but succeeding only in melding the prehistoric past with the present.

Watching the latest three-dimensional version on the
screen, Nick was struck by how little they had understood
ten years ago. Randall's original model had hypothesized
two time ripples created by regular Soviet and U.S. testing
of fission weapons exceeding ten megatons. Later, Emmett
Puglisi factored in the effect of the moon's gravitational
field. Accuracy had improved further when natural explosive
events like Mount Saint Helens and Krakatoa were included.
Still, the fit was not perfect with historical data. There was
some unknown force, or forces, influencing the time waves.

Long ago Phil had inverted the Randall graphics so that the
so-called black ripples were actually black. He had cleaned
up the graphics, created the three-dimensional version, and
programmed options for viewing local, regional, national, or
planetwide effects. No matter how many improvements in the

model were made, however, there was no changing the outcome. Chaos was coming and it was coming soon.

"Show me that regional view again."

Phil complied, the image changing to a view of Central America. The ripples spread through the region as they did the rest of the planet until deflected like waves encountering a protruding rock.

"Show me the moon—you know the region."

The wall image changed again, this time the backdrop gray and pockmarked like the surface of the moon. The background wasn't to scale, created by Phil only for dramatic purposes. Like the waves washing over Central America, the waves on the moon suddenly broke apart and were deflected.

"It doesn't make sense," Nick said aloud.

"Watching it over and over won't change that," Phil said.

Nick watched the model of the effect on the moon repeat, then repeat again and again. While he watched, Phil took a ham sandwich from a paper bag and ate, washing down half-chewed bites with luke-warm coffee.

"Pack it up, Phil. We're going to see the president."

"Hot damn," Phil said. "So which intro should I use? Stuttering Raptor? Twilight Zone T-Rex? Puking Pteranodon?"

"This is for the president of the United States, Phil."

"I understand," Phil said solemnly. "I'll come up with something special."

4 ▪ TROPHY

It may seem preposterous to speak of both Zorastrus and Kenny Randall in the same breath, but both share one trait, the ability to look the ugly truth in the face and not turn away.

—*Dr. Carrie Simpkins, foreword to the second edition of* Mathematics and Prophecy

YAMHILL COUNTY, OREGON

John Roberts turned off the highway onto a poorly maintained gravel road. Most of the gravel had been hammered into the soil by the weight of vehicles, leaving two muddy tracks with gravel in between. There were new-growth firs on either side, planted, he suspected, to help hide the owner's land from passersby and the prying eyes of government spies—government spies included everyone from CIA agents to water-meter readers.

John almost missed the turn, having been there only once before. Although the gravel road continued, it led nowhere, ending abruptly in a stand of trees. The road was designed to sucker invaders past the real entrance to the owner's home. Although he couldn't see it, a tree would be rigged to fall across the road, trapping any trespassers in a killing field at the end of the road.

Calling what John was driving over now a road would be generous. After a quarter mile John came to a small clearing with a small house, large barn, and a prefab steel building. Robert Ripman was waiting, wearing camouflage pants, green shirt, and a holster. His clothes were military but his hair was not—he wore it long, tied in a ponytail.

"Damn, John, how'd you get this far in life without my help?"

"Your help? Let's see, because of you I was almost caught stealing pumpkins, arrested for drag racing, almost drowned swimming across Hague Lake, and was caught skinny dipping with Barb Nelson in her parents' pool."

"You outran the farmer, you won that drag race, you didn't drown, and swimming naked with Barb was the best time you've ever had."

"True enough."

"And life ain't over yet, John."

John smiled, but it quickly faded.

"Yeah, but it would be sweeter if Cubby was here to share it."

Ripman kept his smile.

"He chased his dream until he found it," John said. "That's the best anyone can hope for. It doesn't get any more elemental than that."

Cubby, John, and Ripman had been teenagers when the disaster had struck, wiping out most of Portland and taking Cubby's family and church, and Ripman's father. The boys had been safe in Newberg, not knowing whether their families were dead or alive. The three of them had gone searching for their parents, losing Cubby when he had gone into the Portland time quilt just before the cruise missiles had arrived. They never saw Cubby again, nor anyone from the missing section of Portland. John had also lost his father in a helicopter accident because of the explosions. After that, Ripman had come to live with John and his mother. He was with them for two years.

"I've got a gift for you, John. It's in the barn."

It was dark inside. Ripman flipped switches and the interior was suddenly as bright as a museum. There was a Hummer inside, two pickup trucks, an SUV, three motorcycles, an ATV, and a tractor. A walk-in freezer was built into one corner. There were no animals, hay, feed, or farming implements.

"Just how do you keep your farm exemption? You're supposed to produce something to keep your tax break."

"I have an arrangement with the tax assessor. I keep my exemption and he gets to do a little hunting."

"John, you know I'm with OSS. Dinosaur hunting is illegal."

"Not if you have a permit."

"You get permits? From Dinosaur Control?"

"I have an arrangement."

"Never mind."

Ripman led him to the back of the barn where a tarp hung from the ceiling. Ripman took hold of the tarp, pulling it slowly aside.

"I never really thanked you for taking me in after the time quilt took my father. So I asked myself what would John like more than anything else? Then it came to me—the head of an old friend."

Ripman revealed the mounted head of a Tyrannosaurus rex.

"Ripman, what were you thinking? You can't take trophies. . . ."

John stopped, looking closer at the T-rex. Its right eye was missing. John knew this animal. When searching for their parents, Cubby and John had hidden under a pile of logs but a T-rex had found them, jamming its head under the pile to reach them. John had put an arrow into its eye when it did. The wound gave them time to escape.

"This can't be 'One Eye.' Those rednecks shot him a dozen times."

"Most of those slugs buried in meat; nothing vital. They were using deer rifles when they needed an elephant gun. I spotted One Eye on a hunt three years ago. He had a limp and a bad lung, but he was still hunting. Hunting him down again was easy. Getting the head out of the preserve was the trick."

John looked at the massive head, estimating its weight at a couple of hundred pounds.

"Getting a taxidermist to work on it wasn't easy either."

"Let me guess. You had an arrangement with the man."

"His wife, actually," Ripman said, smiling. "He gave me a discount, too. He needed only one glass eye."

John almost believed the line about the eye. It was the size of a baseball.

"So, John, do you want to pick it up or have me deliver it? No charge."

"I live in a condominium, Ripman."

"Yeah, I know. Alone, too. You are pathetic."

"Really. Why don't I meet your girl while I'm here."

"I'm too screwed up to get a girl. You're supposed to be the normal one."

"I'll never get a girl with the head of a dinosaur hanging on my living-room wall."

Ripman handed John a frame. There was a picture of One Eye in the background and an arrowhead mounted in the middle.

"I cut it out of his eye socket."

"This is great. I . . . I . . . This I can hang on my wall."

"Whatever. Now, why did you want to see me?"

Ripman moved on to business, getting past the warm moment they were having as quickly as possible.

"We're putting together a team to go into the Yucatan," John said. "There's something there, an anomaly. It's putting out an unusual magnetic field. Whatever is in there is hidden by dense jungle. On infrared there appears to be a structure. We want to take a look at it."

"What do you need me for?"

"We're going in by foot. The electromagnetic interference is strong enough to stop an engine. We'll helicopter in as close as feasible, but we'll have to hike the last few miles. Also, for some reason this area has an unusual concentration of Dinosauria."

"It's the electromagnetic field," Ripman said. "I've seen the same kind of behavior under high-power lines. My guess is that in the Cretaceous period the Earth's magnetic field was stronger and used by the dinosaurs for orientation during migration. Now migrating toward the source of a strong field is like going home. You'll also find a high concentration of predators. They know where to find the herds. So, let me ask again. Why me? Why not use dinosaur rangers?"

"I will if you say no, but their experience is with managing dinosaurs, not killing them."

Ripman chuckled.

"Do I get a double-oh number to go with my license to kill?"

"You kill in defense only. This is field research, not a hunt."

John and Ripman had grown up together, and John had often sensed another side of his friend, a hidden Ripman that wasn't shared with anyone, but who sometimes took control of his friend. This other Ripman was dangerous, reckless, and self-amused. John's father had been a psychologist and John had listened often enough to his father to suspect the existence of this hidden Ripman was rooted in the abuse his father had dished out. A father that Ripman never talked about.

"Maybe we can work out an arrangement," Ripman said, smiling.

"I thought we might," John said.

5 · PERSPECTIVE

The concept of a black ripple—a ripple in time—was unheard of before the disaster. In retrospect it seems an obvious result of the creation of transient black holes. How many other obvious, but undiscovered, phenomena are out there, we cannot know.

—*Nick Paulson, Director of the Office of Security Science*

BREITENBUSH HOT SPRINGS, OREGON

Star wrapped her arms around him when he stirred. He pulled her tight for a second, and then slipped out of the bag, pulling his clothes on. Star had just spent six months sitting in a giant redwood tree to protect it from loggers— Gaea, she named it. The stay had sharpened her sexual appetite, but that was spent now, and over the last few days he had begun to think of his other lovers. Despite her liberal talk, Star had a conventional streak and was not willing to share him. There would be tension when he returned to Alaska.

Lacing his boots, he left the shelter, taking the trail that led past the hot springs. It was chilly still, but his light jacket kept him warm enough. In a few hours the sun would top the trees and he and Star would be sunbathing nude in the meadow. Ahead of him he could see three early risers getting ready for a morning soak in the spring. He knew them; three middle-aged nurses from Portland. He had soaked with them before and come away puzzled—how can someone be fat and wrinkled at the same time? When they dropped their robes to climb down into the pool, he detoured. Some things a man should not have to see more than once in a lifetime.

He cut through the woods and came out on the road, and then hiked toward the highway. She was at the turnout, waiting, and she spread her arms and they embraced, then he kissed her deep and long.

"I miss you so much," she said. "I want us to be together, always."

"I know it's hard, but it has to be like this if we're going to change the world."

She smiled at that, knowing she was an important part of the plan.

"That doesn't make it any easier."

She wasn't ready to let go so he let her hold him, slipping his hands into her back pockets. He could feel her heart pounding against his chest. After another minute she let go and then dug into her purse and retrieved a disk.

"Here's the data," she said. "The California quilt isn't in there yet."

He gave her a hard look. She was older than Star by a few years, a professional woman who kept her red hair short, her clothes neat. She was vegetarian, of course, but not vegan. Still, he trusted her.

"You have as much data as they do," she said quickly, afraid she had made him angry. "It was enough for Dr. Paulson to get on the president's agenda."

"What is he talking to the president about?"

"I couldn't find out, but when they offered him a slot next week he refused. They're squeezing him onto the Security Council agenda tomorrow."

Now, she was watching him, anxious for a sign of approval. She was not really his type. She was pretty, but obsessive about her appearance, neat to a fault, tidy to the point of distraction. She liked her sex the same way; neat, clean, carefully orchestrated. Star, on the other hand, was unpredictable, even chaotic as a lover and he liked that. However, he needed her, and she needed to think he loved her. Pulling her close he shoved his hands in her pockets again, pulling her tight against him. They kissed again, then he took her by the hand pulling her into the trees.

"The ground's still wet," she complained, resisting. "But my van is just down the road."

His temper flared but he hid his anger, letting her lead him instead. She was a controlling bitch and he longed for the day when he didn't need her anymore. Then they would do it his way whether she wanted to or not.

6 ▪ SECURITY COUNCIL

Dr. Paulson's hindsight is twenty-twenty. However, when the crisis was on us and President McIntyre needed advice, Paulson had nothing to offer. Nothing! Appointing him as Director of the new Office of Security Science is a mistake I fear we will come to regret.

—*Dr. Arnold Gogh, former science advisor to President McIntyre, interviewed on Fox News Sunday*

WASHINGTON, D.C.

Nick was not a regular member of the Security Council, which dealt with the mundane issues of war, terrorism, and natural disasters. It was the unnatural disaster that created his agency and it was the continuing occurrence of time quilts that had brought him to the Security Council table seven times in the last four years, three of those visits in the last year alone. He was grilled each time about why the time quilts had begun appearing again. He had no explanation—no one did—yet it didn't stop them from demanding a "plan of action."

Mason Clark, Chief of Staff, was there already, always preceding the president, making sure everything was ready.

Agendas were on the table along with pads of paper and pens. There were pastries for those with a sweet tooth, and a variety of vegetables for those watching their weight. There were china plates and cloth napkins. Two pots of coffee sat on a separate table, one a French roast, one decaf. Next to those were a variety of flavored creamers, a pot of hot water and a selection of teas—the Secretary of Defense was a tea drinker. There was also a bowl of ice cooling a half dozen bottles of Diet Coke. The vice president was the only soda drinker and drank it directly from the bottle, much to Clark's disgust. Clark always placed a glass and a straw at the vice president's place, but she would not use either.

There was a coffee mug for each person, emblazoned with the presidential seal and his or her name. Clark was a bit mysophobic and wouldn't dream of drinking from another person's mug even if it had been washed. Disposable cups were too informal for his refined tastes and not used anywhere in the top levels of the executive branch. As he knew there would be, Paulson found a cup with his name on it. He filled the cup with the French roast coffee and found the nameplate marking his place. As usual, he was at the opposite end of the table from the president, with Marliess Krupp, Director of Homeland Security, on his left. To his right the vice president anchored the other end of the table.

The chairs were high backed and comfortable, upholstered in leather. The table was polished maple, the light fixtures brass. Clark had directed the remodeling of the conference room as well as the redecoration of the living quarters of the White House. There had been a little tension between him and the first lady, but there was no doubt about the outcome. Clark had a promising career as a decorator if he ever tired of managing the rich and powerful.

There was no agenda at Nick's place, since he would not stay for most of the meeting. He glanced over at Krupp's agenda. There were two agenda items besides Nick's: The Russian/Muslim Nuclear Connection, and Response Options to Nuclear Incidents. Nick realized he would be competing for the attention of the Security Council with a growing nuclear threat. Given what was now known about the effect of nuclear detonations on the space/time continuum, such explosions were catastrophic in the present as well as the past and the future.

Joel Bass, Secretary of State, entered, nodding to Nick and then filling his coffee cup. Bass would not be a problem, since he usually kept out of discussions, letting others take risky positions. Bass had movie-star good looks—a square jaw, chestnut-colored hair—and stood six feet tall. Jay Leno had once joked that "Bass could have been a network news anchorman except his IQ was too high."

Marliess Krupp arrived, hugging Bass, and then shaking hands with Clark. She was a large woman, big boned, who had enough hair for two women. She was raised Southern Baptist and came out of the big-hair culture of fundamentalists. A former Deputy Director of the FBI, she had spent most of her professional life in Idaho where Republicans were as common as potatoes and Democrats as rare as rain. As Idaho Attorney General she had earned a reputation for tough, inflexible prosecution, disdaining plea bargains. The crime rate had plummeted. Krupp could ask tough questions, but once on your side she was a formidable ally.

There was a rush of arrivals now, the most obvious the Counsel to the President, Courtney LeFavre. LeFavre earned the nickname "Court" as a career lawyer, working her way up the ladder to partner in the third largest law firm in the country. Based in New York, she openly spoke of her ambition of becoming a Supreme Court justice. Supremely self-confident, LeFavre often complained that the only stumbling block in her way was her name, "Courtney." "Cheerleaders are named Courtney, not judges," she once said. She was five-feet-seven with blue eyes, petite features, and perfectly coiffed blond hair. Her clothes carried designer labels, as did her shoes and handbag. She exploited her beauty, encouraging men to dwell on her appearance, thus missing the sharp mind beneath.

The tabloids frequently included LeFavre on their lists of President Pearl's mistresses, but in fact she was happily married to a historian who had retired from academia to be a house-husband and to write historical novels. He was plain and meek, thus proving that opposites attract. Nick had never read one of his novels, but they were popular. However, with the way things were going, "history" could lose all meaning and he could be out of business.

John Flannery, Chairman of the Joint Chiefs of Staff arrived, his physical presence unintentionally intimidating. An army general, former Green Beret and tank commander, he had worked his way up the ranks, making him popular with the service men and women. Single for the last ten years, his wife and two children were lost over the Pacific, most likely to a time quilt. With red hair and eyebrows, green eyes, and ruddy complexion, he could not hide his Irish roots even if he wanted to. A burly man, thick chested, and strong enough to tear the turret off of a tank, he had supported Nick before. Flannery knew he would never get his family back, but he saw the time quilts as a threat as real as North Korean ballistic missiles.

The others arrived now, chatting, greeting each other while they filled coffee cups. Nick was ignored, not one of the inner circle, a man who only brought bad news. When everyone was present, Clark nodded to a female aide who stepped out. A couple of minutes later the president arrived, taking his place at the head of the table. The aide filled his cup, adding creamer and then stirring it and placing it before the president.

"All right, we've got an important agenda today but before we begin I've given Dr. Paulson a few minutes at his request. I'm hoping, Nick, that you've brought us good news this time."

"What I've brought, Mr. President, is a way to proceed. As you know, the time displacements have continued. The most recent confirmed displacement is the one in Northern California. There is also an undocumented quilt site in the north Atlantic, but we are still waiting for confirmation."

"Dr. Paulson, the displacements are becoming more frequent, aren't they?" the vice president asked.

The vice president held her bottle of Diet Coke, screwing and unscrewing the cap, and would do so unconsciously throughout the meeting. Willamina Brown—"Willa"—was young, black, conservative, and ambitious. A former professor of economics, she left academia shortly after earning tenure to run for the House of Representatives in North Carolina. She won and became a favorite on the Sunday morning news shows as the only female black Republican. Her nominating speech at the Republican National Convention for President Pearl made her a media star and Pearl picked her as a running mate in a blatant bid to pull African-American votes. It worked, with Pearl taking 25 percent of the black vote—most of it female. She proved to be an indefatigable campaigner, an able debater, and now the president's most trusted advisor. The fact that Dr. Brown was single had not been lost on the media and every news outlet had run stories about a rumored affair between Brown and the president.

"That's what we thought at first too, Dr. Brown," Nick responded politely. "Because of the gap between the Portland solution and the Alaska displacement, and then shorter gaps between the next couple of displacements, we assumed that this was an event unrelated to the first. New models suggest that the gap between the first event and the subsequent events was merely the eye of the hurricane."

There was general disbelief around the table. Again, Vice President Brown showed the best grasp of the situation.

"Dr. Paulson, the analogy of a hurricane doesn't quite fit the data. The pre–quilt displacements were really micro effects—frogs displaced from a pond to fall on a highway, a person disappearing here or there, others appearing out of nowhere. Since then, the displacements have been much larger. The Alaska displacement covers several square miles."

"Correct, Dr. Brown. The two sides of the eye are not symmetrical. Something is influencing the time ripples. While it appears the post–quilt events are becoming more frequent, that may be because we can't project far enough into the future. What we really have is chaos. However, if you understand chaos theory, you know that out of chaos comes order."

"But when it will emerge is impossible to predict?" suggested Caroline Mauck, the Director of the CIA.

Mauck was sixty, although she dyed her hair blacker than it had been when she was twenty. She looked ten years younger than her age and was full of nervous energy. She drank decaf but it made no difference. With her motor constantly in overdrive, she burned more calories than two women her age. As a result, she was thin, almost to the point of being emaciated. There were rumors Mauck never slept, although she denied it. Still, no one had ever caught her asleep, even on long transpacific flights.

"Normally, yes, although I suspect there are laws that govern chaos just as there are laws that govern the rest of the natural world. I know that sounds contradictory, but there is order to disorder. In this case, however, we're not dealing with simply chaos. Something is affecting the time waves, nudging them this way and that, as if to direct them."

"Something, or someone?" the Secretary of Defense cut in.

Honor Perkins was a former general who had run in the early primaries, fighting Pearl for the Republican nomination. He had dropped out after a bruising fight with Pearl in the South, losing all the primaries. Pearl had hurt himself with the military vote, by ruthlessly attacking the popular general, since he had never served in a branch of the military. Trailing in the polls, Pearl was desperate enough to swallow his pride and mend fences with Perkins, naming him Secretary of Defense before the election.

"I would be looking solely at natural phenomena except for two significant anomalies."

Nick asked the aide to turn on the display system. Screens emerged from the table in front of each person. Normally Nick would have used Phil for his presentation, but Clark strictly limited who sat in meetings.

Phil had prepared a simplified version of the model of the

anomalies—Nick cut his introduction. Now an image showed Flamsteed Crater on the moon. Sitting in the crater was a rectangular structure.

"No!" the president said abruptly. "I will not divert funds from reconstruction just so a few scientists can satisfy their curiosity. Whatever is up there will still be there when we finish getting the country back on its feet."

The structure in Flamsteed Crater had been discovered ten years earlier by the Puglisis, initiating a rancorous debate waged on two fronts. First there was the argument over whether what was in the crater was natural or unnatural. Some compared it to the face seen in images from Mars. When shot from a different angle, or at a different time in the Martian day, the Martian face became simply a jagged rock formation. However, the shape in Flamsteed Crater kept its sharp angles and rectangular shape even when photographed from lunar orbit.

The other debate was over whether to send an expedition to the moon to explore the site. President Pasternak, who had replaced McIntyre, had supported the expedition during his administration, pumping three billion dollars into building a new lunar lander and vehicle to make the trip from Earth. The moon shuttle now orbited the Earth, docked at Freedom Station. However, economic growth was slow during Pasternak's administration and he lost his reelection bid to Governor Costello who promised to redirect reconstruction funds from high tech and defense projects to social services. Once elected, he slashed NASA's budget and many of the basic research and development projects and then raised taxes to fund new social spending. The resulting recession set the stage for Pearl's election. It also meant the politically savvy Pearl was not about to make the same mistakes of his predecessors.

"Mr. President, this isn't just about the structure on the moon. If you will give me a few minutes to explain."

"There better be more to this. Otherwise you are wasting our time."

"Run the simulation," Nick said to the aide.

The model showed waves sweeping across a lunar backdrop.

"This represents the level of time wave activity over the last three years and projects it three years into the future. It's a loop, so it will repeat. You will notice that the waves are smaller, and more numerous, than before the Portland detonations. The time wave created at the Portland site was designed to counteract the effect of the wave that created the mass displacement. While it did not reverse the effects, it did for a time stop the displacements. However, for some unknown reason that giant wave has been broken up, creating many more smaller waves. As you can see there is insufficient convergence in this lunar region for a significant displacement."

Nick nodded to the aide who then changed the view. The image zoomed in, the waves nearly indistinguishable.

"We'll speed it up so that you can see the phenomenon that we are interested in."

The image sped up, now occasional waves could be seen to break up, as if washing over an obstruction.

"What is causing those disruptions?" Krupp asked, the Director of Homeland Security speaking for the first time. "As I understand it, you need either matter as dense as that in a black hole or a thermonuclear explosion of ten megatons or more to create time waves."

"That's true but there may be other influences that we are unaware of."

"Man-made causes?" Honor Perkins asked.

"The disruptions are centered over Flamsteed Crater," Nick said.

Now murmuring spread around the table. Nick caught the president and Mauck glance at each other, and then just as quickly look away.

"Who has the technology to do something like this?" Perkins asked.

"What effect are these manipulations having on the waves?" Brown asked, still playing with the cap of her drink.

"What's the power source?" Mauck asked.

"What can we do about it?" Bass asked.

"All good questions," Nick said. "We don't have enough data to know what the effect of these manipulations will be. I think it would be better to know the outcome rather than wait for it."

"Why?" the president asked. "It would take a nation, or several nations, to construct something on the moon. Undoubtedly we would be one of those nations and we certainly would not participate in a project that would ultimately be destructive."

"If we fully understood what we were doing, that would be true. However, it's not clear that the structure in Flamsteed Crater was built on the moon."

Nick asked the aide to return to the photo of the site.

"If you look closely, there is no construction debris, no equipment, no mounds of excavated soil. There is this one structure here," Nick said clicking to a new photo.

A small, partially collapsed structure stood near the larger building.

"Higher resolution photos show no machine tracks, and no excavation, no equipment. Since it would cost more to return equipment from the moon than it would to deliver it there, where did it go? Even if the equipment was moved to another site, why brush out the tracks?"

"Most of the moon's surface is covered with powder," Brown pointed out. "If there was any seismic activity during the displacement, the tracks could have been erased."

Nick was impressed. Dr. Brown had hit on a reasonable explanation; however, there was another more disturbing explanation.

"There you go," the president said, as if the vice president had answered every question.

"There is something else you should see."

Nick asked the aide to switch to another presentation. An orbital view of the Yucatan Peninsula appeared, then the image zoomed in on a section. Now the familiar time waves swept the region. Then the image zoomed again and, like on the moon, some of the waves were disrupted or deflected.

"Just like on the moon," Krupp said.

"It's a similar effect, but not identical," Nick said.

"But this one is on Earth," Bass added.

With a nod to the aide, a photo appeared; a patch of dappled green.

"This is a satellite photo of the region where the wave effects are occurring. Nothing can be seen through the dense foliage; however, if we look at it through infrared . . ."

The image changed, showing blotches of red.

"Notice the regular shape here. It appears to be a structure."

"Appears to be? You haven't investigated?" Mauck asked.

"We just recently discovered the anomaly. The site is difficult to reach, and the locals have stayed away because of an unusually high concentration of dinosaurs. Remote investigation, however, has also revealed enormous electromagnetic radiation around the site. Almost as strong as the EMP generated by nuclear detonations.

"In addition to the lunar mission, I am proposing to send an expedition to explore this site and identify the reason for the effect on time waves."

The president had been silent since his initial outburst. He had suppressed his objections and become a listener, letting others share their thoughts. He was also a political being, constantly calculating the political costs of this move or that. Anything he missed would not get by Clark.

"Why not investigate this site first?" the president offered. "Learn what you can before we invest a billion to return to the moon?"

"I've already begun to put together an investigative team for the Yucatan. In some ways this site is even more intriguing than the moon site."

"How is that?" Perkins asked. "Weren't both structures time quilted to those locations?"

"No, sir," Nick said. "The Yucatan structure is not sitting in a quilt."

"But you said there were dinosaurs in the area," the president said.

"They migrated there after the quilting."

Now the members of the Security Council began talking among themselves, speculating, worrying, and weighing the risks against the costs.

"There is another reason to be interested in this site," Nick said. "We believe Kenny Randall was trying to get here when he disappeared."

Kenny Randall was famous for predicting the time disruption that had wiped out cities and brought dinosaurs to the present.

"I thought he was hospitalized," Mauck said. "He took hostages."

"He was trying to save his sister from the disaster, and the others with them. After he proved to be right, they never charged him. He was hospitalized because he was catatonic. Gradually he improved and was released. He disappeared almost six years ago in this region."

"Even more reason to investigate this site first," the president said.

"It's risky to ignore the moon anomaly," Nick said.

"It's been there for ten years," the president said.

"Yes, but the new non-Cretaceous quilts have raised the stakes, making it imperative that we understand what is going on. The newest quilts are from the Tertiary Period, specifically Oligocene and Miocene. Primates evolved in this period, Mr. President. Somewhere in here is the earliest branch of the human family. If that is snatched out of our past, then we cease to exist."

"Obviously, that is not going to happen," Mauck pointed out. "We're sitting here, and that's proof that it did not happen."

"You're thinking linearly," Nick said. "The fact that dinosaurs once again roam the Earth tells us that time is not as fixed as we once thought."

Mauck spent her days at the CIA weighing threat matrices, estimating the likelihood of terrorist action. She was right about the evidence for the end of the human line being thin.

"Even if the end of all human life seems unlikely, think of

other possibilities. Once we begin massive displacements from our own past, what might happen to human history? What if a quilt takes Einstein from America? Or Teller? Germany might have completed development of the atom bomb before us and bombed the rest of the world into submission. Jews could suddenly become as extinct as the dodo bird. What if colonial Jamestown disappears from history, does the United States ever emerge?"

"Some changes could be for the better," Brown interjected. "In fact, the whole point of the two structures you discovered might be to establish a certain line of history. Interfering with it might cost us paradise."

"That raises enormous ethical questions," Nick pointed out. "Remaking our past to improve the future is playing God to a level never imagined."

"And that ethical debate took place somewhere," Brown argued. "Those two structures are a sign of that."

"Are they?" Nick asked. "We don't know the origin of those structures or their purpose. We need to explore them. Both of them."

"Mr. President," LeFavre interjected, "if someone is acting to influence U.S. history, they are either private citizens, not empowered by the people to act on their behalf; lower level government or military managers, not authorized or qualified to make such decisions; or foreign nationals who are acting in a way that could alter American history—and that is tantamount to an act of war."

"Sir," General Flannery said, leaning forward on massive arms and looking down the table to the president. "In the past we've debated the threat level of the time quilts, always assuming that it was a natural phenomenon. Clearly that assumption must be questioned."

Now all eyes turned to the president.

"Thank you for your presentation, Dr. Paulson. I'll give you my decision by the end of the day."

Clark made a notation on a pad and pushed it in front of the president. He read it and then nodded.

"I see I have a state dinner tonight. We are welcoming the new ambassador from England—that is of course unless he disappears between now and then."

Only Mauck and Clark laughed.

"You may not hear until after the dinner."

"Thank you, sir," Nick said.

Nick left, uncertain of the outcome. The last time his request to refund the moon expedition was turned down it had been on the spot. Now the president suggested he would not hear until after a state dinner? But why wait until late? Nick knew the decision would be made as soon as Nick left the Security Council. Nick found the lack of a decision almost as disequilibrating as the anomalies in the Yucatan and on the moon.

7 • NIKKI

I'm saving you from the end of the world.

—Kenny Randall, to the hostages in the Oregon Caves, just
before the time quilt

ST. AUGUSTINE, FLORIDA

John passed two pools on his way to Nikki Ryden's second-floor condo. It was just before noon on Saturday so John had hopes of catching her home. She answered the door wearing a jungle safari uniform—khaki shorts, tan short-sleeve shirt, well-worn athletic shoes. Her shirt was monogrammed with her name and a "Gatorland" logo.

"Nikki Ryden?" John asked.

"Yes."

"My name is John Roberts. I'm with the Office of Security Science. I wonder if I could talk with you for a few minutes?"

"Have you found Kenny?" she blurted.

She suddenly flushed, clearly anxious for his answer.

"Kenny Randall? No, but I am here about something related."

"Oh, I thought maybe . . ."

Her disappointment told him a lot about Nikki's relationship with Kenny. Nikki looked at her watch, revealing a scarred wrist. She invited him in. There was a short hall to the right with two bedrooms. They passed a bath and small kitchen as they came to the living room that looked out on the Atlantic. The living room was cream colored, one wall covered with mirrors etched with flamingos. There was a couch and two matching chairs upholstered in fabric created in collusion with whomever designed the flamingo mirrors. Nikki was a young woman, about John's age, with bright blue eyes and short blond hair that was crudely trimmed around her ears.

"Why did you ask if we had found Kenny Randall?"

"Because you are with the OSS. I guessed you were working on the same thing as Kenny."

"Which is what?"

"He predicted the time quilt, you know? After it happened he kept working on trying to understand how it happened. When he heard about what they found on the moon he really got into it. He worked for weeks doing calculations. It took him a year to finish, but he finally did."

"This was when you were in the hospital together?"

"Yes, and after we got out."

As John set up the expedition to the Yucatan site, he had heard from locals that there had been a previous expedition. That had piqued John's interest and he had used the resources of the OSS to access records on Kenny Randall, including his hospital records. Those records included notes about his relationship with Nikki Ryden and the mutually therapeutic benefit. Through interviews, bank records, credit card activity, and phone records, they had pieced together a rough outline of Kenny Randall's ill-fated expedition to the Yucatan. It had taken John only a few days to trace Nikki to Florida.

"He finished what?"

"His prediction. I guess it would be his second prediction."

"What was he predicting?"

"What all prophet's predict! The end of the world."

John was puzzled. Nikki had followed a prophet who predicted the end of the world into a dinosaur-infested jungle and come back alone. Yet, she didn't seem worried.

"When is the world supposed to end?"

"He never said, exactly. That was one reason why we went to the Yucatan. He thought he could learn more when he got to the source."

"Source of what?"

"The source of the time disruption."

"And he thought that was in the Yucatan?"

"He proved it mathematically. Of course I couldn't understand it very well. But he figured it very carefully."

Nikki's eyes lit up when she talked of Kenny. She was a devotee, a groupie, a disciple—whatever descriptor best fit someone absolutely devoted to a charismatic leader. But as such, she was also blind. The calculations could have been nonsense as far as she knew.

"Where exactly did Kenny lead you in the Yucatan?"

"To the Zorastrus temple."

John was shocked. If Nikki was right, then she had already been to the structure they were seeking and it was somehow connected with Zorastrus, who had predicted the time quilting a few thousand years before it actually happened.

"A temple?"

"That's what Kenny called it."

"How did he connect it with Zorastrus?"

"There were markings on it. He could read them."

John was suspicious. Kenny Randall was not a linguist.

"Nikki, what happened to Kenny?"

Now she looked sad, turning her head toward the ocean. There was a light breeze bringing the smell of the sea, gently tossing her short hair.

"He went inside and never came out. We waited nearly a week, but he never came back."

"Didn't you go inside to look for him?"

"Kenny said it was dangerous to go inside. He explored it by himself. Then one day he went in and didn't come out."

That made no sense to John, but he didn't pursue it.

"I'm going to be late," Nikki said.

"Just another minute. Nikki, a group of us are going to go to the temple. Something peculiar is going on in that area and we need to understand it."

"Find Kenny. He could explain it."

"Yes, I'm sure he could, but he has disappeared."

"Yes, in the temple."

"Okay. I wonder if you would be willing to go back there with us?"

"Everyone else died," Nikki said. "The dinosaurs killed them." Nikki was terrified, her voice merely a whisper.

"We will be armed."

"We had guns. Everyone died anyway."

"We'll have professional dinosaur rangers."

Nikki looked out the patio doors at the ocean, silent, thoughtful. "Could we look for Kenny?" she asked softly.

"Yes, if he's still there we could bring him home. If the end of the world is coming, maybe he can help us stop it."

Now she looked back, her voice strong again, her eyes bright with joy.

"Oh, it's okay now."

"What's okay?"

"The world's not going to end anymore. Kenny fixed it."

8 · APPROVAL

SHC [spontaneous human combustion] entered the popular imagination with the case of Countess Bandi of Casena, an Italian noblewoman whose head and fingers were found arranged around a pile of ashes in June 1731. Since then upward of three hundred cases of SHC have been reported . . .

—*Joel Levy,* K.I.S.S. Guide to the Unexplained

WASHINGTON, D.C.

It was nearly midnight when Chief of Staff Clark brought the news. He wore a tuxedo, bow tie, and black shoes polished to military standards. Nick, on the other hand, had jettisoned his suit coat and tie, needed a shave, and had bloodshot eyes from staring at a computer screen for six hours straight. He offered Clark a cup of coffee but had only Styrofoam cups. Clark declined.

"The president has decided to fund your mission."

"It's the right move," Nick said, hiding his surprise, expecting a catch.

"However, as you know there are political ramifications in this decision."

"Mr. Clark, I was not exaggerating my concern about the impact on our planet. Human history, even human life, could be wiped out."

"If you are right, yes. If not, it could cost the president reelection."

"It can't be helped."

"It can."

Nick was sitting in his executive chair, leaning back, sipping his coffee. Clark was in a side chair, on the edge of his seat, careful not to touch more of the cushion with his body than was absolutely necessary. Now Nick leaned forward. He could sense the strings being attached to his project.

"The Secretary of Defense and the Director of the CIA have agreed to fund your expedition to the moon out of black bag funds. There will be no public announcement. You are to tell no one outside of your team what you are doing. You will lead the mission yourself."

"What about training? We'll need to spend a few months at NASA."

"No. You and your team will be carried to orbit by an Aurora out of Groom Lake within thirty days."

"A month? That's too soon."

"The lunar shuttle is already in orbit. Its systems will be checked and the shuttle fueled. The lander will be removed from mothballs and shipped to Groom Lake. The fuel cells will be replaced, and all systems debugged. Lunar environment suits are being assembled as we speak."

"You've thought of everything."

"I've just begun. It will all get done."

"But why the secrecy?"

Clark adjusted his already perfect tie, avoiding Nick's eyes. Nick had never seen Clark uncomfortable. He was a Zen master of self-control.

"There is a project that you are unaware of," Clark said, still avoiding Nick's eyes. "It is designed to explore phenomena related to dense matter effects."

"Clearly that would fall under OSS jurisdiction."

"Not if it is a weapon program."

Clark was avoiding eye contact, still fiddling with his tie.

"You want to use time disruption as a weapon?"

Now Clark was regaining his confidence and he looked Nick in the eye.

"We are not convinced the time quilting was accidental."

"An attack? But we discounted that a long time ago. The Kenny Randall model and the Zorastrus calculations confirmed it was a by-product of transient dense matter created by fusion explosions."

Clark shrugged.

"Once we know what is possible we can better assess

what is happening," Clark said cryptically. "However, the research is into an energy by-product of the time waves."

"An energy by-product? What by-product?"

"It is classified."

"Okay," Nick said with a sigh. "But you came to tell me something?"

Getting information from Clark was as hard as finding out why a teenager had been out past curfew.

"The research involves use of a structure to focus a heretofore unknown energy."

"A structure?" Nick probed.

"Yes."

Nick rocked forward, leaning on the desk, exasperated.

"What kind of structure? A nuclear reactor? A particle accelerator? A plasma generator? A cotton-candy machine?"

"Closer to the latter."

"A cotton-candy machine? Why are you wasting my time?"

"I only mean that it is a low technology approach."

"Impossible."

"I'm sure you know best," Clark said testily. "However, others disagree."

"Who?"

"The names of participants in the project are classified."

"Fine. How big a 'structure' is this . . . this . . . whatever it is?"

"A few stories tall. I've not seen it myself."

"And just how does this mystery building influence time and space?"

"How do you think that the structure on the moon and the one in Yucatan accomplish this?"

That caught Nick off-guard. He had assumed the structures on the moon and in the Yucatan contained some technology that produced the effects. It never occurred to him that the structure itself might be the source.

"I understand the effects are produced by a combination of shape and material composition."

"In what way?"

"I'm sure I don't know."

"Where is this structure being built?"

"It is classified, but I can assure you it is not on the moon." Clark stood to leave.

"It is unlikely that there is any relation between the effects you are interested in and this project."

"Have you finished the structure?" Nick asked.

"Once you return from the moon we will be able to eliminate any connection."

"Have you tested it?"

"Please e-mail me a list of your team members by noon tomorrow so I can complete arrangements."

Then Clark was gone. A few seconds later, Nick shouted one last question at the closed door.

"What the hell is an Aurora?"

9 · BLACK MARKET

Unthinking respect for authority is the greatest enemy of truth.

—*Albert Einstein, quoted in* Black Holes and Time Warps: Einstein's Outrageous Legacy

DUSTIN, NEW MEXICO

He had his suitcase bomb, but only two twenty-megaton warheads. He needed three. Acquiring the third had proved difficult, until now.

In the worldwide chaos following the time quilting, Eastern Europe had lost all semblance of civilization, governments as transient as South American dictators. When order was finally restored, the new leaders had to cope with looted armories, missing aircraft, unaccounted-for missiles, incomplete inventories of nuclear weapons, and unexplained plutonium shortages.

The chaos had made nuclear weapons available on the black market—for a price. That price had been dropping as order was restored and the countries reestablished their borders and their military. As governments tracked down, and ruthlessly retrieved, missing weapons, prices had plummeted. The risk was just too high for weapons dealers. The two hundred thousand dollars demanded for this weapon was a bargain—not that he had two hundred thousand dollars.

He stood alone on the runway as instructed. There was a moderate wind, hot, dry, and stirring up dust from the desert. Occasional tumbleweeds rolled across the cracked concrete. There were faint remnants of yellow paint, thoroughly scoured by years of blowing sand. To the west were three buildings, one concrete, the other two sided with rusty sheet metal.

The plane came in low; two engines, twin tails. The plane shot overhead, waggled its wings, and then began a series of ever-widening circles. He remained where he was, small satchel by his side. Satisfied, the pilot began his approach, coming down into the wind, landing, taxiing toward him, and then spinning around, ready to take off again. The engine still running, a hatch opened in the back. Two large white men jumped out, both carrying rifles. They wore khaki pants and white T-shirts, their brown hair cropped short. Then they circled the airplane, staying clear of the propellers. After a signal, a third man jumped out. The new man had brown skin, a thin mustache, and was a head shorter than the two behemoths that flanked him. He wore jeans and a black sweatshirt with the sleeves cut off. He would be "Bobbie." All three advanced toward him. When they did, he picked up the satchel and began backing up. They stopped.

"What you doin'?" Bobbie yelled.

"I'm unarmed, as agreed. I'm alone, as agreed. You brought two men with guns, not as agreed."

"I said I'd have protection."

"They can protect you from the airplane."

"Who's gonna carry the merchandise? Or didn't you think of that?"

"I don't see them carrying anything except guns."

"Well we ain't taking it out of the plane till I see the money."

He unzipped the satchel and held it open. Now Bobbie signaled the others to wait and came forward, reaching for the money.

"Look, don't touch."

"Man, is you suspicious. We coulda shot you anytime we wanted."

Bobbie bent over, looking inside. Loose hundred-dollar bills filled the interior.

"What kind of sloppy shit is this? Ain't you ever heard of a rubber band?"

"If you start shooting I dump it and you can chase your money all over the desert."

To make his point he took out one of the hundred dollar bills and let go of it. The bill fluttered briefly, then caught by a gust, bounced across the runway just like the tumbleweeds.

"Now you short!" Bobbie said.

"I've got another hundred in my wallet."

"I'm gonna get a better look than that before you waltz outta here with that bomb. And I'm gonna count it too."

"I showed you mine, now you show me yours."

"I oughta get outta here, is what I oughta do. It's gonna take an hour to count that much loose money. We ain't sittin in this piece of hell that long."

"I can count it in less than five."

"Like I'd trust you."

"Count with me."

Bobbie rubbed his chin, looked at the bag, and then made his decision. He signaled his men, who returned to the airplane. They had pistols tucked in the back of their pants. Putting their rifles back in the airplane, they lifted a metal trunk out of the airplane, carrying it forward.

"That's close enough!" he said to Bobbie.

"You gonna look from here?"

"Tell them to put it down and go back to the plane."

"Man, you start'n to piss me off. Things gotta be your way or no way. I had a girl like that once. Three weeks later I threw her rags in the street and her ass right after."

He pulled out a handful of hundreds and held them in the wind.

"All right, but you is really pissin' me off."

Bobbie turned and yelled for the men to stop and then told them to go back to the airplane. They did, standing under one wing in the shade.

"Okay, let's see what you have."

Bobbie led him to the trunk. There was no lock, just two latches. Bobbie released them and lifted the lid. Inside was the promised twenty-megaton warhead complete with detonator. He unzipped the outside pocket of the suitcase and pulled out a scanner, running it over the device. The digital readout told him there were free protons radiating from the warhead.

"Satisfied?"

"The only way to be sure is to detonate it."

"It'll work. It's all original parts, genuine cold war, Soviet fuckin' Union, fry everyone who ain't a commie, killing machine. The only thing better'n these are made in the good ol' USA and gettin' one of those is impossible. Cost you more'n two hundred thou too."

Rivulets of sweat ran down Bobbie's brow. There was a wet "v" on the front of his sweatshirt.

"Looks like I'll have to trust you."

"Then let me get to countin' the money."

"You can count it if you like, but I can tell you it's a little short."

"I know. That hundred you threw away."

"It's a bit more than that. There's only twenty thousand in there."

"That ain't funny."

"Of course if I did have the money I wouldn't give it to an animal murdering sonofabitch like you."

Bobbie's face reddened and his nostrils flared. When Bobbie reached under his sweatshirt he pulled his .32 first, putting a bullet into Bobbie's forehead. Bobbie teetered for a second, and then fell flat on his back, his own gun dropping from his hand, the steel weapon clattering on the concrete.

The report of the pistol shocked the guards into action. Reflexively, they pulled their pistols, and then reached for the rifles in the back of the airplane. At the same time six armed men erupted from the sand along the edge of the runway where they had been buried. Four of them concentrated on the guards, the other two on the airplane and pilot. One guard took multiple rounds to the torso and collapsed, never firing a shot. The other took a round in the shoulder and then tried to climb into the airplane. Bullets tore through his legs and buttocks and he too dropped to the runway. The airplane's tires blew out just as it started to move. The cockpit window shattered, the rifle fire continuing even though the airplane was no longer moving. He signaled his men to stop shooting and advance on the airplane.

One guard was still alive so he shot him in the head. Two of his men climbed into the fuselage, carefully working toward the cockpit. Two quick reports told him they had found someone alive. Pulling a walkie-talkie from his pocket he called for the truck. Then his men began to clean the site. The bodies were deposited in the hollows his men had hidden in and were buried. The airplane was towed to where other derelicts were parked. His men stripped off all identification and ripped out most of the instrumentation. Leaving the doors open, they left it to the soft sandblasting of the desert winds.

Riding in the back of the truck with his prize, he felt like a proud father. He had the last of what he needed to turn the world upside down once and for all.

10 · ELIZABETH

Consistent with section 6001(a) of the Resource Conservation and Recovery Act (RCRA) (the "Act") as amended, 42 U.S.C. 6961(a), notification is hereby given that under Presidential Determination No. 108-36 I exercise the authority to grant certain exemptions from Federal, State, interstate, or local hazardous or solid waste laws that might require disclosure of classified information, under section 6001(a) of the Act. Such exemption is granted to the United States Air Force's operating locations near Groom Lake Nevada, Colorado Springs Colorado, Kings Peak Utah, Bismarck North Dakota, and Fairbanks Alaska.

—Text of a letter from President Pearl to the Speaker of the House of Representatives and the President of the Senate

WASHINGTON, D.C.

Nick and Elizabeth had eaten dinner together once a month since she left the White House, and she frequently picked restaurants like The Right Choice—independent, quaint, and meatless. Nick did not mind, since he could usually find something he liked. She was waiting in front of the restaurant, greeting him with a kiss; enthusiastic, just short of passionate. It was a good start. Elizabeth had been cool to him when he had been science advisor to President McIntyre and she the president's Chief of Staff. Elizabeth had stood by President McIntyre after his controversial decision to use nuclear-tipped cruise missiles to try and reverse the time quilting. Instead, he took the blame for acting prematurely and freezing the dinosaurs in the present and millions of Americans, and others around the world, somewhere else in time. When he ran for reelection the voters punished him for being unable to fix the unfixable. Only after McIntyre's administration ended, and she became a defense lobbyist, did Nick come to see Elizabeth's softer side.

Elizabeth had come straight from her office at Grayson, Weinert and Goldfarb, wearing the feminine version of a pinstriped suit, complete with a tie that hung loosely from her neck. Nick was dressed more casually in slacks, cotton shirt, and light jacket. The evening chill was setting in and they hurried inside, waiting briefly before being ushered to a table. They made small talk while they ordered, then sipped wine and gossiped about political insiders. The new, relaxed Elizabeth Hawthorne was a beautiful, mature professional woman. She still wore her hair long, like a younger woman, but it did not look out of place on Elizabeth. Her hair was unnaturally dark, but then few women her age who moved in the Washington power circles could even remember their natural hair color. Her figure still turned heads and, except for a few smile wrinkles, her skin was as smooth and unblemished as a preteen's.

Elizabeth ordered an artichoke salad and a cheese and pasta dish, Nick a garden salad and eggplant parmigiana. While they waited, Nick asked Elizabeth the last question he had shouted at Clark.

"Elizabeth, what is an Aurora?"

"How did we jump from the Speaker of the House's pregnant mistress to high-tech aircraft?"

"It's just something that came up recently. You say it's an airplane?"

"Actually it's half airplane, half spacecraft. The rumors are that it can reach escape velocity and travel into and out of orbit using a dual propulsion system. The engines don't burn fuel, they detonate it. That's what gives it the speed and lifting power it needs to reach orbit."

"It sounds like the space plane."

"Much more powerful and its primary function is military—first strike capability, spy missions, stealth operation. The funny thing is that every military in the world knows we have it but we still keep our own people in the dark."

The meal came with doughy bread sticks and Nick was satisfied before he was half done.

"Elizabeth, how much do you know about other black bag projects?"

"I was wondering what this was about. Most men ask me out because they want to seduce me, not pump me for information."

"I don't buy you dinner to seduce you. I do that with my charm."

"Trust me, the dinner helps. As for black bag projects, a few of our clients have classified technology under development. Most for the Defense Department. Shouldn't the Director of the Office of Security Science know more about this than a lowly lobbyist?"

"You would think so, wouldn't you?" Nick said, not hiding his irritation.

"I see. Tell me something, Nick, why are the time disruptions happening again?"

"I don't know. After the detonations at the Portland site, the time ripples were disrupted, randomized. They even seemed to be dissipating. Then a new pattern began to emerge with increasing intersections of sufficient strength to let pieces of the past pop into the present."

"I've heard rumors that the new time periods aren't all Cretaceous."

"No, they're not. They are approaching our present."

"And your question about classified projects has something to do with this?"

"I don't know, but the president is holding something back."

"Can you be more specific? The Aurora is strictly a weapons delivery platform, so I can't imagine it has anything to do with this. What kind of project are you talking about? Weapon? Energy source?"

"A building. A structure of some kind. Fairly large, probably several stories."

"A building? The government owns thousands of buildings."

"There's something unusual about this one. And before you ask, I don't know what makes it unusual."

Elizabeth was picking at what was left of her food.

"Well, if it is large, and secret, then it will be on a restricted military reservation like Area 51, or Kings Peak, Utah. I suppose I can look around and see what I can find."

"Thanks. Would I be pushing our friendship too far if I mentioned this is urgent?"

Elizabeth sighed deeply but she was still smiling. Pushing her long black hair away from her face as she leaned forward, she whispered, "You know what you owe me is reaching national debt proportions."

"I'm at your mercy."

Now Elizabeth reached across the table, taking his hand.

"Just the way I like you," she said. "Now let's get out of here."

11 · YUCATAN TEAM

March 1, 1517, somewhere off the northeast coast of the Yucatan Peninsula. Three small wooden ships under the command of Francisco Hernández de Córdoba rock gently in the turquoise waters close by a shore unknown to them before that day. On board one vessel, soldier and future historian Bernal Díaz del Castillo squints toward a shimmering skyline that rises above the trees beyond the beach. "As we had never seen such a large town in the island of Cuba nor in Hispaniola," he later recalled, "we named it the Great Cairo."

—*Gene S. Stuart and George E. Stuart,*
Lost Kingdoms of the Maya

HONOLULU, HAWAII

Carrollee's sense of humor knew no bounds and when it came time to name their children, Emmett gave in to her whimsical side. Their daughter, age seven, was named Emma for Emmett and their son, who had just turned five, was named Lee, for Carrollee. Today, Lee was not feeling well, and Emmett carried him in one arm. Carrollee's mother, Grandma Chen, held Emma's hand, as they trudged to the airport security gate where they would say good-bye.

Carrollee's mother was half Chinese and took to grand-mothering like the matriarch of a herd of monoclonius. Like her daughter, Grandma Chen had a unique sense of style, her graying hair tight in a bun, her short, trim body decked out in a Hawaiian shirt, yellow Capri pants and orange sandals.

Carrollee was pink today, from sandals to shorts, to top, to the sweater she wore over her shoulders. On her head were perched pink-and-white sunglasses. Emmett wore tan slacks, green polo shirt, and Hush Puppies, resisting for a decade Carrollee's efforts to get him to wear "outfits." Emma and Lee, however, were at the mercy of Mom and Grandma and wore matching blue shorts and tops. When they reached the security station, Carrollee pressed her hand to Lee's forehead.

"He's got a fever, Mom."

"Let me see," Grandma said, putting her own hand on Lee's forehead. "Yes. Quite warm."

"Maybe you should stay, Carrollee," Emmett suggested. "Since Lee is sick. They don't have to have a botanist."

With the incident with the entelodonts fresh in his mind, Emmett had argued long and loud with Carrollee that she should not go on the expedition, but refused to stay home himself.

"You think I can't take care of a sick little boy?" Grandma Chen complained. "I raised five of my own and they did well, too."

Grandma Chen was fiercely proud of her children. Two were doctors, one a lawyer planning to run for the state legislature, and two had Ph.D.s.

"You go on your vacation and let me take care of Lee."

"It's not a vacation, Mom," Carrollee said. "It's a research expedition."

"You're going to take pictures. Sounds like a vacation to me."

"Fine, Mom, it's a vacation." Now Carrollee turned to Emmett, speaking firmly. "I'm going, Em. We'll have a satellite phone so I can call every couple of hours until we get close."

"No you won't," Grandma Chen said. "I'm not getting up and down to answer the phone because you don't trust me with my own grandchildren. You call twice a day, no more!"

"Fine, Mom."

Reaching for Lee, Grandma Chen took the sleepy little boy. As small as she was, Grandma Chen was strong and held the boy comfortably, letting his head sag to her shoulder.

"Now, you go."

They both kissed and hugged Emma and then kissed Lee and rubbed his back. Lee did not move.

"Bring me something," Emma called as they joined the security queue.

"Me, too," Lee managed, rousing briefly.

They separated in Los Angeles, Carrollee continuing to Dallas, and Emmett catching a flight to Las Vegas. It was a reluctant separation and they parted with a lingering kiss.

Carrollee met part of her team at the Dallas airport. John Roberts was the team leader. She had worked with him before at the OSS. A lifelong friend of John's, Robert Ripman was to be their guide to the Yucatan anomaly. With his ponytail, jeans, and flannel shirt, he struck Carrollee as odd. Ripman was nearly six feet tall, lean, with tan and weathered skin, sun-lightened brown hair, and myriad scars on his face and hands. He was friendly, but emotionally reserved. An hour later Nikki Ryden arrived from Florida, carrying a small suitcase over her shoulder. She was taller than Carrollee, with blue eyes and short cropped blond hair that looked like it had been trimmed with hedge shears. Her face was round, her lips full, her cheeks pink over deeply tanned skin. Her makeup was poorly applied, and, oddly, she wore a shirt that was monogrammed "Gatorland."

"You wore your work shirt," John said.

Nikki pulled at the front of her shirt.

"It's the only thing I have that seemed appropriate for a safari."

Carrollee sized up Nikki from her ragged running shoes to her patched shorts and Gatorland workshirt, deciding the clothes hid a beautiful woman.

"You safari in East Africa," Ripman said, staring at Nikki intently and shaking her hand. "The proper term for this group would be 'buffet.' "

No one laughed. Nikki didn't flinch, but continued to hold Ripman's hand and said, "Been there. Done that."

"Welcome, survivor," Ripman said, smiling.

"I'm glad you're here, Nikki," Carrollee said, pushing John and Ripman aside. Taking Nikki by the arm she said, "We have a couple of hours before the rest of the team arrives. Let's wander around some."

The two women walked off together, John and Ripman watching them go.

"Are you sure you're up to this?" Carrollee asked candidly.

"You mean because I'm a former mental patient!"

"Yes," Carrollee said honestly.

Carrollee had been briefed on Nikki's mental-health history.

"Well, at least you don't tippy-toe around it. Yes, I'm up to it. I've been there before and I made it back when no one else did. Maybe I used up my luck but maybe it wasn't luck. Maybe there was a reason why I got back. Do you know why I tried to kill myself? Why I ended up in the looney-bin in the first place? It's because I didn't have any purpose in life. No direction. I got addicted to drugs looking for . . . for whatever. But I found the strength to get clean when I met Kenny. He and

I brought each other back to the world. I was able to forgive myself for what I had done and I reconnected with my family. I made friends. Of course, my friends are all dead now."

Her mention of the deaths of her friends was emotionally flat.

"You don't seem concerned about their deaths."

"I mourned for them for a long time but then I realized they died doing something important. They had a sense of purpose right up to the very end. That's why I'm willing to go with you. When I got back it took a long time before I could work again. My grandmother has been giving me money and my parents let me use their condominium. I have a job now but it's not enough, not without Kenny. Honestly, in the last few months I can feel myself pulling away from the world again—don't worry, I'm not crazy yet, and I'm still clean, but I would rather die doing something important than go back to my old life."

Carrollee was satisfied. Nikki still had issues in her life to deal with, but they wouldn't hinder her on this journey.

Carrollee had been steering Nikki through the airport and now she stopped in front of a hair salon.

"We could be gone for quite a while. It's best to start with a good cut."

Nikki looked at the salon.

"I can't. I make minimum wage and I owe my parents and grandparents for money they loaned me for my first trip. I won't borrow anymore."

Carrollee pulled a platinum Visa from her purse.

"This expedition is fully funded by the OSS."

Nikki hesitated and then smiled.

"I've been cutting it myself," Nikki said.

"Really! You do a good job," Carrollee lied.

Nikki was wearing new shoes, shorts, and blouse and pulling a suitcase with its price tag still dangling when she and Carrollee returned. Her hair was professionally styled, her makeup freshly applied by Carrollee. The new suitcase was packed with clothes, cosmetics, feminine supplies, and other equipment purchased at airport premium prices.

Now, Ripman and John hovered around Nikki, joking, finding reasons to be close to her. A half hour later the dinosaur rangers arrived. They were all male and looked both Carrollee and Nikki over in that male way and then concentrated on younger Nikki, thus irritating Carrollee. The biggest of the rangers was six feet four, broad shouldered, with long yellow hair, goatee, and mustache. He looked like he had shown his barber a picture of George Armstrong Custer and said, "Make it so." While he was the most physically intimidating, his name was Marion Wayne.

"My mother loves those old John Wayne Westerns, and 'Marion' was Wayne's real first name," he explained.

The other two were shorter, but only by a couple of inches. They looked more military with eighth-inch buzz cuts that left so little hair it was hard to tell hair color—both brown but slightly different shades. One ranger was quiet, but not shy, the other willing to do the talking for his friend. Both took a back seat whenever Marion spoke. Both also laughed whenever Marion joked.

The talkative ranger was Mitch Hope who had been ten years old and living in Dundee, Oregon, when the time quilt wiped out Portland. When John heard that, they immediately reminisced on all that had been lost in their home state.

The quiet ranger was Jose Ibarra, a Hispanic who had been living in one of the buildings just missed by the New York time quilt. He had been nine then, and he remembered being shocked awake by a sonic boom. Pictures fell from the wall and his baseball trophies tumbled off his dresser. He and his brother were looking out the window when a dinosaur came walking toward their building.

"I thought it was a monster and I was dreaming it," Jose said, staring into space like he was seeing it for the first time. "But my brother was seeing it too. We ducked low, peeking over the sill and watched it come. It was an iguanodon. They look scary to a nine-year-old but they're herbivores."

The others nodded. Even average citizens were experts on Dinosauria in the new world.

"We got out of there fast, but one thing was kind of sad. My dad and mom stopped on the way out to help an old woman who lived in the building. She was kind of a busybody, but she didn't mean any harm by it. Her name was Mrs. Weatherby. She refused to come with us. We had to leave her, but then my dad went back to get her and found her feeding sugar to the iguanodon like it was a pet. She had that animal trained to come to her window and beg. Then some thugs shot the iguanodon and Mrs. Weatherby followed the wounded animal, crying, just like it was her baby. When my dad caught up she was with the iguanodon and dying; a heart attack I think. My dad has told that story a hundred times and he still tears up every time. You know that's the only iguanodon in any of the time quilts? Brought back from extinction and extinguished again in twenty-four hours. That's got to be a record."

A chartered Boeing 737 was waiting to take them to Mexico. Once in the air, Carrollee and Nikki opened the new suitcase and Nikki examined the contents as if it were a treasure chest. Using the scissors from Ripman's Swiss Army knife, they clipped the tags from the new clothes. Next came the fashion show as Nikki tried on her new clothes. The men *ooh*ed and *aah*ed like they were watching a Victoria's Secret fashion show.

Carrollee let Nikki enjoy the attention, mentally totaling the cost of the purchases while the party atmosphere continued. Eventually she fell asleep, practicing her explanation to Emmett of why Nikki Ryden's wardrobe was charged on their personal Visa.

12 · SECRET INSTALLATION

Area 51 is a top-secret military test and development facility, operated by the U.S. Air Force. It is located within the Nevada Test and Training Range (NTTR), 85 miles north of Las Vegas . . . the base was constantly expanded and used for various Black Project developments, including the A-12

"Blackbird," the F-117 Stealth Fighter and the B-2 Stealth Bomber. More recent projects include research on Stealth Technology . . . and a rumored high altitude platform known as "Aurora."

—*www.dreamlandresort.com*

WASHINGTON, D.C.

Hey, Bill?" Elizabeth said, leaning into a colleague's office. "Have you ever heard of a black bag project involving construction of some kind of building?"

Bill Rawlins was forty-five, bald, pudgy, and addicted to chocolate and conspiracy theories. His paranoid tendencies made him thorough to the point of being anal retentive about accuracy. No contract got through the office without his stamp of approval. Bill looked up from the contract he was editing, took his wire-rimmed glasses off, and rubbed his eyes.

"There are a lot of secret bases out there, hiding everything we're not supposed to know about: particle beam weapons, alien artifacts, transdimensional portholes, clones of historical figures."

"Don't go over the edge on me, Bill. In this case the building is the secret."

"Hmmm. Is it made out of something exotic?"

"No idea. I know this is a bit vague."

Bill had already turned to his computer and was accessing the Internet. When the time disaster struck, the Internet proved its resilience. Because the Internet isn't site dependent, the time quilting punched holes in the net that were filled by rerouting around the missing servers.

Elizabeth leaned on the back of Bill's executive chair. Bill smelled faintly of cologne and peppermint. There was a picture of his wife and two kids in a silver frame next to the monitor. All three were pleasingly plump. Selecting from his bookmarks, Bill found one he liked and logged onto a chatroom.

"Before I start poking around, is there any reason I shouldn't be doing this?"

"Like what?"

"Like I could get killed."

"No, it's nothing like that," Elizabeth said quickly, suddenly unsure.

Bill logged into the chatroom, and then typed an inquiry.

"ANYONE HEARD ANYTHING ABOUT THE CONSTRUCTION OF A SECRET BUILDING? THERE WOULD BE SOMETHING UNUSUAL ABOUT THIS BUILDING."

A minute later a ping announced a reply.

"THERE ARE SAUCER HANGARS AND LAUNCH TUNNELS NEAR KIEV IN THE UKRAINE," Cyber Sam sent.

"NOT WHAT I'M AFTER," Bill responded. "THE BUILDING DOESN'T HOLD A SECRET, IT IS THE SECRET."

"THE U.S. HAS BEGUN CONSTRUCTION OF A SPACE ELEVATOR IN PANAMA. IT IS MADE OUT OF DIAMONDS," Warpman offered.

Bill looked over his shoulder at Elizabeth.

"Well?"

"I don't think that's it. Any chance he's right about the space elevator?"

"No, that's silly," Bill said. "Everyone knows the space elevator is being constructed in the Florida Keys."

Elizabeth wasn't sure Bill was kidding. When she leaned over to check his face, he was smiling. She thumped him on the shoulder in punishment. Another ping and another response.

"THE ANTARCTIC ACCESS PORT TO THE EARTH'S CORE IS BEING REPLACED WITH FORCE FIELDS. THIS WILL FACILITATE UFO ENTRY AND EXIT."

"Ignore that one," Bill said. "It's from Nanonator. He still believes the Earth is hollow and that UFOs are from an ancient civilization living inside. Everyone knows that civilization was wiped out when Atlantis sank to the center of the Earth."

Elizabeth didn't look to see if Bill was smiling this time but began to wonder if she was wasting her time.

Another ping.

"I DON'T KNOW IF THIS IS WHAT YOU ARE LOOKING FOR BUT IF YOU STUDY THE PHOTO OF THE MYSTERY STRUCTURE ON THE MOON IT LOOKS VERY SIMILAR TO A BUILDING AT THE RESTRICTED MILITARY INSTALLATION NEAR FAIRBANKS."

The message was from someone calling herself Spacebabe.

"That's worth checking," Bill said, sending a "THANK YOU" to Spacebabe and then scanning his bookmarks.

Elizabeth found it slightly disturbing that Bill had a bookmark that took him directly to a photo of the anomaly in Flamsteed Crater.

"Bill, what do your friends on the Internet think is in that crater?"

Bill searched the Web while he talked.

"Most think it's a secret U.S. base. There were rumors for a decade before the time quilt that the U.S. had bases on the moon, Mars, and in deep space. They think the Puglisis inadvertently discovered the location of the base and disclosed it before they could be silenced. Blabbing what they knew probably kept them alive. There was no point in killing them once the secret was revealed."

"But how would anyone get to a base on the moon?"

"With the Nautilus. It's a secret spacecraft driven by magnetic fields."

"And does it exist?"

"Here we go," Bill said, ignoring Elizabeth's last question. "Commercial satellites don't have the same resolution as the CIA birds, but they give decent photos. There's a Web site that purchases and posts orbital photos of most secret military bases." Then pointing to an array of thumbnail photos, Bill said, "These are of sites in Alaska and the Arctic."

The photos were tiny and difficult for Elizabeth to see. Bill leaned close to the screen, head tilted back so he could use the maximum magnification in his glasses.

"This one looks right," Bill said, double clicking on one tiny photo that expanded to fill the screen.

Reducing the image to half his screen, Bill then dragged the photo of Flamsteed Crater next to it. With the two rectangular structures side by side the resemblance was startling.

"I'll be damned," Bill said. "Spacebabe is onto something."

13 ▪ MOON TEAM

Although frogs and fish are the most common contents of a strange fall, dozens of other creatures and objects have been reported falling inexplicably from the sky. These include insects, mussels, rats, lemmings, worms, alligators, and even a small troll, which is supposed to have fallen on the Swedish town of Norrköping in 1708.

—K.I.S.S. Guide to the Unexplained

LAS VEGAS, NEVADA

Nick dug for his ringing cell phone, finding it in the bottom of his briefcase.

"Hello."

"Nick, it's Elizabeth."

"Hi, Elizabeth."

"Where are you? I called your office and they said you were out of town."

"I am."

"Where?"

Nick looked out his window at the bright lights of the Las Vegas strip and decided not to tell her.

"I can't say."

"Really. Seems like everything you are into now is classified."

"Sorry."

"I may have something for you on that building you are interested in. It seems there is a building in Alaska that looks very similar to whatever it is in Flamsteed Crater on the moon."

Nick was stunned. The president, Clark, and Caroline Mauck, the CIA director had been holding back critical information.

"Nick? You still there?"

"How similar?"

"I'll e-mail you the photos so you can take a look."

"Use the PresNet. It's secure."

"Nick, I got these off the Internet. They are public record."

"Yes, but I don't want anyone to know I've made the connection yet."

"I don't have access to the PresNet anymore."

"I'll set you up for access, just pick your password."

"Use iownnickpaulson."

Nick laughed. "That's too many characters."

"Then use iownyou."

"Done. And thanks for doing this."

"I'm not done yet, Nick. Now that you've got my curiosity piqued I'm going to snoop around a little more. By the way, there isn't anything dangerous about this, is there?"

"No, nothing like that," Nick said quickly, then had a brief pang of doubt.

"I'll call again when I find something useful."

"I may be out of touch for a while but you can e-mail me on the PresNet."

"Aren't you becoming Mr. Mysterious?"

"Sorry, Liz."

"Fine, get me access to the PresNet and I'll e-mail you."

Nick said good-bye, worrying about Elizabeth. She was a little obsessive–compulsive, just like Clark. Nick guessed a touch of neuroticism made them both successful chiefs-of-staff. It also meant that Elizabeth had low tolerance for ambiguity. She wouldn't let go of the mystery of the building easily.

Nick set up his computer and logged onto the PresNet, a

secure Internet available only to a network of scientists. The speed and quality of the data exchange were superior to public access Internet. He added Elizabeth to the permissions list and recorded her password. A few minutes later her message arrived. He opened the photos and put them side-by-side. The similarity was uncanny. For some reason the president had authorized the construction of a duplicate of whatever was on the moon. But why? There was nothing obviously remarkable about the shape of the building. Was there something about its composition? Its interior? But how would they know what was in the interior of the moon structure? Infrared and radar observation had revealed little. Clark had said something about the interior being "quite complex." Until Nick had opened Elizabeth's photos Nick thought he knew more about the mystery structure on the moon than anyone else on the planet. Now he wondered what was being withheld and why?

He met the rest of the moon team the next morning for the drive out to Area 51. Phil Yamamoto was there, although Nick still regretted his decision to include him. He was too old and out of shape. Yamamoto was there because Clark had insisted that Nick limit who knew about the mission, and because Yamamoto had important computer skills. Nick was secretly disappointed when Yamamoto passed the physical.

Emmett Puglisi earned his spot on the team by identifying the moon anomaly in the first place, not to mention he knew more about time ripple phenomena than Nick. Regina Bates rounded out the team. Reggie was a physician and astrophysicist who had distinguished herself as a creative problem solver. She was also the most fastidious woman Nick had ever met and, as one of his associate directors, she kept Nick on task, on time, and well organized.

Reggie wore her sandy-colored hair short and always carefully combed. Her eyes were hazel, her teeth bright white, her makeup carefully applied. Her features were small, regular, and as neatly arranged as her hair. She was slim, but not skinny, and turned the heads of men younger than her thirty years. She had no shortage of suitors, al-

though she rejected them all. Although she never talked
about her personal life, Nick knew she frequently spent
weekends out of town with a "friend."

The airman that took them out to Area 51 was tight-lipped,
talking only about the weather and football. The base at
Groom Lake, a long-dried-up lakebed, was seventy-five
miles northwest of Las Vegas. The public was kept far away
from the base and its two-mile-long runway. Surrounded by
nine thousand acres of desert, and sprinkled with motion detectors capable of tracking a jackrabbit, trespassers never got
within binocular range of the facility. They passed through
three checkpoints with armed military guards before they finally saw the base.

Area 51 was legendary, among ufologists. Ultimately, the
super-secret base was ordinary, and therefore disappointing.
There were four large hangars bordering the runway, several
unmarked smaller concrete buildings, a couple of low,
concrete-block administrative buildings, a housing complex, and an octagonal structure that was odd looking, but
not exotic.

They were taken to the housing complex and assigned
rooms that were appointed like motel rooms, including little
bars of soap and neatly folded towels. There was no minibar.
A guard kept them in their rooms. Nick took the opportunity
to shower and nap. At dinnertime they were escorted to a
small dining room. The few people they passed on the way
looked them over, but did not talk to them or even respond to
greetings. The meal was served by equally tight-lipped airmen who were polite and helpful, but not loquacious. Joining
them for the dinner were the pilot and copilot of the Aurora,
the half airplane half spaceship that would carry them to orbit
and the lunar shuttle. The pilot was a middle-aged African
American with military short-cropped hair. There was a
slight drawl in his speech, and he spoke slowly and carefully.

"I'm Captain Jonathan Smith. I'll be driving the bus. This
is Rosa Perez, she'll be our navigator and will also pilot the
lunar lander to the surface."

Nick tried to hide his surprise. Smith was fortyish, five foot ten, husky, and fit looking. The kind of man that instantly commanded trust. Perez was much shorter, maybe five foot five, with brown hair and eyes. She was pretty, but Nick guessed that when she stood in front of a mirror she would wish to have slightly less in the hips and slightly more in the bust. But it was her youth that bothered Nick. Perez couldn't be thirty yet.

Nick shook hands with both, then introduced them to the rest of his team. Smith and Perez were talkative, friendly, and good company. The stewards brought food, which was served family style, and soon they were passing salad, boiled red potatoes, roast beef, carrots, homemade rolls, and butter up and down the table.

"I notice you're a vegetarian," Captain Smith said to Reggie.

Nick looked at her plate and saw that it was filled with salad and carrots. He had worked with Reggie for five years but did not know she was vegetarian.

"Yes," Reggie said, smiling. "That's not a problem, is it?"

"No," the captain responded. "We'll just make sure we pack enough freeze-dried veggies for the trip."

Captain Smith and Phil hit it off particularly well since both had lived in Atlanta before it was taken in the disaster. The chunk of the Cretaceous period that had replaced it had kept most of its flora and fauna, since the climate was more compatible than other quilts, including New York, Portland, and all the Canadian quilts. Both men had been back to visit, taking helicopter tours over the Atlanta dinosaur preserve, estimating where their homes had once been.

Emmett and Rosa discovered a mutual love of sailing. Emmett had been on the faculty of the University of Hawaii and he and Carrollee still loved the ocean; sailing, sea kayaking, or snorkeling whenever they got the time. Rosa was telling Emmett that her love of sailing developed because of the disaster. She and her family had been sailing off the coast of Florida the day a chunk of the Cretaceous past dropped into the ocean. When the sailboat capsized, they managed to get the entire family into a life raft only to lose it to a drowning dinosaur that tried to climb in with them.

"Incredible," Emmett said. "But if you were miles off-shore without a life raft, how did you survive?"

"We managed to climb on the back of a passing apatosaurus."

Rosa paused, waiting for disbelief.

"I saw you on the news," Emmett said. "I remember the story. Didn't the apatosaur die saving you?"

Rosa's smile softened, then looked forced. "The apatosaur had a baby that was swimming with it. We called the baby Pat and the mother Patty. Naming them was probably a mistake because we began to think of them as friends. It made what happened next harder to take.

"They were heading for shore and the mother didn't seem to want to waste any energy knocking us off her back, so we just kept quiet and kept riding. She was very buoyant and it was working until a pod of killer whales showed up. They went after the baby first. Patty tried to protect Pat but there was little she could do in the water. She finally realized it was futile. The orcas had torn him apart. I remember my brother and I cried for Pat.

"Then the orcas went for Patty. I don't even think they were hungry. They seemed to know the apatosaur didn't belong in their world and, at Mother Nature's direction, decided to correct the error. Anyway, they attacked."

"With you on Patty's back?" Emmett asked.

"Yeah, at first. I was so scared. Mostly for Patty, believe it or not. The orcas kept circling, darting in and slamming into Patty. There was so much blood in the water that when we finally jumped off we were covered in it. The orcas left us alone, though, and we managed to get to land. I remember the foam along the shore was pink. Patty washed ashore a little while later."

There was silence now. Phil and Captain Smith had broken off their conversation and were listening to Rosa's harrowing story.

"So how did that experience lead you into a love of sailing?" Emmett asked.

"It was my stepfather. He loved sailing and bought another boat a year later. At first we wouldn't leave sight of shore but eventually ventured farther. We sailed twice to the Bahamas. My stepfather insisted I learn to navigate and it turned out I was pretty good at it. I originally joined the Air Force to fly a shuttle or space plane. Then this opportunity came along."

"The Aurora?" Nick asked.

"The X-33-C," Captain Smith said. "It's a single-stage-to-orbit ship capable of carrying you and your crew from here to Freedom Station."

"Amazing," Emmett said.

"If you think that is amazing, you should see the TR3-A Pumpkinseed," Phil said. "It can do Mach 50 intra-atmosphere."

"Ridiculous," Emmett said. "That would be 38,500 miles per hour. It would circle the globe in less than an hour."

Nick noticed that both Captain Smith and Rosa were silent.

"Is there such a ship?" Nick asked.

"I can neither confirm nor deny the existence of such a vehicle," Smith said.

Rosa stabbed the last piece of potato on her plate and ate it, carefully avoiding Nick's eyes.

"How do you know about the Pumpkinseed?" Nick asked Phil.

"The Internet."

The Internet was Elizabeth's source for information on the secret building as well. Nick made a mental note to spend more time surfing the net.

"Would you like to see the Aurora?" Captain Smith asked.

Smith and Perez led them from the dining room outside and across the housing complex toward the hangars. It was

dark now, but the air was still desert warm. A slight sunglow
lit the western horizon. The base was more active now, men
and women moving about. When they left, the gasket-lined
doors quickly sealed the light in again.

"We do a lot of our work at night," Captain Smith explained as he led them across the compound. "Even though
civilians are kept well away from the base, darkness gives us
that little extra layer of protection."

"An infrared satellite could map you anyway," Emmett
pointed out.

"True, but we won't let anyone park one of those over the
top of us."

"You go straight up and that's where they've stationed a
Crystal Seven defense satellite," Phil said with authority.
"Missiles, lasers, and focused electromagnetic pulse, everything they need to make accidents happen to snooping
satellites."

"Crystal Seven?" Nick probed.

"I can neither confirm nor deny—"

"Never mind," Nick said, cutting off Smith.

They came to the first hangar in line along the runway. It
was large enough to hold a 747 with a little room to spare.
They entered through a door that led to a security check station, where their ID cards were scanned and their finger-
prints checked. Finally, they were through and got their first
look at the Aurora.

The ship was huge with no visible engines. A torpedo
nose quickly widened out into a delta-winged craft with two
vertical tails. The wings and the tails were so thin Nick
couldn't imagine they could function. Nick thought the ship
looked eight months pregnant. The convex hull made the
ship a lifting body that would allow it to slow coming down
through the atmosphere with minimal energy utilization.

"Where are the windows?" Phil asked.

"Windows create drag," Captain Smith explained. "Drag
creates friction. Friction creates heat. Heat is our enemy."

"No windows?" Phil exclaimed.

"Are you claustrophobic?" Smith asked.

"Just wondering how you see where you are going"

"It's computer controlled and fly-by-wire. Technically, I don't need to be there. If it wasn't for upper atmosphere anomalies they would probably save the weight and jettison me and Lieutenant Perez.

"Up front I get a CGI of what's coming—computer-generated image. But, just to reassure you, there is a retractable window in the nose that I use during takeoff, landing, fueling, and docking."

Phil looked relieved. Nick was too.

"When do we go?" Nick asked, interrupting the exchange.

"As soon as you are ready. This won't be like a NASA launch dependent on two hundred flight controllers and engineers spread around the world. We just fuel the ship and take off. We just need to get you new fish ready. We'll start the training in the morning."

"Train us to do what?" Nick asked. "Aren't we just cargo?"

"Train you not to throw up," Rosa said, smiling. "Although, usually the best we can do is train you to get most of it in a bag."

They returned to their rooms but Nick wasn't ready to sleep. Instead he logged onto the PresNet looking for a message from Elizabeth. There was one.

NOTHING NEW ON THE MYSTERY BUILDING IN ALASKA. MAY HAVE TO TAKE A FEW DAYS OFF AND TAKE A LOOK FOR MYSELF.

Nick's instinct was to tell her not to go but his fingers hovered over the keyboard. It was a government project, after all. There shouldn't be any danger.

14 · NORTH TO ALASKA

Everyone knows of the relationship between mass and space-time. There is also a lesser-known relationship between form and space-time. This little understood phenomenon was exploited for centuries but abandoned just as technological advances would have significantly improved the power of this energy.

—*Liam Cordoba,* Shape of the Future

ALASKA, NOVEMBER

Elizabeth Hawthorne tested her personal courage, as each leg of her journey to Alaska required a smaller airplane. When the last bumpy, stomach-dropping, vomit-enticing, fear-engendering flight from hell ended with a skidding stop on a frozen lake in the dark, Elizabeth's jaw ached from non-stop clenching. They say that any landing you can walk away from is a good landing, but whoever said that had never landed in an airplane equipped with skis. Eilene Stromki waited, holding a lantern, and dressed in a fur-trimmed parka.

It was three o'clock in the afternoon and already getting dark.

"Elizabeth Hawthorne?" Eilene asked, holding out her hand.

Eilene asked it as if she were in Reagan International Airport, searching the faces of passengers disembarking from a 747.

"Yes," Elizabeth said, shaking the gloved hand.

The pilot dumped Elizabeth's bag in the snow.

"Got anything going out?" the pilot asked Eilene.

"Did you bring the money?" Eilene asked Elizabeth.

Elizabeth reached into her down-filled parka and pulled out a folded envelope. Eilene looked inside but did not count it.

"Nope, Randy, you can go."

The pilot trudged back to the idling airplane.

"Cash in hundreds? I feel like I'm making a drug deal, not hiring a guide," Elizabeth said.

"Uncle Sam doesn't have to take a piece of every dollar I make, does he? Grab your gear. My cabin is about a quarter mile up this way."

Eilene's suitcase was made to be rolled through an airport, not dragged cross-country, and she soon gave up, attaching the strap and carrying it over her shoulder. The roar of the airplane's engine grew louder now and then more distant as the pilot taxied the length of the lake and then lifted into the air, disappearing into the darkening sky, leaving Elizabeth in the wilderness.

The snow was thinner under the trees, the bulk of it caught in the canopy with most of the remaining twilight. A layer of dry snow covered the surface, easily scattered by their steps. Underneath was a firmer, frozen pack that was slippery where the powder was scoured away. Elizabeth could hear the sound of an engine ahead and soon she saw the glow of cabin lights.

It was a classic log cabin on the outside, built out of the same trees felled to create the clearing where the cabin stood. There were two sheds behind, a kennel complete with barking dogs, and a smaller building Elizabeth recognized—an outhouse. "Nick, you are so going to pay for this," she muttered.

After the gathering dark of the forest, the cabin felt bright and comforting. Eilene stirred the fire in a wood-burning stove, adding a few small sticks, and put a kettle on to boil.

The cabin was one room with two doors, the one they had entered through and one in the back wall that led toward the sheds and the outhouse. The logs making up the walls had been skinned, leaving blond wood that accented the glow of the electric lights. There was a bed in one corner, a small, rough-hewn, wooden table with three chairs and two large Adirondack chairs, with leather cushions and red wool blankets draped over the back. There were cabinets and cupboards in the "kitchen" area and a sink with a faucet.

There was a wood stove close to one wall, the stovepipe reaching through the ceiling. A pile of blankets next to the stove stirred and Elizabeth found herself looking at a wolf. Big patches of its fur had been shaved. The animal came confidently toward Elizabeth, sniffing. Elizabeth froze.

"That's Kamiak. He won't bother you."

"Isn't he a wolf?"

"A little bit. Mostly he's husky."

"Is there something wrong with him?"

"What? Oh, he's still recovering from his wounds. Got into a fight with a raptor."

"Velociraptor?"

"Yeah. Three of them."

"And he survived?"

"The rest of the team didn't. That's why you're getting a guided tour of a classified military installation. I need the money to improve my team. Do you mind telling me why you want to get to that military reserve?" Eilene asked, just as the teapot started to steam.

"Curiosity."

"So you said on the phone," Eilene said, pouring hot water into two mismatched mugs. "Don't you think the government is entitled to a secret now and then?"

"Depends on the secret," Elizabeth replied carefully.

Eilene repeatedly dipped a tea bag in one of the mugs and then dropped the bag in the other mug. She handed Elizabeth the first mug. The mug had a picture of a dog sled team and the words IDITAROD: THE LAST GREAT RACE.

"This secret have anything to do with why dinosaurs keep dropping out of the sky?"

"It might."

"No games. Does it or doesn't it?"

"Honestly, I'm here to find out."

"I'll tell you what I think. I think the government is behind what happened. I think they caused the first mess and now they can't stop it."

Elizabeth did not ask Eilene for evidence. An angry person didn't need evidence.

"So, are you here to stop it, or not?"

"I'm not the one to stop it, but I know the right people."

Eilene sipped her tea.

"How close a look do you want?"

Elizabeth hesitated. Eilene Stromki turned out to have a strong anti-government streak, not uncommon in westerners. Like rattlesnakes, they were harmless when left alone but irritated they bite.

"Close. I want to learn as much as I can."

Eilene smiled.

"Then close is what you'll get."

Eilene showed her around her land after that, until Elizabeth was shivering uncontrollably. Kamiak limped along with them. Then they ate supper and played pinochle until Eilene decided it was bedtime.

"Let's get some sleep. We've got a piece to travel tomorrow."

Elizabeth looked at her watch. It was eight-thirty. Eilene pulled a mattress from under the one bed and dragged it close to the stove. Then she took a sleeping bag from on top of a cabinet.

"This will have to do. Don't mind Kamiak if he curls up with you. He misses sleeping with the team and just does it for the company. Oh, and if you need the toilet it's through that door. There's tee-pee and a flashlight by the door. There's a *Reader's Digest* there, too. Don't move the bookmark."

After a slow cold trudge through the snow to the outhouse, Elizabeth got back to find the cabin dark. Leaving the flashlight by the door, she walked carefully to her sleeping bag and crawled in. Eilene began to snore. In the near perfect dark she wondered what she was doing lying on a cabin floor, listening to a crazy woman snore, about to sneak up to a secret military installation. She wanted to blame Nick for this, but she had gone further than he asked. That didn't matter. She was still going to blame Nick. Then she heard snuffling and the soft padding of Kamiak. When his cold wet nose touched her face she flinched. He wasn't offended and did a full turn before laying down next to her on the mattress, body pressed against hers. She remained stiff for a minute, then relaxed and stroked the dog's head. The dog rolled its head back so she could get at his ears.

"Nick, you owe me your soul for this," she whispered.

15 · PREDATORS

We found a large number of [Mayan] books . . . and, as they contained nothing in which there were not to be seen superstition and lies of the devil, we burned them all, which they regretted to an amazing degree, and which caused them much affliction.

> —*Bishop Diego de Landa, cited in Gene S. Stuart and George E. Stuart's* Lost Kingdoms of the Maya

MEXICO

Carrollee's crossword puzzle–working friend was part of the helicopter crew.

"What's a four-letter word for a Hindu melody?" he asked, leaning close so she could hear him over the roar of the rotors.

Tom Naylor was called "Nachos" by officers and other airmen, for no discernible reason. He wasn't a big man, maybe five foot seven, with blond hair and a beard so light it looked like he could shave with a washcloth. He had an endearing grin that he never lost, didn't seem to take anything seriously, and did his jobs efficiently and without complaint.

"Raga, I think," Carrollee shouted back.

He wrote it down.

"Isn't the point to figure out the puzzle yourself?" Carrollee asked.

"I just like putting the letters in the little squares," Nachos explained. "All those empty boxes just look so naked without their letters."

"Makes sense," Carrollee said, even though it didn't.

This flight was far different from the flight Em and she took to find the indricothere herd. The air was hot and sticky and the hatch was open to cool the passengers. Carrollee sat next to Nikki, both wearing nylon cargo shorts. Nikki's were new. They wore T-shirts, Carrollee's white, Nikki's robin's egg blue. Carrollee's back was soaked with sweat. There was a wet patch on Nikki's chest. John, Ripman, and the rangers were deeper in the helicopter's belly, all but Ripman asleep. Ripman wore a camouflage-patterned baseball cap that nearly covered his eyes. Carrollee could see he was awake, watching them, or at least Nikki. He was an odd man and Carrollee didn't trust him.

Two crossword puzzles later they landed just outside a small village. The jungle had been cleared for a quarter mile. Some of the stumps were fresh. Ripman saw her looking at the freshly cleared land.

"They expanded their kill zone," Ripman said, indicating the cleared ring around the village. "They think it makes them safer because it keeps the carnosaurs from sneaking up to the village."

"Makes sense," Carrollee said.

"No it doesn't," Ripman said. "The clearing just attracts herbivores and the hunters follow the prey."

Ripman's know-it-all attitude irritated Carrollee.

"Since you're such an expert, what would you do if you lived here?"

"Move," Ripman said, and then winked and directed the unloading.

Thirty people stood on the edge of the clearing, gathered to watch the helicopter land and unload. Ripman called to the villagers in a language Carrollee couldn't identify, although she recognized a few Spanish words. Men and boys came forward, carrying supplies into the village where two yellow Hummers waited. A dirt road split the village and then crossed open space until it vanished in dense foliage. From the village the jungle was a beautiful emerald green, but its beauty belied the fact that it was at war with civilization; had always been at war with civilization. It had beaten the Maya, who had fought it to a draw for centuries, by cutting, chopping, and burning away waves of invading leafy tentacles. Eventually, with the help of conquistadors, the great Mayan cities, temples, and pyramids had been reclaimed, swallowed in great loamy mouthfuls until the last stone house was infiltrated, overgrown, and ruined. Modern civilization had fared as well or better than the Mayans, but then the time quilt had happened, bringing allies from the past to the fight. Once again, the jungle was making inroads.

A boy and girl approached, carrying a basket filled with bottles of Coca Cola.

"One dollar," the girl said in a fair approximation of English.

She was about ten, wearing a dirty white dress with a pink flower pattern. She had a round face, like most of the villagers, and eyes the brown of coconut shells. The boy was about two years younger with a big smile showing large white teeth, but with blue eyes that seemed anachronistic in a village filled with descendants of indigenous peoples.

Carrollee fished in her pocket and bought bottles for her and Nikki. The boy expertly pried off the caps with a bottle opener, handing them the bottles. The Coke was warm, but to the two dehydrated women, it really was the pause that refreshes.

Carrollee used the satellite phone they carried to call her mother. It would be early morning in Hawaii, but her mother would be up. The connection was poor, the background static nearly a roar. Carrollee walked off from the others so she could shout into the phone.

"How is Lee, Mom?"

"It's the measles. Didn't you have him vaccinated?"

Carrollee knew Lee was up on his vaccinations, but also knew there were always new strains, many blamed on bacteria brought back with the time quilt.

"Did you take him to the doctor?"

"Carrollee, who do you think raised you? Of course I took him to the doctor. I gave him Tylenol and the fever is down. Don't you worry about him."

"I know he's in good hands," Carrollee said, still worried.

There had been some nasty strains of flu and measles since the time quilt and an outbreak of smallpox that shocked the modern medical world.

The background noise was nearly as irritating as her mother, so Carrollee said good-bye and hung up. She left the phone with the small amount of supplies they would leave in the village. It would be useless a few miles in.

Ripman paid the helpers, who continued to mill around, looking for more opportunities to earn a little money. Ripman passed out a few more bills and sent some of the men off. Then he and John talked briefly. When they were done, John called them all together.

"The locals say there have been carnivores hunting the area. So, get your weapons ready and check your gear. We'll take the Hummers as far as the road goes. There will be pack mules waiting for us."

Everyone got to work then, checking equipment, finding and filling packs. Carrollee helped Nikki with her new gear. There hadn't been much of a selection of hiking boots in the airport shops, but Carrollee had found Nikki a pair that were supposed to be so comfortable that they didn't need breaking in. They were expensive, of course.

"If you ladies have a minute, I'd like to check you out on weapons," Ripman said, his shadow covering them where they sat, tying up their packs.

"We aren't carrying guns," Carrollee said. "That's what the rangers are for."

"You can show me," Nikki said, jumping up. Then to Carrollee she said, "You should come too. Please."

Nikki was pleading, remembering her last expedition to the Yucatan. Reluctantly, Carrollee agreed and followed Ripman past the village general store into the clearing. The men Ripman had spoken to were setting up logs. One was twenty yards away, one fifty, and the last a hundred yards distant.

Ripman carried a rifle with the biggest bore Carrollee had ever seen. The rangers crowded around, examining the weapon. One by one they hefted it and held it to their shoulders.

"It's lighter than it looks," Jose said.

"It's a prototype. The man who put it together built it according to my specs. He and I have an arrangement."

Carrollee saw Ripman wink at John.

"The barrel is composite, the stock unbreakable plastic. The clip holds nine rounds, the bolt has a short pull."

Ripman demonstrated the bolt action, which took little more than a flick of his thumb.

"Why not semi-automatic?" Mitch asked.

"Semis are less reliable. Too many moving parts. This one is simple and can be broken down and reassembled easier than an M-16."

Marion was now hanging back, scowling as Mitch and Jose continued to admire the weapon.

"Give it a try," Ripman said, inserting a clip, then handing the weapon to Jose. Jose worked the bolt, located the safety, then held the weapon to his shoulder, aimed at the nearest log and fired. The report was sharp and loud. A geyser of splinters erupted from the log. When the particles settled they could see the log had nearly been split in half.

"Wow," Jose said. "There wasn't much kick. What caliber is it?"

"Fifty," Ripman said. "Air compression cylinders in the stock absorb most of the recoil."

Mitch took the rifle and fired at both the fifty-yard and one-hundred-yard logs. He took two tries to hit the fifty-yard log and three to hit the one at a hundred yards. The impact diminished with distance but was still impressive. Finally the weapon was handed to Nikki who let Ripman stand close and help put it to her shoulder. She fired at the closer log and hit it.

"Nice job, Nick," Ripman said, hand on her side.

Carrollee stepped forward, pushing between them.

"Let me give it a try."

She ignored Ripman's attempts to show her how to work the weapon, put it to her shoulder, aimed at the twenty-yard target and pulled the trigger. Her shot went wide, burying in the moist earth beyond.

"Maybe you should move the target closer," Mitch suggested, snickering.

"Carrollee, if you let a tyrannosaur get closer than twenty yards, you're dead," Ripman said.

"Nonsense," Marion said. "I've been closer than that."

"So have I," Ripman said. "I said if *she* lets a tyrannosaur get that close."

Furious, Carrollee slowly expelled her breath as she aimed, then squeezed the trigger. The recoil drove the stock painfully into her shoulder. Thankfully, her round hit the log low, a large chunk splitting off and falling to the ground.

"Good work," Ripman said. "I have three more of these guns for the rangers."

"Not so fast," Marion said, stepping forward. "We're rangers, not hunters. We're here to manage any problematic dinosaurs, not murder them."

Ripman reacted to the word "murder."

"Murder? They're animals, not people."

"They are living beings and have as much right to live as we do."

"They aren't even supposed to be here!" Ripman countered.

"It doesn't matter how or why they are here, the fact is it is our job to protect them."

John stepped between the two men who had been inching closer together. Marion was bigger than Ripman, outweighing him by thirty pounds, but Ripman showed no sign of backing down.

"I'm in charge," John asserted, hand on Marion's chest. "I decide whether we kill or not but this isn't a preserve, it's wild and unprotected. It's been hunted so the dinosaurs will be skittish, giving us a wide berth. We probably won't have any trouble."

"Ah, John?" Nikki said, breaking in. "When I was here before, the dinosaurs didn't avoid us. In fact they acted kind of weird."

Now all eyes were on Nikki.

"Weird in what way?"

"Confused. Very aggressive."

"It's the magnetic field," Ripman said.

"You're not a biologist," Marion said angrily, leaning against the hand on his chest. "You're not even a hunter. I could respect a hunter. You're nothing but a poacher using high-tech weapons to help rich men trophy hunt into extinction a species that has been given a second chance."

Ripman held up the rifle designed for dinosaur hunting.

"This is the first expedition I've had this weapon for. Do you know why I designed it? Because I haven't been on an expedition for predators yet where we didn't take casualties. Even with weapons like this, I doubt it will be enough for what's ahead of us."

That sobered the group but Marion continued to assert his authority.

"You're the guide, but I'm the senior ranger. If we meet any dinosaurs, predators or not, I'll handle them."

"Marion, on this expedition the goal is more important than the dinosaurs," John said, reasserting his own authority.

"Don't bother, John," Ripman said. "I'm happy to let the dino-scouts deal with any beasties we meet."

John was surprised his friend had given in so easily.

"I guess that means you won't be wanting the dinosaur rifles."

"I'll take one," Nikki said.

"Me too," Carrollee said, hating her dependency on Ripman even as she said it.

John took the last rifle and the rangers carried standard issue over and under weapons that fired rubber bullets from one barrel, nine millimeter from the second.

Given the tension, Ripman, John, Carrollee, and Nikki

rode in one Hummer and the rangers in the second. The vehicles were air-conditioned but Ripman insisted they not use
it. He wanted the windows open to listen to the jungle
sounds. Carrollee was going to complain that no one would
be able to hear the approach of a dinosaur over the roar of
the engine but remembered the bellowing of the indricotheres. Carrollee noticed the rangers were riding with
their windows up.

The track through the jungle resembled a road for the first
few miles, but once they passed through an abandoned village the correspondence ended. The countryside was mountainous, the road either climbing in sharp curves, or
dropping into deep valleys. After an hour of bumping along,
Ripman suddenly braked hard. In the backseat Carrollee
and Nikki rocked forward against their seat belts and then
snapped back. Looking between the seats they could see a
triceratops in the road. It had its head in the dense vegetation, eating, while the rest of its huge body blocked the
road.

Carrollee had seen many dinosaurs, some in the wild, but
she still hadn't lost her wonder that something so massive
could be alive. A sharp rap on the roof startled her. Marion
bent down and looked in Ripman's window.

"We'll move that little lady for you," he said.

The rangers walked down the road confidently, holding
their rifles casually. They stopped only ten yards from the
triceratops that continued to ignore them.

Next Marion pulled something from his pocket, held it in
the air and suddenly it shrieked—an air horn. The great
beast started; moving surprisingly fast, it brought its massive
head around. Mitch raised his rifle and fired into its rump,
the hard rubber slug hitting with an audible thump. Another
blast of the air horn was too much for the triceratops and it
turned, bulldozing through the vegetation. Marion stopped
by Ripman's Hummer window on the way back to his own.

"And that's how it's done, poacher."

Ripman didn't reply. Carrollee wasn't sure she liked Marion any more than Ripman, but enjoyed the dig. She piled on.

"Well, there's no doubt about the courage of those rangers."

"It's not their courage I doubt, it's their intelligence."

They drove on. In the backseat Carrollee and Nikki were bounced and jostled, rocked and tumbled together. After losing her grip again and falling into Carrollee's lap, Nikki began giggling. Carrollee caught the mood, realizing how ridiculous they looked, jiggling, bouncing, and slamming into each other. Laughing now, the two of them fed off each other, nearly hysterical. Ripman and John looked over their shoulders, puzzled. Seeing the two laughing women, they smiled, then laughed. Ripman swerved back and forth a few times, sending everyone colliding, triggering a new round of laughter. Then without warning, the engine began misfiring.

"Something has changed," Ripman said. "We're still a kilometer from where the mules are waiting."

"What do you think that means?" Nikki asked Ripman.

"Well if it were a sign it would read 'I'd turn back if I were you.'"

The engine continued to miss, sputter, and cough as they bumped along.

"There's the clearing," Ripman said.

Most of the journey had been through foliage so thick it was like driving through a green tunnel. Now they broke into a clearing that opened to their left and the spectacle of lush hillsides occasionally split by precipitous rockslides. Directly across the clearing was a ruin, so overgrown that Carrollee could barely recognize it. While little more than a pile of stones now, it hinted at what once must have been a three-story building. There was a dark gap to the left—a doorway?—and to its right set high on one of the visible piles of stone was a carving. Carrollee guessed it was a highly stylized conception of an animal.

Suddenly, Ripman hit the brakes, the sputtering engine dying immediately. Carrollee and Nikki hit the front seats again but this time there was no giggling.

"What's wrong?" Carrollee asked.

"There should be mules and two wranglers named Hector and Banana waiting."

Ripman picked up his rifle and stepped out of the Hummer. Carrollee reached for her gun, but then left it on the seat, standing just outside the Hummer, hand on the door. Nikki stood on the other side. John came around to stand with Ripman. The rangers joined them.

"Smell it?" Ripman asked.

"What?" Mitch asked.

"Blood," Ripman said.

"Bullshit, you can't smell blood," Marion said.

Ripman turned and smiled at him, took a pair of sunglasses out of his pocket and put them on.

"Really!"

Then Ripman walked forward through grasses and shrubs that came nearly to his knees, rifle held with both hands, pointed low. John followed a pace behind and to the right. The rangers fanned out, weapons ready. Carrollee and Nikki grabbed their rifles and hurried after the men. Ripman was twenty yards ahead, almost to the ruins, when a cloud of black flies erupted from the grass. Ripman stopped after a few more yards, the others coming up next to him. The vegetation was torn up, large clods mixed with blood, flies hovering, settling, then taking off again, and giving the remains an illusion of motion.

"Don't move," Ripman said suddenly.

Carrollee and Nikki froze, but Marion continued to chafe under Ripman's arrogance.

"What now?" Marion demanded.

"Don't you feel it?" Ripman asked.

Now they all stood still. Carrollee felt it. A vibration. Then she heard crackling and rustling, and slowly, the massive head of a Tyrannosaurus rex appeared above the ruins. Seeing intruders standing next to what was left of its kill, the tyrannosaur bellowed a warning, and then started around the ruin.

"Okay Marion, here's your chance. Wrangle him!"

16 • ALTERNATIVE ENERGY

Orgone energy was the least understood and least respected scientific concept, that is until the claims of cold fusion knocked it down a peg.

—*Dr. Chester Pilcher*

FOX VALLEY, ALASKA

Toru Kawabata waited for his printer to finish. He had accidentally selected the option of printing the document from the back forward, so he had to wait to read it. It was on his screen, of course, but he hated staring at glowing flat screens. It made his eyes hurt. He rubbed them now, pushing his wire-rimmed glasses up on his virtually bare scalp. Dr. Kawabata was impatient with his printer. It was slow, noisy, and inexpensive, but he would not replace it. He managed a billion dollar budget but watched every dollar as closely as he did his personal finances. He brought his lunch to work in a paper bag, which he reused, neatly folding it after lunch and putting it in his back pocket. It was not the lack of restaurants in Fox Valley that made him bring his lunch, or even the poor quality of the canteen food. Dr. Kawabata simply refused to pay six dollars for a mediocre sandwich. There was also a coffee bar in the canteen, selling four-dollar cups of fancy coffee. Dr. Kawabata had never spent a dollar on that coffee. Instead, Dr. Kawabata had his receptionist keep a coffeemaker in his outer office, making his own coffee with generic coffee grounds. He insisted that anyone who took coffee from his pot, put fifty cents in a Styrofoam cup. He sold enough cups each month to pay for the coffee and a little more. He had used the profits of his coffee sales to buy his printer and now to pay for the ink cartridges it consumed at a disquieting rate.

Dr. Kawabata walked to the large window overlooking the

end product of nearly a decade of research and construction. The structure he had babied from conception to birth was essentially finished, and already they had begun to collect more orgone energy than his models predicted. Not that they could measure orgone energy directly. Instead, they measured it in terms of the anti-entropy effects on iron oxides. In early experiments they used organic material—hamburger—but the smell bothered his executive director.

Kawabata was a proud father and grandfather, and past the usual retirement age. Many of his classmates at M.I.T. had long since retired, making fortunes in industrial research or engineering careers. Kawabata carried on. He owned a condominium in Houston, purchased so his wife could live near her grandchildren. He had been married to his work even then and justified the purchase of the condominium as the price of marital harmony. When his wife died there was no marital harmony to be concerned with and he let his passion for his work consume him. A grandson and his wife lived in the condominium now, Kawabata using a spare bedroom when the airlines had sales on airfare to Houston. His frugality had earned him the respect of granting agencies during his academic career, and now with his benefactors in the Department of Defense—or wherever his funds actually came from.

The largest part of the structure was the open space he looked into. It was there they had built the structure, constructing it with composite materials designed to conduct orgonic energy. One end of the building was dedicated to manufacturing, offices and dormitories. Many of the workers had families, but they were kept far from the facility in government housing. The workers were regularly rotated between the village and the facility, working two days on and one day off. Dr. Kawabata slept in his office.

The printer finished and he took the sheets and sat in an old rocker he had brought from home. He had returned from work one day to find this favorite chair in the garage, and a new leather chair in its place. "I can't hide the holes with doilies anymore, Toru," his wife had explained. It pained him to see the old friend waiting to be hauled away as garbage, so he took it to his office where it had served him five more years, and served him still.

The article he had downloaded was about Dr. Chester Pilcher. Dr. Pilcher and his longtime friend, Dr. Coombs, had been unknown eccentrics before the time quilt, but now were widely regarded as prescient. Kenny Randall had studied with these men, taking Drs. Pilcher and Coombs in a direction neither anticipated. Kawabata had read everything these men had written, and was now reading what others had to say about them. In the original works, Kawabata could identify the mind behind each of the ideas, distinguishing Pilcher and Coombs's contributions from others, including Kenny Randall. Dr. Pilcher was a genius, but once he encountered Kenny Randall they fed off each other, reaching a new level. Kawabata understood Dr. Pilcher's excitement about Kenny's theory, because it tied so many historical loose ends together. But Kawabata was disappointed that Dr. Pilcher had never made the connection to some of his earlier work with orgone energy.

There was a light knock on the door. Phat Nyang was there. Phat had been part of Pilcher and Coombs's group before the time quilt. He had known Kenny Randall and had worked with him on building the model that so excellently predicted time quilts.

"Doctor, would you please come down to the floor with me? There is something you should see."

Phat was always polite and that pleased Kawabata. His family had come to America from Vietnam when he was ten. They had not allowed him to adopt the bad manners of most young people and Phat was now teaching those manners to his own children. If only he would bow, Kawabata thought.

Phat had come to Kawabata's office because there was no intercom connecting the assembly floor with the office. Kawabata could see no purpose in an intercom and had used his red pen to cross intercoms off the purchase list. When the lab was not too cold—Kawabata never let it be heated above sixty degrees—he kept the window open and the workers below would shout up to him. Shouting at one's boss may not be respectful, but Kawabata tolerated it because it was less expensive than wiring, speakers, and receivers.

Kawabata followed Phat down to the construction floor. The structure towered above him. The huge containment building was virtually empty, since they now only worked one shift. What had once been a beehive of activity now had the feel of a shopping mall on a Sunday morning. The only reason there were any workers this late at night was because they had begun to see results as they retracted the baffles that controlled the energy flow.

Out of the corner of his eye Kawabata saw two workers hurriedly hiding scrap material. Without moving his head, Kawabata noted the location. He would inspect for waste in the morning.

Phat led him into the structure. The interior was a bit of a maze to those who first entered it, but Phat and Kawabata had no problem making the correct turns, climbing, then dropping into the center. Marissa Welling was there, leaning over a microscope, studying something. Marissa was a stocky woman, hair a mass of short curls, kept out of the way by a headband. She wore a white jumpsuit like Phat, although the cleanliness restrictions had been canceled and they did not have to wear the full bunny suit.

"Good evening, Doctor," Marissa said, turning to face them.

Another polite young person. Kawabata approved. Marissa was also efficient, careful with resources, and one of the regular contributors to the Styrofoam cup in front of Kawabata's coffeepot.

"We pulled the plate from the focal point when we realized what had happened," Phat explained.

Kawabata adjusted the eyepieces on the stereoscope so that he could see the rusty metal plate that they used to measure the orgonic energy. He could see no rust. Kawabata systematically slid the plate back and forth. Grid lines had been scratched into its surface, creating tiny boxes. No rust.

"Very curious," Kawabata said.

"Curious!" Marissa exclaimed. "It's impossible."

"Nonsense," Kawabata said. "If it happened, it is not impossible."

"Sixty percent of the plate was oxidized when we began, sir," Phat said. "It reduced to forty-seven percent in two days. We removed the remaining baffles this morning and tonight the rust is completely gone."

Kawabata was still studying the plate. Now he stopped and stood, sniffing the air.

"Do you smell something?"

Now both Phat and Marissa sniffed.

"Yes, I can," Marissa said.

"It smells like . . . like . . . mildew," Phat said.

"Phat, there is a hydrometer on my office wall. Bring it down here."

"I understand, Doctor. I can feel it, too," Phat said, hurrying up the ramp.

Marissa put her finger in her mouth, wet it, and then held it up. The only lights were work lamps, aimed at the monitoring equipment. The corners and space above them were deep shadows.

"I think there is a breeze," Marissa said, walking around randomly.

She licked her finger again.

"I can't tell the direction."

Suddenly Marissa bent and pulled something from beneath her shoe.

"A leaf," she said, puzzled.

It was fresh and green. She handed it to Kawabata who deftly dropped his glasses to his nose with a sharp nod of his head.

"I don't know this leaf," Kawabata said.

"Some support staff have plants in their offices," Marissa said. "Maybe it came from one of those."

"Perhaps," Kawabata said, doubtfully. "Let us check."

Leaf in hand, Kawabata led the way out. As they exited

they could feel a slight breeze at their back. The breeze was definitely moist. The intense Alaskan cold meant the air could hold little water so static electricity was a constant problem in the lab. When they stepped out, Kawabata spotted his executive director in the exit, the large steel doors—blast doors—slowly closing. Three men were with him, all dressed in parkas. They had a large crate. Kawabata checked his watch. He knew that two of the men with his assistant were security personnel, and not scheduled to work. The third was an engineer, due to be released since his portion of the project was finished. The security personnel were contracted, not military, and as such, union workers. Working extra shifts would require overtime pay. Kawabata would have to talk to Dr. Walters.

Phat came in with the hydrometer and headed into the structure. Kawabata let Marissa wander from office to office and through the dormitory, matching the leaves. While he waited, he walked around, looking over the shoulders of workers. He knew it made them nervous and he liked that. It kept them on their toes. Marissa returned, mystified.

"It doesn't match any horticultural plant in the building and it's too fresh to be left over from summer."

Then Phat came out of the structure.

"The humidity in the core is over sixty percent and climbing. The temperature is going up, too. It's turning into the world's most expensive sauna. It doesn't make sense, sir."

"In what way, Dr. Nyang?" Kawabata asked, always polite, always formal.

"All of our models show orgone energy as anti-entropic. Heat is a possible by-product, but water? Impossible."

Kawabata stepped toward the opening, palm open.

"I can feel the heat," Kawabata said.

"What does it mean?" Marissa asked.

"It means that I can turn the furnace down," Kawabata said.

17 ▪ MURDERER'S LAKE

Sightings . . . of Venus, the so-called Star of Ishtar . . . and other astronomical observations were used to predict the future and, as markers of time, are accurate enough for historians to be able to establish the dates of early Babylonian kings . . .

—Mesopotamia: The Mighty Kings, *Time-Life Books*

SOUTH OF FAIRBANKS, ALASKA

Eilene Stromki alternated between running and riding on the runners behind Elizabeth, occasionally calling out "Gee" and "Haw," the dogs turning right and left. The lead dog was called "Mack" and was a magnificent animal, larger than the rest of the team, dusky gray with white boots. Elizabeth was awed by the dog's power but during one of their breaks Eilene called him a "mediocre" lead dog.

"He's got the stamina, all right, courage enough for two dogs, even the heart for the lead, but he doesn't have a nose for the trail. He led the team onto thin ice the first time I gave him the lead. The next time I tried him he buried the whole team in powder so deep I had to unhitch the team and shovel the sled out. Still, he's got potential. I use him for stud, crossing him with bitches that have better trail sense."

Eilene's negative assessment did not diminish Elizabeth's admiration of Mack. Elizabeth was essentially baggage, with the dogs doing most of the work. During the brief daylight, the dogs ran nearly constantly, tongues lolling, panting great steaming breaths, but they slowed during twilight, running only over open ground. When they lost the last of the twilight the moon rose, the blanket of snow reflecting enough of the half-moonlight to navigate.

Elizabeth was snug in the sled bag, wearing a borrowed

parka. When they dressed to leave, Eilene had examined Elizabeth's new snow coat declaring it "designer crap," then insisting Elizabeth use her old one. It was stained, with rips sewn up with large Frankenstein stitches. The hood was trimmed with fur. Riding in the sled bag, she wasn't sure why Eilene had insisted she change coats. She was warm enough, and Eilene wouldn't let her help with the sled. Elizabeth felt useless, a feeling she had seldom had in her long career. Even fresh out of college, working for a congressman's election, she had quickly risen in responsibility, earning a job in his Washington office when her candidate defeated the incumbent. Every few years after that saw increased responsibility and power and now suddenly she was reduced to baggage, sitting on an axe between dog food and a rifle.

A little after eight P.M. they stopped, unhitched the team, fed them, and then left them staked. Eilene and Elizabeth carried flashlights, but they kept them off, the moonlight bright enough to show the way. They climbed a rise and crossed to where it dropped sharply to a valley. To the left the hills rose along the sides of the valley like stair steps, each hill higher than the last. Elizabeth could not see the end of the valley but there was the glow of electric lights. Eilene pushed back the hood of her parka.

"That's Fox Valley. What you're looking for is in there."

Elizabeth strained to see something but at this distance nothing could be made out but the glow. When she started to walk along the ridge Eilene grabbed her arm.

"Hold it," Eilene commanded. "See there," she said, pointing.

It took Elizabeth a minute to see a black box mounted on the side of a tall evergreen.

"What is it?" Elizabeth asked.

"It sends some kind of signal. If you pass it, they come zooming out of the valley on snow machines."

"I'd like to avoid that," Elizabeth said.

"Me, too. The last time we met they made it clear I had trespassed for the last time."

The security told Elizabeth Eilene had brought her to the right place.

"I can't see anything from here. How much closer can we get?"

"Legally, this is about it, but you paid for the deluxe tour," Eilene said.

When they got back, the dogs were curled up in the snow, tails covering their faces. They let them sleep, Eilene pouring Elizabeth coffee from a Thermos. They ate trail mix for energy, then Eilene spread a tarp and handed Elizabeth a sleeping bag.

"My turn in the sled bag," Eilene said, as if it was a privilege.

Elizabeth unrolled the sleeping bag, took off her borrowed parka, then climbed in and zipped it up to her neck. Ten minutes later she put the parka back on. Fifteen minutes later she pulled her head inside and zipped the bag over her face. Without activity, the cold was seeping through her multiple layers. Eilene roused at ten and got the team up and hitched. Elizabeth stayed out of the way, stamping her feet, rubbing her arms, thankful for Eilene's efficiency. Gratefully, Elizabeth climbed into the sled bag, pulled the sleeping bag over her legs, not caring if she was cargo.

If there was a trail, Elizabeth couldn't discern it as Eilene directed the team on a switchback course through trees and down a steep slope. Eilene frequently dragged behind the sled, keeping it from running into the dogs. Elizabeth was hopelessly lost by the time they got to the bottom and then broke into the open.

"This is Murderer's Lake," Eilene said as the dogs picked up the pace.

The lake was long frozen and covered by a thick blanket of snow. Seeing the steep slopes and towering evergreens on both sides, Elizabeth imagined it was even more beautiful in the summer.

"Murderer's Lake fills the valley that parallels Fox Valley," Eilene explained, riding the runners, the dogs finding good footing and easy running. "The restricted area starts up the ridge a ways, so we can run on the lake without any-one knowing. No one lives around here now, but about fifty years ago a couple of prospectors found a small vein up here a ways. They worked it together for nearly twenty years, bringing out small amounts of gold. Neither of them got rich but they made a living, paid their bills and bought rounds of drinks now and then. Then one spring only one of the prospectors comes out for supplies. You don't have to be a detective to think it's suspicious that after twenty years of them coming into town for supplies together that something might be wrong. Bull Petroski was the prospec-tor's name that came out. His partner was Charles Paley. Two state troopers went in a couple of weeks later to inves-tigate. Paley couldn't be found. Petroski claimed he didn't know where Paley was. Said he just up and left one day when Petroski was working the mine. The problem was that all of Paley's personal belongings were still in their cabin. Still, they couldn't pin anything on Petroski until his partner's body bobbed to the surface of the lake. Paley's skull had been split by an axe."

"They spent twenty years together!" Elizabeth said. "What could possibly have driven Petroski to murder?"

"According to Petroski, they were cabin bound for a month because of bad weather. Paley got some sort of intes-tinal disorder that he couldn't shake and had to break wind pretty often. Petroski got tired of it and told him to go out-side to break wind. Paley refused. Petroski said he warned him not to break wind in the cabin again but Paley did it any-way. Petroski snapped and killed him."

Elizabeth couldn't turn around far enough to read Eilene's face, but she told the bizarre story as if it was true.

"No one would kill someone over something like that," Elizabeth said.

"Really," Eilene said. "Why do you think I live alone?"

The lake ended in pitch darkness under a thick canopy of towering evergreens. Eilene unhitched the team, led them into the trees and fed and watered the dogs, then checked their feet, replacing the boots on the paws of two dogs. Then she pulled two sets of plastic snowshoes out of the sled bag and handed a pair to Elizabeth.

Elizabeth put them on but had to be helped to her feet by Eilene. Clumsily she followed Eilene through the trees, Eilene breaking trail. Even so Elizabeth found the going tough and her legs soon ached.

Eilene led Elizabeth up a gentle slope that seemed to be leading to the sensor line. The snow was deep, and even with the snowshoes Elizabeth sank several inches. Elizabeth was about to ask for a rest break when they came to a cabin. The window was broken out, the door gone.

"Did they hang Petroski?" Elizabeth asked, as they passed the long-deserted cabin.

"Nope. They tried him twice and got a hung jury both times. Seems enough people around here have spent time in a cabin with a flatulent friend and considered it justifiable homicide."

"You're kidding!" Elizabeth suggested.

"Nope. Petroski worked the mine himself for another five years and then one spring didn't come out for supplies. They found him dead in the cabin. He'd put his shotgun in his mouth and pushed the trigger with his big toe. He left a note that said 'Sorry Chuck.'"

A few stumps pushed through the snow and the terrain quickly became too steep to climb. There was a gulley to one side and Elizabeth could picture a stream running there in the spring. Then Eilene stopped, turned on her flashlight and shone it on the boarded-up entrance to the Petroski-Paley mine. They took off their snowshoes and then Eilene tore loose a board. Then she pushed on the heavy wood door that sealed the entrance. It swung open. Elizabeth had to duck under the remaining boards, getting on her hands and knees to follow Eilene into the mine. Eilene pulled the snowshoes inside, closed the door, then lit a match and touched it to the mantle of a propane lantern. The mine was nothing more than a tunnel with wooden beams shoring up the roof.

"Is this safe?" Elizabeth asked, looking at the old timber.

"No," Eilene said. "Follow me. Don't touch anything I don't touch."

Eilene could stand up in the mine, her head barely clearing the top of the tunnel, but Elizabeth had to walk slightly bent. There were occasional side passages, but when Elizabeth explored them with her flashlight she found them to be dead-ends filled with rubble.

"Two men dug all of this?" Elizabeth asked, whispering.

Eilene answered in full volume.

"Sure. If all you did for twenty years was dig, you could do it, too. Of course some of this was blasted. Like I said, it was a piss-poor vein and they had to crush tons of rock to make a living. That's why no one's ever picked up the claim."

Eilene led her deeper into the mountain, then abruptly turned left into a short side passage. An old wooden ladder led up into darkness.

"This is a ventilation shaft," Eilene said. "Follow me."

Still holding the lantern, Eilene started to climb. Elizabeth tested the first rung with her weight even though Eilene outweighed her. Then she climbed, seeing nothing above her but Eilene's bottom. The passage was tight, barely bigger than her body. It meant it was almost impossible to fall since it would be easy to jam oneself between the rock and the ladder, but it was also claustrophobic. There were cobwebs, most cleared by Eilene, but enough left to tickle Elizabeth's skin and trigger imaginary spiders skittering across her face and hands.

Then Eilene paused and blew out the light. She fumbled with something metal, then climbed and pushed and with a thump there was faint light and fresh air. Gratefully, Elizabeth followed Eilene out of the shaft.

"We're inside the fence and their detection devices," Eilene said.

Still looking for imaginary bugs, Elizabeth did not look up right away. When she did, she could see the secret of Fox Valley. Taking her satellite phone she held it up and took a picture, and then she used the satellite connection to access the Internet and typed in a brief message for Nick. Attaching the picture, she sent it.

"Let's get closer," she whispered to Eilene.

"Wait," Eilene said. "Someone is coming."

18 • ORBITAL FLIGHT

They said to each other, "Come, let's make bricks and bake them thoroughly." They used brick instead of stone, and tar for mortar. Then they said, "Come, let us build ourselves a city, with a tower that reaches to the heavens, so that we may make a name for ourselves and not be scattered over the face of the whole earth."

—*Genesis 11:3-4*

GROOM LAKE, NEVADA

There was little diversity but much repetition in their training for their flight on the Aurora and their work on the lunar surface. On the trip up, they would ride in a windowless chamber, strapped into padded seats in a semi-reclining position, wearing helmets and special pressure suits designed to compensate for the g-forces they would experience. They were taught to operate the radio, regulate their air supply, and monitor each other for signs of respiratory or cardiac stress. However, once in flight, nothing could be done except abort. Packed like sardines in a can, locked in the hold, and accelerating to 25,000 miles per hour, emergency aid was impossible. There was no escape system for the cargo— Nick and his crew—or even for the pilot, Captain Smith, or navigator, Rosa Perez.

Most of the training was for the lunar surface where they would have to work in clumsy environment suits in one-sixth of Earth's gravity. The simulator used counterbalancing weights to imitate light gravity. Nick expected weighing less would conserve energy, but he constantly overestimated the effort necessary to move or lift and then had to compensate with other muscles to slow or stop his motion. It was exhausting. Slowly, they reprogrammed their muscles for a low-gravity environment. There would be as much time spent in a micro-gravity environment. However, they had not trained for that environment since they had no duties other than to keep out of the way and not push any buttons.

While astronaut training would normally take months or even years, they had only a few days' worth. Since no one knew what they would find in Flamsteed Crater, they had no idea of what to train them for. What tools would be needed? What skills? What knowledge? With nothing for the mission planners to work with, and a short timeline before launch, they were trained to walk, breathe, eat, and eliminate in environment suits. They practiced with a variety of instruments used to examine the structure and with a variety of tools they would bring with them, learning how to pry, twist, hammer, and jab in one-sixth of normal gravity. They were essentially lunar tourists.

Nick had finished his last day of training before the flight and was back in his room, computer hooked up to the Internet. He had permission to access the PresNet, but to read only, not to send without screening. He had accepted the limitation and now logged on and downloaded e-mail messages. There was one message from Elizabeth with an attachment. Nick opened it.

LEAVING FOR THE SITE NOW. I THOUGHT YOU SHOULD KNOW I SLEPT WITH SOMEONE ELSE LAST NIGHT. HE IS THE ONE IN THE FUR COAT. HIS NAME IS KAMIAK.

Jealousy flared in Nick. Although he and Elizabeth had no more commitment to each other than friendship, his jealousy suggested the depth of his feelings for her. He always guessed that she had other lovers but he repressed the thought. Now he grew angry. Why would she send him a picture of a lover? Why tell Nick his name? He almost deleted the photo, but perverse male curiosity made him open it. It was a photo of a dog with patches of fur shaved off. Nick was embarrassed. He fell for Elizabeth's trick, but found himself thinking about Elizabeth in a different way.

The crew of the Aurora and Nick's team ate dinner together, but only Captain Smith and Rosa were talkative. Even Phil made only a few comments about the afternoon's training. Phil continued to surprise Nick with his stamina. He was faring as well or better than Nick. Smith and Rosa left immediately after dinner to preflight the Aurora. Nick, Phil, Emmett, and Reggie went back to their rooms.

Nick tried to sleep but could only toss and turn, worrying about Elizabeth's quest for the secret building. He was still awake at midnight when they called him to the preflight room. Nick logged on one more time before he left, typing a message to Elizabeth, scolding her for the joke, but wording it carefully so that she got some hint that it made him jealous. He then sent the message to the security officer, with others he had written earlier, who would screen it and release it in a day or so if the mission was going well. The delayed e-mail messages would give the illusion that Nick was still on the planet and checking in occasionally. Nick was about to log off when he checked his inbox out of habit. There was another message from Elizabeth with another attachment.

HERE'S YOUR DAMN BUILDING. YOU WOULDN'T BELIEVE WHAT I WENT THROUGH TO GET THIS PHOTO. DOESN'T LOOK SPECIAL TO ME. I'LL SEE WHAT ELSE I CAN FIND OUT. MORE LATER.

The photo was poor quality, the lighting bad, but Nick was at once elated and disappointed. The structure looked rectangular, and could or could not be similar to the structure on the moon. While the size was hard to judge, it was at least a few stories tall, but nothing to suggest it was some exotic form of power. Nick studied the photo more closely. He could tell nothing about its composition but as he studied the building one thing did strike him as unusual. The framework of this building was on the outside. It was as if the building's skeleton was never intended to be covered. Nick knew that the skin of buildings was often designed to add strength. Certainly, one could engineer a building without an exterior skin, but why do it? In a northern climate, the space between the interior and the exterior was insulated to conserve heat. Where was the insulation?

Nick, Emmett, Reggie, and Phil were helped into their flight suits. The tight black flight suit exaggerated curves making Reggie voluptuous and Phil comic. Nick tried not to stare at Reggie during the dressing process and especially after she had her suit on. Nick also tried not to think about what he must look like to Reggie and was glad there were no mirrors.

They were loaded into the belly of the Aurora through a top hatch. Phil went in first, then Emmett, Reggie, and Nick. Lined up like bobsledders, each seat reclined into the lap of the one behind. Hoses and cables attached to their suits, their black helmets locked onto the collars. The visors were open and airsickness bags were taped to the seat in front of each passenger. Captain Smith and Rosa entered through a second hatch and as soon as they were in place, their hatch closed. There was a dim light to keep it from being pitch dark and a screen to show them what the pilot was seeing. The screen glowed blue.

The Aurora flew only under cover of darkness and even now, patrols were scouring the perimeter lines of Area 51 for ufologists, conspiracy freaks, and sightseers. Once fueled and loaded with its crew, the Aurora was then covered with a camouflage tarp and towed to the runway. Only when air traffic control confirmed the surrounding airspace was clear, and there were no foreign or commercial satellites overhead, did the tarp come off. At that point, Captain Smith did not waste time. The engines were fired up and tested, and then the Aurora began to roll. The Aurora's secret was most vulnerable when it sat on the runway. Once in the air, nothing could catch it.

An image appeared on the screen at the front of the cabin. With no lights, Nick could barely make out the runway. Either Smith had an infrared view, or he was going to take off by memory. Instantly, the Aurora accelerated down the runway much faster than any commercial jet. Then the Aurora's nose snapped up, and the craft shot into the air. The screen showed nothing but blackness.

Started in a reclining position, their heads were now tilted down, blood forced toward their heads. Their pressurized suits helped to control blood flow, but Nick could feel the pressure in his head. The airframe vibrated, but as they climbed, the vibrations diminished. Gratefully, the vertical flight ended more gently than it began as the Aurora leveled off. The screen showed darkness with bright twinkling stars on the top edge of the screen.

"Everyone okay back there?" Smith radioed.

The helmets fit tight and the headphones were built in.

"Let's go," Emmett said.

"Sure, no problem," Phil replied.

"Fine," Nick managed, trying to sound calmer than he really felt.

"I could use another bag," Reggie said.

Nick tore one of his airsickness bags loose and forced his arm between the seat and the exterior wall that was lined with tubing. Nick barely had enough room to get his hand back far enough for Reggie to grab the bag.

"Was that the worst part of the flight?" Reggie asked hopefully.

"Depends on what makes your stomach churn," Smith

said. "We don't have any more climbs quite that steep left, but the biggest g-forces are still ahead."

"Oh," Reggie said, disappointed.

"You can relax for a few minutes while we refuel. The next leg takes every drop we can carry."

Nick knew that the air tanker coming to rendezvous with them carried a different kind of fuel. The Aurora had many smaller fuel tanks, which were baffled in such a way that sections could be closed off and filled with different fuel. Most of the fuel for normal air flight had been expended at this point and those cells would be refilled.

The air tanker appeared on the screen as the Aurora closed quickly. Just when collision seemed likely, the Aurora slowed and the tanker extended a refueling probe. The ships coupled and then Nick felt the vibration of refueling. The tanker was in position only a few minutes, and then veered away.

"Now the fun begins," Smith radioed. "We need to make a small adjustment in our flight path and in about three minutes we will reach our launch window."

Again, without wasting time, the Aurora tilted right, like a normal airplane, and then leveled. A minute later it tilted slightly left, wobbled a bit, then steadied with its nose in the air, and their suits pressurizing.

"Stand by," Smith said cryptically.

There were no armrests on the seat, so Nick gripped the harness that held him in place. Then there were motor sounds as windshield, antennae, and other exterior features were retracted and the wings reshaped.

"Here we go," Smith said.

Now Nick fully understood the concept of "g." He felt like he was in a vise, the back of the chair one of the clamps, the other invisible on his chest. His pressure suit hissed, and the pressure across his chest eased.

The engine roar became a thrum, made up of hundreds of individual detonations so closely timed as to be indistinguishable. Consuming fuel at an obscene rate, the Aurora became lighter, letting it climb through layers of the atmosphere. The screen lightened as they raced toward the rising sun, but it was also changing color, the atmospheric filter thinning.

"Coming up on insertion point," Smith radioed.

Now the pulse detonation engine became a rocket as the Aurora switched to onboard oxygen and hydrogen. The Aurora leaped toward space, the remaining tons of fuel combined in nozzles in a mix designed to maximize explosive power. The pressure became painful now, as they literally rocketed through what was left of the atmosphere, breaking free of Earth's gravity. Limited to short gasps, Nick felt he was suffocating, his ribs bending, threatening to collapse and crush his internal organs. He knew nothing of Reggie, Phil, and Emmett. Just when he thought he would pass out it ended abruptly.

Gasping for breath like a drowning man pulled to the surface, Nick luxuriated in the ability to breathe again. It was several seconds before he thought to look at the screen. It was blue again.

"I hope you enjoyed your flight," Smith called. "I can tell by the monitor you are all alive so the question is are you all still conscious?"

"Yes," Nick said, irritated.

"Yes, I just wish I wasn't," Emmett said.

"I think I reached a new level of consciousness," Phil said. There was a pause.

"Reggie?" Nick probed.

Another pause.

"I'm okay," Reggie said, softly.

"Good, you can relax for a while," Smith said.

"Oh no!" Reggie said suddenly.

"What's wrong?" Nick and Phil both exclaimed, the radio cutting their voices together as it tried to switch back and forth.

"My barf bag is floating."

"Please catch it," Phil pleaded.

Nick pulled his remaining airsickness bag free and let go of it. It floated before his eyes, drifting toward his chest on ventilation currents. Nick tapped it with his finger putting it into a spin. Like every visitor to space since Yury Gagarin, Nick experimented with an environment that few had experienced. Soon, Nick was queasy and stared at the screen instead. Then with a blink, Nick could see the Earth curving below. Thankfully, it was mesmerizing and he forgot about his stomach.

"Beautiful," Reggie said.

Those in the cargo hold were quiet now, enjoying the spectacular scene. Soon, an object appeared—Freedom Station. Despite orbital speed, the Aurora crept up on the station and soon Nick could distinguish large solar panels, and tubular modules. He could see the craft that would take them on the next leg of their journey docked at one of the modules. It looked nothing like the sleek Aurora.

19 · THIRD LEG

At the heart of the universe is a steady, insistent beat: the sound of cycles in sync. It pervades nature at every scale from the nucleus to the cosmos. . . . In every case, these feats of synchrony occur spontaneously, almost as if nature has an eerie yearning for order.

—*Steven Strogatz,* Sync: The Emerging Science of
Spontaneous Order

FOX VALLEY, ALASKA

Vince Walters avoided his boss's eyes as the steel doors slowly closed. Kawabata was a cheap old bastard, and far too nosy for his own good. He had been suspicious since the beginning of the project, snooping, probing, questioning every decision that Vince made. "Why must the walls be a foot thick?" he asked. "Why so much steel? Why not aluminum? It is much cheaper." Vince had hidden his needs behind the canard of "emergency containment" in case of catastrophe. Kawabata scoffed at this, too. "No one around here to be killed except us," Kawabata pointed out.

Fortunately for Vince, the Defense Department had been easier to manipulate. Accustomed to spending outrageous amounts on black bag projects, Vince found it easy to convince DOD to authorize the type of structure he needed. It helped that Vince had supervised the construction of the containment building while Kawabata had remained in Houston, completing design and materials development. Most of what Kawabata considered unnecessary had been authorized and expended by the DOD before he knew about it.

With the doors open, Vince's face stung. He pulled the cords dangling from his hood, pinching his hood tighter around his face. He loved the purity of Alaska, but he hated the weather. He should not have to suffer such conditions to live free of strip malls, traffic-jammed highways, and polluted air. If this worked, he would be one step closer to what the world had once been.

A flatbed snow machine waited. The crate containing the nuclear weapon was on a dolly and they rolled it forward until it buried in the ice that surrounded the building. Lifting the crate, four of them placed it on the flatbed. Working in gloves, they lashed the crate down with nylon rope. When it was secure, they walked to the shed where the snow machines sat, plugged into wall sockets to keep their engines from freezing.

Vince led the way, the snow truck and the other snow machine trailing. Building the bunkers for the warheads had been the most difficult step to keep secret from Kawabata. The bunkers—called anchors then—were poured early, ostensibly as part of an early design for the containment building, which included cable supports, which Vince later claimed to have abandoned. With the bunkers, Vince could secure the warheads as he acquired them, and monitor them remotely. Headlight on, traveling slowly, he followed the trail up into the trees. There were three identical sites equidistant from the containment building, with warheads already installed in two. The empty bunker was just ahead.

The trail became a switchback, the dimly lit containment building below. Kawabata had grudgingly authorized minimal exterior lighting, but rejected funding for a basketball court, which the employees had requested. "Plenty of places to walk if you need exercise," Kawabata had said. The result of his penurious nature was that the exterior was clean, the only exterior structure the sheds where the snow machines were kept.

They finished the climb, leveling out, and reached the empty bunker. As the others unlashed the crate, Vince shoveled snow from the entrance, and then pulled off a glove and took a key from his pocket. The silicone-lubricated padlock unlatched easily. He pushed the heavy steel door open. The ceiling was low, his head nearly scraping the top. He hit the light switch, the fluorescent tube blinking to life, casting a pinkish glow. Kawabata had never discovered the connection to the site's power grid, the cabling laid even before the bunkers were poured.

There was little room inside, so they lifted the crate off the back of the snow cat and pried the crate open with a crowbar, setting it aside. Then the four of them lifted the warhead straight up and out of the crate. Carrying it down into the bunker's entrance, Vince took half the weight, backing in. Then they set it down carefully, the frame nestling over four bolts. While a man attached nuts and wrenched the bolts tight, Vince connected the sockets wired into the warhead to those connecting to the containment building. The control panel came to life with a flash of confused symbols, and then CONDUCTING SYSTEM CHECK. Reprogramming the device's computer to display in English had been relatively simple, compared to integrating three timing circuits. The man with Vince slapped him gently on the back.

"It's going to work. We're actually going to do it!"

Whitey had been an early convert to Vince's movement, and like so many other men, seduced in by a woman. Whitey's girlfriend was in prison now, caught burning SUVs at a dealership in Detroit, but Whitey had proved a true believer, staying the course when the sex that hooked him was gone. Recruited out of the University of Michigan, Whitey graduated summa cum laude in materials science and engineering, the perfect background for infiltration into Kawabata's project. Despite his appearance, Whitey's nickname did not come from his colorless hair and skin so fair he could be an albino. Whitey was actually his name—Lawrence Whitey.

Whitey had gray eyes and did tan, if you considered changing from the color of paste to the color of eggshell a tan. He was not an attractive man, broad shouldered with thick arms, broad hands and feet, round face, sparse hair and a flattened nose that gave him a faint Asian appearance. The co-ed that had seduced him, at Vince's request, only stayed with him because Vince insisted. It helped that Whitey was kind and generous, but she did not love him—she loved Vince.

Vince patted Whitey's gloved hand, overcome with his own emotions. With this warhead in place, he had the third leg of a giant who would lift the world above the filth it wallowed in, elevating human and animal in symbiotic equality. Justifiably proud, Vince knew that only he had the genius to imagine the new future, and new history, that could be attained if only someone had the courage to reach for it. Vince had that courage, and that new world was coming, a world he was fashioning.

NO SYSTEM ERRORS DETECTED. SYSTEM STATUS: STAND BY.

The timing on the detonations was critical, but the computer would update the timers on the individual bombs every few seconds to make sure that they were synchronized. The computer itself was kept accurate from time pulses broadcast by satellites of the rebuilt Global Positioning System.

"Bring down the detonator," Vince called out the opening.

Then giving in to his emotions, he hugged Whitey and they slapped each other on the back.

"Nothing can stop us now," Vince said. "Nothing."

20 · BUNKER

About four P.M. yesterday, Good Friday, a small cloud
passed over Mr. Chas. H. Clarke, and several of my ser-
vants, a few paces from the south bank of the Pamunkey
River in the lower end of Hanover County, Virginia, on the
estate called Farmington, and discharged around the
parties . . . various pieces of flesh and liver, too well defined
in each sort to allow any mistake in their character.

—*G. W. Bassett, 1850, reported in* Unexplained!

FOX VALLEY, ALASKA

Elizabeth and Eilene shrank into the shadows of the trees,
crouching, listening to the approach of snow machines.
They were still below them but climbing.

"Let's go, Eilene, they're coming for us."

Eilene hesitated, head cocked to one side.

"No, they're not. They're coming too slow to be after anyone. There's another vehicle too. Something bigger."

Elizabeth listened but could not tell one engine sound
from another. Now Eilene grew bolder, creeping forward until she could see down the hill. Elizabeth crept up next to her,
looking over the edge. It was another minute before the vehicles came into sight. Catching brief glimpses of the vehicles through the trees, Elizabeth realized there was a road
below them. Elizabeth distinguished two snow machines and
a larger vehicle that ran on tracks. Something was tied down
on its bed.

"Kind of late to be making deliveries," Eilene observed.

"Where would they deliver it to around here anyway?"

"Nowhere in that direction," Eilene said.

The engines died, the forest returning to the still of deep
winter. Without a breeze, not even a rustle disturbed the forest. Then they heard the sound of digging.

"Let's get a little closer," Eilene said.

They kept to the trees as much as possible where the snow was not as deep. When they did cross open ground, Eilene broke trail. Elizabeth followed closely in her footsteps, but they were leaving a deep track. Soon they came to the path the snow machines had followed.

"We'll follow their track for a ways," Eilene said.

Walking in the snow machine tracks was easier and they made good time. Soon they could hear people ahead. Eilene led them into the trees again, then broke off a branch and tried to erase their tracks. At best it smudged their trail.

They approached slowly now, keeping trees between them and the voices. Soon they could see the snow vehicles parked next to a concrete structure. Men in dark parkas were lifting a crate off the back of the snow truck. They watched as the crate was pried open, the crowbar tossed aside. Then they lifted something out of the crate. Eilene could make out a metal framework containing cylinders and not much else. They carried whatever it was down into the concrete structure, three of them waiting outside. A few minutes later someone called out from inside, his voice clearly heard in the winter stillness.

"Bring down the detonator."

Elizabeth and Eilene looked at each other, both mouthing the word "detonator" at the same time.

Something was passed through the opening to whoever had called for it. Some minutes passed now, the cold creeping through Elizabeth's down parka. She began shivering, partly from the cold, mostly from the anxiety.

The men worked for another fifteen minutes, lashing the crate to the back of the snow truck, taking something from the cab of the snow truck, then passing it inside. Then there was the distinctive flash of a welding torch. A few minutes later the torch was passed back out and then the last of them climbed out of the building, turned off a light and closed the door. Then there was hugging and back slapping. Seeing the congratulatory behavior, Eilene and Elizabeth exchanged puzzled looks. Then the workers started up their machines, circled the building, and were gone.

"You ever party like that after finishing a job?" Eilene asked.

"Only when we won an election," Elizabeth said. "Not when we unpacked a crate."

"Let's take a look," Eilene said, moving forward.

Elizabeth had unleashed an uncontrollable force in Eilene. Leaving an easily followed trail, they walked to the building. Eilene walked down three steps, almost disappearing in the deep shadows at the bottom. Suddenly she flicked her flashlight on. Eilene jumped as if she had fired a gun.

"There's a padlock."

Eilene climbed out of the well and Elizabeth walked down, looking at the lock. It wasn't impressive, just a sturdy Master lock.

"There couldn't be anything worth hiding in here," Elizabeth said. "The entire security system is a padlock."

Eilene came back, carrying the crowbar the men had left behind.

"Don't underestimate the Master lock company," Eilene said. "That lock isn't coming off that door even with this."

"Then what are you doing?"

"If the hasp makers were as good as the Master lock company, we'd be out of luck."

Eilene jammed the hasp with the crowbar, the sound startlingly loud.

"Eilene, they might hear you," Elizabeth whispered, holding out her hand to stop her guide.

"They can't hear nothing but the roar of their engines."

Eilene repeatedly attempted to get the pry bar under the hasp. Finally, she managed to bend up an edge. With a small high spot to work with, Eilene worked diligently now, alternating between jamming and prying. Finally, the hasp broke free with a screech that sent Elizabeth running up the stairs to look down the trail. Eilene was inside the building now, the light on.

The interior was lit by a single fluorescent tube, the harsh light too weak to banish all the shadows. A strange device was sitting in the middle of the room. Framed in steel, it was box shaped, with two cylinders, one larger than the other. Wires connected to devices on the sphere at several points. More wires led to a black box that looked like a computer complete with keyboard and display panel. There was a second smaller round display mounted on top of a cylinder that rested next to the sphere.

"What is it?" Elizabeth asked, still whispering.

"You heard them as well as I did," Eilene said in her normal voice.

Elizabeth cringed, even knowing their voices could not carry far.

"He asked for the detonator," Eilene said. "This is a stinking bomb."

"Okay, I heard that, but why would someone put a bomb out here?"

"I suppose it could be some sort of security device. Maybe it's supposed to go off and destroy that base if they are invaded."

"It would have to be a very powerful bomb to destroy that building from here!"

Now the women looked at each other again, both the weathered Eilene and the polished Elizabeth coming to the same conclusion. Elizabeth ransacked her memory from her White House days, remembering pictures of nuclear weapons. Most were in steel casings, ready to be launched, but some memories were of the guts of these weapons. There was a close match.

"Nuclear?" Elizabeth said. "It makes no sense. If their secret was that precious then why wouldn't they just guard it better?"

"I suppose they could be terrorists," Eilene said, sounding doubtful. "Maybe they planted the bomb to destroy the base? Maybe they hid it here so they would have time to get away."

"But they came from the direction of the base. They weren't being secretive."

"Traitors?"

A red glowing LED indicated power, but the panel was

dark. Studying the keyboard, Elizabeth pushed the return key and the panel came to life. Glowing red letters marched across the screen.

NO SYSTEM ERRORS DETECTED. SYSTEM STATUS: ARMED. TIMER MODE: COUNTDOWN.

Stunned, Elizabeth touched Eilene's arm, pointing at the display.

"What did you do?" Eilene demanded.

"Nothing. I hit the return key, that's all."

"Try delete."

Doubtfully, Elizabeth hit the delete key but nothing happened. Then she punched it twice. Then three times. Now punching it over and over there was still no response.

"It just says 'countdown mode,' it doesn't say it is counting down," Eilene pointed out.

Elizabeth studied the keyboard, finding a button labeled "reset." She punched the key. The screen went blank for a few seconds, then PASSWORD: appeared.

A few seconds later, the screen changed again. NO SYSTEM ERRORS DETECTED. SYSTEM STATUS: ARMED. TIMER MODE: COUNTDOWN scrolled across the screen. Then a new message appeared. TIMER SYNC INTERRUPT: 02:17: TIMER SYNC RELOCK. NO SYSTEM ERRORS DETECTED. SYSTEM STATUS: ARMED. TIMER MODE: COUNTDOWN.

"Back where we started," Elizabeth said.

"Maybe we can pull the detonator out?" Eilene suggested, leaning into the device, looking at its guts. "I've worked with dynamite and blasting caps."

Elizabeth frowned.

"Don't say it, Elizabeth! I know that is the dumbest-ass thing you've ever heard."

Elizabeth pulled her satellite phone out, stepped back, and took a picture of the device. Then she stepped outside and punched up the menu, and logged onto her e-mail. She typed a brief message, attached the photo, and sent it. Then she hesitated. Who to call for help? State police? FBI? Homeland Security? She couldn't imagine the federal government would set off a nuclear device above ground on the continental U.S., but what if there was a reason they would? Then calling federal authorities would do no good.

"Call the state police," Eilene suggested as if she read her mind. "I don't trust them farther than I can spit, but that's a damn sight farther than the feds."

Eilene didn't have a number for the state police, and she had only dialed direct with the satellite phone. She wasn't even sure how to get directory assistance. Instead of trying to get an operator, she decided to call Bill in Washington. He could relay the message. As she worked her way back to the telephone's menu she heard the sound of engines.

"Run for it," Eilene said, bolting down the road.

Elizabeth's heart pounded from fear and exertion. The roar of the engines was loud now, and Elizabeth could see headlights flickering ahead. Eilene turned into the trees, Elizabeth following, the two of them hiding, waiting. While Elizabeth waited she pulled out her phone again, connected to her e-mail, composed a message and then sent it to Bill just as the snow machines roared by, two men to a vehicle. Eilene waited a few seconds, and then jumped up and used a branch to smudge their tracks.

"Let's go," Eilene said.

They ran under the trees where the snow was shallower, venturing into open space only when unavoidable. Elizabeth's legs burned from exertion. She couldn't hear the snow machines now, not over her heavy breathing and pounding heart. Nearly exhausted, she stumbled, planting her face in the snow. Eilene paused, hands on her knees, gasping for breath.

"I'm too old for this," Eilene said.

Getting to her knees, Elizabeth heard the engines idling.

"Come on," Eilene said, turning to go. "They're looking for our trail."

Elizabeth got to her feet, looking ahead. It was all uphill to the mineshaft. Now the engines roared. Elizabeth forced her legs to move, picking up speed, trying to catch Eilene. Suddenly the pitch of the engines changed. They had found their trail and they were coming fast.

21 ▪ STRANGER

Gernon had just taken off in his Beech Craft Bonanza from Andros Island in the Bahamas, bound for Palm Beach, Florida. Gernon remembers accelerating quickly to avoid the thick cloud, but it seemed to rise to meet him . . . this was no ordinary cloud. . . . The plane seemed to pick up unnatural speed and for several seconds, Gernon and his father experienced weightlessness. . . . Through the haze, he spotted an island and, calculating his flight time, thought it must be the Bimini keys. Minutes later, Gernon recognized it as Miami Beach instead. . . . A trip that normally took him about seventy-five minutes had taken only forty-five, and he had burned twelve fewer gallons of fuel than usual.

—Mysteries of the Unknown: Mystic Places,
Time-Life Books

FOX VALLEY, ALASKA

Kawabata was displeased with his project assistant. Dr. Walters had returned from whatever errand he was on, without his crate. Kawabata was supervising Phat and Marissa who were charting the increase in humidity and air temperature. Immediately after Dr. Walters returned to his office, he came racing out, putting on his parka as he ran.

"What is the emergency?" Kawabata called, concerned.

Dr. Walters looked stricken and irritated at the same time.

"There may be a security breach," he said. "It's probably just another damn moose."

The exit door was open just wide enough to pass through when Dr. Walters and the same three men squeezed in, then reversed the door. Kawabata did not believe his story. If a moose had triggered the motion sensors it would have enough mass to be screened out by the ID program.

Phat and Marissa seemed to be making good progress,

Phat typing on the keyboard, Marissa kibitzing. Kawabata walked up the stairs to the office level and to his assistant's office. Dr. Walters supervised security among his other duties, but it was unusual for him to respond to alerts personally. Stranger yet was why he took one of their engineers with him.

Dr. Walters had been Kawabata's second choice for the project, accepting him only after his first choice, Dr. Joyce Niles, had been killed in a car accident. While her death had been a tragedy it had not greatly affected the nascent project since Dr. Walters proved an able engineer and project manager, although he lacked the ability for theoretical work.

Now stepping into his assistant's office, Kawabata was reminded of another of Dr. Walters's fine qualities. His office was neat, although not spartan. His desktop was clear of clutter, free of dust, and well polished. A desk pad sat in the middle, a pen-and-pencil holder sat at the edge of the desk, equally distant from each side. The pictures on the walls were all wilderness settings, each identically framed, well spaced around the room. Dr. Walters had added throw rugs to his office, at his own expense, covering large sections of the industrial quality carpeting Kawabata had authorized reluctantly since he wasn't sure carpeting was a necessity in a research facility. There was a three-cushion couch, and two side chairs upholstered in chenille the color of toast.

Dr. Walters's keyboard and screen sat on a sidebar and Kawabata walked over, sitting in his assistant's chair. The computer was in energy saving mode—Kawabata approved—the screen blank. A click of the mouse and the computer came back to life. "TIMER SYNC INTERRUPT: 02:17: TIMER SYNC RELOCK. NO SYSTEM ERRORS DETECTED. SYSTEM STATUS: ARMED. TIMER MODE: COUNTDOWN" scrolled across the screen.

Kawabata frowned. He had never seen this display. He guessed it was part of the security program, which Walters supervised, but Kawabata prided himself on knowing all of their systems. He studied the message, becoming convinced that it indicated some sort of security breach, but saw no connection with a moose. The part about the COUNTDOWN made the least sense. Pushing his glasses up onto his forehead he rubbed his eyes. "Very curious," Kawabata said.

Kawabata tried accessing the security system but none of his passwords would get him in, the screen returning to the one message after rejecting his passwords. He gave up, planning to have a difficult conversation with his assistant.

Back on the construction floor Phat and Marissa were running a model that projected that the humidity would plateau at 92 percent, the temperature at 38 degrees Celsius.

"Who's that?" called one of the assembly specialists.

Kawabata turned with the others, looking back at the structure. There was a man standing in the opening. He wore camouflage pants and a long-sleeve shirt with large pockets on the chest. His face was dirty and streaked by rivulets of sweat. There was a belt around his waist with a water bottle and pouch, and a holster. He looked as confused as those who stared back.

"Call security," Marissa yelled.

"No, wait!" Kawabata countermanded.

Kawabata studied the man. He knew him from somewhere.

The man stepped out, looked around, and then up at the ceiling. Then he backed away from the structure a few steps, studying it.

"Who are you?" Marissa asked.

The man turned, looked each of them over, then trotted back to the opening and disappeared inside. Marissa and Phat followed, Kawabata hesitating, his sharp mind systematically considering the possibilities. Then he realized who the man was and he muttered, "Not possible," immediately correcting himself. "If it happened, it is possible." Quickly, he followed his rash assistants into the structure, knowing what they would find even as he did.

22 ▪ PURSUIT

The continuing debate over Russia's command and control
of its nuclear arsenal intensified on September 7 when retired General Alexander Lebed, former secretary of the
Russian Security Council, told the CBS news program *60
Minutes* that he believes more than 100 . . . nuclear
weapons are unaccounted for.

—*Craig Cerniello, Arms Control Association, 1997*

FOX VALLEY, ALASKA

Eilene was opening up a gap, the tough old bird's legs
breaking trail and still outpacing Elizabeth. Lungs burning, legs aching, barely able to stumble after Eilene, Elizabeth was ready to surrender. They were from her
government, after all, and she and Eilene weren't spies.
Well, not foreign spies. Elizabeth knew all this, yet she still
ran. Whatever she had stumbled across, it wasn't like any
government secret she had ever been privy to.

The snow machines were roaring so loud, Elizabeth was
afraid to look behind her, fearing she would find herself
face-to-face with them. The trees thickened as they reached
the crest. Stumbling, she could see the shrubs that hid the
shaft. They were close now, but so were the snow machines.

Eilene reached the shaft, pulled up the hatch, and then
started down. She paused long enough to yell.

"Hurry, they're almost on you!"

Suddenly one engine died, then another. Now men could
be heard tromping through the snow. Eilene disappeared into
the shaft. Elizabeth ran through the brush, reaching the
hatch. The opening was black. She jumped the last few feet
and landed on her seat, legs in the opening. Feeling for the
rung, she had to turn to put her feet on the ladder. The lead
man was only a few yards away and he had a gun. She

started down the ladder but when she did he fired. A puff of snow to her left marked where the bullet had just missed her.

"Don't shoot!" she called. "I'm an American citizen."

She was too terrified to be embarrassed and pleaded with them.

"I'm not a spy!" she yelled.

"Get down here," Eilene whispered below her.

The men surrounded her.

"Don't shoot!" Elizabeth repeated, estimating her chances.

"Now, before it's too late," Eilene said.

"Get out of there!" she was ordered, four guns pointing at her.

"I'm an American citizen. I'm not a spy."

"Climb out of that hole and whoever is with you, too!"

The man giving the orders pushed his hood back. He wore a black stocking cap underneath, and goggles. Now he cocked his gun dramatically.

"One, two," he said.

"All right, I'm getting out. I told you I'm not a spy."

Elizabeth climbed out, talking as she did.

"I'm a lawyer, and I know my rights," she said.

As she climbed out she put her hand on the top of the hatch, pushed herself out the rest of the way and then pretended to stumble, pushed the lid down, and fell on top of it.

"Dammit!" the leader yelled. "Get her off of there."

Elizabeth could feel the hatch being latched. Then there were two quick knocks and a muffled "Thank you."

Elizabeth went limp, and then when they tried to drag her off, she suddenly twisted, jerking free, falling on the hatch again. Now grabbed under the armpits, she was angrily dragged off to the side and dropped. Elizabeth rolled over, watching. While one man kept a gun on her, the leader leaned over and tried pulling up on the hatch. It wouldn't budge.

"Damn."

"Who's in there?" he demanded.

Elizabeth shook her head.

Frustrated, he fired five rounds into the lid.

"Stop, you'll kill her!" Elizabeth blurted.

"Where does this go?" The man demanded.

Elizabeth shook her head.

"Pick her up!" the leader ordered, pointing the smoking weapon at her.

"Where does that go?"

Elizabeth glared at him.

"One," he said, cocking his gun.

What had Nick gotten her into? Elizabeth wondered.

"I don't believe you will shoot me," she said, trying to sound confident. "Government agents don't murder suspects."

Now he smiled.

"Two."

"Are you counting to three? Ten? One hundred?" Elizabeth asked. "Shouldn't I know for this to be effective?"

Pointing out his incompetence was a mistake. His lips tightened, and his hand trembled. Now he put the gun to her forehead, the heat of his first shots already sucked away by the bitter cold of the night air. It felt as if a Popsicle was being pressed against her forehead. She closed her eyes waiting to die. She started counting her life in seconds. Then the gun was pulled away. She opened her eyes to see the man calmer now, even puzzled.

"I know you," he said softly. "You're Elizabeth Hawthorne."

He released the hammer, and then scratched the side of his head with the pistol, pushing the gun under his stocking cap.

"Who sent you here? What do you know?"

Relief flooded Elizabeth. She was going to live until he found out what he needed to know. He studied her now, lost in thought, thinking through the implications of finding a former presidential chief of staff sneaking around a secret military installation in the middle of the Alaskan winter. Suddenly his eyes fixed on something by her face. He took off his glove, then reached out and felt the trim on her hood.

"That's real!" he said ominously. "You murdering bitch!"

"It's not—"

Before she could finish, he punched her in the face. Somewhere between the blow and hitting the ground she lost consciousness.

23 ▪ MUTINY

The *Apocrypha*'s book of *Bel and the Dragon* relates . . . that in the temple of Bel, Lord of the World, Nebuchadnezzar's favored god, the priests kept a "great dragon or serpent, which they of Babylon worshipped." The king challenged the Hebrew prophet Daniel, who had been sneering about nonliving gods of brass, to dispute this god, who "liveth, and eateth and drinketh; you canst not say that he is no living god; therefore worship him." To remove himself from this quandary, Daniel poisoned the animal.

—Jerome Clark, Unexplained!

FOX VALLEY, ALASKA

Toru Kawabata followed Phat and Marissa into the structure after the mystery man who had disappeared back inside. The younger assistants ran ahead, negotiating the turns, climbing and dropping into the center. They were about to search the rest of the structure when he called to them.

"Stop! Do not pursue him."

"What? Why?" Marissa asked.

"Sir, I do not believe he is part of the project team. He is a trespasser."

"Yes, Dr. Nyang, but I do not think you will find him."

"Sir? But he did not pass us. So where did he go?"

"That is the right question. Look for evidence."

Kawabata began examining the floor, systematically pacing off the interior. Marissa and Phat looked, still puzzled. The interior was sultry now, and they were soon sweating in their coveralls.

"Dr. Kawabata," Marissa said suddenly. "There is sand on the floor."

Kawabata and Phat hurried over, and squatted. Marissa had pushed several grains together, making a tiny pile. Phat looked up the ramp behind Marissa.

"There is more," Phat said, duck-walking a few steps.

"Collect it. We will examine it in the materials lab."

Marissa folded a piece of paper into an envelope shape, and then Phat swept her small pile of sand into the holder. With their armpits soaked through and sweat running down their necks, they headed to the exit.

"Sir, something has changed," Phat said, pausing.

Phat stood by one of the baffles. The baffles were retractable and were used to control the flow of the orgonic energy.

"This baffle was fully retracted before."

Kawabata looked the baffle over, lips pursed.

"Phat, check the baffles between here and the central chamber. Record their positions, but do not change them. Do not cross the central chamber. Examine only this side."

His instructions mystified Phat, but he would obey.

"Come immediately after you have made your observations."

Sand in hand, Marissa followed Kawabata to the exit, the air in the containment building warmer than Kawabata's approved temperature, but still twenty degrees cooler than the interior of the structure. Wet with sweat, the abrupt change sent a chill up Kawabata's spine.

As they exited the structure the motors on the exit door started up and the heavy doors slid apart. Dr. Walters was there, hood thrown back, wearing a stocking cap. He had his gloves in one hand and with the other he held the arm of a woman wearing only a sweater. There was blood on

her face. One of the other men held a bloodstained parka
in his hand.

"Dr. Walters, Dr. Whitey, what is the meaning of this?"

Vince rolled his eyes, his disrespect palpable. Kawabata
would not tolerate it.

"Dr. Walters, you will come to my office!"

His assistant looked uncertain, still holding the arm of the
woman. Finally, he made his decision. He unzipped his
parka, pulling a pistol from his belt. Now all of his men
pulled out pistols, all except Dr. Whitey.

"Yes, we will go to your office, but I'll do the talking."

"What is the meaning of this?" Kawabata demanded,
coming forward fearlessly.

Someone pulled Kawabata's arm behind his back.

"Please, sir. They have guns," Phat said, coming up behind.

Vince Walters shouted orders, further insulting Kawabata.

There were three other workers in the assembly room besides Phat and Marissa. They all froze, looking to Kawabata.

"Do as he says," Kawabata said, always a practical man.

"What is going on?" Kawabata demanded again.

"You have no idea, do you, old man? You don't even know
what you've built here!"

"It is a collector of orgonic energy," Kawabata said, confused.

Dr. Walters laughed derisively.

"Yes, but why? Don't you understand the connection to
the time quilting? To the black ripples that have given our
animal brothers and sisters a second chance?"

Kawabata was seeing his assistant in a new way, an ugly
way.

"Don't be disrespectful, Dr. Walters. I was the first to see
the connection between time ripples and orgonic energy and
I was the first to document the confluence of energies. You,
however, are an engineer, not a scientist. You build what I
design. You are a workman, not a creator."

The scolding had the desired effect. Dr. Walters shook
with rage.

"A workman, am I? You are the fool, Dr. Kawabata!" He spat. "Even now, the greatest discovery in human history is under your nose and you can't see it. History is rushing at you and you don't even know it."

"And you made this discovery?"

"You're damn right I did!" he screamed. "Tell him, Marissa! Tell him who it is that is going to change history!"

Kawabata and Phat turned to their coworker and friend. Distinctly uncomfortable, she inched between them, then turned and backed toward Dr. Walters.

"Dr. Welling?" Kawabata said, disappointed in the bright young woman.

"Tell him!" Walters shouted again, purple with rage.

"Vince—I mean Dr. Walters, he discovered an anomaly in Phat's model. It was created when we factored in the influence of orgonic energy and the first test model. The collector not only focuses orgonic energy, but the extraction of the energy influences the time ripples."

"That's right, Toru," Dr. Walters said, using his given name in disrespect. "How did a penny-pincher like you get as far as you have? Nickel-and-diming may impress the bureaucrats, but it's no substitute for genius. *You* are the workman, Toru, and *I* am the creator, the creator of a new world."

"There was no anomalous data," Toru insisted. "Phat?"

"There was something early on but it cleared up," Phat said tentatively. "Marissa assisted me with that part of the model. Marissa, what did you do?"

"I created a subroutine to screen the anomaly from you and Dr. Kawabata."

Marissa continued to back away, head down, ashamed.

"Now, Toru, don't you feel foolish?" Dr. Walters said tenderly, adding to the scientist's humiliation.

"Vince, something's happened that changes things," Marissa said.

Walters's mood swung back and forth like a manic-depressive's.

"What are you talking about?" he growled.

Marissa cowered, just outside of Walters's reach.

"The orgonic energy met our expectations, but there has also been heat and moisture generation."

As if he was just now feeling it, Walters looked around the enclosure, and then sniffed the air.

"Then a stranger appeared from inside the collector," Marissa continued. "Before we could talk to him he ran back inside. Now we can't find him."

Walters turned to face the woman he held, pointing his gun at her head.

"How many are with you?"

Kawabata studied the woman's face. It was a day for recognition.

"Dr. Hawthorne?" Kawabata asked.

Hawthorne was shivering, her sweater soaked from melted snow. Her skin was purplish. She was unresponsive.

"What have you done to her?" Kawabata demanded. "She is suffering from hypothermia."

"She was wearing fur!" Dr. Walters hissed. "I would not allow her to wear the skin of one of our animal brothers or sisters."

"You would let her die?"

Grabbing the bloody parka from Dr. Whitey, Walters held it out. "How many animals died to produce coats like this? Do you know how much they suffer in those fur factories? Yet your only concern is for the murderer, not the murdered."

The containment building was quiet, even those with Walters uncomfortable with his ranting. Sensing he had exposed a side of himself he did not want them to see, he pulled himself together.

"Search the facility, inside and out. Find the intruder."

With orders, confidence in their leader returned and his followers scattered to their tasks.

"Take them to the dorm and lock them in," Dr. Walters ordered.

One of his men moved forward, motioning with his gun. The three technicians, Kawabata and Phat began to move but then stopped. Walters took the arm of Hawthorne and was about to lead her away when he, too, stopped in his tracks, eyes wide. Turning, Kawabata understood. Standing in the collector's opening was a dinosaur.

24 · IN TRANSIT

The great anomaly chronicler Charles Fort asked a friend, writer Miriam Allen deFord, to go to Chico to investigate personally [rock falls]. There she, in her words, "saw a stone fall from some invisible point in the sky and land gently at my feet." Fort noted that, whether by coincidence or inexplicable design, fish had fallen out of a clear sky in great numbers and landed on a roof and surrounding streets in Chico some forty years earlier, on August 20, 1878.

—*Jerome Clark,* Unexplained!

EARTH ORBIT

During the transfer to the space station from the Aurora, Nick had been distracted as he negotiated the connecting tunnel from the tomblike hold of the Aurora, to the relative spaciousness of the space station. Now, however, he was useless; just another piece of flotsam floating in and out of the way.

The stay at the station would be brief, as the moon shuttle was fueled and flight checked by Rosa Perez and Captain Smith. The three astronauts currently in residence in the space station had duties, although they were chatty when they had the chance to talk to someone besides their crewmates.

The arrival of the Aurora balkanized the station, with Nev Rhyakov, the Russian station commander, and the French astronaut restricted from the module where the Aurora docked. It was a tissue-thin security measure, but the fiction kept peaceful cooperation alive in space when tensions on Earth were high. The Americans returned the courtesy when certain Russian craft arrived.

At the request of ground control, Reggie circulated among both Nick's team and the space station crew, doing medical checkups. Phil, whose powers of adaptation continued to astound Nick, followed the American astronaut around, asking questions, offering to help with programming glitches. To Nick's surprise, Phil was put to work. Emmett connected with the French astronomer who was tracking an asteroid with orbital perturbations from an unexplained source. Emmett was soon immersed in the problem, going over the Frenchman's calculations. Nick found nothing for a bureaucrat to do, and spent the time looking over shoulders, staring out the porthole at Earth, and trying to sleep. Shortly before they were to leave for the moon, Nick tracked down Commander Rhyakov.

She was a stocky woman, wearing red coveralls, her short brown hair a mass of natural curls. Rhyakov floated upside down, holding a clipboard, studying a display and recording data. She was singing an old Monkees tune.

"Cheer up Sleepy Jean, Oh what can it mean . . ."

"Commander Rhyakov," Nick said, getting her attention.

"Call me Nev," the Russian said with only a touch of an accent.

"Is it possible for me to log onto my e-mail from here?"

"Of course. Communications is what Russians do best. But why would you want to? Aren't you on vacation?" she asked playfully. "What other reason would you have for being here? Next time fly Russian spacecraft. Much cheaper than flying in your secret space plane and you get free vodka."

"Really?"

"Absolutely! No one would fly in Russian spacecraft unless they were full of vodka."

Rhyakov laughed at her own joke, a deep masculine chuckle. Still chortling, she motioned toward the other end of the module.

"Pull down the keyboard. I'll patch you in."

"It needs to be a secure connection."

"Of course! Security is what Russians do best."

Nick found the keyboard and folded it down to reveal a screen. Soon Rhyakov had a dial-up program displayed and Nick used it to connect to the PresNet. Nick looked down the corridor and called to Rhyakov.

"I've got the connection. Thanks."

"No problem," Rhyakov said.

Nick waited until the Russian pulled herself up into another module. Over the constant hum of the circulating air, he could hear "One pill makes you larger, and another pill makes you small."

Now Nick started to type but found that keyboarding was enough action to set him to drifting away. Locating straps along the floor, he hooked his feet. Now anchored, Nick went directly to his e-mail and found a message from Elizabeth.

WE FOUND THIS NEAR THE BASE. WE THINK IT MIGHT BE A NUCLEAR BOMB. I'M CALLING FOR REINFORCEMENTS AND THEN GETTING THE HELL OUT OF HERE.

Nick's heart stopped when he saw the words "nuclear bomb," but quickly reason took over. Elizabeth would not know what a nuclear bomb looked like, and nuclear weapons were not lying around where Elizabeth could find one.

Nick opened the attachment and the screen filled with a dim picture of cylinders, cabling, and unidentifiable electronics. Nick had no idea what he was looking at, not having any more experience with nuclear weapons than Elizabeth. Then the screen flickered, the image rebuilding. Nick looked down the corridor but Rhyakov was nowhere in sight. Nick listened—no singing.

Leaving the connection open, Nick pulled himself down the corridor, and then peeked into the tunnel where Rhyakov had gone. Empty. Now Nick pulled himself up to the next module, looking over the edge. Rhyakov was at another station, Elizabeth's photo displayed on her screen.

"Commander," Nick began, startling Rhyakov, "I thought security is what Russians do best?"

"A common misunderstanding," Rhyakov said, recovering from being caught. "Spying is what Russians do best."

Nick pulled himself fully into the compartment.

"Since you've had a look at it, do you know what it is?"

"And this is located where?" Rhyakov asked.

Nick hesitated. There were tensions with the Russians over their carelessness with their nuclear arsenal and now over the rumors of Russia arming Arab countries with nuclear weapons to counter the Israeli arsenal. He decided to be vague.

"Alaska."

More tongue clucking.

"Officially, I do not recognize anything in this image, especially the Russian twenty-megaton warhead in the middle of the screen. I regret that I could not be of any help; however, I can put you in touch with a reliable Russian recycling specialist that would be happy to collect that junk."

Nick was surprised by her candor.

"There should be a junk collector on the way by now."

"Very good!" Rhyakov said, and then broke the connection. "My apologies for eavesdropping but we get so bored up here."

Now she moved off again, singing, ". . . When your shoes get so hot you wish your tired feet were fireproof . . ."

Nick returned to his station suspecting that Rhyakov was still monitoring his communications. Now it didn't matter. She knew about the bomb and his only remaining decision was how best to deal with it. Who could he tell? Who had Elizabeth told about her discovery when she called for "reinforcements"? Nick knew the president and Clark had held back information, and based on the reactions in the Security Council meeting, the CIA director, Caroline Mauck, was party to the secret. The Secretary of State was too ambitious to trust, and Honor Perkins seemed as out of the loop as

General Flannery. That left the director of Homeland Security, Krupp, and the vice president. Krupp was rigid and would want to follow proper channels. The vice president was ambitious, but willing to speak her mind.

The vice president could be accessed through the PresNet, and Nick typed her a message and attached the two photos from Elizabeth and sent the message. He had done what he could until he returned from the moon. Until then, at least Elizabeth was out of it. Now that Nick had sent the message he had second thoughts, worrying that the vice president would go directly to the president and not act independently. If she was coerced, or part of the secret, then he had done nothing about a Russian nuclear device on American soil. Nick found he did not quite trust his own government. However, there was another option.

Nick found Rhyakov mixing powdered soup and hot water in a plastic bag.

"Nev, can you contact your recycling specialist friend discreetly?"

"Of course," she said, smiling. "Discretion is what Russians do best."

25 ▪ CHAOS

Marlene Smith of Kempton, Tasmania, woke up on the morning of November 3, 1996, to find "queer stuff, white/clear jelly, oodles of it," on the concrete in front of her house. "I've lived here for 56 years," she said, "and I've never seen anything like it. We could have got a bucket of it." The previous night had seen a rainstorm preceded by the fall of a yellowish fireball that Barry Smith, Marlene's husband, observed. A quick analysis in a laboratory revealed that the material contained unspecified "micro-organisms."

—*Jerome Clark,* Unexplained!

FOX VALLEY, ALASKA

Toes and fingers frozen, limbs numb, Elizabeth was hypothermic, seeing in blurry snapshots. Nose bloodied, cheekbone bruised or broken, she had been stripped of her parka, then made to ride behind the leader. Without the parka, the windy ride sucked out her body warmth, the wind like sandpaper on her exposed skin. Halfway back she began to shiver violently. The shivering passed as she became sleepy and then stuporous. By the time they reached the building she had to be half-carried inside. Elizabeth managed to stand as they entered, held by the leader.

Still groggy, understanding came hard. She thought she was inside the building she had come to Alaska to see. The man who had hit her held her by the arm, shouting at a small group of people. She didn't know any of them. Clarity came with the rhythm of ocean waves. One moment awareness came rushing over her, her apprehension sharp. Then, with the receding wave, clarity left her, visual and auditory details were lost. What was understood perfectly moments before would suddenly be jumbled, like pieces of a puzzle dumped on a tabletop. The tide of awareness was coming in again, clarity returning. She noticed the backdrop behind those standing in the building. It was a flat black wall, but as she widened her view she realized there was a corner and an edge and that the edge sloped inward. Following the sloping corner upward she saw that the structure tapered—it was a pyramid.

Elizabeth's face was a pincushion now, hundreds of needles pushed through her skin as the blood returned. Elizabeth Hawthorne, Washington, D.C., lawyer and lobbyist, former presidential chief of staff, had traveled to the wilds of Alaska, snuck onto a secret military installation, been chased, assaulted, nearly frozen to death, and held at gunpoint only to discover that the U.S. government's best kept secret was a pyramid.

Through Elizabeth's confusion she saw movement—a dinosaur looking out of the opening, convincing Elizabeth her senses were still scrambled. A jerk on her arm and the leader said, "Lock them in," and then they all stopped, looking at the pyramid, seeing what Elizabeth thought she had dreamed.

The dinosaur was bipedal, maybe three feet tall with long thin legs. Its feet were three toed, its hands four-toed. Its jaws were beak-shaped and Elizabeth could see several teeth in its open mouth. The skin was mottled, green and cream with freckles of forest green. The neck was long and thicker than the legs. It had large eyes and a thin mane that ran from its head along its spine to the tip of its tail. The animal was breathing hard, mouth agape, eyes wide, taking in the scene. Still too fuzzy to trust herself, Elizabeth thought the animal looked terrified.

"Don't anyone move," her captor said. "We're scaring it. It won't harm us if we leave it alone."

Those nearest the animal were not as confident and began inching back. With a snap of its neck, the dinosaur looked back inside just as the sound of thumping emanated from the opening. Those closest to the pyramid backed toward the men with guns. Suddenly, the dinosaur leaped from the opening and more of the creatures poured out, scattering in all directions. In the middle of the stampede, the humans ran for cover.

"They will not harm you!" the leader shouted, releasing Elizabeth. "Stay calm."

Then with a screech, a new dinosaur leaped from the pyramid.

This one was larger, bipedal, clawed hands and feet, and one big claw on its middle toe. It carried its stiff tail straight out for balance, running with its head low. Its jaw was lined with rows of inch-long pointed teeth. Then, three more of the carnivores leapt from the pyramid. Now the herd loose in the building reached a new level of frenzy, clawed toes clicking on the concrete vainly looking for traction. With feet built for turf, concrete was as friction-less as ice. Prey and predators slipped, skidded, and fell as the pursuit continued.

The humans fled through a set of double doors down a

corridor, and Elizabeth followed, awkwardly. She couldn't run, let alone dodge the fleeing beasts. After only a few steps she was knocked to the floor by a skidding dinosaur. Then, the dinosaur stepped on her for traction and pushed off. As she tried to get up someone took her arm.

"This way, Ms. Hawthorne."

An older Asian man had her by the arm. Gratefully, she let him lead her through the madhouse. Then from the side she saw one of the predators angling toward them. Elizabeth cringed but just then one of the prey came running by, the carnivore's attack timed to intercept it. Powerful jaws clamped on the thick neck. Blood spurted from the wound as the two tumbled to the ground. The hunter had found an artery.

As they reached the doors they opened and they were pulled inside, the doors closed. Through the windows Elizabeth could see green dinosaurs running in all directions. In the middle of the chaos, one predator ate its meal.

"Open the exit doors," Elizabeth's helper said.

A man in a jumpsuit ran down the hall and a minute later Elizabeth heard the rumble of the doors she had entered. Then through the window Elizabeth saw movement. There were people still in with the dinosaurs.

"Hold the doors!" her rescuer shouted.

Elizabeth leaned against the door in front of her as others helped. Someone pushed from the other side but there were six of them holding the door. Looking through the window Elizabeth could see the man who had punched her. He shouted at them.

"Open the door! Now!"

No one budged. Elizabeth looked back to see his face just on the other side of the glass. Then he stepped back and raised his pistol, pointing it at Elizabeth's head.

"Get down!" she shouted, ducking.

A second later the glass shattered, everyone cringing. A hand came through the glassless frame holding the gun.

"Get back!"

They obeyed and the men with the guns came in. Behind

them Elizabeth could see the green dinosaurs scampering out the now open doors into the Alaskan wilderness.

"Whitey, close those doors," he ordered, and a man ran down the hall.

A few seconds later, the exit doors reversed, rumbling in the other direction.

"They can't survive the cold, Toru!" the man said, pointing the gun at Elizabeth's helper. "You just condemned them to death."

"And what was your solution?"

The man shook with anger but said nothing.

"There are still some enjoying their lunch," Toru pointed out. "Perhaps you would like to deal with them?"

Through the window Elizabeth could see one of the predators, jaws bloody, shredded flesh hanging from its mouth, watching the doors closing.

"I will, when the time is right, and I won't murder them!"

"Vince," a young woman said, coming forward. "I'm sorry about those dinosaurs too, but where did they come from? I don't understand how they got inside the collector."

Vince was a stew of anger, confusion, and fear. Seconds of indecision passed.

"Lock them in the dorm!" he finally ordered.

Herded down the hall, the Asian man called Toru held Elizabeth's arm.

"What is going on?" Elizabeth asked.

"More than he knows," Toru replied.

26 · VICE PRESIDENT

Allah has given us the tools to destroy the decadent infidels, atheists, and Jews. If America does not repent its sinful ways and withdraw its troops from the lands of the holy people, we will burn them out with nuclear fire.

—*Warriors of the True Prophet (posted on the Internet)*

WASHINGTON, D.C.

Willa Brown had aides who opened her mail, her packages, collected faxes and answered her e-mail. Only a very few people besides the president had access to her private e-mail address, and only one person could send her messages over the PresNet. So it was that the unusual icon caught her attention.

VICE PRESIDENT BROWN, I'M SENDING YOU THIS IN CONFIDENCE. WHEN APPROVING THIS MISSION MASON CLARK MENTIONED A CLASSIFIED PROJECT THAT INVOLVED A STRUCTURE THAT WOULD INTERACT IN SOME UNSPECIFIED WAY WITH TIME RIPPLES OR AN ASSOCIATED PHENOMENON. I ASKED ELIZABETH HAWTHORNE TO RESEARCH THIS PROJECT. SHE FOLLOWED A LEAD TO ALASKA WHERE SHE FOUND THE STRUCTURE BUT ALSO WHAT MAY BE A RUSSIAN THERMONUCLEAR DEVICE. SHE REPORTED THE FIND BUT I THOUGHT IT WOULD BE BEST IF AT LEAST TWO PEOPLE IN AUTHORITY KNEW ABOUT THIS. I'M ATTACHING TWO PHOTOS THAT ELIZABETH SENT. WE LEAVE ORBIT SHORTLY SO IF YOU NEED MORE INFORMATION, PLEASE CONTACT ELIZABETH.

Willa read the message again. Twenty years in government had brought many surprises across her desk, but nothing like this. She opened the photos. One showed a building in the distance—nothing remarkable. The second was purportedly the nuclear device. There were at least three mysteries here. First, what was Jared Pearl keeping from her? Second, what was the secret project in Alaska? Third, was there really a Russian nuclear weapon in Alaska? There was precious little information in Paulson's message. The Alaska location was unspecified. There was no information on how he knew the device in the photo was nuclear, let alone Russian, and how had Elizabeth Hawthorne tracked it down? Hawthorne was a lobbyist, not a secret agent. If the message had come from anyone but Nick Paulson she would have considered it a joke.

Willa was also suspicious. Rumors of Russian nuclear weapons in the hands of Muslim terrorists were rampant, although the best the CIA could do was confirm that Russian weapons were for sale on the black market. The Security Council was split over the seriousness of the threat, although the president seemed to be siding with those who saw it as a move by the Russians to weaken the United States and reassert Russian influence. Without concrete evidence, the president had refused to rattle the saber of the U.S.'s considerable nuclear arsenal. Now suddenly, here was a purported Russian weapon in the U.S.'s own backyard. It was too convenient.

Picking up her phone she asked her executive assistant to track down the phone number for Elizabeth Hawthorne. Then she leaned back in her leather executive chair and wondered whom she could trust.

27 · FIFTEEN MINUTES

We have persistent intelligence reports indicating that Russian nuclear weapons are being offered to, or are in the possession of, terrorists. We consider this a grave and gathering threat to our nation.

—President Jared Pearl, press conference

WASHINGTON, D.C.

Willa managed to get fifteen minutes on the president's schedule, catching him between a meeting with Republican leaders of the Senate, and his flight to Michigan for a fundraiser. Mason Clark agreed only when she disclosed that she had information about a Russian nuclear weapon.

The president's meeting ran over, Pearl coming out with the senators, shaking hands, promising to have them to the White House for dinner. Clark stood behind him, looking at his watch, glancing at Willa.

"Willa, come on in," President Pearl said warmly. "Mason, do we have time for a cup of coffee?"

"No, sir."

"Get us some anyway."

Mason stepped to the door and spoke to the president's secretary. The president sat in one of the guest chairs, Willa taking another. Mason perched on the edge of the couch.

"I'm headed up to your old stomping grounds," the president said.

"I believe you are going to Ann Arbor, Michigan, sir. I was a professor at Ohio State University."

"That's right. I shouldn't mention the Buckeyes, should I?"

"Not if you want to carry Michigan again."

"Your speech mentions the Wolverines," Mason assured the president.

The coffee came and the president thanked his secretary.

Then he leaned back, sipping. It was too hot for Willa and she preferred Diet Coke.

"Now what is this about Russian nuclear weapons?"

"There's more to this than just the weapon."

Willa took a photo of the bomb from the folder she carried, handing it to the president. Clark got up and stood behind the president.

"We'll need to have it authenticated, of course," Willa said, "but if it is fake, whoever built this has seen the real thing."

"Where did you get this?" the president asked.

"Nick Paulson e-mailed it to me before he left for the moon. Elizabeth Hawthorne sent the photo to him. She took this in Alaska."

"I know Ms. Hawthorne," the president said. "What does she have to do with this?"

The president had kept his distance from all members of the McIntyre administration, since they were widely blamed for freezing the dinosaurs in the present and permanently cutting off millions of Americans from their homes.

"Dr. Paulson asked her to find out something about a secret project that Mr. Clark told him about. It has something to do with the time ripples that continue to plague us."

Willa passed them the second photo. Now the president looked at Clark, who reddened—anger or embarrassment?

"She didn't seem to have any trouble tracking it down," the president said, frowning.

"The device is near this facility. Is there a legitimate reason for a Russian nuclear weapon to be there?"

"Of course not," the president said derisively.

"Sir, that may sound like a stupid question, but I have been kept out of the loop. Is there something going on that I should know about?"

"This is on a need-to-know basis," Clark said.

The president waved his hand dismissively.

"She already knows about it, Mason."

Now the president put his coffee cup down and laced his fingers.

"The project is designed to explore a new kind of energy that somehow interacts with the time-wave phenomena that plague our planet. The director of the project is Dr. Toru Kawabata and he's convinced that this energy may have the remarkable quality of slowing or even reversing entropy."

"Entropy? The tendency for systems to move from order to disorder?" Willa said.

"Correct. If this works I'm going to turn it loose on my private office."

No one laughed. Now the president returned to serious.

"There is a possibility that this energy in some way could regulate the rhythm of the time waves. If we can understand this, potentially we would have a tool to influence time itself. But there is another reason for this project. As you know, Dr. Paulson himself suggested that the time waves are behaving in a way that suggests manipulation. That's something that I've long suspected and there aren't many countries in the world that have the sophistication to pull this off."

"Russia," Willa said.

"Exactly, and if this is real," the president said, tapping the photo, "then we would have the confirmation we need that Russia is behind the manipulation of the time waves."

"But they have been hit by the time quilts, too," Willa argued. "They lost a quarter of Moscow."

"That was before the manipulation. They know something we don't and we need to catch up before it's too late. You heard Dr. Paulson at the Security Council. He believes something big is coming."

Willa wasn't convinced of a Russian connection. They seemed so eager to expand cultural and economic ties and had cooperated fully in joint space efforts. They were especially anxious to enter into a mutual defense treaty to ward off Chinese border machinations. Could all of that be a smokescreen?

"Then I had better check on this bomb," Willa said, moving to keep herself involved.

"That won't be necessary," Clark said quickly. "We'll send someone."

Willa ignored Clark, looking at the president.

"Thanks for bringing this to our attention," the president said. "I will have someone look into it right away."

Willa was being dismissed. Thanking the president for his time, she left, wondering if she really could let it drop. She waited by the door for a few minutes, noticing that the president did not hurry off to make his flight.

28 · THE MOON

Much of what has been considered the superstition of past civilizations is now proving to be the core of an ancient secret science; many a modern discovery betrays its origin and basis in this secret science. Certainly, pyramid power is at the forefront of these rediscoveries.

—*Max Toth and Greg Nielsen,* Pyramid Power

EARTH TO THE MOON

They managed to cut half a day off of the time Apollo took to journey to the moon, their voyage uneventful, even boring. The lunar explorer was a bus compared to the lunar command module that had taken the Apollo astronauts to the moon in the sixties and seventies. The bulk of the ship was devoted to fuel tanks, since next to oxygen, reaction mass was the most precious of all commodities in space. There was ample living space since they did not carry most of the cargo anticipated when the lunar explorer was designed.

"Is having only one pilot really a good idea?" Nick asked Rosa as they strapped in for departure. "What if something happens to you?"

"Relax, you don't need me either," Rosa replied. "The computer does the flying. You have to remember the computers on the original lunar spacecraft had the computing power of a modern digital watch. This craft has the equivalent of a supercomputer. If something happens to me, just get back in the lander, push the 'up' button, and away you'll go."

They rocketed straight out from above Africa, accelerating to 25,000 miles per hour. The Earth slowly shrank; at first only the mottled red and green continental rifts filled one window, then entire continents, and then the whole Earth. Then, just as slowly, the stark beauty of the moon swelled in the portholes, until Nick could see details even the most powerful telescopes on Earth could not discern. With a deceleration burn and a slight course correction, they dropped into lunar orbit and prepared to land.

The shuttle was an ugly craft, built for space where aerodynamics had no meaning. All cylinders, composite framework, solar panels, rocket nozzles, and antennae, she was an asymmetrical bug of a craft. With a slight jerk, the lander separated from the shuttle, Nick still wishing someone had stayed behind to housesit while they were gone. He had no clear idea of what someone on board could do to help them if they got in trouble, but he clung irrationally to the belief that there would be something.

Like the original lunar lander, the ship they were riding in relied on hypergolic propellants for fuel. Once the fuel and the oxidizer came into contact, they ignited. Like the original lander, this lander used dinitrogen tetroxide and Aerozine 50 as propellant and oxidizer for propulsion, and injected helium to control the thrust and act as a throttle. Unlike the original lander, the combustion took place in an intense magnetic field that increased efficiency.

The descent began with an ullage burn; seven seconds of deceleration that brought the fuels to the bottom of the tanks, where they could be fed to the nozzles. Then they began their twelve-minute descent. Wrapped in vertical hammocks, the passengers were kept out of the way while Rosa monitored the flight. Their target was in Flamsteed Crater, and they approached from the east with the sun behind the ship, casting clear shadows. Rosa watched the display, ready to override the computer as it measured the height and width of the rocks and small craters below and made landing decisions. Flamsteed Crater had been overflowed by basalt somewhere in lunar history, creating a flat plane and many good landing sites. However, regular meteorite activity had pockmarked the surface, leaving a regolith of uncertain depth and composition.

Flamsteed Crater was 110 kilometers in diameter, so the rim looked like distant mountains as they dropped inside. The computer-controlled descent combined feedback from landing radar and infrared, and then adjusted thrust and nozzle angle two hundred times a second. However, when the ship was six feet from the surface a simple rod touched first, shutting down the engines. They dropped the last six feet, landing with a soft thud.

Without air to diffuse light, the moon was a world of sharp contrasts. The sky was black, the stars hot white pinpoints. The lunar surface was colorless, its features in sharp relief, the shadows crisp. They rested on a flat plain, the crater rim looking like a gray palisade completely surrounding them. To the east was the rim shadow, and somewhere in that direction was the structure they had come to see. Knowing their time on the surface was severely limited, they shook off the reverie and began the arduous process of donning their portable life support suits—PLSSs.

The first layer was a tight-fitting capillary suit that circulated water to cool the body. The underwear also included sensors to monitor heart rate, respiration, blood pressure, and other information, which was relayed to the computer to make diagnostic judgments about the health of the wearer. Nick avoided watching Reggie as she donned her underwear, and afforded Rosa the same courtesy. Nick noticed Emmett kept his eyes averted as well. Phil, however, had no willpower. Nick watched Phil try three times to put his right leg into his underwear, missing each time.

"Try looking at your foot, Phil," Nick suggested.

Caught watching, Phil shrugged it off. If the women were aware of Phil's ogling, they ignored it. Once into the underwear, they helped each other into the suits, locking top to bottom, gloves to sleeves, and finally, helmet to the locking ring around the neck.

When the suits were double checked by humans, and the computer confirmed all PLSSs were functioning optimally, they pumped the air from the chamber, released the latches and opened the hatch. With no air to carry sounds there was no *hiss* or *pop*, just the sound of Nick's own breathing and light so bright his eyes clamped closed while one of his three visors slid into place.

Rosa went first, releasing the ladder that slid slowly down its track, stopping a foot above the surface, locking itself into place. Then Rosa climbed down, moving slowly, carefully. Nick went next, mimicking Rosa's slow movements, finding it easier than the simulation at Area 51. Nick and the PLSS combined would weigh three hundred and fifty pounds on Earth. Here it was closer to fifty pounds. He dropped the last foot, feeling almost no impact. Then with the bunny hop motion they had practiced, he hopped away from the lander. The surface was covered with an inch of powder, which compressed, leaving waffle footprints. Nick noticed that stomping down did not raise a dust cloud. With no air to compress or carry the dust motes, only a few particles surrounding his foot danced from the vibration.

Gaining confidence, Nick found he could leap six feet at a time and hopped randomly across the surface, giddy with a sense of power. Soon he realized everyone but Rosa was hopping and leaping across the surface in all directions.

"Let's get the gear and get moving," Nick said, broadcasting to the others.

They gathered back at the lander, retrieving equipment from compartments built into the bottom. Each person carried a set of tools. Once equipped, they set out, walking single file, Nick in front, followed by Reggie, Emmett, Phil, and then Rosa. Using directional signals sent from the lander and the orbiting shuttle, Nick led them toward the retreating rim shadow, all three sun screens in place now. Nick soon abandoned the bunny hop and adopted a motion more like a cross-country skier, moving his fifty-pound weight with muscles accustomed to nearly four times that. They had only gone a short distance when he realized he could see their destination. Radioing the others, he slowed to a walk and then stopped, pointing.

"There it is."

The building could be seen just inside the rim shadow. It was a twin of the one in the photo that Elizabeth had sent. They resumed course and speed and made good progress; soon the building loomed over them. They stopped when the surface suddenly changed.

"Look at this, Emmett," Nick said, pointing. "See the clear demarcation?"

The two textures were distinctly different.

"It's a neat line," Emmett said.

The others came up and stood shoulder to shoulder, no one ready to step across the line in the sand.

"I've seen this before," Emmett said. "The same thing happens at the edge of a time quilt. How easily the two time segments connect physically is limited by density, number of converging ripples, length of the convergence, and many other factors."

Phil unsnapped a scoop from his belt. The long-handled scoop worked like salad tongs. Reaching across the line he pinched the regolith, picking up a sample, then dumping it in his gloved hand. There were fibers in the dust.

"What are those?" Reggie asked, poking through the sample.

"It's organic," Emmett said.

"I can't tell what color they are through these filters, but they look like pine needles," Nick said.

"That answers one question," Emmett said. "We can rule out the theory that this was built on the moon. It's a time quilt."

"It explains the lack of construction debris," Nick said, then made the connection to Elizabeth's building. Could it be the same one? If so, how did it get here, or better yet, when?

"Any reason not to step on this?" Rosa asked, foot hovering over the line.

"Not that I know of," Nick said.

Rosa's foot plopped down on new territory—and nothing happened. Sighs were audible in Nick's helmet.

Nick led off again, certain he knew where the building had come from, but not certain of what they would find inside. There was an odd exterior framework to the building, supporting interior walls, which seemed to be reinforced concrete. There were no windows but there was a large door on the side they were approaching. There was also a smaller, collapsed structure to one side. Nick led the group there and they gathered around.

There was a large piece of sheet metal and wood beams collapsed at one end, but partially standing at the other. Walking along the length to where they could look underneath, they could see a vehicle.

"Is that some sort of lunar excursion vehicle?" Phil asked.

"Not with an internal combustion engine," Rosa said.

"It's a snowmobile," Nick said.

"Where there are snowmobiles there are people," Phil said ominously.

Now they moved toward the door and deeper into shadow. When they got within ten feet of the door a light came on. The light was above them, mounted behind a thick clear plate in a housing that protruded from the wall.

"Power?" Emmett said. "This structure was time quilted here and has been sitting in a vacuum for a decade and still has power?"

"That means it was no accident," Phil said. "Whoever built this, built it for a lunar environment."

There was a transparent panel to the left of the door. Nick tapped on it and it lit up and began flashing. A few seconds later the words OPEN appeared at the top and CLOSE at the bottom. Nick's sunscreens had retracted when he entered shadow, but the faceplate was a polarized filter designed to screen out the invisible spectrum. Even so, he could tell the OPEN was in green, the CLOSE in red. Nick stood looking at the two options, thinking.

"You want me to decode those instructions for you?" Phil offered.

The others laughed.

"I feel like Hansel and Gretel standing outside the gingerbread house," Nick said. "It's just too tempting."

"We didn't come all this way not to push the damn button!" Phil said.

"Push it," Emmett said.

"Do it," Rosa said.

Reggie said nothing. Nick had noticed she had grown silent as they approached the structure.

Nick reached up and pushed OPEN. Silently, the doors slowly slid apart, revealing a chamber with another set of doors on the other side. Cautiously, they walked in. On the inside was another panel. Nick pushed CLOSE and the doors obeyed. Now they turned to the other wall and found an option for EQUALIZE PRESSURE in red. Nick pushed it and then put his hand on the wall. He could feel vibrations and soon his suit was rippling.

"An airlock," Emmett said.

Nick noticed that Reggie was staring at her feet.

"What's wrong, Reggie?"

"There's a brown stain on the floor."

She was right. The stain covered half of the space.

A minute later, the EQUALIZE PRESSURE option was green. Nick pushed the OPEN option on the interior wall and the doors slowly slid apart, lights flickering on in the interior. Nick had imagined a lot of possibilities for what he would find if he ever got to the structure on the moon, but not in his wildest imaginings had he pictured what he now saw. Inside the building from the future was a pyramid.

"We took a wrong turn somewhere," Phil said. "We ended up in stinking Egypt."

"I'm just a pilot," Rosa said. "So would one of you geniuses explain to me why there is a pyramid on the moon?"

No one had an answer. They stepped inside, closing the doors behind them. Nick started to release the lock on his helmet.

"Let me do it," Phil said, pulling Nick's hand away. "You can carry me back to the lander if I pass out, but I can't carry you."

Phil released the lock, gave the helmet a twist, and lifted it an inch off the collar. He breathed in and out several times, then lifted the helmet all the way off. He said something now but no one could hear him. Then he made the okay sign and signaled the air was breathable. One by one they lifted their helmets. Back on Freedom Station the air had been stale, the result of endless recycling. This air was different. The atmosphere was humid, dank, and something else.

"It smells like something died in here," Phil said.

29 • RECYCLING SPECIALIST

We categorically deny any involvement in the distribution of weapons of mass destruction. The Russian people held out the open hand of friendship only to have it slapped aside by President Pearl's unwise and unfounded accusations. We can only conclude that President Pearl has an ulterior motive in rejecting our offer of friendship.

—*Gennadi Petrov, President of Russia*

APPROACHING FOX VALLEY, ALASKA

Anatole Baranov squatted in the helicopter, back against the wall, chewing a wad of gum. The wad had lost its flavor an hour ago but he chewed it anyway. If he did not chew, he smoked, and his wife would not kiss him if he had smoke on his breath. So, he chewed, keeping his breath fresh for love.

Dressed in white from head to toe, Baranov and his men

carried American weapons. All spoke English. Launched with only a few hours of planning, they had crossed into American airspace after lying about their purpose and course. They were deep into the Alaskan wilderness. If caught in the air, they would claim navigation errors. If they succeeded in recovering the weapon, they could not afford to be caught and would take the recovered weapon into the sea with them rather than surrender. Terrorists were spreading rumors that the Russians were passing out nuclear weapons like party favors. The Americans were stupid to believe such nonsense, but believe it they did. Baranov's superiors preferred not to irritate the Americans any further.

This would be the fifth recovery mission for Baranov and his Spetsnaz team. He had lost men on three of the previous missions. With fifteen troops split between two helicopters, each ship could carry the entire team if one was lost. Every man on board was expendable and knew it.

They were at treetop level, Baranov's ship in the lead, the proton detector in the nose, busy sniffing out what should not be in rural Alaska. The land below them was much like his home: heavily forested, frozen, and thinly populated. There were more moose than people and little risk anyone would report their helicopters.

They skirted even small villages, beelining for where their intelligence people thought the weapon might be. The information had been sketchy, but the image of the building in the valley matched a satellite photo of an isolated facility of unknown purpose in their intelligence database. The Fox Valley facility supposedly conducted environmental research, but then Russian trawlers supposedly fished. Highly placed moles in the U.S. government assured them that the Americans did not possess any Russian nuclear weapons, so if such a device was indeed in Alaska, it was there for nefarious purposes.

From analysis of the photo, the nuclear device was definitely a Russian design, modeled on a stolen American design, but then all nuclear weapons in the world were based on stolen American designs. Baranov chuckled to himself.

Perhaps it was fitting that they were retrieving another fusion egg from the mother hen of the nuclear age.

His men were young, multilingual, highly intelligent, professional soldiers. Even in the new Russian democracy, there were privileges for the military. On call twenty-four hours a day, fighting Russian Mafia, Chechnyan rebels, and Muslim extremists, his men earned the extra rubles in their paychecks. Fighting Americans would be a first he hoped to avoid.

The proton detector in the nose of the helicopter was the most sophisticated in the world, based on a stolen British design, but improved with Russian ingenuity. Bent over the display, earphones tight to his head, the technician raised his hand and waved it. Baranov came forward, leaned over to study the display, and then spoke to the pilots with the microphone built into his helmet. The ship turned now, reversing course. They could not risk detection. Suddenly the technician waved his hand again, calling Baranov back. The display had changed. Normally, they would operate with three helicopters, triangulating on a source. However, penetrating American airspace on a pretext was risky enough, so they had come with only two ships, taking multiple readings from both to detect the location of the weapon. The computer was having difficulty locating the source.

"Much interference," the operator said.

Baranov ordered the pilots to fly in ever expanding circles until finally the computer resolved some internal conflict and placed the source near, or in, the structure in Fox Valley. Now satisfied, Baranov squeezed the shoulder of the technician and then signaled his men to get ready.

They put a few kilometers between them and the beginning of the detection zone and then came down in a small clearing, Baranov's squad fanning out, securing the site. Then the second helicopter came down. Troops stepped into cross-country skis, and then skied out to establish a wider perimeter. Six men would stay behind to protect the helicopters and secure an escape route back to the ships. Baranov would lead nine more to the site to recover the weapon. With surprise, Baranov was confident they could handle a force of up to thirty, more if they were gangsters and not soldiers.

With scouts ahead, they started across country, the ground sloping upward. A scout sped ahead. Using the American GPS satellite system, they kept in a straight line, hiding their numbers, minimizing the trail breaking and conserving energy. They made good progress, the skies overcast but an approaching snowstorm holding off. Sweating lightly, his men were conditioned to keep this up for hours and still fight at the end. Suddenly, a shot echoed through the trees ahead. Without a command, his men dispersed, taking cover behind trees. Baranov put his hand to his head, pushing on the white hood of his parka, pressing the earpiece deeper, waiting.

"One civilian with a dog," came the economical transmission in English, lest someone pick it up. "Terminate?"

Killing local citizens was rarely a good idea, and killing American citizens on American soil the worst of all ideas.

"Hold, I'm coming."

Signaling his men in hiding, Baranov skied ahead, coming up behind the scout who hid behind a tree, rifle trained on something ahead.

"He ambushed me from those trees," he whispered, showing the hole in his parka where the bullet had entered, stopped by his bullet resistant vest.

Leaning out, Baranov could see nothing.

"He's good," Baranov said, appreciative of hitting a moving target through dense trees.

"I can flank him," the scout offered.

"We'll talk first," Baranov said, spitting his wad of gum into the snow. "You in the trees," he called. "You almost shot my friend!"

"I did shoot your friend and I'll shoot you, too, if you come any nearer."

It was a woman's voice.

Baranov scowled at his scout.

"It hurts just like being shot by a man," he said.

"Why are you shooting at us?" Baranov called.

"Because you shot me first, you bastard."

"We aren't even armed," Baranov lied.

"Your friend was carrying an M-16," she shouted back.

Baranov thought for a minute.

"I surrender. I'm coming to you unarmed and with my hands up."

"I'll shoot you dead if you come near me."

Now the scout scowled. The scout was the younger brother of Baranov's wife's sister. Leonid would carry this tale back to the family.

"What happens in the field, stays in the field, Private," Baranov said firmly.

"Dah," Leonid said. "If you survive."

Kicking off his skis, Baranov leaned his rifle against a tree, and then took his pistol off the belt. He left his knife in the sheath, knowing she could not see it under his parka. Waving his arms, he stepped out, keeping his hands high.

"Please don't shoot, I have a wife and three children, thank you very much!"

"Get back in your hiding place, you skunk," the woman shouted.

"I am unarmed. You wouldn't shoot an unarmed man."

A bullet buried at his feet, the report echoing through the trees. He had to stop her firing. Rifle reports could carry for miles in this wilderness.

"Don't shoot, I am not going to harm you, and I really do have a wife and three children."

Now he could see her, leaning against a tree, the rifle resting on a low branch. He could see blood on her parka and bright red dots in the snow. A dog stood next to her. He was close enough now to hear its growl.

"You are hurt," he said.

"Thanks to you," she said, weapon pointed at his chest.

"Not me," he protested, still moving forward.

"Then one of your men."

"No, not us," he said.

"You came in those black helicopters, didn't you?"

He thought about lying, but she had not believed one of

his lies yet. Now she slipped to her knees, the rifle pointing up to the sky. He could rush her, but she was a remarkable shot, and there was the dog. Instead, he held his ground, letting her reposition the rifle, again aiming it at his chest. Now the rifle barrel wavered, the woman too weak to keep it steady.

"My name is Andy," he said. "We did come in those helicopters."

"Then you're with the damn government, just like the ones who shot me."

Baranov chose his words carefully.

"I am with a government, but not the government that shot you."

Taken by surprise, she thought for a minute, still holding the rifle on him.

"An Earth government."

'Of course."

"Then what the hell are you doing here?"

"I've come to recover something that was stolen from us."

"Russian?" she asked.

"Dah!"

"Thank God."

She dropped the rifle, turned, and sat, leaning against the tree. Baranov signaled the scout to bring the team. He walked slowly forward, the dog growling.

"Easy, Mack," the woman said.

The dog stopped growling but watched Baranov warily. It was a sled dog, part of its harness still hanging from its chest.

"They killed some of my team and scattered the rest. That's why I thought you were them."

"Like I said, we are here for another reason."

"The bomb, right?"

Baranov could not suppress his surprise.

"I thought so. You can't sneak into that base. They have sensors all over the valley."

"They usually do," Baranov said, unzipping her parka and looking at the wound.

He had seen worse, but he had seen men die from less. He took off his pack and pulled out a dressing, pressing it against the wound to stem the bleeding. The woman moaned, her eyes closing. Mack growled, stepping toward Baranov's face.

"Easy, Mack," Baranov said.

Suddenly, Mack's ears pricked up and he turned toward the trees behind them.

"You're a confident sonofabitch," the woman said, eyes fluttering open.

"Thank you very much," Baranov said.

"Now we'll see how good you black helicopter sonsof-bitches really are, because here they come."

30 · INTO THE JUNGLE

The paleontological and geological evidence suggests that a herd of 400 or more of these 4-ton animals [Monoclonius] attempted to cross a river in flood. They may have been good swimmers as individuals, but many of them appear to have drowned when they interfered with each other . . .

—*Byron Preiss and Robert Silverberg (Eds.),*
The Ultimate Dinosaur

YUCATAN PENINSULA

Ripman turned his back to the approaching tyrannosaur, walked to the nearest Hummer, and then leaned nonchalantly against the grill, dinosaur rifle slung casually across his chest. Carrollee, Nikki, and John backed up to the Hummer, eyes on the tyrannosaur but leaving the rangers to handle it. Carrollee held her dinosaur gun tight, pointed in the general direction of the tyrannosaur, which continued its slow approach around the ruins. Nikki stood in a similar posture on the other side of Ripman. John stood to one side, watching the three dinosaur rangers spread out, ambivalent about whether to help them or not.

"You sure those popguns are gonna be enough for you?" Ripman asked.

Marion and the others ignored the jab, cocking their rifles. The tyrannosaur came on, so heavy even the soft soil could not absorb the vibrations.

"Those are the dumbest bastards I've ever met," Ripman said.

"Aren't you going to help them?" Carrollee asked.

"No," Ripman said.

Carrollee started forward, feeling for the trigger.

"I wouldn't do that if I were you," Ripman said.

Carrollee stopped, turning.

"The bigger the pack, the more threat the tyrannosaur is going to feel, and trust me, you don't want to piss off something that eats stegosaurs for breakfast."

Carrollee hesitated, then backed up, eyes on the tyrannosaur, ready to help if Ripman would not.

Marion was in the center, Mitch to the right, Jose to the left. They walked slowly, confidently. They avoided the bloody vegetation, keeping to the clean grasses. At a command from Marion, Mitch pulled something from a pouch on his belt and tossed it toward the tyrannosaur. The device bounced once, and then landed at the T-rex's feet. The rex ignored it, coming on. Then the device burst, emitting a yellowish cloud. Surprised—and it did look surprised—it dipped its head, sniffing the smoke. Then it snorted, shook its head and then sneezed, a sneeze louder than a hundred human sneezes combined. Then it sneezed again and Carrollee could see tears running from its eyes and mucus from its nose. A shake of its head and another sneeze, and mucus was dripping from its nostrils.

The rangers held their ground, not advancing, not retreating. Now the tyrannosaur bobbed its head, uttering a guttural sound that turned into a hacking cough. With the coughs racking its body and its neck stretching out, the great beast opened its gaping jaws and coughed up a twenty-pound wad of phlegm. Turning away, the T-rex retreated several steps from the cloud, and then stretched its neck and tail out, repeated the series of violent coughs, and spit up another slimy mass. Then it disappeared into the jungle, coughing and sneezing.

Jose, Mitch, and Marion returned, looking smug. Ripman applauded.

"Cute," he said. "What do you call that, a snot bomb?"

"It's an aerosol that irritates the nasal passages and induces nausea."

"Glad we didn't get to see it retch," Nikki said.

"Yes, since that rex would have thrown up three men and two mules," Ripman said.

Nikki blanched, and Carrollee's temper flared at Ripman's insensitivity.

"You don't know they died," Marion said. "The tyrannosaur would target the mules."

"Really, Mr. Ranger? That's good to know. Too bad we're fresh out of mule bait."

John stepped between the two men, but Ripman would not let it go.

"That snot bomb trick would be useless if that tyrannosaur hadn't just fed. They're a bit more pugnacious when they haven't had lunch."

"Seemed to work well enough to me," Carrollee said, deliberately smiling at Marion.

"I hope you have a lot more of those stink bombs. You're going to need them," Ripman said. Then calmer, "There's still plenty of daylight left, so let's repack everything; we're carrying it all now."

The rangers hesitated, looking to John who was in command. John nodded agreement.

"Let's get far away from the remains of that kill," John said. "The smell will attract scavengers."

Ripman was already pulling packs and supplies from the back of the Hummer. They joined him, making decisions on what to take. Marion argued for more food and less ammunition, Ripman insisting on the opposite. John made the compromise decision. Everyone agreed on the water, first-aid kit, vitamins, water purification tablets, knives, hatchet, two machetes, solar blankets, change of clothes, insect repellant, mosquito netting, knives, Leatherman tools, two pack shovels, and flashlights for everyone. The remaining supplies were left in the Hummers. As they walked away, John turned, pointed the remote at the Hummer and clicked it twice, the horn giving a brief good-bye beep. Then John dropped the keys in his pocket.

"John, you might as well toss those keys," Ripman said.

"You said yourself the locals don't come this far into the forest, so who's going to steal them?"

Ripman gave his life-long friend a pitying look, and then picked up the pace, taking the lead. Then John understood, and he smiled at Carrollee.

"He's always been like that," John said. "He won a set of tires at a church raffle once, and then complained because he had to spend his Saturday mounting the tires on his truck."

Carrollee and Nikki were kept in the middle of the line, a remnant of male chauvinism she chose not to protest. They exchanged words occasionally, but the terrain was steep, the footing treacherous, and the heat stifling. Carrollee and Nikki wore trail pants and during a brief break detached the legs, stuffing them in their packs. The insects quickly found the bare skin, mosquitos and flies tasting them despite the DEET coating their legs. When they stopped again, they put the legs back on. The men all wore long-sleeve shirts and trousers. Ripman's was camouflage, the rangers tan with Park Service patches on the sleeves and dinosaur ranger insignia below that. Everyone had a hat; Ripman a camouflage baseball hat, the rangers broad-rimmed hats with cords that hung under their chins. Carrollee and Nikki wore nylon hats they had found in the airport mall. The hats could be folded up to the size of a package of gum but when unfolded covered their heads and shaded their face and neck. They were flower-print, Carrollee's yellow, Nikki's blue. Carrollee's head was hot with the hat, the heat unbearable without.

Three hours of walking found them deep in a valley, at a crossing between two animal trails. One was ten feet wide, the equivalent of a freeway in the dense foliage. The other was narrow with overhanging vegetation. Ripman paused, studying the tracks. John squatted next to him while the rangers fanned out, taking protective positions. Ripman took out his compass, studying it.

"I think this might be one of those occasions where we take the road less traveled," John said.

"Look at the compass, John. Notice anything?"

The compass needle kept a steady point. Then he looked at where the sun was getting low on the horizon.

"It's not pointing north," John said. "That's to be expected because of the magnetic field that is being generated by whatever is in there."

"Now look at the trail," Ripman said.

Then John noticed the wide trail did not line up with the compass needle.

"You think the dinosaurs should be drawn toward the source of the field?"

Marion had inched closer, listening.

"Like homing pigeons," Ripman said.

"They're not pigeons," Marion protested.

Ripman looked up at the ranger, sunglasses reflecting the setting sun.

"Isn't the theory that dinosaurs evolved into birds? So where did the birds get the homing instinct?"

"It's not that simple," Marion protested.

"Ripman's the guide," John said, asserting his authority. "He picks the route."

"Besides, you're going to be busy," Ripman said.

"Yeah, doing what?" Marion asked.

"Dealing with them," Ripman said, standing and pointing behind the ranger.

Emerging from the jungle behind them were stegosaurs. They were herbivores, large armor plates along their backs and tails.

The rangers directed the others off the intersection, Ripman casually following orders. It was a small herd, one large male, a dozen females, a few immature males and calves. The male angled toward them, the herd shying in the other direction. The male suddenly charged, then skidded to a stop, pawing the ground.

"It's just posturing," Marion said. "Don't move."

The stegosaur snorted and pawed until its family had passed, and then with another impressive show of force, it followed.

"We have to get out of here," Nikki said, suddenly.

Nikki was pale, agitated, pulling Carrollee's arm.

"A carnivore will be here soon. They follow the herds."

Everyone turned to Ripman, not John.

"It's a small herd but it may have picked up a juvenile carnivore," Ripman said. "Just to be safe, let's give them some space."

Ripman led them down the narrow path and soon they were out of sight of the jungle freeway. Nikki did not relax until they had put a couple of miles between themselves and the trail. Then it was time to camp for the night.

Carrollee was exhausted and glad for the short first day. They ate cold rations, buried their waste, and then climbed into trees to spend the night. Carrollee tied herself to the limb she was reclining on, draped mosquito netting over herself and used her pack for a pillow. Exhaustion helped her sleep, but she woke periodically, animals moving underneath, others scampering in the branches above. When dawn broke, she found she was already sweating. She ate an energy bar and washed it down with sips of water. Soon, Ripman called them down, ready to resume the trek. When she stood, her joints ached and her head hurt. She took two aspirin. The others were stretching, walking stiff-legged, trying to get their circulation back.

"How long does it take to get used to sleeping in trees?" John asked Ripman.

Ripman snapped his finger to his lips, shushing John and the others. Slowly he turned, bringing the rifle off of his shoulder. Carrollee picked up her rifle, Nikki doing the

same. The rangers were a few steps away, relieving themselves. The carnivores came in low, heads down, slicing
through the soft undergrowth. They were bipedal, three feet
high, long flat snouts, stiff tails held straight out, skin camou-
flaged in greens and browns. Ripman killed the first one with
a shot to its chest. The report of the rifle startled the other
two, but inertia kept them coming, one at Nikki, one at John.

John turned to reach for his rifle just as the dinosaur leaped,
center toe claw extended, ready to rip John open. Carrollee
fired, hitting the leaping dinosaur in the side, the slug passing
through, blowing out guts. John took the full weight of the at-
tacker, arms up protectively. The two went down in a heap,
John pushing up with his arms, tossing the dinosaur over his
head as they fell. The predator was convulsing even before it
hit the ground, flopping around, screeching, taking its time in
dying.

Nikki missed the other onrushing dinosaur with her first
shot, but the second crumpled a leg, the carnivore collapsing, and then tumbling head over heels toward her. She
jumped sideways, stumbling but not falling. The wounded
dinosaur was flopping on the ground, trying to stand, its
nearly severed leg collapsing. Holding the gun at her waist,
Nikki shot the dinosaur, punching a hole through its chest.
Then she shot it over and over, splattering pieces of the dinosaur across the clearing. She stopped only when the clip
was empty. She was crying when the rangers reached her,
Mitch putting his arm around her shoulders and pulling her
close. She leaned into him, burying her face.

Ripman walked up to the dinosaur that had attacked John.
It had stopped thrashing around but still twitched, still drew
breath. He cut its throat and then helped John sit up. There
was blood on his shirt.

"How much of that is yours?" Ripman asked.

"Some," John said.

Blood had plastered his shirt to his chest. Ripman helped
pull his shirt over his head. There was a gash high on his
chest.

"We should stitch that," Ripman said.

"It's not that bad," John said.

"John, you were a wuss when you were fourteen and you're a wuss now. I've stitched up worse wounds than that on my own body."

"Just bandage it," John said.

"Can't do it, John," Ripman said. "A few drops of blood in the ocean will bring every shark for miles. We have to stitch it tight."

"You're overestimating their olfactory abilities," Marion said, opening a first-aid kit.

"Really! At least I knew enough to have something besides my dick in my hand when they attacked."

"You got lucky," Marion said defensively. "Those are from the Tyrannus family. Probably eotyrannus. Tyrannosaurs don't come much smaller than these."

"Isn't it funny how often I get lucky?" Ripman said.

"I don't think it's eotyrannus," Jose said, trying to defuse the tension.

Jose squatted to look at the carcass.

"The eyes are together in front, the nasal bone seems to be joined like the tyrannosaur family, but eotyrannus wouldn't be contemporary with Tyrannosaurus rex. It's probably another unidentified species. The fossil records the dinosauria is built on were incomplete."

"Get out of the way," Nikki said, pushing through to John and taking the first-aid kit from Ripman. "He's still bleeding."

She put the kit on John's stomach, and then selected a curved needle and surgical thread. John's eyes went wide.

"Have you done this before?" he asked.

"Many times," she said, sadly.

When Nikki pushed the needle through his skin for the first stitch, he put his forearm over his eyes, leaning back. He winced with each stitch.

"From now on," John said between stitches, "we piss one at a time."

Ripman set to work burying John's shirt. Mitch, Marion, and Jose examined the carcasses.

"I think Jose is right," Mitch said. "This species hasn't been catalogued."

"It's a terrible loss," Marion said.

After stomping the soil covering John's shirt, Ripman gave Nikki a bottle of water to wash the blood off of John's chest. Ripman inspected her work when she was done.

"Nice even stitches," Ripman said, approving her work.

Then they bandaged John's wound, wrapping gauze all the way around his chest. While Nikki helped John into his spare shirt, Ripman took his machete, walked to the dinosaur that Carrollee killed, and hacked the claw off one of its feet.

"Taking trophies is illegal," Marion said.

Ripman paused briefly, glared, but said nothing. Then he used his knife to clean the rest of the flesh from the claw, washed it with water, and dropped it into a side pocket of his pack.

John was up now, tucking his shirt into his pants, taking charge again.

"Let's change tactics," John said. "I think it was a mistake to avoid the herds. Now we know the carnivores aren't just following the herds, so it isn't really any safer. If we stick close to a herd the predators will be just as likely to take one of them as us. My guess is they'll eat what they're familiar with first."

"They'll eat what they can catch," Ripman said.

"I agree with John," Marion said. "Once herbivores realize we're not hunters, they'll ignore us. We might even be able to get inside the pickets, let them protect us."

Ripman was giving Marion a peculiar look, then looked at John the same way.

"That the way you want to play it, John? It's ballsy, that's for sure."

Before John could answer, Ripman turned to Nikki.

"What about you, Nikki?"

"We never tried mixing with the herds, only following their trails. Following was the worst. We lost the most that

way. Making our own trails helped some, but they kept finding us, killing us."

Nikki was near tears. Carrollee stepped close, putting her
arm around Nikki's shoulders.

"All right, John," Ripman said. "Let's get elemental."

It was midday by the time they found a herd of monoclonius, moving in the direction they wanted to go. With three
horns, and a large bony collar, the quadrupeds lumbered
slowly but steadily, wary of the humans and unsure of what to
make of them. The clump of humans followed for two hours,
gradually closing the gap. When the herd reached a stream,
the humans waded upstream to refill their water bottles. When
the leaders started the herd moving again, stragglers stopped
to drink. Now when the stragglers had drunk their fill, the humans found themselves with monoclonius in front and behind. Ripman smiled at John, mouthing "El-ah-mental."

They traveled with the herd the rest of the day, walking
slowly, keeping toward the rear. Gradually, they inched as
close to the herd as possible, the monoclonius seemingly indifferent to their presence. When they passed through mead-
ows, the herd would spread out, slow down, and graze. The
breaks were short.

"It's not normal," Mitch said to Carrollee during one
stretch where they walked side by side. "They're moving
much faster than any herd I've ever seen. Ripman might be
right about them being drawn to the pole of the magnetic
field."

Mitch kept his voice low, not wanting Marion to overhear
the ranger agreeing with a poacher.

Occasionally a calf would wander their way, curious, too
young to appreciate the danger. The humans would veer
away, giving the calf a wide berth until a bellow from a worried parent would bring it trotting back to the herd. In places
the terrain made it impossible to stay close without merging
with the herd, so they would cut through the jungle, the men
taking turns hacking through the foliage with the machetes,
the rest alert, guns ready.

At dusk the leaders circled the herd, stopping the migration. They were on a lightly wooded hillside that sloped steeply down to water. None of the monoclonius approached the stream, instead spreading out through the trees, grazing, rubbing up against trunks. A few of the calves got into shoving matches, grunting and snorting in mock battles. Gradually, the play settled down, the milling herd becoming still, settling in for the night.

The spot the herd had selected couldn't have been worse from the humans' perspective. The trees were too small to sleep in and when they moved in close to the herd they were greeted with lowered heads, wicked horns, and aggressive posturing.

"Their eyesight is so poor, they won't be as tolerant at night as they would be during the day," Marion said.

Ripman grunted. Carrollee took that as grudging agreement.

"There were some larger trees back about half a mile," Jose said.

"No, not back," Nikki said quickly.

"She's right. We'd be better off sleeping right here," Ripman said.

"I agree," Marion said.

They moved a little way down the hill, giving the nearsighted monoclonius space, then picked the flattest spot they could find.

"Two on guard at all times," John said. "Mitch and I will take the first shift, then Ripman and Carrollee, Marion and Nikki, then Jose and me."

"No, you're wounded," Ripman said. "I'll pull the double shift."

"Fine," John said.

Carrollee made sure the rifle's safety was on. She spread out her solar blanket, put her pack at one end. Then she mixed lukewarm water with soup mix and ate it with crumbled crackers. Then she stretched out, head on her pack. The moon was nearly full and Carrollee stared up at it, trying to

locate Flamsteed Crater. It was too small to see with the
naked eye but she knew it was in the southwest quadrant.
Was her husband there looking back at her? She found the
notion romantic, warming to the thought, but the time table
for the launch was classified. He could still be in transit.
What would he find? What would she find?

Carrollee dug out two more aspirin, unable to shake a
persistent headache. She was still perspiring too, even
though the evening had cooled from unbearable to uncomfortable. She thought of her children, knowing they were
safe with her mother, at least for now. Their world had become unstable in a way the world had never known. Not ge-
ologic instability or climatic, which the world had suffered
through periodically, or even stellar instability that had
brought the great comets twice into collision with Earth, ex-
tinguishing virtually all life. This new threat, this temporal
instability, a by-product of human foolishness, was a threat
unlike any other. Mother Earth had a way of recovering
from catastrophe, but often at the cost of dominant species.
That was a price Carrollee and Emmett weren't willing to
pay, not personally, and they certainly wouldn't let their
children pay. So here she was, and somewhere out there was
Emmett. At least there weren't dinosaurs where he was going.

Carrollee was bruised in two dozen places when she laid
back down after her shift on guard duty, the bruises a result
of repeatedly pinching herself to stay awake. Three days a
week at the gym didn't prepare one's body for real exertion.
Her exercise routine was designed to flatten her tummy, not
prepare her legs for hiking up and down hills, her back for
carrying a pack, her shoulder to carry a rifle, and her feet to
carry all of it. She was just about asleep when someone
shook her shoulder. She rolled over to see Ripman leaning
over her.

"Good work this morning," he said. "Only one man in
twenty could have made that shot."

"That explains it," Carrollee said. "I'm not a man."

Ripman smiled.

"A souvenir of your first kill," he said, dropping something on her chest.

Ripman walked away, laid down, turning away from her. On her chest she found the claw he had cut from the predator she had shot. He had bored a hole through it and strung it on a leather bootlace. She examined the claw from the needle point to the serrated edge. She realized John was lucky to have survived the attack.

She admired the claw, discovering she was proud of what she had managed to do, even knowing it was dumb luck. Slipping the lace over her head, she tucked the claw inside her shirt, then rolled over on her side. She didn't wake when the guard shifts changed later, and was still sound asleep when the tyrannosaurs attacked.

31 • LOSS

... It is likely that tyrannosaurus hid among the trees, to ambush its prey. It would have leapt out on a passing victim in a short burst of speed. Charging with mouth open wide, the force of the impact would have been absorbed by its strong teeth, sturdy skull and powerful neck.

—*Dougal Dixon, Barry Cox, R. J. G. Savage, Brian Gardiner,* Macmillan Illustrated Encyclopedia of Dinosaurs and Prehistoric Animals

YUCATAN PENINSULA

Suddenly conscious, Carrollee was moving, grabbing for her rifle. Whether it was the sound of the tyrannosaur tearing off tree limbs in its rush, or the warning bellows of the monoclonius that woke her, she never remembered. She came up on her knees with her rifle ready, seeing the monoclonius stampeding toward her. Someone yelled "run" and

she ran, grabbing her pack. Then it was a headlong rush
down the hill toward the stream below. Right behind, the
monoclonius herd thundered over the ridge. Over the noise
of the herd was the screech of an attacking predator.

With the sun just breaking, there was barely enough light
to avoid crashing into trees. Carrollee stumbled, but kept her
feet. The forest slowed the herd as they threaded their massive bodies through the trees. Smaller trees were run over,
uprooted, and trampled.

The ground leveled as Carrollee approached the stream.
Carrollee had seen other human silhouettes angling left and
she mimicked the move, trying to get out of the path of the
stampeding herd. Then the trap was sprung. Two more
tyrannosaurs charged from the far side of the stream.

Carrollee pulled up, trying to stop. One of the tyrannosaurs rushed right at her. She slipped, hit the ground, landing on her hip, and slid right toward the tyrannosaur. The
tyrannosaur lowered its head, jaws gaping. Now in an uncontrollable slide, she fumbled with her rifle. Then the jaws were
right above her and with a lunge the tyrannosaur reached
over her, clamping down on a monoclonius calf. Instantly,
Carrollee picked up her feet, completing her slide through the
legs of the tyrannosaur. She cleared the back foot just as it
changed position to support its grip on its struggling prey.
The feeding tyrannosaur created a breakwater, and like a
river around a boulder, the panicked monoclonius streamed
to either side. Carrollee got up, running full speed into the
stream. It was soon chest high, slowing her nearly to a stop.
Monoclonius hit the water on either side of her, the waves
knocking her back and forth. Rifle held high, pulling her
pack behind her, she fell, got her footing, slipped again and
was washed toward the monoclonius churning the stream.
She slammed up against a monoclonius whose pumping legs
created so much suction it threatened to pull her under.

Forced to choose, she threw the pack toward the shore,
hearing it splash. Pushing against the monoclonius, she got
her footing, and managed to move far enough away to clear

the suction. Then she angled toward clear water, the feeding tyrannosaur still creating a gap. She dragged herself ashore, exhausted. The monoclonius were slowing, still moving fast, but the panic was subsiding. The tyrannosaurs were feeding now, not hunting. Crawling away from the stream, she hid behind a tree, letting the herd move into the forest. Panting, half from exertion, half from fear, she cowered, watching. The monoclonius were calming, but they butted and swatted each other when touched.

As the last of the stragglers moved past, Carrollee heard the sounds of the tyrannosaurs feeding. She leaned around the tree, looking back up the hill. The T-rex that had passed her up for a bigger helping was on the hillside, ripping out entrails. With a great mouthful, it leaned its head back, snapping its jaws and jerking its head, the intestines sliding down its throat. To its left was another feeding T-rex, its prey still twitching as chunks of flesh were torn from massive haunches. Then just over the hill, another raised its head, a silhouette against the rising sun.

Fearing scavengers, Carollee took the rifle, and moved, scampering from tree to tree. She found her pack a hundred yards downstream. It had been partially unzipped when she had used it for a pillow, and some of the contents were gone. The pack was waterproof, but the interior had filled, sinking it in mud, making it as heavy as if it were full. With difficulty she pulled it out, and then retreated to the trees, dumping out the water.

Now she looked for the others, risking a shout.

"Anyone there," she called, just above a whisper.

No answer.

"Anyone out there!" she tried louder.

"Over here," came a reply.

Carrollee found Nikki crawling out from under a log. She had her pack, but not her rifle. Three bleeding scratches marked the left side of her face. Carrollee dug in her pack—she had one water bottle left. She used it to wash the dirt from Nikki's wounds.

"I ran into a tree," Nikki explained. "I just about knocked myself out. That's why I hid under there."

"Where's your gun?"

"Where we camped, I guess. It happened so fast."

Carrollee looked back to the hill and the feeding tyrannosaurs. There was no thought of retrieving the rifle.

"Where did the boys go?" Nikki asked.

"They outran us," Carrollee said. "Damn that women's liberation stuff."

Nikki laughed, then the sound of monoclonius bones breaking got them up and moving. The ground was churned to muck by the stampede, so they walked the rocky stream bank. Soon they heard the sound of digging.

"Is there someone there?" Carrollee called softly.

"Yeah," came the reply.

Jose was in the trees, digging a hole. There was a body on the ground opposite the growing pile of soil.

"Oh, no," Nikki gasped.

The body had been trampled, arms and legs broken, chest caved in, skull crushed.

"Who?" Carrollee asked softly.

"It's Mitch," he said, tears dribbling down his cheeks.

Jose went back to digging, talking while he shoveled.

"We were running together and he tripped. I reached out to catch him. I missed. There was nothing I could do. They were right behind us."

"You would have helped him if you could," Nikki said.

They let Jose dig, not offering to help. It was more than a burial, it was penance.

Jose had his rifle but not his pack. Mitch's rifle and pack had been trampled with him, destroying the weapon and most of the pack's contents. Carrollee retrieved the pack, salvaging dried soup, a dozen energy bars, and a half-filled water bottle. Carrollee knocked the mud off of the bag, finding one strap had been torn loose. She transferred some of her food and set the pack aside for Jose.

It took Jose another hour to get the hole deep enough for

his satisfaction. Then Carrollee and Nikki helped him gently lower the crumpled body into the hole. Now Jose hesitated.

"Can I pray for him, Jose?" Nikki offered.

"Please," Jose said gratefully, reaching into his shirt and pulling out a cross hanging on a gold chain.

"Heavenly father, please accept the soul of this good man. He was a gentle man, kind to his friends and to strangers. I only knew him for a short time, but I never heard him take your name in vain, lie, or say an unkind word about his colleagues or friends or anyone. He loved your creation and especially animals, and he dedicated his life to protecting them. Please, Lord, open the gates of heaven for this man. Amen."

Jose crossed himself and then kissed the crucifix.

"That was nice, Nikki," Jose said, then he scooped up a shovelful of dirt.

"Wait," Carrollee said.

Carrollee stripped leaves from trees, and uprooted ferns and other vegetation. Then she carefully covered the body with the leaves. Nikki worked with her until Mitch was covered from head to toe. Now the soil would not touch Mitch's body directly.

"I should have thought of that. Thanks," Jose said, and began filling the hole.

Carrollee and Nikki gathered the biggest rocks they could carry, stacking them next to the grave. The hole was nearly filled when John and Ripman came through the trees. John had his rifle, but not his pack. Ripman had his pack and his rifle.

"Mitch or Marion?" John asked.

"Mitch," Jose said, without pausing.

"I'm sorry, Jose," John said.

Ripman and John helped gather rocks. Once Jose finished covering his friend, they built a small cairn.

"That will keep the scavengers out," Nikki said.

Carrollee saw Ripman's eyes flick toward Nikki but he said nothing.

"Anyone seen Marion?" John asked.

No one had.

"Any idea of which way he ran?"

No one knew.

John sent them out in pairs to search; Ripman and Nikki, John and Carrollee. Jose was left by the grave. John set up a search pattern in the shape of half of a spoked wheel. John reasoned that if Marion had not made it to the stream he was dead, since every square inch of the hillside had been churned to muck. They started by going in opposite directions along the stream, walking out a kilometer, and then arcing back to the grave. They repeated the pattern, gradually working around the wheel until the two search parties met. In that terrain, and with dense vegetation, no search could be "thorough," but they covered enough territory to be sure Marion wasn't lying in the open.

Halfway back on their last search spoke, they were surprised by a dozen small bipeds running across their path, heading in the direction of the feeding tyrannosaurs. They were two feet high, green, with storklike snouts, lined with rows of needle teeth.

"Uninvited dinner guests," John said. "We have to move."

Without proof of death, it was hard to leave a comrade who might be injured, needing help. Although no one would speak it, they all believed that Marion was dead. At the very least they would never know what had happened to him.

Despite the stampede, John still believed in the protection of the herd and they fast-walked, trying to catch it, mindful that they were now trailing it, just as the tyrannosaurs had. They caught the monoclonius late in the afternoon, working their way inside the pickets just as before. Now they slowed, sharing the remaining water bottles and food. Running low on water, and dehydrating fast, Ripman took a pack full of empty bottles and angled into the jungle alone. The herd had started its dusk routine of settling down before Ripman returned, passing out the bottles, everyone refreshing themselves.

"That's two good days for you in a row," Ripman said, passing Carrollee a water bottle.

"What do you mean?"

"You and I were the only ones who kept both their pack and gun," he said, smiling.

"This isn't a contest," Carrollee said irritably. "No one is keeping score."

"Yes it is, and God is keeping score. So far it's humans three, dinosaurs two. The problem is that they have more players than we do."

Ripman walked away, leaving Carrollee angry and disgusted. That man didn't think like any human being she had ever known.

"Hey, look!" Jose shouted. The nearest monoclonius snorted, and then lowered their heads, presenting the bony neck collar. "It's Marion."

He was coming out of the jungle, walking slowly, clothes filthy. Jose ran to greet him, falling in, telling him about Mitch. Marion nodded sadly, and nothing more was said. When he reached the others, Carrollee could see his hair was caked with blood. He was also carrying his rifle and his pack.

"What happened to you?" John asked.

"I tried to get out of the path of the herd and pretty well made it. I was still ahead of the leaders when I hit the stream bank and turned, letting them charge across. There were still stragglers but I dodged all of them—except one. It clipped me from behind. When I woke up I was face down in the mud."

"But you kept your pack and gun!" Carrollee said, looking at Ripman.

"Of course," Marion said. "There's a ruin a half kilometer over there we might be able to shelter in," he suggested.

Everyone liked the idea better than sleeping in the open again, and they followed Marion. The ruin turned out to be so overgrown it was nearly unrecognizable. The ancient structure was up against a hill, swallowed by an ancient landslide. Ripman still had his machete, and hacked away at vines, small trees, and overhanging limbs, exposing a few standing walls. Finally, he found an opening, exploring it with a flashlight. Then he was back, carrying the body of a snake he had beheaded.

"What do you think?" John asked.

"We're safer in there than near the herd—unless there's an earthquake."

They decided to risk the earthquake. They set up camp, which amounted to finding a comfortable place to lie down. The room they were in went back thirty feet, but they stayed near the opening. Ripman skinned and filleted the snake, and then created a half dozen shish kebobs, minus the vegetables. Ripman sprinkled them with something from a small plastic container he carried and then built a fire and roasted them. Carrollee was trying to force herself to eat another energy bar when Ripman offered her a stick with a half dozen pieces of skewered snake meat. Hating herself, she accepted.

The snake was spicy, with a slightly gamey taste, but palatable. Sliding off a second piece, she realized she was enjoying the fresh meat. Only Marion refused the snake. Jose took a loaded skewer but looked guilty. Now there was an extra skewer of meat, so Ripman offered it around and everyone took another piece. Full of warm, fresh meat, feeling safe in their human-made cave, and happy to be alive, they settled into a general sense of well-being. Only Jose was sad, grieving his friend's death.

"Hey, Ripman," Marion said. "Have you ever seen tyrannosaurs hunt like they did today?"

"Not with an ambush," Ripman said, both arms behind his head, watching the sky. "I once saw four of them rip into a herd of zebrasaurs—those striped dinos with the crests."

"Paralophosaurus," Marion said.

"Yeah, that's them. They angled in from opposite sides driving the zebrasaurs toward each other. Two zebrasaurs ran head on into each other. Knocked themselves out cold! The tyrannosaurs just snapped their necks and started eating. Yeah, coordinated hunting, but never an ambush."

"I haven't seen it either but ceratopsians are tough to hunt in a herd. They like to circle up and put those big heads down. Even king rex can't get past those horns and collars."

"I've seen them do that," Ripman said. "Getting them moving was a good way to get around that armored head problem. Hey, Marion, you ever see a T-rex take on a shunosaurus?"

"Never."

"I did once and it was the funniest thing I ever saw. I don't think this T-rex had ever seen one before and didn't know what was coming."

Ripman paused, realizing the others might not know the species.

"Shunosaurus is a four-legged herbivore. Looks something like an apatosaurus but a little smaller and with a thicker neck and a long tail. Apatosaurs use that tail like a whip but with a lot more stopping power. Shunosaurs have a whip tail but it has a club on the end."

"Shunosaurs and tyrannosaurs didn't range together before the time quilt," Marion said. "That tyrannosaur had probably never hunted one before."

Now Ripman was smiling, enjoying his story.

"Old Mr. T comes charging into the herd, which stampedes every which way. Mr. T is still coming when one of those shunosaurs does a pivot turn and whips that tail around. Mr. T is expecting it and angles his head around opening his jaws. I think he was going to try and clamp down on it like it's an apatosaur tail. Well, the tail comes snapping around and that shunosaur conks Mr. T on the side of the head with that club."

Ripman chuckled at the memory.

"Mr. T doesn't go down, he just stops in his tracks, standing there with this surprised look on his face. His mouth hung open, his tongue was drooping out one side. He was so stunned it wouldn't have surprised me if tweety birds started flying around his head."

Everyone was smiling or laughing now.

"Then . . . then . . . I swear this is true . . . Mr. T shook his head making a noise like Curly from the Three Stooges and then smacked himself on the side of his head with one of his tiny arms."

"I've heard that sound!" Marion said excitedly. "It's that nyuck, nyuck, nyuck sound."

"Exactly," Ripman said, and then mimicked it, sending everyone into convulsions. "The funniest thing I've ever seen."

Carrollee, John, and Nikki exchanged surprised looks. The bulls had temporarily unlocked horns. Even Jose had enjoyed the story, briefly forgetting that morning's tragedy.

The sun went down and still they sat at the mouth of the cave. They kept the fire going to discourage local and imported fauna, but sat outside, leaning against the ancient wall, waiting for the stars to come out—they never came. As the sun set, the moon rose, its face a smear of rainbow colors. As dark finished filling the forest, the sky shimmered with waves of red and green. The only stars were just above the skyline.

"What's happening?" Nikki asked. "It wasn't like this when we were here before."

"It wasn't like this yesterday," Jose said.

"The radiation is ionizing the gas in the atmosphere," Carrollee said. "But I've never seen it this intense. Maybe we better move inside."

"Is it dangerous?" John asked.

"Probably not," Carrollee said. "Probably."

As of one mind, they retreated under cover, peeking out at the beautiful but disquieting sky. Suddenly there was a flash as bright as lightning and the sky cleared, the stars came back, the moon returned to the accustomed white.

"Any theories, Carrollee?" John asked.

Carrollee trained as a botanist, but had picked up significant knowledge of dinosauria, and even some understanding of basic astrophysics through her work with Emmett and the other physicists in the OSS. When Nick Paulson picked her for the expedition, it had been considered strictly a "look-see-report" mission. She was to photograph, observe, record, not explain electromagnetic phenomena.

"No, except that energy had to be discharged somewhere or in some time."

"A lot of energy went somewhere," John said. "I just hope no one was in its path."

32 ▪ DESTINATION

The new time quilt in the Witsundays confirms the return of the time disruption, but also raises new questions since the size of this event is significantly less than those from the first disaster. Even more troubling are reports that this event brought humans from the past to the present. Australian witnesses report that a small castle dropped into the sea and that two Spanish-speaking soldiers were rescued. Authorities found the fifteenth-century soldiers in a pub, drinking beer with their new mates.

—*Caroline Mauck, Director of the CIA,*
Presidential Daily Briefing

YUCATAN, MEXICO

It was midday, the temperature in the nineties, and the humidity nearly as high. They were resting, letting the herd move past them. Ripman, Marion and John were bent over a map, an overlay on top, deep in discussion. Nikki had taken off her shirt, wearing only her sports bra, and was sewing up a rip. Jose sat next to her, the two talking about movies. Carrollee knew Jose would have discussed needlepoint if it kept him close to a pretty girl in her underwear.

Carrollee cleared her throat and coughed softly. Her throat itched, she had another headache, and she was running low on pain medication. At home with Emmett, being sick meant special privileges. Carrollee would lie on the couch under a blanket while Em made dinner, fed the kids, bathed them, read them a story and put them to bed. He would bring her tea whenever she asked and let her pick what to watch on TV. Sick time was almost as good as vacation time at home, but there would be no special privileges here.

"Shouldn't we be there?" Carrollee asked, as John and Ripman and Marion noticed Nikki.

"What? Oh. Yeah," John said, tearing his eyes away. "But we're going to have to leave the herd. We don't think they are heading toward the source of the electromagnetic field anymore. They seem to be going into orbit around it."

"Won't the predators do the same?" Carrollee suggested.

"They should," Marion said.

"The attacks got worse the closer we got," Nikki said with the voice of experience.

Nikki slipped her arms into her repaired shirt, buttoning it as she spoke.

"I think they hunted us because there wasn't any other game. At least we didn't see any."

Keeping close to the herd of monoclonius had kept most other dinosaurs away, but regularly they would see hadrosaurs, anklosaurs or stegosaurs. Once they had seen heads of apatosaurs lift above a copse of trees. The jungle was alive with a mix of dinosaurs and local wildlife.

When the herd turned south they angled east through the forest, finding narrow paths bulldozed here and there by the aimless wanderings of confused dinosaurs. Using the ready-made paths where they could, they zigzagged through the forest, occasionally cutting their own with a machete. The farther from the herd, the fewer trails they found and the slower the going.

Carrollee had specialized in marine botany, but she recognized some of what they were hacking through, and she identified it for Nikki as they walked—hardwood trees, coconut palms, gum trees and even an occasional almond or fig tree. With the local game, it was a veritable Garden of Eden.

Carrollee knew there was a time quilt nearer the coast where the ocean breezes generally kept the temperature in the eighties. That little piece of the Cretaceous past had thrived, dinosaurs spreading beyond their time quilt, driving away local fauna, and, over the last decade, the ancient angiosperms and other Cretaceous vegetation had been mixing with their descendants. Three coastal tourist towns had been abandoned. New businesses were built at a safe distance, offering visitors guided tours of the new dinosaur preserve.

Two hours later the sound of breaking limbs froze them in their tracks. They listened for a few seconds. It was coming toward them. They hid behind tree trunks, rifles ready. Something large was moving through the growth just out of sight, snapping off limbs, crushing rotten logs, bulldozing bushes and small trees. The racket peaked, then began to recede, all of them sighing with relief. When the noise was well distant, they moved forward. A hundred yards deeper into the forest they came to the recently bulldozed path. The men squatted around a print that was larger than a meat platter.

"Apatosaur," Ripman said.

"Big one, too," Marion said.

"It's unusual for them to travel alone," Jose said.

"Herds always have rogues, but I'll bet that if we could autopsy that apatosaur we would find it's sick," Marion said.

"I could arrange an autopsy," Ripman offered.

Marion glared briefly.

"If you shoot it, you have to eat it," Marion said.

"Damn, and I had a big lunch," Ripman said. "Maybe for breakfast."

Carrollee found she was mildly disappointed that Marion and Ripman were getting along now, like she had lost an ally. They were about to move on when five velociraptors came trotting out of the woods, following the apatosaur path. The humans froze. Then, one of the velociraptors noticed the clump of humans, honking a brief warning. The predators stopped, heads low, tails high, studying the humans.

Velociraptors came in a variety of sizes. Even the smallest of those across the clearing was bigger than any in the pack that had attacked them earlier.

"We'll handle them," Marion said, signaling Jose to join him.

"Don't do it, Marion," Ripman said softly. "Stay still."

"Watch and learn," Marion said, starting forward.

Jose moved with him but at an angle, the gap widening as they approached. Slowly, Marion took a grenade from his belt, pulling the pin with his teeth, his rifle in his right hand. The raptors were interested, not afraid—prey ran away, not approached. Now the raptors lifted their heads, tails settling to the ground. They were six feet tall, heads cocked, puzzled by the behavior of the humans. Now the largest raptor made a sound like a deep-voiced crow. The other raptors bobbed their heads, birdlike.

"Don't move," Ripman whispered, and then followed the rangers.

Carrollee wanted to stop Ripman, but knew any sound or motion could trigger an attack. Thankfully, Ripman moved carefully, weapon at shoulder level. Marion rocked back and threw the stink grenade. It arced through the air, beginning to smoke as it flew. All five raptor heads snapped toward the quick move, and then tracked the object. It was still ten feet off the ground when one of them leaped, snatching it from the air.

Smoke poured out of both sides of its mouth. The raptor tried crushing the smoker but started gagging, and with a whip of its head, threw the device twenty feet away. The raptor then went into a coughing fit, the others snapping and snarling, blaming him for the irritating fumes. Now their heads came down again, tails straight out.

"Here they come," Ripman said in a near shout.

As of one mind the healthy raptors charged. Ripman ran to the side, trying to get a better angle on the raptors. Marion and Jose opened fire, the sounds of their guns distinctly different. Marion fired rubber bullets, Jose his nine-millimeter ammunition.

John ran the opposite direction from Ripman, mimicking his move, trying for a better angle. Nikki pulled on Carrollee's arm, dragging her back to a fallen tree. The two of them hunkered down, Carrollee using the log to steady her rifle. Marion went down first, the raptor burying a toe claw into his belly, then ripping down while its jaws went for Marion's throat.

Jose hit the first dinosaur to reach him, but a second leaped over his wounded comrade. Ripman shot it mid-flight. Jose, bringing up his rifle to deflect the attack, disappeared under the dinosaur. John opened fire, he and Ripman shooting at the remaining attacking raptor. It yelped, and then retreated, the sick raptor following it into the woods. No one moved for a few seconds, guns ready, ignoring the dying raptor flopping on the ground. Then they raced to the injured. John reached Jose first, where the raptor was still thrashing about. John shot it in the head. Ripman checked the raptor that Jose had shot—it was dead.

"Damn, you people are lucky shots," Ripman said, shaking his head.

Carrollee and Nikki helped John drag the dead raptor off of Jose while Ripman stood guard. Jose was alive.

While John and Nikki attended to Jose, Carrollee walked with Ripman to where Marion had fallen. The dead raptor partially obscured Marion's body. He had been eviscerated, intestines partially pulled from his body. The raptor had managed to clamp on his neck before dying, and tore out a large chunk. Blood pooled around Marion's head.

The sound of the surviving raptors could be heard in the woods, making the crow sound, one raptor coughing intermittently.

"We have to get out of here," Ripman said.

"We should bury him," Carrollee said.

"We can't," Ripman said. "They are calling for reinforcements."

Carrollee believed him. Jose was sitting up now, cradling his left arm.

"Broken?" John asked.

"It better be," Jose said. "It hurts like hell."

"Let me feel it," Nikki said.

"Not here, not now," Ripman said, eyes on the forest, listening to the calls.

John dug in Ripman's pack and pulled out his spare shirt, tying the arms around Jose's neck to make a sling. When Carrollee tried to give Jose aspirin, Nikki stopped her, producing two yellow capsules.

"Mental patients have the good stuff," Nikki said, smiling.

John took Marion's pack and Nikki his rifle. Helping Jose to his feet, they followed the apatosaur-dozed path a half-mile until it crossed a stream. Then they waded in the stream for another half mile before resuming course. They did not rest until they had put the site of the attack a couple of miles behind.

Helping Jose down, they leaned him against a tree trunk, and then Nikki felt his arm. Jose didn't flinch.

"I have to set this," Nikki said.

With Ripman and John standing guard, Carrollee assisted.

"Sit in his lap facing him, then wrap your arms around him and hold the tree trunk," Nikki ordered.

Carrollee did as she was told, Jose looking dazed but pleased as she pressed up against him and wrapped her arms around as much of the trunk as she could.

"Why Carrollee, I thought you were married," Jose said, speech slurred.

"Hold him tight," Nikki said.

Carrollee pulled herself tight against the ranger. Then Nikki put one foot in the crook of his arm, took his wrist in both hands and pulled. Jose gasped, reaching for his broken arm, but Carrollee's body prevented it.

"Got it," Nikki said. "Ripman, get me some splints."

Ripman pulled the machete and began hacking at branches. Jose was panting now. Still pressed against him, Carrollee could feel his heart racing.

"You can let him go now," Nikki said.

Carrollee got off. Jose was white, sweaty and breathing in short shallow gasps. Nikki finished splinting his arm, and then put it in the shirt sling.

"Carrollee, Nikki, stand guard," John said.

Ripman examined Nikki's splint while John opened the map.

"Nice splint," Ripman said.

Nikki flashed him a quick smile. Ripman smiled back, and then joined John, leaning over the map.

"Maybe a couple of more hours," Ripman said, tracing a path.

"How are you doing, Jose?" John asked. "Do you need to rest?"

"If we sit still, we're lunch," Jose said.

"Got that right," Ripman said.

John helped him to his feet. Rifle in his good hand, Jose fell in with the others, Ripman in the lead, John protecting the rear. Hacking a path, they worked up an incline, the rain forest too thick to see more than a few meters. Sweating, weak, her throat raw, Carrollee struggled to keep up. Finally they started down, the route soon becoming a steep decline, the composting ground cover treacherous. Nikki was helping Jose, steadying him, but keeping up, embarrassing Carrollee who needed a break. Then ahead was a lake.

"It's on the other side," John said, pausing.

The rain forest on the opposite shore was dense, vegetation interwoven, opaque. Carrollee flopped down, resting.

"Carrollee, you don't look well," Nikki said, studying her face.

Carrollee laughed. Nikki's new clothes were spotted with green and brown stains, her repaired shirt ripped in two new places. The knees of her pants were brown and her boots caked with mud. Sweat ran down her dirty, sunburned face. Her recently styled hair hung in greasy clumps. Carrollee laughed, ignoring her headache.

"I don't look well?" she chortled.

Nikki giggled.

Controlling herself, Carrollee said "Nikki, you have a smudge on your nose."

Now the two women burst into laughter. Nikki dropped next to Carrollee, arm around her shoulders. The men looked at them as if they were insane, and then one by one smiled—even Ripman. They might have broken out into laughs too, except for the vibration. Ripman felt it first, but the others were sensitized now, quickly sobering. Ripman put his hand in the air.

"Damn, we're upwind."

Briefly, the rhythmic vibration stopped. Then it came again, but faster.

"It's big, isn't it?" Nikki said.

"Yes," Ripman said. "And it has our scent."

33 ▪ TEMPLE

Almost no one knows how to visualize this arena [space-time], which is a hybrid form of three-dimensional space woven onto a dimension of time. . . . Objects do not move in space-time, they simply exist at all stages of their travel from start to finish along their history . . .

—*Sten F. Odenwald,* Patterns in the Void

YUCATAN PENINSULA

Split up, run, or fight?" Ripman asked, laying out the options for John.

"Run," Carrollee voted.

"Fight," Jose said.

Now all eyes were on Nikki.

"Run," she said.

"Ripman, get us out of here," John said.

Ripman led them in the opposite direction of the approaching predator. The footfalls were steady, growing louder, accompanied by another vibration, a different rhythm.

"I think there's more than one," Carrollee worried out loud.

"Two, at least," Ripman said.

Weak, joints aching, Carrollee struggled to keep up. The sickness had complete hold of her now, making her groggy, and affecting her judgment. One moment she would fail to lift her leg high enough to clear a root, stumbling, and the next she would choose poor footing and slide. She became aware of a hand holding her arm—John steadying her.

Ripman led them toward the lake. The shore was hidden under tangled roots locked in a fight for water rights. The overhanging canopy was thick, creating deep shadows along the shore while the lake sparkled with diamonds of sunlight. The jumble of thick roots was slippery and treacherous. Now they helped each other, up and over, placing boots consciously, ever mindful that they were being stalked. The crack of breaking limbs, the swish and scrape of massive bodies forcing their way through the forest paralleled their moves.

The forest was ancient, the trees thick, giving the monkeylike humans protection from the tree-sized predators. The hunters tracked them by scent, keeping pace somewhere out of sight, but not out of sound.

"Persistent bastards," Ripman said.

"All five of us wouldn't fill one of those things up," John said. "Why aren't they hunting the herds?"

"It's the magnetic field," Jose said. "It's an addiction. If they leave it they go through withdrawal, so they hunt what they can find."

An hour later they had rounded the lake and were now opposite of where they had first contacted it. The hunters were silent now but no one doubted they were out there.

"Now it gets tricky," Ripman said. "We need to leave the shore."

Ripman slapped the trunk of one of the trees.

"As long as we stay in old growth the tyrannosaurs can't get to us."

They kept weapons at the ready. Occasionally, there was movement in the distance, the tyrannosaurs shifting position, still at a safe distance but close enough for them to feel the vibration. Carrollee watched the trees, noticing the girth declining and spacing increasing. Still, the behemoth tyrannosaurs would find it impossible to maneuver between them

and these old growth trees were well rooted and not easy to
bulldoze. Without speed and surprise, even massive tyrannosaurs could be brought down. But yard-by-yard, the forest
was thinning, the ground vegetation increasingly lush.

"Don't worry," Nikki said. "The forest is just like this
around the site."

"You came this way?"

"Not exactly. I don't remember a lake."

Carrollee was not reassured. Then, through the trees they
saw a ruin. They approached slowly, the tumble of stones a
hive of hiding places. Trees grew from the piles, roots
snaking into the soil, overlaying rubble like veins. The wall
of tumbled buildings and trees effectively blocked their
path. The ground was spongy, the air dank, the smell of rot
pervasive.

"I don't remember this," Nikki said.

"It's been here a while," John said.

Carrollee wondered in the age of time quilts how anyone
could make such a statement?

Ripman led them along the wall of rubble, looking for an
opening.

"We could climb it," John suggested.

"I could," Ripman said.

Again, Ripman's arrogance irritated Carrollee.

"You don't think I could climb this?" Carrollee asked
angrily.

"What!" Ripman said, honestly confused. "Not you. Jose!"

"He's right," Nikki said. "Jose couldn't make it with that
arm."

"I could if there was a T-rex after me—and there is," Jose
said confidently.

As sick as she was, Carrollee was not sure she could make
the climb.

Ripman ignored them, his machete out, hacking off
branches randomly, studying the piles of stone. Now he bent
down and hacked furiously, revealing close-fitting wedge-
shaped stones.

"What do you make of this, John?" Ripman asked.

John stooped, tracing the shape of the stones.

"Looks like the top of an arch."

"Hmmm," Ripman said.

Ripman moved on while one by one the others bent to examine the stones. Carrollee agreed, it did look like an arch and that meant the land had filled in since the structure had been built.

Now Ripman was hacking a tunnel through small trees, looking for a way through the ruins. Soon he disappeared in dense foliage, well past where he should have contacted the wall of debris. John stood at the opening, looking inside, watching Ripman work. Behind her, Carrollee heard the sound of breaking branches. Carrollee and Nikki spun, rifles ready.

"A tyrannosaur couldn't get through those," Jose assured them, his rifle nestled in his good arm.

Nikki looked at the spacing, picturing one of the monsters from the first attack; they had been fifteen to twenty feet tall, forty feet long, and five or six tons in weight. It didn't seem possible one could force its way through and if it did, it would come slowly and be vulnerable. Then somewhere out of sight, but close, they heard the bellow of a tyrannosaur.

"See, I told you," Jose said. "We're protected by the trees."

Despite the reassurance, Carrollee kept her weapon ready. Then she saw movement. Squeezing between the trees was a small tyrannosaur. Nikki spotted it, lifted her dinosaur gun and fired. Now Carrollee opened fire, but the protection of the trees was afforded to all, their rounds merely tearing chunks from trunks. Startled by the noise, the small tyrannosaur changed direction and they lost sight of it.

"Come on," Nikki said, pulling Carrollee's arm and then Jose's.

Backing up, they kept their eyes on the forest. John was covering them now at the edge of the opening Ripman had created.

"Inside," John said, indicating Ripman's tunnel.

Nikki pushed Jose in, ignoring his protests. Then she shoved Carrollee ahead of her.

"Hurry," Nikki said.

Nikki was insistent, but not panicky. She showed a competence Carrollee had not seen when they first met in the airport.

Ripman had hacked a path tall enough for himself, so Carrollee had plenty of headroom. Sunlight sifted through the dense overhang, the interior a kaleidoscope of greens. The path was narrow, lined with machete-sharpened limb spears. Carrollee caught up to Jose. She could see nothing but his back, but she could hear Ripman's machete work ahead. Suddenly, Ripman gasped.

"Ripman!" Jose yelled, then ran.

As Carrollee followed, Jose suddenly tried to stop, turning sideways. Carrollee crashed into him, knocking him forward where the ground gave way. Jose whipped out his good arm, his rifle flying. Flailing, he grabbed at anything and everything. Carrollee lunged for him, landing flat. She grabbed his good arm with one hand, slowing his fall, but she could not hold him. Dropping her rifle, she held him with two hands but found she was sliding after him. Jose's head sank out of sight. Then she slid to the brink, legs splayed wide, still being pulled into the hole. Suddenly, Nikki jumped on her legs, hooking her hands over the waist of Carrollee's pants. Carrollee stopped sliding, but Jose's dead weight was too much. The ground sagged, limbs cracked and Carrollee was falling.

She released Jose as she fell, tucked her head and tried to roll midair. Nikki let go of her and they separated. Carrollee hit shoulder first, bounced head over heels, and then landed flat on her back, sliding down a steep slope, feet first, then burying her legs deep into soft muck.

Blind with pain, Carrollee lay still, letting the shock dissipate, waiting for the dull aches of serious injuries. Soon she opened her eyes. Looking back up the slope she could see deep shadows. It took her a few seconds to realize that Ripman's tunnel had led over a low point in a wall but then onto the lowest level of the forest canopy. A canopy so thick with broken limbs, and composting leaves, that it supported their weight. Now legs appeared from the hole and John lowered himself, hung by his arms, and then dropped, absorbing his landing with his knees.

Jose was sitting up, moaning, and holding his broken arm. Nikki crawled to him, checking the splint. Ripman stood a few yards away, legs gray to the knees with muck, wiping mud from his rifle. Carrollee pulled her legs out, nearly losing a boot to the suction. Now she stood, John coming up behind her. Looking around, she felt as if they were in a bowl, the wall and trees behind them running in both directions. The center was sprinkled with trees, much smaller than the giants outside. Over the tops of these trees they could see a structure.

"That's it," Nikki said, standing. "That's the Zorastrus temple."

"Temple?" Carrollee said. "Nikki, that's a pyramid."

Then there was a rumble behind them, the cracking of foot-thick limbs, and with an ear-splitting screech, a tyrannosaur fell through the canopy into the bowl.

34 ▪ JUVENILE REX

One of our adult tyrannosaurs is nearly forty-seven feet long. That means that if one of you stomped on its tail you would have nearly eight seconds to escape before the nerve impulse reached its brain. I don't recommend trying this since eight seconds is about the same amount of time you would have left to live.

—*Marion Wayne, dinosaur ranger, speaking to a tour group at the Everglades National Dinosaur Preserve*

YUCATAN PENINSULA

Carrollee looked for her rifle. It had fallen through the canopy with her and rested next to the tyrannosaur now struggling to its feet. This tyrannosaur was smaller than those that attacked and killed Mitch—ten feet tall, maybe twenty feet in length, weighing a couple of tons. Not the monsters they had seen before, but with the same massive jaws and hunter's instinct. Size made no difference; Carrollee was just as afraid. Then the canopy parted again and another tyrannosaur fell through, landing on the first, setting off a deafening fight.

"Juveniles," Jose said.

"Let's go!" John yelled, shoving Carrollee.

Nikki was already running, Ripman trotting alongside, still struggling to clean his weapon. They ran toward the pyramid, losing sight of it as the vegetation thickened. Soon the squabble behind them ended. The juvenile tyrannosaurs would be sniffing out their trail soon.

The ground was firmer now and they made good time. Even without her rifle, Carrollee struggled to keep up. Nikki was running with Jose, ready to catch him if he fell. John kept in the back, frequently looking over his shoulder.

The pyramid was ahead now, barely distinguishable in the trees, enveloped by vines and runners. The base of the pyramid was virtually invisible, hidden by trees, vines, ferns, and other growth. When they reached what looked like one side, they stopped, turning, watching, listening. Carrollee, still not experienced enough to know which of the soft sounds meant danger, started at every rustle.

"Do you hear them, Ripman?" Carrollee asked.

"No, but they're out there."

Ripman worked the bolt on his rifle—it jammed open, a shell partially ejected.

"There's an opening somewhere," Nikki assured them.

"Let's find it," John said, now taking the lead as Ripman struggled with his rifle.

They tried to keep their backs to the pyramid, but growth forced them to deviate out, around, and over, so many times that Carrollee often lost track of where the pyramid was. Finally they reached what must be a corner as they angled in a new direction. The terrain fell off sharply, dropping lower. Carrollee realized the pyramid was half buried just like the buildings they had climbed over.

"This is familiar," Nikki said excitedly. "We're close to the opening."

They picked up the pace, still wary, watching for the tyrannosaurs. Finally, satisfied that his rifle was clean, Ripman took the lead again, easing their path with his machete. Gradually the ground leveled, the trees thinned, and they came to a small clearing with two overgrown ruins set close to the base of the pyramid. Vines and even small trees rooted in the pyramid's seams, but from this side, looking up, the structure was impressive.

"That's where Kenny went," Nikki said, pointing between the two structures. "There's an opening in there. But he never came back."

"What's inside?" Carrollee asked.

"Nothing. At least not as far as we went. Kenny told us it was dangerous to go inside."

"Dangerous? How?" John asked.

"I didn't understand," Nikki said.

They moved between the two smaller buildings guarding the entrance. Ripman hacked away some of the greenery, revealing one building. The ceiling was gone, but the walls still stood, the interior an arboretum. They crossed to the other side and Ripman cleared away more of the growth, revealing what once had been an identical structure. Only two walls remained, supported by trees that had sprouted in the interior. High on the wall, Carrollee noticed a small opening. Something was resting in it. She pulled it out, wiping away grime. It was a calculator.

"That's Kenny's," Nikki exclaimed, grabbing it. "I gave it to him for Christmas."

Nikki held it out for all to see. Then she pushed the "On" button, and the screen came to life. She held it to her chest like it was precious. Now they moved toward the pyramid, looking for the way in. Ripman hacked away, revealing a rectangular shaped opening that was ten feet high. The interior was black.

"I don't know what Nick Paulson was expecting, but I don't think it was this," John said.

Carrollee agreed. Nick had no idea of what they would find, but certainly an ancient Mayan pyramid was not on the list of possibilities.

"Maybe he should have expected it," Ripman said.

"Why?" Carrollee snapped, set off by Ripman's know-it-all attitude.

"Pyramids are said to have special powers. That's probably why cultures on two different continents devoted their wealth to creating the structures. Chalking that kind of sacrifice up to a king's ego, or religious mumbo-jumbo, is short-sighted. Whoever built these things expected something in return and I don't mean regular rain and bumper crops."

Carrollee knew both the Egyptian and Mayan pyramids were developed—perhaps perfected—over centuries, as designs were improved, structures enlarged, and interiors modified. The Egyptian pyramids had been tombs, or so she thought; the Mayan pyramids, temples to their gods.

"But there are other pyramids both here and in Egypt. Why aren't they having the same effect?" Carrollee asked.

No one answered.

"What have we got left?" Ripman asked. "Looks like we're down to two rifles."

Ripman flashed Carrollee a disappointed look for losing hers. Nikki had lost a second rifle while trying to keep Carrollee from falling through the canopy. Jose had tossed his rifle, trying to save himself with his good arm. Only John and Ripman had rifles.

Exhausted from the rush through the forest, Carrollee now realized she was feverish. She sank to the ground, next to the pyramid, taking off her pack. The others dropped packs too, fishing out water, sharing energy bars. Carrollee passed up the food, but took water and then found her camera in her pack, and belatedly began taking pictures.

She took pictures of the two small ruins, and then the front of the pyramid. She was too close to take the whole structure in, so she started to back up. Ripman shook his head no. She stopped. He was one of the least likeable men she had ever met, but his instincts were uncanny. She took two pictures, one of the top, and one of the bottom. She then took some close-ups of the stones that made up the structure.

"There were markings here," Nikki said, pointing to one side of the opening. "Kenny thought they were important."

Ripman chopped away, exposing rows of figures.

"They're Babylonian," Nikki said.

Now all eyes were on Nikki.

"Akkadian, actually. That's what Kenny said."

"Did he tell you what they meant?" John asked.

"No. But I think it's an equation and some of the symbols at the bottom say 'Zorastrus.' "

Everyone knew of Zorastrus and his prediction of the time quilt. How anyone in the Yucatan would know of a Babylonian prophet was anyone's guess.

"What makes you think it's an equation?" Carrollee asked.

"Because he entered them into his calculator."

"Let me see," Carrollee said.

Reluctantly, Nikki turned over the calculator. With John leaning over one shoulder, and Ripman the other, Carrollee turned the calculator on. She located a menu on the small screen and found everything had been deleted except one file. She called up the file and a graph appeared. A small NEXT flashed in the corner. Carrollee clicked on it and a new graph appeared.

"Does this make any sense to anyone?" Carrollee asked.

It didn't.

"Let me hang onto this for a while, Nikki? I'll take good care of it."

"I'll get it back?" Nikki said anxiously.

"I promise."

Now Carrollee fished out her flashlight. Ripman and John also had working flashlights. Then Carrollee started into the pyramid. Nikki dragged her back a step.

"It's not safe, Carrollee. Kenny went in and he didn't come back."

"But you went in and did," Ripman pointed out.

"Just in there, that first part. Not deep inside."

"Then we'll just go as far as you did for now," John said.

"Let's just go home. Take some more pictures and let's leave."

Considering their losses, Carrollee couldn't believe entering the pyramid could be more dangerous than going back the way they had come. Then the decision was made for them. The juvenile rexes attacked.

Ripman's rifle came up first, but jammed. John got off one shot, as everyone bolted into the pyramid. Carrollee was first, turning on her flashlight. The floor sloped down, and then branched. She turned right, continuing down, a small cone of light illuminating a few yards at a time. She came to another branch and stopped, afraid of getting lost. Jose pulled up behind her, and then Nikki crashed into him. They stumbled, trying to keep their feet.

"Run!"

John's shout echoed off every surface. Carrollee flicked her flashlight past Nikki and Jose and spotted Ripman and John running recklessly, flashlights bobbing. Over John's shoulder she could see the head of one of the tyrannosaurs. Carrollee's light startled it and it snapped its head up, cracking it on the ceiling. Screeching in pain, it hesitated only briefly, and then came on again, channeling the pain into hunting.

They ran, Carrollee in the lead, legs pumping, chest heaving. Recklessly she navigated the complex interior of the pyramid. She knew others were behind her, but not who or how close. She came to another branch; one corridor went up, another down. She slowed, hesitating. Then there was movement. Aiming the flashlight down the corridor, she saw one of the young rexes.

"It's not possible," Carrollee said. "It couldn't get ahead of us."

"Run!" Nikki said, pushing her from behind.

The tyrannosaur charged up the ramp. Nearly delirious, Carrollee was slow to react. Nikki shoved Carrollee out of the path of the juvenile rex. Jose was right behind. He didn't make it. The tyrannosaur clamped its jaws on his shoulder, the sound of breaking bones audible. Jose's scream was cut off when the juvenile rex snapped its head, opened its jaws wider, and got a better grip, crushing Jose's chest.

Nikki took the flashlight from Carrollee and led the way. Stumbling along behind, the mix of shock, fever, and exhaustion left Carrollee in a surreal nightmare. As they ran, Carrollee realized that Ripman and John were not with them. She also knew there was nothing she could do for them.

Now she realized the interior had changed. The surface was smoother, the walls blacker. Then her stomach fluttered like she had shot up in an elevator and she felt stronger, capable of keeping up without being pulled. Then just as suddenly, her stomach fluttered again. She was nauseated and weak, as if carrying a great weight. The pyramid seemed different again, and then Carrollee saw daylight ahead.

35 • AMBUSH

To: Carolyn Mauck
From: John Flannery

Carolyn, we have been unable to contact the Fox Valley facility. This is most likely due to the unusual amount of atmospheric radiation. I am dispatching a Delta team to investigate Elizabeth Hawthorne's claim.

—*John Flannery, Chairman of the Joint Chiefs of Staff*

NEAR FOX VALLEY, ALASKA

There were six men on three snow machines, coming slowly, following the old woman's tracks. Baranov's men were invisible, partially buried in the snow. The unconscious old woman lay in the snow, her dog still guarding her. Spotting the pair, the men on the snow machines dismounted, approaching slowly. The dog snarled, and then barked a warning. One of the men raised his rifle.

"Surrender, you are surrounded!" Baranov shouted from cover.

The man snapped toward the sound of Baranov's voice and fired. Only two of the other Americans managed to get off a shot before they were killed. Baranov directed his men to search the bodies, finding identity tags, with a corporate logo Baranov knew to be a CIA front, the letters FVERS SECURITY, and FOX VALLEY ENVIRONMENTAL RESEARCH STATION in smaller letters below. The dead men carried wallets, one clip of spare ammunition, and radios. Baranov turned one on— nothing but white noise. They were not U.S. military quality.

Baranov frowned. Six dead Americans was not good.

"That was too easy," Leonid said.

"Yes. They weren't military."

"Gangsters then?"

"Perhaps," Baranov said, doubtfully. "But gangsters don't usually work security for secret American government installations."

Baranov ordered the bodies to be hidden and the old woman to be taken back to the helicopters for treatment. When they tried to pick her up, the dog bit one of his men.

"Easy, Mack," Baranov said, approaching slowly.

He held out his hand to the snarling dog, letting him sniff it.

Keeping a respectful distance, he spoke to the dog in English, using its name. When he signaled his men, they knelt slowly, then locked hands under the woman and lifted her. Watching intently, Mack uttered a soft growl.

"Go with her, Mack," Baranov said.

With the dog growling at their side, his men carried her back toward the landing site.

"Drop her and that dog will have your arm for lunch," Baranov called.

"I'll take the point," Leonid offered, reaching for his skis.

"Not necessary. This time we go American style," Baranov said, indicating the snow machines.

Baranov selected Leonid and four others to go with him. The six Russians took off their snow camouflage, putting on the parkas of the dead security men. Then with the hoods of the parkas covering their heads, they followed the trail back to Fox Valley.

36 ▪ LOOSE ENDS

Once on a journey, a philosopher encountered an old man and asked the old man to describe the world's place in the universe. "That's easy," the old man said. "The world is a great ball resting on the back of a giant turtle." "But what is the turtle standing on?" the philosopher asked. "Another, larger turtle," the old man replied. "And what is this turtle standing on?" asked the philosopher. "You can't trick me," the old man shot back. "It's turtles all the way down."

—*Nick Paulson*, Infinity Is Forever

FOX VALLEY, ALASKA

Vince Walters was a charismatic man when he was in control. He was a hypnotic speaker, physically intimidating, and had a tender touch that never failed to arouse the women he wanted. With neatly trimmed black hair, dark eyes, and fair skin, he had been a brilliant student, earning top grades until he reached graduate school. There he ran into self-

promoting professors who assigned him meaningless prob-
lems with no reasonable chance of discovering a solution.
When he failed in his assignments, they dared to criticize his
"problem-solving ability." Feeling his degree slipping away,
he seduced a promising first-year student and convinced her
it was a privilege to work on an older student's project.
Blinded by love, the ploy worked and Vince made progress,
completing the requirement of two published articles and
earning his degree. He slept with his ghost researcher one
last time at his graduation party, and then never saw or wrote
to her again.

He took a position at the University of Michigan but soon
realized the faculty were dumping the least qualified graduate students on him, students too dimwitted to complete the
projects he assigned. Three years into his career he knew the
senior faculty would block his tenure, and he would not settle for a second-tier university. After his fourth year, he took
a job with the government, where civil service gave him protection from incompetent managers. There he discovered a
gift for administration, managing the work of others and taking the credit. He began climbing the ladder.

Vince Walters was not charismatic when he lost control,
and he was on the edge now. He didn't like surprises, especially surprises he could not explain. Elizabeth Hawthorne, a
stranger from the pyramid, and then dinosaurs! None of this
was part of his plan.

Vince sat in Kawabata's cheap executive chair, feet on his
poor quality desk, thinking. He was in Kawabata's office not
because it was comfortable—it was not—but because it was
a symbol. Whitey was with him, worrying.

"Marissa and I have been talking, Vince. Maybe we should
delay a day or two," Whitey said. "At least until we can figure
out where those dinosaurs came from. That stranger, too."

Vince feigned confidence.

"It's not important. The stranger was probably with
Hawthorne and is now hiding in the pyramid. You said yourself that Kawabata would not let you search thoroughly. As

for the dinosaurs, they were the result of an aberrant time wave that opened a hole, letting a few slip through."

Whitey shifted his weight, uncomfortable in Kawabata's worn side chair.

"Yes, that's possible. Marissa thinks that drawing the orgonic energy may have pulled an unpredicted confluence to this exact point, but I don't like that it wasn't predicted. It should have shown up. I mean if we missed that, then what else did we miss? Maybe we could delay just a few days. I might be able to fit this into the model and figure out what is going on."

"No delays," Vince snapped. "The employees we gave extra vacation days will come back. Worse, the families of those we locked up will wonder why they haven't received calls or e-mail. Don't forget Elizabeth Hawthorne! What is she doing appearing mysteriously in the middle of the night, breaking into one of our bunkers? And then there's the one in that shaft—dead? Alive? If the security team doesn't find her, then someone will certainly come to investigate. No, Whitey, we're past the point of no return. We have to stay on schedule. Besides, you're the one who picked the timing. The conditions are perfect, right?"

"Yes. It'll be another month before conditions are acceptable and even then they would be marginal."

Now Whitey paused, avoiding Vince's eyes, and nervously shuffled his feet.

"There might be another way to understand what happened," Whitey said.

Vince waited.

"Marissa says that when they were in the pyramid, after the stranger appeared, that Kawabata instructed them to take recordings of the positions of the baffles. He seemed to have a hypothesis about what happened. We could ask him."

Vince erupted.

"Kawabata is an overrated, penny-pinching, half-wit. I carried him on this project. He never understood the potential of the collector, never really understood the connection with time waves. I was the one with the vision. If anyone could explain what has happened it would be me and I say that it is an insignificant side effect."

"Sure, Vince, sure. It was just an idea."

"We stay on schedule. The building conversion will be completed soon and then we can leave."

Again, Whitey shifted in his chair.

"You know what will happen if we leave Dr. Kawabata and the others here."

"We can't take them with us, Whitey," Vince said more gently. "At least this way they have a chance to survive."

"But we know they don't," Whitey argued.

"Not true. For all we know, the government has kept the truth from the public."

Vince was losing his temper again. Whitey had too many questions and he too few answers.

"What about Ms. Hawthorne? If someone knew enough to send her, won't they be expecting to hear from her?"

"We stick to the timeline. By the time they decide something has gone wrong it will be too late."

Suddenly Vince realized he had overlooked something. Finding Elizabeth's parka lying over one of Kawabata's Goodwill-quality chairs, Vince searched its pockets, finding a satellite phone. Swearing, he tossed the phone to Whitey.

"Find out if she made any calls!"

Trembling with rage, Vince was anything but charismatic and Whitey slunk from the room.

37 · SPECIAL DELIVERY

Are there any lengths our movement wouldn't go to, any laws our people wouldn't break in order to achieve the greater good of healing this planet? No!

—*Star Koslowski, quoted in "Inside the Pro-Earth Movement," Portland Weekly*

WASHINGTON, D.C.

Bill Rawlins was a man of habits. As was his custom, he ate oatmeal for breakfast not because he particularly liked oatmeal, but because it helped control his cholesterol. He drank his usual glass of orange juice, took his cholesterol medicine, joked with his children, then kissed them and his wife good-bye, leaving home by 7:00 A.M. for the thirty-minute drive to his office. He parked in his parking space in the garage across the street from his office building and then stopped by the newsstand for the stack of newspapers Mel had ready every morning. He paid and overtipped the disabled vet and took the express elevator to his floor, arriving before the staff. Next he leafed through the newspapers, looking for stories relevant to the defense industry and particularly their clients. After clipping three articles, he logged onto the web for the latest defense and international news, and then checked specialized Web sites that kept him up on news the mainstream press ignored. Now came his least favorite chore—phone messages. Bill worked through the messages, making a list of who had called and what they wanted. When the messages were all cleared, he assigned a rating to each call. Those he would ignore got a three. He assigned a two to those he would delegate to an assistant. Ones he saved for those he would answer personally. Virtually all of the "ones" were current clients, potential clients, or congressmen. The ones he ranked in order of the size of the contract or the importance of the committee the representative sat on. Finally, he turned to his e-mail messages. Experience told him that sixty percent of the messages would be spam and he quickly deleted messages from a Nigerian national seeking help smuggling cash out of her country, an ad for vitamin supplements claiming to restore hair—he knew these didn't work—three notices of the latest travel bargains, an offer for dance lessons and an invitation to buy "art from starving artists." When thirty-five spam messages were in the trash, he ordered the messages by when received, then began with the earliest, opening them, taking notes on what they were about, then moving on before answering. The messages came in from all parts of the world, from all time zones.

He was halfway through the messages when his administrative assistant arrived with her customary "Good morning, Mr. Rawlins." She would make the first pot of coffee now, Bill making the ten o'clock pot. Bill had worked with Mrs. Jeter for six years and they had a symbiotic relationship. She was widely considered the best administrative assistant in the firm. Other partners had tried to lure her away, but she had remained loyal, and would remain loyal as long as Bill matched their salary offers.

Bill was nearing the top of his e-mail list when he came to one from Elizabeth Hawthorne. He opened it.

BILL, I FOUND WHAT I WAS LOOKING FOR IN FOX VALLEY AND MORE. THERE IS A NUCLEAR BOMB HERE. SEND HELP.

Bill read the message again. Wondered for a few seconds if it was a joke, then remembered it was from Elizabeth. He reached for his phone, pausing. Who to call?

There was a knock on his doorframe. A skinny young woman stood there holding a basket of flowers. Her hair was long and greasy, her skin pale. She wore jeans and a T-shirt with words that were obscured by the flowers. If she had breasts they had insufficient volume to influence her shirt.

"Yes?" Bill said, impatient with the interruption.

"Bill Rawlins?"

"What is it?"

"I have flowers for you."

Bill frequently received unsolicited gifts from clients. The firm had strict limits on what he could accept in hard goods and cash, but no limits on consumables and disposables like play tickets, sports tickets, food, and flowers. He preferred tickets to the Redskins to another vase of flowers.

"Leave them with my assistant. If she's not there, put them on her desk."

The woman came forward, setting the basket on Bill's desk. Worried that it would leave a ring, he started to stand. Before he could, she lifted her shirt, pulled a revolver with a silencer and shot him in the chest. He collapsed back in his chair, the pain in his chest expanding like a swarm of agitated bees around a hive. He tried to speak, to ask "Why?" but he couldn't force enough air from his one functioning lung. The young woman came around to his side of the desk, looked at his e-mail, and then deleted Elizabeth's message.

"Too easy," she said.

Then his killer rapped on Bill's mahogany desk.

"It's people like you that are killing the rain forests, dead man!"

Then she turned to Bill again. He could read the words on her shirt now. They said "Flower Power." Then the skinny young woman shot him in the head.

38 ▪ TRAPPED

Even if the boundary condition of the universe is that it has no boundary, it won't have just a single history. It will have multiple histories. . . . There will be a history in imaginary time corresponding to every possible closed surface, and each history in imaginary time will determine a history in real time. Thus, we have a superabundance of possibilities for the universe.

—*Stephen Hawking,* The Universe in a Nutshell

FOX VALLEY, ALASKA

Elizabeth was lying on a lower bunk, covered in a pile of blankets. The stinging had left her toes and fingers, and she could control her shivering now. The man named Toru brought her a cup of tea. She sat up, covering her legs with blankets. Toru pulled another around her shoulders.

"Thank you," she said.

"You are welcome, Ms. Hawthorne."

Elizabeth was used to being recognized, although the longer she had been out of the White House the less it happened.

"I am Dr. Kawabata. I am director of this facility. May I ask what are you doing here?"

Elizabeth hesitated, sipping her tea. She had committed at least one felony, and possibly contributed to the death of Eilene Stromki in getting here, but she had stumbled onto something more than a mystery building. Deciding her fellow prisoners were likely to be allies, she answered. Another Asian American came up behind Toru. He was younger, thirties, intelligent eyes, his face wrinkle free, hair black. He seemed intensely interested.

"Dr. Nick Paulson, the director of the OSS, asked me to look into rumors of an unusual building being constructed. He seemed to think it had something to do with the return of the time quilts."

Both men looked surprised.

"I know of Dr. Paulson," Kawabata said. "But you say he does not know of this project?"

"No. He didn't even know where to look."

"Sir, how is it possible Dr. Paulson does not know?" the younger man asked.

Dr. Kawabata held up his hand, silencing him.

"That is Dr. Phat Nyang."

Nyang nodded his head.

"I am curious about why Dr. Paulson believed that what we are doing here could cause time disruption?"

"He didn't explain. Frankly, I wouldn't have understood even if he did. But you did create a time quilt, didn't you? I saw the dinosaurs come from the pyramid."

"That was unexpected," Kawabata said, clearly puzzled.

"Who are the men with the guns?"

"My former executive director, Dr. Vince Walters, and our

security force. I apologize for how they treated you. It is not consistent with policy."

"The fur on my parka collar set him off. He acted like he was a member of the Animal Liberation Front."

Kawabata paused, thinking.

"Where did they find you?" he asked.

"Not too far from where Eilene Stromki and I—she's a local resident—found the bomb. We were trying to get away and they caught me. I think they killed Eilene."

"I am sorry for your loss at the hands of my employees," Kawabata said, apologizing for something he had nothing to do with.

"Bomb?" Nyang probed.

"Yes. They carried it on the back of a snow cat and installed it in a small concrete building. We broke in to see what it was. I think it's a nuclear weapon."

Kawabata was shocked.

"Would you know such a device if you were to see one?" Kawabata asked.

"When I was at the White House I saw photos at security briefings."

"Describe what you saw, please."

"There were two cylinders, one larger than the other. Wires connected with the larger sphere at several points. There was a computer display. It all sat in a steel framework. Cabling. Other devices."

Kawabata frowned, pushed his glasses up on his head and rubbed his eyes. Now he put the glasses back on.

"Could it be, Dr. Kawabata?" Nyang asked.

"Yes," Kawabata answered.

"Oh, and the display indicated that the bomb is armed and counting down," Elizabeth added.

Kawabata stared blankly for a second, then smiled, tried to repress it and then laughed. He had a soft "ho-ho" of a laugh. Nyang could not hide his surprise at Kawabata's reaction.

"Sir, what is funny?"

Kawabata quickly sobered.

"Before Ms. Hawthorne told me the bomb was counting

down I was thinking that things could not get any worse."

"At least we have our health," Elizabeth said.

All three laughed out loud now, the others in the room looking at them as if they were mad. The laughing made Elizabeth's cheek and nose hurt. She touched her cheek lightly.

"I don't have any ice to put on that," Kawabata said.

"That's okay, your executive director pretty much froze me solid on the ride back. I don't think I could put ice on it even if we had some."

Elizabeth looked around the room. There were eight people, most in pairs, holding each other.

"I managed to call for help before they caught me," Elizabeth said. "But I didn't know who to trust so I called a friend and left a message." Now she looked at her watch.

"He should be finding the message soon."

"Very good," Kawabata said. "However, we may not be able to wait for help. Matters may be in our own hands."

"But sir, what can we do locked in here?" Nyang said.

"Nothing. We will leave this room when the time is right."

"Sir, I admire your confidence but why are you so sure we can escape this room?"

"Because this is a dormitory, not a prison. The door hinges are on the inside."

39 · REPORT

A dramatic find in Mongolia during 1971 revealed two fossilized skeletons—Velociraptor locked in combat with the horned dinosaur Protoceratops. . . . No scene could be more indicative of the ferocious lifestyle of the dromaeosaurs in general, and Velociraptor in particular.

—*Dougal Dixon, Barry Cox, R. J. G. Savage,*
Brian Gardiner, Macmillan Illustrated Encyclopedia
of Dinosaurs and Prehistoric Animals

FOX VALLEY, ALASKA

Vince put down his phone, pleased with the efficiency of his network of young, idealistic men and women. There was no shortage of reckless young people he could manipulate. Vince had just heard that Rawlins was dead, and Vince was insulated from the crime by three layers. While he had closed one leak, there was still the problem of Hawthorne's other message sent on the PresNet to Nick Paulson. He had no idea of whether Paulson had received the message, but Reggie was with him, and she would warn Vince if Paulson got wise. Besides, it would be over before Paulson could return.

Whitey knocked on Vince's door.

"The modifications are finished. It's as ready as we can make it."

"Good," Vince said, checking his watch. "Time to get out of here."

"There's one problem. The security guards you sent to find Elizabeth Hawthorne's partner haven't come back yet."

Another loose end. Vince's composure began to slip, and he cursed under his breath.

"I can go look for them," Whitey offered.

"Don't be stupid," Vince snapped, and then calmed himself. "Gather everyone on the construction floor. If they aren't back in an hour, we go without them."

"Vince, the velociraptors?"

Standing, he turned to Kawabata's observation window and looked down to the construction floor. The bloody remains of a half dozen dinosaurs littered the floor. He blamed Kawabata for those unnecessary deaths.

"They're gone," Vince pronounced.

"Are you sure?"

Vince withered him with a sharp look.

"Gather in the corridor! We'll go to the exit together."

Whitey left, relieved. Alone again, Vince called Star who should now be on Murderer's Lake, waiting with an airplane. She answered after the first ring.

"We're here," Star said simply.

"We're leaving in an hour or less."

"That's calling it close," Star said.

"Just be ready to go," Vince snapped.

Relaxing back into Kawabata's chair, he congratulated himself. For what he was about to accomplish his name would go down in history, history that would be written by him. Another rap at the door. Whitey was back.

"Good news. We spotted the security team on the monitors. They should be here soon."

Now Vince smiled. One less loose end. Meanwhile, down on the construction floor, nestled together on the far side of the pyramid, the velociraptors slept off their meal.

40 · SECURITY BREACH

The Pearl administration is conspiring to hide the size and extent of the new disruptions in time. Sources tell me that many small time quilts have been sprinkling across the globe during the last six months. Developing . . .

—*Tawni Lochte,* The Scoop *(political gossip blog)*

FOX VALLEY, ALASKA

Baranov drove the lead snow machine, another man riding behind him. His nephew and the other men followed. They had wiped off as much blood from the parkas as they could, but, even so, the deep red stains on navy blue would be hard to see. Driving toward the large double doors, he spotted the parking shed to the side. He turned into the structure and parked his machine next to two larger vehicles, one a flatbed truck, the other a small bus. His men mimicked his move, parking in a line, and then joining him at the entrance. Mortikov stepped forward to study the security lock, ready to pop off the cover, connect his pocket computer, and decode the access pin. The simplicity of the mechanism surprised him. There were two wide panels, both blank. There was no keypad. Mortikov touched the pad and it lit up. One word said OPEN and the other CLOSE. Mortikov looked at Baranov.

"Open and close?" Mortikov mouthed.

Baranov had seen Mortikov crack a seven-lock system in thirty minutes. He was a genius with electronic security systems. Now, he seemed stymied by an open invitation. Baranov reached past him and pushed OPEN. The double doors slowly slid apart. They were much heavier than normal security doors and thick enough to stop an RPG. Inside was a small chamber and another set of doors. This was unexpected and unwelcome. He and his men stepped into the small enclosure. The open door they had just passed through had two options, with the CLOSE option lit, ready to be pushed. The opposite panel had the open and close options and a new one that read EQUALIZE PRESSURE.

"Equalize pressure," Leonid whispered. "What kind of facility is this? Biological warfare?"

Baranov shrugged. His immediate concern was trapping his men in a small enclosure with foot-thick doors on either side, but the longer they delayed, the more suspicious their behavior. He pushed the close button, sealing them in the chamber. Confirming there were no cameras in the chamber, he had his men take off their parkas and get their rifles ready. Baranov stood in the front in his borrowed parka, pistol in hand, hidden behind his back. Then Baranov pushed the button to equalize pressure.

"Get ready," he whispered. "We don't know what will be waiting for us on the other side."

41 · CROSSING OVER

During the past hundred years, pyramids have been recorded with varying degrees of accuracy as to location. Most of these have been sighted by military pilots flying over uncharted areas during their flight missions. Although a few of these unusual pyramids have been photographed, some of the pictures, it seems, were subsequently lost or misplaced.

—*Max Toth and Greg Nielsen,* Pyramid Power

FOX VALLEY, ALASKA

Vince found his people by the doors to the containment building, in a party mood, almost giddy. He smiled, feeling joy born of success.

"Brothers and sisters," he said, feigning the deep resonant voice of a revival preacher. "We are at the banks of the Jordan ready to cross to the Promised Land. I said the Promised Land!"

Six women and five men were gathered, three of the men and two of the women with weapons. Vince kept a pistol in his belt. Vince pulled Marissa Welling forward, kissing her. Her ability to worm her way into Kawabata's trust endeared her to Vince. His followers "oohed" approval. Marissa beamed.

"Brothers and sisters, are you ready to cross over to the Promised Land?"

"Ready," they shouted.

"Can I hear an amen?"

"Amen," they cried.

"I said, can I hear an amen?"

Now they screamed their reply.

Vince stood with his back to the doors leading to the assembly floor, facing his followers. He dropped the evangelist routine.

"Star and the others are waiting on the lake for us. We'll meet them there and be ten miles away before the detonation and in our California bunker when the new world is created."

They cheered. He bathed in their adoration.

"Mother Nature has taken all the abuse she can take, and now, with a little help from yours truly . . ."

They laughed, letting him take all the credit.

". . . she is going to hit back."

They cheered, and then hugged each other.

"Time to go," Vince said, turning to the double doors, and looking through the glassless window frame. Everything was clear. He released the belt holding the doors closed, tossing it to one side, and then led his flock onto the construction floor like Moses crossing the Red Sea. As he did, he saw the exit doors begin to slide open. His security men would be inside. At the same time there was the distinctive sound of claws clicking on concrete.

Stopping, he saw four velociraptors charging along the length of the pyramid. Vince's confidence vanished, replaced by terror and indecision. One of his men raised a rifle. Vince knocked the barrel down, spoiling the aim. The gun fired, the bullet ricocheting off the concrete and then off a distant wall.

"We're not murderers!" he shouted.

Then the first velociraptor leaped.

42 · ATTACK

My dad died in a helicopter crash, but before the accident, he was nearly killed by a velociraptor that attacked them during one of their landings. The velociraptor tore the seat out from under my dad. Maybe that's why I've always been more afraid of the velociraptors than the tyrannosaurs or allosaurs.

—*John Roberts, personal communication*

FOX VALLEY, ALASKA

Phat was lying flat on the floor, looking through the crack at the bottom of the door.

"She still hasn't come back," Phat said.

"That's long enough," Kawabata said. "Take off the hinges."

The eight people in the room had managed to turn up a metal nail file, a set of keys with a penknife, and the treasure of all treasures, a Swiss Army knife embossed with "Jennifer" on it. Jennifer DeWitt had become a momentary hero. Using the orange peeler blade, and a shoe, Phat knocked the pins out of the hinges. The door remained in place, held by the deadbolt. Now they used the largest blade of the Swiss Army knife, the penknife, credit cards and car keys, to pry the hinge side of the door out. Many fingers pulled on the door when enough of it was exposed.

"Pull," Kawabata instructed, letting the younger people do the work. "It will break if you pull!"

"Are you sure?" Elizabeth asked, fingers wrapped around the edge of the door.

"Very sure," Kawabata said. "Cheapest door on the market."

And break it did. With a crack the wood around the deadbolt crushed, and the other side now cleared the frame, letting them slide it out and lean it against the wall. Phat peeked around the corner.

"It is clear."

The plan was to sneak to the rear exit, then get to the snow machines. While some of them went for help, Kawabata, Phat, and Elizabeth would go to the bombsite and see if they could disarm it.

The exit was to the right and a short way down the hall. The door had an alarm but Phat carried the Swiss Army knife and was prepared to disconnect it. They could hear distant cheering. It gave them confidence and they hurried to the back door. It had been welded shut.

"Why would they do this?" Phat asked.

Kawabata didn't know.

"We must surprise them," Kawabata said. "Get their guns."

Elizabeth could see no other option. As they crept toward the sound of "amens," Kawabata assigned men and women hiding places along the corridor. If they failed to get control of the guns, they would retreat down the corridor and those in hiding could ambush Dr. Walters's people.

They reached the corridor leading to the containment building just as the last of Walters's people stepped through the double doors. As the doors swung closed, they hurried forward, keeping low. Just as they reached the door there was a gunshot. Now they heard screaming. Elizabeth stood, looking through the window frame just in time to see a velociraptor leap into the knot of people. To the right, the exit doors were opening, security men with guns were entering and spreading out. Then, in panic, velociraptors leaping, the men and women rushed the doors they were hiding behind.

"Look out," Elizabeth yelled, trying to back away from the doors.

Phat and Kawabata could not back up fast enough. The double doors burst open, knocking them into the people behind. They went down in the stampede, bodies piling up in the entry, propping the doors open. Pressed under two struggling people, Elizabeth tried to drag herself free. The woman on top managed to roll off, then stood, trying to run down the corridor. Suddenly a velociraptor leaped into the pile, slashing and biting. It jumped on the fleeing woman, tearing into her neck and shoulder, ripping and twisting, breaking the woman's neck. Now standing on its victim, it snagged a man trying to get past it, holding him by the shoulder with its jaws and clawed hands, then stood on one leg and raked his chest and stomach repeatedly with a clawed foot. Elizabeth looked away, trying to crawl out from the body pinning her legs. Then the man on Elizabeth stood, backing away from the velociraptor. "No, not that way!" Elizabeth said, watching the man back into the containment building.

Suddenly he went down under another velociraptor. Now Elizabeth got to her knees, Phat next to her, helping Kawabata. The velociraptor in front of them had finished eviscerating its latest victim and was watching with intelligent eyes and bloody jaws. Now it surveyed the corridor, then turned back to the three of them. Stepping off its victim, it lowered its head and straightened its tail. Elizabeth recognized the posture. It was going to attack.

43 · SLAUGHTER

Four dromaeosaurs were transported to the present with the time quilt: Oviraptor, Deinonychus, Velociraptor and Baryonx. Oviraptor is an egg thief and four-legged Baryonx nothing more than a very efficient fisherman. Deinonychus and Velociraptor are in a completely different class. They are fast, smart, vicious and hunt in packs.

—*Marion Wayne, dinosaur ranger, speaking to a tour group at the Everglades National Dinosaur Preserve*

FOX VALLEY, ALASKA

As the doors cracked open, Baranov saw a pyramid, towering nearly to the ceiling of the structure. It was so big that ninety percent of the building was devoted to that one structure. Between them and the pyramid was a small group of people. Suddenly, one of them fired his rifle. The men behind Baranov shrank back, seeking cover. Baranov dove through the partially open door, landing flat, looking for a target. All he saw were backs. Then above the heads of the people he saw a dinosaur flying through the air, taking down a man.

Baranov took aim on the dinosaur but people were running every direction. Baranov got up, pushing his way through the panic to the dinosaur that was busy tearing the leg off of his victim. Rocking and rotating, the dinosaur was a moving target. Other dinosaurs were attacking, scattering panicked humans. He could not hesitate any longer and save the man's life. Baranov steadied his pistol with two hands and fired.

The bullet struck the dinosaur high on its left haunch. With a squeal, the dinosaur stumbled back, biting at the wound. Baranov hurried forward, reaching for the injured man. Then Leonid was next to him and they took him by the armpits, dragging him back to the entrance, passing him to more of his men who dragged him through the doors where a medic was ready to go to work.

The injured dinosaur was licking his wound. Baranov threw off his parka, dropped the pistol, and unslung his M-16. With the heavier weapon he felt more secure. Now the dinosaur lowered its head, eyes locked on Baranov. Behind him humans were being torn to pieces.

"Kill the beasts!" Baranov said, taking sides in the conflict.

Leonid raised his rifle, but the animal was gun-wise and ran. Leonid and Baranov tracked him but couldn't risk a shot. The dinosaur ran to an opening in the pyramid and disappeared inside.

Now Baranov led his men forward, lining up shots, ready to kill the rest of the dinosaurs. Then a sharp honking sound came from the pyramid and the dinosaurs stopped their attacks, heads up. More calls and they bolted for the pyramid and ran inside. Baranov remembered seeing one dinosaur leap over the human pile into the corridor. Now he hurried in that direction. It was there, crouching, facing a woman and two men struggling to their feet. The dinosaur leaped, clawed feet first. Baranov fired. Three rounds struck its chest at an angle, one passing through, spattering blood across the floor. Dying, the dinosaur's momentum carried it into the woman.

Baranov rushed forward. The woman was kicking at the twitching dinosaur. Baranov shot it in the head. The twitching stopped but the woman kept kicking it. He let her work it out. The sound of clicking caught his attention. He turned to see the dinosaurs racing from the pyramid, ambushing his men from behind. From the entrance where his medic had been working on the injured man, a rifle fired, once, twice, the last dinosaur in line going down. But before his men could turn, the two remaining dinosaurs were on them. It was not a hunt, it was revenge. The dinosaurs slashed, bit, and tore their way through his men, wounding, but not killing, disabling and then moving on to another. Men and dinosaurs were hopelessly mixed together. Mortikov was on the ground, bleeding from a neck wound. Half of Prosol's arm was gone, his rifle at his feet. Prosol staggered, then fell to his knees. With his left arm he pulled a knife, his knife hand chewed off with a quick snap of jaws. Prosol fell next to Smirnov who was clutching his stomach, holding his intestines in.

"Help them," Baranov ordered Leonid.

His nephew lifted the woman and an old man to their feet. The third man led them down the hall. As they cleared the double doors they swung shut. Baranov stood his ground watching the doors. Nothing happened. Then he crept forward, keeping his head below window level. He pushed one of the doors open a few inches. The floor was littered with dead—three of them his own men. There were no dinosaurs. The exit doors were closed now. Baranov pushed the door open wider, surveying the room. No dinosaurs. Baranov pulled out his radio and turned it on. Nothing but static.

Frustrated, he turned off the radio. He had more men waiting at the helicopters, but he had no way to contact them. He could not even reach Mishtov, his medic, who had been in the entrance alcove. He studied the dark opening in the pyramid. The dinosaurs had waited in ambush before. He thought there were only two left, now, but he could not be sure. Baranov backed through the doors, and then retreated down the corridor, looking for his nephew.

44 · EXIT

Deinonychus and Velociraptor are unusual predators in one respect. They not only hunt to eat, but they also hunt for sport. Like a cat that can't help but attack a moving object, these predators will kill even when they are not hungry.

—*Marion Wayne, dinosaur ranger, speaking to a tour group at the Everglades National Dinosaur Preserve*

FOX VALLEY, ALASKA

Vince was lying on the floor of Kawabata's office, a gash in his leg running from thigh to knee. It was deep at the top, but merely a scratch by the time it reached the knee. It was bleeding profusely. Marissa and Whitey were working on his leg while another guarded the door. Two women huddled in the corner, crying. They had lost four of their people to the velociraptors—four of his best educated, best prepared, most adaptable men and women. They were irreplaceable.

Marissa finished bandaging his leg, letting him sit up, leaning against the wall. They had used his own knife to cut away his pant leg. Irrationally, he struck out.

"How am I supposed to go outside now?" he complained. "I'll freeze to death before we get to the lake."

"You can ride in the snow bus," Marissa said.

She was right and it angered him.

"You've got to think before you act, Marissa. This isn't over yet."

"Yes, you're right," she said meekly, handing his knife back to him.

Vince wiped blood from the blade, then folded it and put it in his pocket. Whitey stepped close to Marissa, hand on her back, whispering encouragement. Then he turned to Vince.

"Vince, we're behind schedule. We should be to the lake by now."

"There is a margin of error, Whitey," Vince said, irritated.

Despite his bravado, Vince checked his watch—there was precious little time to spare.

"Help me to my feet," Vince ordered.

Once standing, he kept his weight on his good leg. A trickle of blood ran down the outside of his bare leg.

"What about our security people?" Vince asked.

"See for yourself," Whitey said, indicating the observation window.

Hobbling to the window, Vince looked down on the carnage.

"They came in during the attack. I think they're all dead."

Vince studied the scene. Something wasn't right.

"They weren't carrying M-16s," Vince pointed out.

Whitey and Marissa looked back to the floor.

"I don't recognize him," Marissa said, indicating the one man lying face up.

Vince was taken aback, mumbling out loud.

"Who could they be?"

"I don't know," Whitey said. "Federal agents?"

Vince regretted showing weakness.

"Of course they are, but how much do they know? Whitey, are the bombs still online?"

"I have to go to my office."

"Then go," Vince said impatiently.

Now he studied the space around the pyramid. The velociraptors had been hidden on the far side of the pyramid. Vince would have known that if Kawabata hadn't vetoed funding for closed-circuit video cameras. The man's stinginess had cost him some of his best followers.

Whitey was back, nodding his head as he came in.

"Yes, all three are still armed and the countdown is on schedule."

"Then they don't know about the bombs," Vince concluded.

Vince looked back to the floor and made his decision.

"We are going to get out of here. We may have to shoot the velociraptors if they attack again."

He expected protest. He got none.

"One man with a rifle in front, one in the back."

There were four weapons left. Two rifles, Vince's pistol, and a pistol carried by one of the women.

"Shoot to wound if you can, but be prepared to sacrifice them if they force you. Remember the greater good."

The two men with rifles nodded.

"Let's go."

With an armed person in front and another in back, they went down the hall to the stairs, Vince limping, leaning on Whitey. Empty. The bare wood stairs creaked as they went down and again Vince cursed Kawabata for being too cheap to carpet the stairs. They turned into the corridor leading to the containment building. There were two bodies on the floor ahead and much blood. Someone started weeping.

"Be strong," he said. "His sacrifice will be remembered."

Skirting the bodies, they reached the doors, checking through the window to see if the containment room was still empty. There were body parts and blood everywhere, but no velociraptors. Once through the doors, Vince pointed along the base of the pyramid.

"They came from over there last time," Vince said. "Watch for them."

All weapons were now aimed in that direction. Nothing appeared. As they passed a body, Vince paused, retrieving another rifle, handing it to Marissa. They reached the exit doors, everyone watching over their shoulders. Vince pushed the open button.

"Vince," Whitey said.

Vince turned to see a velociraptor peeking out of the pyramid.

"Don't shoot unless it charges," Vince ordered. "It's been pulled out of its natural environment. That's why they are so violent. Normally they would only hunt to eat."

Vince's little pep talk steadied the nerves of his followers while they waited for the exit doors to open, eyes on the velociraptor. Then behind him he heard movement. Frozen with fear, he forced himself to slowly turn. Inside the airlock, two dead bodies lay in an oval pool of blood. A velociraptor was standing over one of the bodies, jaws bloody, staring at Vince. Only Vince had seen the velociraptor. Only Vince saw it drop into attack posture. And only Vince had enough time to dive out of the way.

45 · ALLIES

Utahraptor may be the deadliest dinosaur yet known. It appears to have been a large, early member of the Dromaeosaur family. . . . Utahraptor was equipped with a huge claw on the middle toe of each foot. Wielding that claw in a single, leaping strike, Utahraptor could have slashed another dinosaur to death.

—*Don Lessem and Donald F. Glut,*
Dinosaur Encyclopedia

FOX VALLEY, ALASKA

Elizabeth, Toru, and Phat were back in the dormitory with the two other survivors. The door was propped back in place, guarded by two strangers with rifles. Elizabeth had added a gash to her injuries, and now held her sweater high while Phat cleaned the wound along her rib cage, and then applied an ointment and bandage. Two others were receiving first aid; none of the injuries were life threatening. When finished, Elizabeth dropped her sweater, then pulled her knees to her chest.

"Thanks for saving my life," Elizabeth said.

The older man turned and squatted. He was in his forties, with short-cropped brown hair and eyes. A scar ran through his lip and down his chin.

"You are welcome very much," he said.

His English was good but not native.

"You are not one of our security personnel," Kawabata observed.

The man took a package of gum from his pocket, offered a piece to the others, then took a stick for himself. He unwrapped it slowly, stalling, thinking.

"I came because of the bomb?" he said finally.

"Then you got my message?" Elizabeth said excitedly.

"Who are you?" he asked, puzzled.

"I'm Elizabeth Hawthorne. I sent the message about the bomb. Who called you? Bill Rawlins? Nick Paulson?"

"The information came from Freedom Station."

"Nick! He came through."

"Dr. Paulson, the Director of the OSS?" the man said.

"Yes," Elizabeth said, puzzled by his lack of information. "Are you Delta Force? Green Beret?"

"What's in a name?" he asked, smiling.

"Are you American?" Kawabata asked.

Now the man smiled broadly.

"I represent an interested third party," he said. "Call me Andy. His name is Leo."

Leo turned and waved, then resumed watching the door.

"We are here to retrieve the bomb. You took a picture of it, so can you tell me which part of the building it is in?"

"It's not in the building. It's outside about a half mile from here."

Andy looked confused, pulling a device from his pocket. He turned it on and looked at the display.

"We took readings and triangulated on the source and set my GPS tracker. I could not have missed it by that much."

"I can explain," Kawabata cut in. "There is more than one nuclear device. Your detectors were not programmed for more than one source. The devices are equally distant from where you sit right now."

Andy cursed in Russian. He pulled a radio from his pocket and turned it on. He seemed surprised when it worked. Walking to a far corner, he spoke into the radio. Then he returned to the group.

"I have men coming to search for the bombs now," he said. "Who is trying to destroy this place?"

"My executive director, Dr. Vince Walters," Kawabata replied, "but he isn't trying to destroy this facility, he is trying to transport it."

"Explain," Andy said.

"As you must know, the time distortions that have wracked our planet are the result of dense matter effects on the flow of time. The detonation of nuclear weapons of sufficient yield compresses matter temporarily to the density of black holes. That dense matter propagates a black ripple—a time ripple if you will. It was the convergence of several of these that created the original time disruption."

"I know the history of this," Andy said.

"My renegade executive director is going to detonate multiple warheads simultaneously. Each of these will send out a time wave. If he planned carefully, this structure is sitting at the point those three time waves intersect."

"And we'll be sent through time," Elizabeth finished.

"But why, sir?" Phat asked. "For what purpose?"

"That I do not know," Kawabata said. "But it would be best to stop him. There is reason to doubt his competence."

Distant screams brought Andy to his feet, rifle ready.

"Guard them," he ordered, and then pushed past Leo, squeezing out the door.

Elizabeth heard him running toward the sound of the screams.

46 · COUNTDOWN

Sometimes I fantasize about sitting my animal and human cousins down at a great round table and asking, "Why can't we all just get along?"

—*Star Koslowski*

FOX VALLEY, ALASKA

Baranov ran toward the screams, barely checking side corridors and doorways. Now there was gunfire. Racing down the corridor, the double doors ahead, he skirted the bodies on the floor and crashed through. The dinosaurs were attacking a group of people by the exit. Two dinosaurs were holding victims to the ground, tearing them apart, other people were running or crawling away. A man by the wall raised a pistol and fired. One of the people fell. They were killing each other.

Fast walking, Baranov came on confidently, switching the M-16 to full automatic. The closest dinosaur sensed the threat, lowered its head, straightened its tail, then pushed off of the body it was standing on and charged.

Baranov knew the animal's leaping ability and didn't wait for it to get in jumping range. Ignoring the danger to the bystanders, he opened fire. His aim was good, most of the bullets impacting chest high. The dinosaur made it three more steps, before going into a face-first skid.

The remaining dinosaur ran for the pyramid. Baranov brought the rifle around, held his fire when a civilian got between him and the beast, then opened fire when he had a clear shot. The animal was fast and his shots missed, the dinosaur disappearing into the black interior. Baranov ran to the pyramid, flattening against the wall, listening. Nothing. Now he peeked around the corner. The interior was dimly lit. There was a corridor that led straight into the interior, and then turned a brief way in. There was a blood trail on the floor.

Baranov debated whether to go after the beast. He and his brothers had killed more of his men than Muslim terrorists. Looking back at the survivors, he saw the one who had shot one of his own people aiming at Baranov.

"Drop the gun!" Baranov yelled. "Everyone drop your guns."

Three people dropped weapons but not the man by the wall. Baranov fired a shot that ricocheted off the concrete next to his head. He dropped the pistol. He was a dark-haired man with one pant leg cut off, his leg bandaged. The others were now gathering around him. Baranov ordered them all to sit against the wall. Two others were dead or dying. Inside the exit doors Baranov found two more bodies. One was his man, Ivan Mortikov. He swore again. He had served with Mortikov's father.

Now Baranov ordered the remaining men and women to get up and march to the back. Every head turned toward the man with one pant leg when he did, identifying him as the leader. Baranov pointed his rifle at the man, who looked at his watch.

"Get up or I will shoot you!" Baranov ordered.

A man and a woman helped the leader up.

"Down the corridor!"

Again all heads turned to the leader. That would be Vince Walters, Baranov remembered. Walters hesitated, looking at his watch again.

"We have to get out of here!" Walters said.

Baranov switched his rifle to semi-automatic, lifted it to his shoulder and took aim at the man's head.

"Why must we get out of here? The dinosaurs are dead or gone."

"It's not the dinosaurs."

Walters refused to volunteer more.

"Tell him," said a man helping to support Walters.

He was a burly man with thick, hairy arms, thin brown hair, and gray eyes.

"Tell him, Vince! Before it's too late."

Walters pushed away those helping him stand, grimacing

as he pulled himself to his full height. Again he looked at his watch.

"We have to get out of here because there are three nuclear devices set to detonate in eighteen minutes. We can still get a safe distance away."

"What is the yield of the weapons?" Baranov demanded.

"Twenty megatons each," Walters said proudly.

"Then we're all dead. Even on the snow machines you could not get a safe distance away."

"But we can," Walters argued. "Straight down the valley to the lake. There are airplanes waiting. We'll be miles away before they detonate."

"You are an idiot," Baranov said, shaking his head. "You would need to be one hundred kilometers away to be safe from such an explosion."

Baranov had exaggerated. If the detonation had been airburst, they would need to be one hundred kilometers away, but here in this valley, the explosion would be contained, and probably channeled toward the lake. With the mountainous terrain, it might be possible to be within twenty kilometers and survive. However, they had no chance of getting even that far, without abandoning everyone else.

Walters and his people were quiet at first and then began arguing and finger pointing. Baranov pulled out his radio and called his men.

"Karl, turn around. There is going to be a sixty-megaton detonation in seventeen minutes."

"Please repeat," Karl radioed back.

"There is going to be a sixty-megaton detonation in seventeen minutes."

"What about you?"

"No options."

"I understand."

Baranov turned his radio off.

"We can make it if we go now," Walters pleaded.

"What about the others here? Some are injured. We would have to retrieve them, get them dressed for the weather, and help them outside. Is there enough room for everyone on the snow machines out there? What about in your aircraft? Will they carry everyone here? If not, who would be left behind? The innocent? Perhaps you, since you are responsible for the bombs? Can you do all of that and get far enough away in fifteen minutes?"

"Yes, we would have to leave some behind, but there is more at stake here than you know. The detonations are just a stepping stone to something bigger, something world changing."

Again, Walters looked at his watch.

"It's now or never," Walters said.

"Never," Baranov said.

Now Walters was furious, red-faced, sputtering.

"You have no right to keep us here. We're leaving."

Walters stepped toward the exit, feigning courage but watching Baranov's rifle. Baranov fired a round into the wall in front of him. Walters gave a satisfying yelp, slapping his arm where a bullet fragment had stung him.

"Vince," Baranov said in a mocking tone, "the host does not leave the party before it has started."

Walters's bravado was gone now, those who looked to him for leadership were lost, wavering, or confused.

"We couldn't make it now, anyway, Vince," the large man said. "But you did a good thing. The world will be a new Eden, just like you promised."

Walters ignored him.

"Remember, there is a chance we can survive. The government may have kept it a secret."

"Shut up!" Walters snarled.

Baranov marched them back down the corridor, conscious of the pyramid opening. He took them to the dormitory room, lining them up against the wall.

"I regret to inform you that the nuclear devices will detonate in eight minutes."

"Can't we get away?" a young woman asked.

"No. It will be a sixty-megaton detonation. You could not get far enough away to survive."

There was general gloom.

"Perhaps the way to survive is to stay where we are," Kawabata said.

"Then you believe we will be transported?" Phat asked.

The others were listening now.

"I am confident in the theory, not in Dr. Walters's calculations."

Walters was glaring now, his ego pricked.

"While Dr. Walters is a serviceable manager, he is not a theoretician."

"Shut up, you old miser," Walters spat. "We're minutes away from the most momentous event in human history and you don't have any idea of what is going on. Yet, you sit there and insult my abilities? It was right under your nose, you myopic fool, and you never saw it. But I saw it! I saw the potential."

"You saw what Dr. Welling pointed out to you," Kawabata said. "Who actually made the theoretical leap, Dr. Walters? Dr. Welling? Dr. Whitey? In all the years we have worked together the only skill you have excelled at is taking credit for other people's work."

Walters started to get to his feet, wincing when he did. Baranov pointed his rifle at him and Walters slid back down the wall.

"If you are so superior, then tell me, Toru, what is going to happen next?"

"Three converging time waves will open a hole in time and this facility will be swept up in it," Kawabata said.

"Is that all you have deduced?" Walters mocked. "Can't you tell us where we will go? Can't you tell us what time period we will be displaced to? I can."

"We will be displaced ten years into the past," Elizabeth Hawthorne said.

Walters's people said nothing, while Dr. Kawabata's group gasped.

"And we will travel to the moon," Hawthorne finished.

Now Walters sagged, his ego fully deflated.

"And I know something else," Hawthorne continued. "Even if we survive the displacement, we will not live for long. I know this because this is the building that appeared on the moon when the first time displacement occurred, and no one has traveled to the moon to visit the structure since it was discovered. When they do, they will find our bodies because there is no way we can survive in a vacuum."

"Three minutes," Baranov said.

No one spoke, each coming to terms with certain death.

"Is this the safest place to be when it happens?" Phat asked finally.

"It's as good as any," Dr. Whitey said. "I'm sorry about this, Phat. We wanted to get everyone out of the building but we couldn't work it out."

"My wife and children?" Phat said.

"I know. I'm sorry," Dr. Whitey said.

Elizabeth Hawthorne struggled to her feet, and went to an end table next to a bunk. There was a cup holding a variety of pens and pencils. She pulled out a black permanent marker and then wrote in big letters on the wall "ELIZABETH HAWTHORNE WAS HERE."

"In case this doesn't work as expected," Elizabeth said, sitting back down. "I want someone some day to know what happened to me."

"If Dr. Walters's calculations are wrong, nothing will be left," Phat said.

"Let us hope that Dr. Welling did the calculations," Kawabata said.

"One minute," Baranov said. "Everyone sit with their back to a wall."

Those who were standing found a place to sit. Leo, who was still guarding the door, sat in the doorframe, rifle in his lap. The room was still, the tension palpable. Someone whispered a prayer. Most were silently counting down, but Baranov knew his timing was just an estimate. As it was, the fusion bombs detonated forty seconds earlier than expected.

47 ▪ REACTION

Mr. President, there has been a nuclear detonation on American soil.

—*Mason Clark, Chief of Staff to President Pearl*

WASHINGTON, D.C.

The secret service picked Willa up at the vice president's residence at the Naval Observatory, taking her to the White House and then to the situation room. Visitors to the situation room were always disappointed to find that it bore little resemblance to the high-tech versions in Hollywood movies. In reality, the situation room was a plush conference room on the first floor of the White House. Surrounding it was a communication center with access to every information source on the planet. Staffed with a minimum of three duty officers and a communications officer, the staff sifted through the steady flow of information, creating summaries of relevant information. Normally, summaries were sent to the president twice daily. During a crisis, the president was a door away and demanding immediate updates.

The president was in transit on Air Force One and would be joining them by digital video. Mason Clark was with the president, so everyone turned to Willa to run the meeting on this end. Without Clark's ministrations, there was only one kind of coffee and a stack of Styrofoam cups. No one complained.

When the president was connected, the image was fuzzy, with varying amounts of snow. The nuclear explosion had been too distant to account for the interference.

"Everyone hear me okay?" the president asked. "All right. Carol, give us the basics of what has happened."

Caroline Mauck put on reading glasses, opened a red binder, and began.

"A little over two hours ago there was a nuclear detonation

in western Alaska, in Fox Valley, where we operated a research facility engaged in classified work. The detonation was of unusual megatonnage. Estimates of the yield are still being refined; however, the detonation was at least fifty megatons and may have been as high as one hundred megatons."

This was all in the intelligence summary Willa and the others had read on the way over, but nevertheless everyone was shocked.

"Loss of life will be significant, although the project had reached a mature phase and the number of workers on the site greatly reduced—less than forty remained, some of those on furlough. Initial indications are that there was Russian involvement. First, prior to the blast, we had intelligence that a Russian thermonuclear device was present in Alaska.

"Second, only the Soviet Union produced weapons of this megatonnage, and only Russia retains them in its arsenal.

"Third is the probability of Russian soldiers in the area at the time of the detonation. At least one Russian helicopter may have slipped into American airspace earlier today.

"We have teams en route to the site to look for survivors and to gather additional data including the plutonium signature so we can pinpoint the origin of the bomb."

Carol Mauck was professional and concise, but her report raised so many questions, Willa could barely wait until she had finished.

"I'm puzzled by the yield of the bomb," Willa said. "It doesn't match the estimates I heard for the bomb Elizabeth Hawthorne photographed and if it does exceed fifty megatons, it would be the biggest bomb ever exploded above ground. If it truly had that kind of yield, then it certainly couldn't be in a package the size of the one supposedly found in Alaska."

"That would be right," General Flannery said. "The likely yield on a device the size of that in the photo would be twenty megatons, upgradeable to thirty with the addition of more fissionable material, but not without a significant increase in weight and size."

"The Russians may have made advances in weapons design that we are unaware of," Mauck argued.

Mauck was never defensive or hostile during discussions. However, Willa knew she had a stubborn streak and would defend her positions past reasonable.

"There is another possibility," Willa suggested. "Could there have been multiple detonations on the same site?"

Now the president cut in.

"To what purpose? Even a small warhead would be sufficient to destroy the complex in Fox Valley."

"Why is that facility so important?" Joel Bass asked.

Like the others, the secretary of state had been briefed on the research in Fox Valley and, like the others, did not know what to make of it.

"We believe that the Fox Valley research facility was destroyed in order to maintain Russian technological superiority in orgone energy production and utilization," Mauck said. "Moreover, we believe that this energy is being used to manipulate the time quilting to American disadvantage."

Now those around the table broke into individual conversations.

"Carol," Willa said loudly, getting everyone's attention again, "Intelligence reports have led us to believe that the Russians were using Muslim fundamentalists as their surrogates and arming them with nuclear weapons. There is no indication of a Muslim connection. And if the Russians are trying to accomplish their goals surreptitiously, then why send Russian helicopters into American airspace, especially since the bomb was already in Alaska?"

"We don't know for sure that Russians penetrated our airspace, or if they did, what their mission was," Mauck said. "This could be wholly unrelated."

Mauck had just argued against part of her own evidence.

"Mr. President, have you spoken to the Russian ambassador or the president of Russia?"

"President Petrov denies Russian involvement," the president said.

"As you would expect," Marliess Krupp cut in.

"Do they deny that Russian weapons were used?" Willa asked.

Now the president paused, looking off camera, then coming back into the center of the screen.

"Adamantly, and he denied the presence of any Russian troops on U.S. soil, but something is going on. There are new confirmed time quilts in Alberta, Alaska, Mississippi, and Australia and unconfirmed reports in Spain, Indonesia, Kenya, Greenland, and the Falkland Islands. Suspicious ocean debris has been washing up all over the globe and the events are getting closer and closer together."

Willa noticed that the time quilts weren't limited, nor even focused on America and pointed this out.

"No, but this is all leading up to something and I suspect we will be the focal point," the president said.

"We need to contact Nick Paulson."

"He's on the moon, Willa," the president said. "It's not practical to consult with Dr. Paulson. Willa, don't think I've closed out other possibilities. We're investigating every angle, but I've got the safety of the country to think about so I'm ordering our armed forces to go to DEFCON two."

Willa sagged back in her seat. DEFCON two was one step away from a nuclear strike. While the U.S. and Russia had dismantled many of their older missiles and bombers, the U.S. maintained its Trident submarine–based state-of-the-art missiles with MIRV warheads as well as a partial missile defense system. From intelligence reports, Willa knew that the Russians had not kept pace. The antiquated antimissile system around Moscow would be near useless and half of its nuclear arsenal was in need of maintenance. The Russians had to know they would fare badly in a missile exchange with the U.S. Moving to DEFCON two would put President Petrov's finger on a hair trigger.

There was silence around the table as members of the Security Council thought through the ramifications. Then the president disappeared from the screen. They broke into individual conversations again, Willa listening to Krupp as she constructed excuses for not intercepting the bomb.

"Congress keeps interfering with our budgeting," Krupp whined, "mandating that we distribute Homeland Security funding by population, not threat. We've spent more on New York than all the states west of the Mississippi, except California, combined. Alaska is so undeveloped it should be a territory not a state."

Willa mumbled something Krupp took as agreement.

"If they want to protect secret facilities, then don't put them in such remote sites."

Now the president was back on screen, asking for attention.

"A message has been posted on a terrorist Web site taking claim for what happened in Alaska," the president said, now looking down at a paper he held. "The message mentions Fox Valley by name. They are demanding that all U.S. forces be withdrawn from bases around the world to U.S. territory. All military aid to Israel is to be halted. We are to stop the distribution of 'the immoral and heretical filth from Hollywood,' stop stealing oil from Muslim countries—there's more of the same. Well I think this confirms it. The Russians are behind this."

Murmurs of agreement spread around the table. Willa saw no direct confirmation in the message.

"Go to DEFCON two. In the meantime I'll draft a letter to President Petrov demanding a stop to the arming of Muslim terrorists and that he immediately provide us information on the groups they have already armed. He's going to know that we will hold his country responsible for any new nuclear attacks on U.S. territory."

Willa could imagine President Petrov's response—his finger tightening on his own nuclear trigger.

48 · CARCASSES

From Newton we understand that for every action there is an equal and opposite reaction. Since the universe must always be in perfect balance, it is logical to assume that there must be a reaction or counterpart to all perceived forces and entities.

—*Max Toth and Greg Nielsen,* Pyramid Power

FLAMSTEED CRATER, THE MOON

The pyramid filled the large space they had entered. To the left were a series of workshops, storage compartments, tool bins, and stacks of crates and piles of what looked like black plastic. The only break was a set of double doors. A window was set in each door. One of the windows had been broken out. A light flickered in the window. High on the wall was another wide window. It was dark. Near the ceiling a crane sat on a rail that ran the length of the building.

Nick pulled his radiation detector from his belt, scanning for gamma rays to microwaves and everything in between. Nothing. Phil walked directly to the pyramid, peering inside the opening. Emmett began taking pictures. Rosa walked toward the double doors. Reggie walked a few steps and then knelt, unlocking one of the rings holding her glove on. She removed the glove and then touched the floor.

"There's more of that brown stain," Reggie said.

Nick joined her, kneeling in his bulky suit.

"I think it's blood," Reggie said.

"Maybe. But whatever happened, happened a long time ago."

"Or hasn't happened yet," Reggie said.

Nick understood. The building had been on the moon for a decade, but they had no idea what time period it came from.

"I don't know what this was built out of, but it sure isn't stone," Phil said from just inside the pyramid. "There's more of that brown stain in here, too."

Now Phil walked to one corner of the pyramid and began pacing it off. However, the low gravity gave him bounce, throwing off what accuracy there was to pacing. Dressed in his PLSS he looked like a high-tech Pillsbury Doughboy. When he reached the corner he turned, continuing his bouncy pacing.

"Each of the four sides will be the same length," Emmett pointed out.

"And we'll know that for sure when I'm finished," Phil shot back.

Now Nick scanned the radio and television frequencies. Nothing.

"Hey, you better come and see this," Phil shouted.

He was standing at the far corner of the pyramid. They all bounded to where he stood. Turning the corner of the pyramid they found bones, lots of bones. Reggie gasped.

"They're animal," Phil quickly pointed out.

"They're dinosaur," Emmett said, squatting.

The bones were scattered along a quarter of the length of the backside of the pyramid. Now Emmett walked among the bones, pushing them here or there, finding bits and pieces of skin.

"Looks like two species. Something from the dromaeosaur family—smaller than utahraptor but bigger and heavier than troödon. Probably deinonychus. Large brains, stereoscopic vision, toe claws as big as a sickle," he said, pointing to a large claw on the remains of a foot. Now he pointed at another set of bones. "This was the prey. Bipedal, maybe ornithomimus."

"Do you see any human bones?" Reggie asked.

Emmett walked through the bones, pushing them apart with his foot.

"No, but I just noticed something. See how the bones from the two species are scattered and intermixed? You can see how clean they are. To get them this clean you would have to boil them, and if you did that then why arrange them like this? I think insects cleaned these bones. So where are the insects?"

"The building was sealed—had to be sealed, given where it is," Nick said. "So someone laid out a dozen dinosaurs, let insects and scavengers clean the bones, and then sealed up the building and sent it to the moon?"

"That's too crazy even for me," Phil said.

"We're missing something," Rosa said. "I say we take a look through those doors. It looks like an office complex."

The suits were bulky, and with the helmets off the PLSS cooling system shut down.

"So, do we have to wear these suits?" Phil asked. "I'm going to drown in my own sweat."

"What's controlling the temperature?" Nick asked, realizing the air temperature was tolerable. "This structure is sitting in the shadow of the crater right now, but it will be in full sunlight soon. The interior should alternate between frozen and baking."

"Well, I'm baking," Phil said.

Nick agreed. The air temperature had to be near eighty degrees.

"There are air circulation ducts up there," Emmett said, pointing to ducts running the length of the ceiling and then at vents in the walls. "And this building seems well insulated. I can hear the hum of circulation fans."

"Rosa, any reason we have to keep the suits on?" Nick asked.

"Oxygen," Rosa said, as she read the monitor on her suit. "The oxygen level is acceptable for now, and there is quite a bit of volume in here so it will take some time to use it up. We can dispense with the suits for now but we should keep them close."

The other reason for not shucking the suits was that it left them walking around shoeless, in the tight-fitting underwear. All chose comfort over modesty, but dragged the suits with them to the double doors. Stopping on this side, Nick pointed out the empty window frame.

"No broken glass," Phil said, indicating the floor. "Someone's cleaned up."

They pushed through the doors, finding a corridor with sheet-rocked walls and a concrete floor stained with the now familiar brown. Reggie studied the floor, looking pale. She seemed almost phobic about blood, Nick thought, a strange reaction for a medical doctor.

They stacked the suits inside, helmets on top. Without the three hundred and fifty pounds of suit—earth weight—now they felt they could fly.

There was a room to the left marked STORAGE. They opened the door and found it filled with office supplies, including boxes of paper, pens, mechanical pencils, and yellow tablets.

"If this is from the future, it's a pretty depressing future," Phil pointed out. "Same crap we use."

The next room was a copy room with a large copy machine, more paper, and a large paper shredder.

"That's the same model copier as the one in our office," Emmett said.

"So either they were using really old copy machines, or wherever this came from is pretty near our present," Phil said.

Nick thought of Elizabeth and the building she had discovered in Fox Valley. He had a growing sense of panic.

A door marked MAINTENANCE revealed cleaning supplies and two dozen green oxygen cylinders connected together and to a pipe leading out of the storeroom.

"Someone planned ahead," Emmett observed.

Rosa examined the gauges on the cylinders, and put her ear to the pipe.

"They are all full and I can hear gas flowing. It's not a lot of oxygen given the volume of this building, but we won't have to worry about oxygen for a while."

They passed a stairway on their right, ignoring it for now. Next came a reception area with four desks, computers, displays, phones, and file cabinets, all dating the structure to their present. On the right was a row of vending machines. The glass on the front of the candy and snack machines was dirty. All the food and drink was gone.

"Someone broke in," Emmett said, pointing to a twisted lock.

Just past the vending machines was a small cafeteria. A coffee cart sat in one corner, a small kitchen at the other end of the room. There was no food in the cafeteria and no coffee. There were bottles of flavoring behind the coffee bar, the contents dried up. Round blue plastic tables with chrome legs and matching chairs sprinkled the room. There was a newspaper lying on one of the tables. Nick picked it up. It was a copy of *USA Today* and carried yesterday's date.

"Oh, no," he said out loud, passing the paper to Emmett.

"Nick, maybe we better—" Emmett started.

Reggie's scream cut him off. They hurried back into the corridor to find Rosa holding Reggie, her face buried in her neck.

"In there," Rosa said, pointing to an open door.

The light in the room was on, revealing a body. Nick pushed the door open wider. Bodies were lined up the width of the room.

"Emmett, would you take a look?" Nick asked.

"I'll examine the bodies," Reggie offered, recovering her composure.

Nick hesitated.

"It was the shock," she explained. "I've participated in autopsies before. I'm the best qualified to determine cause of death."

"That won't be hard," Emmett said from the room where he was holding up a leg bone. "This leg was torn off. The collarbone on this one was broken. You can see the teeth marks in it. It's consistent with a dromaeosaur attack."

"Let me see," Reggie said, stepping inside.

They left Reggie to work, then finished exploring the first floor. There were two bathrooms with three toilets and three showers each, one for men, one for women. On the left was a room marked LAUNDRY, but inside they found six large units that looked like air conditioners. They were attached to the ventilation system. Rosa examined them and decided they were air scrubbers.

"Someone knew where this place was going," Rosa said. "But the oxygen and air scrubbers are add-ons, not integrated into the HVAC system. Given the age of this building, I'm surprised they still function."

Opposite the laundry room was a mechanical room that held circuit breakers, data nodes, and telephone switches.

"I wonder where the electricity is coming from," Emmett asked.

On the far end of the corridor were two rooms. A sign on the wall marked one as the MEN'S DORMITORY in English and Braille. The other room was marked WOMEN'S DORMITORY. The corridor continued to an exit door with a sign reading ALARM DOOR: EMERGENCY EXIT ONLY. The steel door was welded closed, the seamless bead running the whole perimeter of the door.

The men's dormitory door was open and held three sets of bunk beds, dressers, three small desks, and personal items—clock radio, electric razor, suitcase, and sunglasses. The beds were neatly made. They found clothes in the dressers and in a small closet. In one corner of a drawer full of underwear Rosa pulled out a box of condoms.

"Are those lubricated or non-lubricated?" Phil asked.

Rosa started to check, and then caught herself. Phil and Emmett laughed. Rosa gave them the finger.

They crossed the hall to the women's dormitory. It was nearly identical except they realized the door had been removed. They found it leaning against a wall inside. These beds were made as well. There was a layer of dust on everything.

"Nick, look at this!" Emmett said.

Nick turned to see writing on one of the walls. It read "ELIZABETH HAWTHORNE WAS HERE."

Nick left the room on the run, hurrying to the room with the bodies.

49 ▪ MYSTERY

Some physicists believe that the Pyramid is not only an accumulator of energies, but also a modifier of these same energies. We know that any object within which energy vibrates is capable of acting as a resonating cavity. . . . Thus we can conjecture that the pyramid may act as a huge resonating cavity which is able to focus energies of the cosmos like a giant lens.

—*Max Toth and Greg Nielsen,* Pyramid Power

FLAMSTEED CRATER, THE MOON

They shed the sensor laden NASA underwear, and searched drawers, closets, and suitcases for anything comfortable. Most of what they found was cold weather gear, and they cut and trimmed to make it suitable to the near tropical conditions. Phil settled for a pair of warm-ups that were six inches too long for his stubby body. He cut the legs off at the knee and then found a bulky sweatshirt, and cut off the sleeves.

Rosa and Reggie had taken the most care putting together outfits. Reggie had elicited an approving whistle from Phil when she emerged in red boxer shorts with the flap pinned closed with a large safety pin, white tank top, and red flip-flops. Rosa had managed to find a pair of cotton overalls that she wore over a V-neck men's T-shirt. After watching Rosa sweat for ten minutes in the overalls, Reggie took her into the women's bathroom and they emerged a few minutes later with Rosa's overalls turned into short-shortalls. Phil whistled again. Rosa gave him the finger, then slipped on white deck shoes.

Nick's choice was the most boring—a pair of coveralls he found in the maintenance room. Like Rosa, he cut the arms and legs off a few minutes after he put it on. Emmett found a pair of bicycle shorts and a black T-shirt emblazoned with fire and brimstone and a rock group called "Brides of Satan." The musicians were all women, all buxom, and all bulging from leather outfits.

"That's the only shirt you could find in this entire building, Emmett?" Rosa demanded.

"What can I say, I'm a music lover."

"If Carrollee sees you in that you'll have some splainin to do," Phil said, slipping into a Ricky Ricardo accent.

"She's not here, and I control the only camera," he pointed out.

There was more joking, then they gathered in one of the offices on the second floor, scrounging working light bulbs so that the room was brightly lit. It was the only office with a window looking out on the pyramid. Inside thick walls, they were out of touch with the lander, and were overdue. Nick decided to let the mission handlers worry since they were safe for the moment and not using precious oxygen. However, they had no food and no potable water. In a couple of hours, he would send someone back to the lander to relay a message to Earth and bring back food and water.

Phil went to work dismantling the computer on the desk, cleaning it and checking connections.

"Not much risk of static discharge," Phil observed, commenting on the humidity.

Emmett sat on the floor, working on a second machine they had retrieved from the office next door. After his initial panic, Nick forced himself to wait for Reggie's report on the bodies. There were fourteen of them. Eight men and six women. Six of the males had nametags that identified them as security personnel for something called Fox Valley Environmental Research Station. None of the other bodies had identification, but on the wall above each body someone had written names. None of the names were Elizabeth Hawthorne. Strangely, the names above the bodies of the men with security tags did not match the names on their badges. The bodies were too decomposed to match the photos on the ID tags, but at least for one of the bodies, the hair color did not match the hair color in the photo. Four of the names were clearly Russian. One person had been shot in the head, and another possibly shot in the chest, but the rest had died from severe trauma, likely the result of animal attacks.

Nick couldn't help but wonder whether there was a connection between his conversation with Nev Rhyakov and the bodies of Russians on the moon? He also thought about Elizabeth's claim to have found a nuclear weapon near the Alaskan site she was investigating. Using a yellow pad and a pencil he found in desk drawers, he began doing calculations. He quickly estimated the yield it would take for a single bomb to displace a facility the size of the structure they were in and dismissed that possibility. It would take a comet striking the Earth to compress enough matter to the density necessary. Also, the bomb Elizabeth found was not at the site, just near it. He thought about the distance and it suddenly made sense. A ring of small fission weapons could accomplish the displacement. The larger the weapons, the fewer needed.

Nick stood, looking out the window, wondering where Elizabeth was. Clearly she had made it to the site, found her way inside, and for some reason, wrote her name on the wall. But what about the animal and human remains? What had happened? If she, and whoever was with her, got out before the structure was transported, then why weren't the bodies removed, too?

Nick looked at the pyramid, wondering what role it played in all of this? He decided to explore the structure while Phil and Emmett got the computers working. Reggie and Rosa came along, the oddly dressed trio finding their way back through the complex to the pyramid.

Nick examined the material it was constructed out of. Without removing the skin, he couldn't see the superstructure, but the exterior seemed to be a composite, the interior lined with a flat black material.

"Feels like Mylar," Rosa said.

The surface was nearly frictionless and absorbed light and sound. Using LED flashlights designed for use in a vacuum, they entered the pyramid. Lights were strung along the ceiling but either they were burned out or not turned on. Using the flashlights, they worked their way deeper into the pyramid. The passage soon branched. Rosa suggested splitting up, but Nick vetoed the idea. He wouldn't split them up until he knew what the structure was for. They stuck together, coming to another branch, one corridor going up, and one down. They went up. Occasionally they came to movable panels that could be slid in or out of the walls or up and down from the ceiling or floor.

"Do either of you detect a pattern to these passages?" Nick asked.

"No, it seems random," Rosa said.

Reggie just shook her head, although she seemed intensely interested in every aspect of the pyramid. Nick made choices at each intersection, noticing now that there was debris along the passage. They pointed their flashlights down, illuminating a smattering of dry leaves, sand, and soil.

"Turn your lights out for a second," Rosa said.

When they did they could see a glow. The light led them down a long passage and then into a large chamber with working lights. At one side of the chamber was a table. A stereoscope sat on the table. In the middle of the chamber was a tripod with a small clamp on the top. Scattered beneath the tripod were green leaves. Nick picked one up.

"These are fresh," he said.

"How is that possible?" Rosa asked. "They've been here at least a decade."

Reggie said nothing.

Now they examined the table and the stereoscope. There was a piece of metal under the lenses. Nick cleaned the lenses, and then looked through the eyepieces. The image was fuzzy but he could see the piece of metal was marked off into squares. Both Reggie and Rosa took a look.

"It's some kind of experiment," Rosa said.

"I agree, but nothing like I've ever seen," Nick said.

Again, Reggie said nothing.

"Let's head back and see if they've got the computers running."

Phil had his computer cleaned, reassembled and running, when they got back. Emmett was just beginning to reassemble his.

"This machine belongs to someone named Toru Kawabata," Phil announced. "The software is fairly current and I mean in our time, not ten years ago. By the way, this is off the shelf hardware. Give me an hour and I will pull a couple of other computers in here and set them up to run parallel. Give me three hours and I'll wire up five and give you the speed of a Cray."

"Phil, we're on the moon," Nick said. "We need to gather as much information as possible and get out of here."

"I'm just saying I could do it," Phil said. "Some of the files on the hard drive are corrupted and the directory is totally gone. I've reconstructed most of it. Besides commercial programs, there are two kinds of files; open access documents and locked and coded files. Where do you want to start?"

"The locked files," Nick said.

"My kind of boss," Phil said.

"But they're coded?" Rosa said.

"Only for another few minutes," Phil said confidently.

It took Phil ten. Once opened, they had access to all of the computer's files. There wasn't any engineering data on Kawabata's computer, but there was budget information, purchase orders, correspondence, personnel files, and the original proposal for the project. Without a functioning printer they all huddled around the screen, reading.

"Have you ever heard of orgonic energy?" Emmett asked.

"Never," Nick admitted, now tapping the arrow keys on the keyboard to scroll forward. "It seems to be some sort of entropy dampening force originally discovered by the Egyptians."

"I've heard of it," Phil said. "Some people use pyramids to sharpen razor blades and preserve food. The Egyptians used pyramids to focus orgonic energy and stop the decay process. That's why mummies are so well preserved."

"They're embalmed," Emmett pointed out, still working on his computer.

"So's my great grandmother, but you won't find any skin on her bones after all these years, not like they find on those mummies."

Nick walked to the dusty couch and sat down. Phil took control of the keyboard again and began recovering more files. The existence of orgonic energy could explain a number of anomalies in Emmett's model, if it truly was an anti-entropy force. Nick would need Emmett to modify his model to confirm his suspicions, but if orgonic energy did dampen entropy, and if this collector was pulling significant amounts out of the system, then the acceleration and modification of the time displacements could be explained.

"Nick?" Phil called suddenly. "I found a folder with a number of letters in it. One of them is addressed to you and it's from Elizabeth."

50 · HOPE

Either the geometry of the pyramid is in substantial error, which would affect our readings, or there is a mystery which is beyond explanation—call it what you will, occultism, the curse of the pharaoh, sorcery or magic; there is some force that defies the laws of science at work in the pyramid.

—*Dr. Amr Gohed, quoted in* The London Times

FOX VALLEY, ALASKA

Outside the building where Elizabeth sat, a nuclear fireball vaporized everything for miles in all directions. The holocaust in Fox Valley did not affect Elizabeth and the others, since the epicenter for the time displacement had been accurately calculated. The containment building was dropped through a hole in time and space, guided by some undiscovered laws governing the relationship among time, space and matter, to Flamsteed Crater on the moon. The valley that was left behind would be uninhabitable for a century.

Everyone felt nausea and disorientation, although whether from time travel, instantaneous transportation to the moon, or abrupt adjustment to one-sixth gravity, Elizabeth could not know. The building shook, then groaned, as loads shifted, and the building adjusted to new forces. Whoever had designed the building for vacuum had done their job well. It held together.

When Walters and his followers had made plans to prepare the containment building for surviving in a vacuum, air handling systems were readied for the addition of oxygen supplements and for CO_2 scrubbing. The wiring was in place to accept the solar cells and power converters, and for heat radiators to be installed on the roof. They had simplified the entrance and exit controls so that some future visitor could get easy access, and then set up a trigger for power so that the facility would come to life when someone visited the site. They had no idea of who would visit, or when, but for their purposes they knew it was important for the pyramid to remain intact, functional, and out of reach, until they could accomplish their goal. The preparation of the building also helped ease the consciences of his followers since they knew some of their colleagues would be sent with the building.

Walters and his group had not planned to travel with the pyramid to the moon, so when planning they did not conceive of leaving the building nor did they think about a desire to look outside. There were no windows engineered into the walls and the external cameras were disconnected as the building was sealed. They had no environment suits. While they had been willing to strand Kawabata and some of his staff on the moon, they had not put up stores of food and water. The water in the hot water heaters, the toilet tanks and bowls, bottled water in the canteen, canned soda and additional stock for the soda machine, were all confiscated and rationed. Food was treated the same way. With a dozen people in the facility, Baranov estimated they could survive for a month.

"Two months if we execute those who did this," Baranov pointed out.

"Give them water," Kawabata said and Baranov complied.

The interior of the building was hot and humid so everyone wore as little as possible. Snow parkas were piled in a corner. Everyone had come in cold weather clothes and now searched the building for something lighter, or cut the legs and sleeves off of what they wore. Andy and Leo stripped off their snow pants, walking around in cotton pants and military green T-shirts. Elizabeth found a pair of stretch exercise shorts and wore those with a cotton blouse. She added a pair of men's running shoes with no socks. After three days of constant complaining, Baranov relented, giving Walters and his people a pair of scissors, and then holding a gun on them while they made their clothes more comfortable.

Phat Nyang and Dr. Kawabata divided their attention between the pyramid and information found on the computers of some of his renegade employees. Neither Marissa, Whitey, nor Walters would help, so they concentrated on the pyramid, taking readings, and making short forays inside.

Baranov had Walters's people police the building. The dead dinosaurs were collected and stacked behind the pyramid. With limited freezer space, and no way to preserve the flesh, they ate dinosaur for the first few days. Walters's group refused to eat the flesh of "murdered" animals. Baranov let them go hungry. Eventually, they begged for food, eating what was offered.

They removed the furniture from an office on the main floor, and laid the bodies shoulder to shoulder. Jennifer took the time to write the names of each person on the wall above their heads. Walters was allowed to gather with his four surviving supporters to eulogize his fallen friends, calling them "green warriors." They sang songs, recited poetry, and chanted. Elizabeth, Phat, Jennifer, and Valerie, a materials control assistant, gathered for a Christian ceremony. Phat led the songs and prayers, reciting scripture from memory. Kawabata spent a few minutes by himself with the remains of his employees but said no prayers. Andy and Leo performed the simplest ceremony, speaking the names of their fallen comrades, and then saluting them.

The first indication of something odd was when Leo was found cooking more dinosaur meat, a week after it had been left to rot.

"It's still good," he declared, offering samples. "Perhaps it's because this is the moon and the environment is sterile."

"We brought all the necessary bacteria with us," Kawabata pointed out. "Perhaps we should examine the remains of the others," he suggested cautiously.

They had stuffed towels along the bottom of the door to control odor, and now they removed these and Baranov opened the door slowly. There was little odor. Looking in, the bodies looked much the way they had left them, although there were signs of decay—dark blotches on bloodless skin, hollow cheeks, but no bloating.

"In this temperature they should be—" Kawabata started, then softened what he wanted to say, "—further along."

"What's going on, Doctor?" Baranov asked.

"Orgonic energy," Kawabata said. "The pyramid shape is especially suited to collecting orgonic energy, much like different shaped antennae are better at collecting UHF signals, other shapes VHF. But pyramids made out of stone were poor collectors. Our pyramid was constructed of a composite material that facilitates collection and focus."

"But what is orgonic energy?" Baranov asked.

Kawabata paused, closing the door to the bodies, then pushed his glasses up to his forehead.

"I will explain this way. The second law of thermodynamics is based on the observation that the physical world is active and will dissipate energy whenever there is a differential in energy potential creating a gradient."

"Sir, that is too complex," Phat said respectfully. "If I may?"

Kawabata nodded.

"The second law of thermodynamics states that order moves to disorder. We call this entropy. A cup of hot tea cools. Ice melts. Rivers flow to the sea."

"Good, Dr. Nyang," Kawabata said, taking over again. "However, recently we have observed an anomaly that is counterintuitive. In certain circumstances when a less efficient dissipation of potential is taking place, and a different, more efficient dissipation potential presents itself, the system will reorganize. Thus violating the basic assumption of entropy."

Kawabata looked at the puzzled faces in the hallway, rolled his eyes, and nodded at Phat.

"If we were to puncture a hole in the wall of this building— excuse the poor choice of analogy—the air would rush to the hole and stream out. This is entropy in action. However, if we were then to open the exit doors, the systems that were already equalizing pressure would reorganize themselves to a more efficient system, and the air would rush out the door. So, in this example, disorder creates a different, more efficient order."

"But you could explain that through other physical laws," Elizabeth said.

"Yes, in this example," Phat conceded. "In other examples, no."

"To explain the increase in order that we can observe in the midst of entropy, we hypothesized a force that works in opposition to entropy," Kawabata said. "This force is orgonic energy. The Egyptians were aware of this energy, and many cultures since then. However, they were inefficient at collecting this energy."

"Our collector turned out to exceed expectations, and now

we know that our colleagues were withholding important data," Phat added.

"We now know our collector is storing and radiating orgonic energy, thus slowing decomposition," Kawabata said.

"A fountain of youth," Leo suggested.

"To a degree, yes," Kawabata admitted. "But not a miracle. We can still starve to death, although it is likely that starvation will be prolonged."

Everyone blanched at that realization.

"What about the dinosaurs coming from the pyramid? And the man that appeared and then disappeared inside?"

"That may be our salvation," Kawabata said, smiling.

"Through the pyramid?" Elizabeth asked.

"Perhaps, but there is still much I do not understand. It is virtually certain that the pyramid connects to somewhere on the Earth. However, when and where is not possible to know. Also, the path to that location is not clear. Phat and I have explored the interior but have not found our way to anywhere but here. Still, the air is moist, laden with pollen, and fragrant with the smells of vegetation. None of that is present on this side of the pyramid."

"How is this possible?" Elizabeth asked. "It sounds like a wormhole. What's powering it? Orgonic energy?"

"No," Kawabata said flatly. "Orgonic energy could not create such a force. There is another factor. Since the original time quilt, there has been an increase in orgonic energy. For a reason I do not fully understand, orgonic energy has been liberated by the time disruption. I now believe that the connection between time waves and orgonic energy is more intimate than I knew."

"So if the way out is through the pyramid, why don't I organize a systematic search of the passages?" Baranov suggested.

"There is some danger," Kawabata said. "That should be our last resort."

"We will arrive at the last resort very shortly, Doctor," Baranov said.

Baranov agreed to wait, but in the end it did not matter.

A week later everyone was bored, having explored every nook and cranny of the facility, read every book, and knew everyone's life story. Exercise was limited because it increased food and water consumption, so card games passed for activity.

"Perhaps we should destroy the pyramid," Baranov said to Kawabata one day at a lunch of Fritos and cheese crackers. "If Walters and his bunch like what this thing is doing, then I am against it."

"We would not be able to escape," Kawabata said after some thought.

"A price that may need to be paid," Baranov said.

"Perhaps, but destroying the pyramid would not be easy. The material it is constructed of is very resistant. Without explosives, it would be difficult to do enough damage in the time we have left," Kawabata said.

"I would be willing to try, thank you very much," Baranov said.

"You should also know that the pyramid functions as a battery and it is charged with orgonic energy. It would work against your efforts."

"That, I do not understand!"

"The pyramid will repair itself as you damage it."

"Self-repairing systems," Elizabeth noted. "No wonder you got black bag funding for this."

"There is another concern," Kawabata said. "If we modify the interior, we may modify the outcome. It would be dangerous to put us on a new course without knowing what that course would be."

No one disagreed, and they dispersed after the meager lunch to various tasks. Elizabeth was just outside when she overheard a snippet of conversation.

"Sir, they have overlooked the most obvious danger," Phat said.

"Yes."

Elizabeth moved on, wondering what they had missed.

Elizabeth worked with Leo to build a moisture collector out of the refrigerator and the pyramid construction material, managing to impress even Kawabata with its efficiency. It bought them a few more days.

Neither of the Russians was talkative, refusing to reveal anything about their mission and precious little about their personal lives. They did learn Andy was married and Leo was single.

Andy had a dry sense of humor but was businesslike much of the time. He couldn't help but take charge, issuing orders like he was in command and then apologizing when he realized what he had done. No one minded. He and Kawabata took to playing chess, the games lasting hours.

Leo flirted shamelessly with Jennifer and Valerie, and both teased back, even though both claimed to have boyfriends. Elizabeth set clear boundaries, and Leo respected these, but with two younger women, it was easy to do.

"Come see! Come see!" Leo shouted one day.

Everyone but the prisoners responded to his excited calls. He was standing by the far side of the pyramid where the dinosaur carcasses had been laid out. Elizabeth could smell rot, as she got close. The orgonic energy had lost the fight with decay.

"Look, look," Leo said, encouraging them around the corner.

Elizabeth turned the corner to see the dinosaur carcasses writhing with maggots. She gagged, and then threw up. Thirty minutes later they gathered in the cafeteria. Walters and his bunch shouted down the hall, demanding to know what was going on. Everyone ignored them.

"The maggots are a good sign, aren't they Dr. Kawabata?" Leo asked.

"Yes. The maggots are larval flies. Since there are no flies in the building, they must have come from the pyramid. But, it is not easy to follow a fly. We must wait for a better guide."

Fly watching became a popular activity, until the stink of the decomposing carcasses drove the watchers away. As the flies on the carcasses hatched, they infested the entire building and were even seen crawling under the door to the makeshift morgue. After that, the towels were replaced and no one opened the door. Their water was almost gone when the "better guide" showed up.

One day Phat discovered a thin black line of ants stretched from the pyramid, around the corner, to the carcasses. The ants were half an inch long, black, and hairy. The line of ants was made up of two columns, those coming and those going. Those going were carrying bits of meat.

"Army ants," Kawabata declared.

"Does that help you pinpoint the time era?" Baranov asked.

"Somewhere between now and the mid-Cretaceous period," Kawabata said. "Ants evolved before humans."

"Is there really a choice?" Elizabeth asked.

There wasn't, and they made plans to leave. Baranov wanted to leave Walters and his group behind, but Kawabata insisted they come. They each wrote letters to leave behind on Kawabata's computer, not knowing if they would ever be found. They offered the opportunity to Walters and his followers, but each refused. They gathered what water and food was left, and then distributed the weapons and ammunition that Baranov had collected. There were enough weapons for everyone to have one, but precious little ammunition. Baranov and Leo were fastidious, and policed the building one more time, even making beds in the makeshift jail. Then they pulled the towels from the bottom of the door to the morgue. Time to let nature do her work.

Leo herded Walters and his people to the entrance of the pyramid. They stared at the ants, fascinated and puzzled. Elizabeth found it disconcerting that the creators of the mess they were in didn't know what was going on.

"Never lose sight of the person in front of you," Kawabata instructed.

Then Kawabata led them into the pyramid.

51 · LETTER

We interrupt this broadcast to bring you a special report. There has been a nuclear explosion in western Alaska. I repeat, there has been a nuclear explosion in Alaska. While the site of the explosion is remote, we understand that there have been casualties.

—Richard Anders, ABC News

FLAMSTEED CRATER, THE MOON

Dear Nick,

You are in my debt forever, although it looks like I will never be able to collect what you owe me.

After I sent you the message about finding the bomb, I was captured and taken inside the facility in Fox Valley. Since you are reading this, I can assume that you know the building you were interested in contained a pyramid. The pyramid is constructed out of a composite material that attracts orgonic energy. Read Dr. Kawabata's letter for details. Unfortunately, I arrived during a mutiny. Dr. Vince Walters, the executive director of the project, took control. He had stolen and planted three twenty-megaton nuclear warheads around the facility. His motives for doing this are not clear. We believe he hopes to influence the time disruptions in some unspecified way. He never intended to be transported to the moon but was stuck here after we were attacked by velociraptors that came out of the pyramid. I believe I have you to thank for sending the Russian soldiers who saved us. Why you sent Russian instead of American soldiers, I'll never know. Unfortunately, the velociraptors killed four of them. In fact, fourteen people died from velociraptor attacks. I won't dwell on that horror. The names of the dead are listed in Dr. Kawabata's letter. Their personal effects and identification are in the lower desk drawer.

At first we thought there was no way out for us. Then we discovered that insects were coming from the pyramid to feed on the dinosaur carcasses. We decided to follow an ant trail back to its source. We are sure the source is on Earth, but we don't know where or, most important, when.

There are twelve of us left, although five are prisoners. Since I am writing this ten years before your time, I can only assume that wherever we end up is not in the recent past otherwise I would have found a way to get a message to you. Perhaps we will journey to the future, if so, I'll look you up and meet your grandchildren.

I love you. I don't think I knew how much until I realized I would never see you again. I know this is an unfair way for you to find out, but I couldn't let my last chance go by without telling you.

Love,

Elizabeth

P.S. Would you look up a woman named Eilene Stromki for me? She was my guide in Alaska. Vince Walters may have killed her in a mineshaft near Murderer's Lake. If she is alive, thank her for me and let her know I got out safely.

Nick read the letter again with a deep and profound sense of loss growing. By the end of the second reading he was dealing with grief and guilt. He had sent Elizabeth down the road that led to this, and like Elizabeth, only now did he realize how important she was to him.

Reluctantly, Nick relinquished the screen, letting Emmett read Elizabeth's letter. Until then, no one on the team knew of Nick's suspicions about the secret building that Elizabeth discovered in Alaska. Emmett's expressions while he read ran the gamut of emotions—surprise, wonder, concern, anger, sadness.

"This is the building that Elizabeth found in Fox Valley—wherever that is?" Emmett said.

"Elizabeth discovered that the structure on the moon looked similar to the one she found in Alaska. They have to be the same building."

"Russian soldiers?"

"Elizabeth sent me a photo of a nuclear device. It turned out to be Russian. I shared it with Nev on the space station. She made a contact for me. I suppose that's where they came from."

"Nick, there's a lot you haven't been telling me," Emmett said, his anger growing.

"The connection seemed so remote," Nick explained.

"What have you held back from my wife? Is she going to get blown to the moon too? Or just blown up?"

"Believe me, Emmett, I didn't know anything about nuclear weapons being involved. I'm sure Carrollee is safe. John is with her and he took a hunter and three rangers."

Emmett wouldn't be mollified, but he let it go. The others had been listening intently, fascinated by the cryptic references to everything from Russian soldiers to nuclear weapons in Alaska. Clearly worried, Emmett slipped out of the chair and went back to work on the computer he was refurbishing. Rosa, Reggie, and Phil all rushed to fill his spot, tilting the screen this way and that until they agreed on an angle where they all could read at the same time.

Rosa's reaction was wonder. Phil's was puzzlement. Reggie began to cry.

"Reggie, what's wrong?" Nick asked.

Reggie wiped her eyes with the back of her hand.

"Just the stress, I guess."

"Maybe you should prescribe something for yourself," Nick suggested.

They carried a small supply of pharmaceuticals.

"After reading this I could use a hit myself," Phil said.

Reggie ignored him, hurrying from the room, her sobs receding down the corridor. They gave her the privacy she needed.

Emmett finished reassembling the second computer. The computer belonged to the Vince Walters mentioned in Elizabeth's letter. Those files not corrupted were correspondence, internal memos, and work schedules.

"Let's take the hard drive with us. I can recover any wiped files when I get back to Earth," Phil said.

"Nick, I need to go outside and contact mission control," Rosa said. "We're long overdue."

"I'll go with you to the lander," Nick said. "We can carry back food and water and then spend more time going through these records."

Nick also wanted to contact the vice president to find out whether there had been an explosion. Phil and Emmett would stay and continue to work on recovering files and refurbishing computers.

Downstairs they helped each other into their PLSS suits. On the way to the exit they found Reggie standing in front of the pyramid, looking inside. Reggie's reactions continued to puzzle Nick. They seemed out of proportion and often inappropriate. Letting Reggie work through whatever issues she had, they headed for the exit, then suddenly stopped, startled by loud noises.

Reggie backed away from the pyramid opening, the low gravity giving her an exaggerated, slow-motion movement. Then, from the dark doorway two men burst, arms around each other, rifles in their hands. Tumbling out of the door, they lost their footing, bouncing, releasing each other. Then there was a booming bellow that echoed through the chamber, and out of the pyramid came a tyrannosaur.

52 · STRUCTURAL DAMAGE

We tend to confuse mass and weight because we tend to measure mass in pounds or kilograms. But weight is only the result of gravitational force. If there were no gravity, an object would be weightless, but it would still have mass. Accelerate a weightless mass and it will still have force when it strikes a stationary object. Fire a gun in the space station and the bullet will be weightless. The effect on any object the bullet meets would be the same as if it were on Earth.

—*Nick Paulson, Fundamentals of Physics, Guest Lecture,*
University of Georgia

YUCATAN PENINSULA

John Roberts and Robert Ripman had been friends since high school when their first period teacher called out "Ripman, Roberts," and assigned them to share a locker. They quickly found they both hated the teacher, and whispered defiantly in class. John introduced Ripman to Cubby, one of John's oldest friends, and the three bonded. All were too shy to talk to girls; all liked to talk about girls. They spent hours driving around in Cubby's van, a gift from his evangelist father. Ripman usually drove, Cubby in the front passenger seat, John leaning between the seats, cracking jokes.

Their friendship was tested when the world was time-quilted, and they decided to search the Portland quilt for Cubby's and John's parents. Ripman never admitted he was worried about his father, but Ripman did search for his own house. Ripman never spoke much about his father and his mother had died before he could shape memories of her.

John's father was a psychologist, and he once asked John about his choice of friends. "John, you selected a wannabe survivalist and a fundamentalist preacher-in-the-making for your friends. What does that say about you?"

"We just like to mess around together, that's all," John said defensively.

Before his father's death after the Portland Quilt, John hated being his father's guinea pig, but now he would give anything to have another conversation with his father, even an awkward one. Over the years John had tried to understand his friendships with Ripman and Cubby. Partially it was based on mutual need. All three were shy, and all three just a little out of sync with their peers. They were a team, and loyal to each other. They stood up for each other in an argument and covered for each other when they made mistakes. And they did all that without the need for a word of thanks.

There came a time when Ripman needed to fight his own battles, face down the bullies himself, rejecting help from John and Cubby. Ripman had a need to feel independent, and bragged of his ability to survive on his own, to the point of arrogance. Still he hung out with John and Cubby and never failed to come to their aid when needed. When he lived with John and John's mother after the time quilt, he had seen what family could be. Still, after high school graduation, he moved out. But their friendship had deep roots and Ripman had come when John asked. Helping others had always been easy for Ripman. It was taking help that was hard.

So when Ripman stumbled in the dark interior of the pyramid, going down hard, breaking his flashlight, he slapped John's proffered hand away.

"Run, there's no time," Ripman yelled.

John ignored him, squatted, and wrapped an arm around his friend. Cursing John for his stupidity, Ripman got up, then nearly collapsed, one ankle sprained. Refusing to let go of him, John supported his limping friend, following Carrollee's and Nikki's flickering light. Then, rounding a corner, they ran into a juvenile tyrannosaur making a meal out of one of their team members.

"Shit!" John shouted, veering left, down a passage. "Who was it?"

"Jose," Ripman said. "We should kill it, John."

"We will," John said, continuing to run.

The other tyrannosaur was still on their trail, its olfactory abilities giving it an advantage in the dark, but its size hindering it.

"Left," Ripman yelled as they came to a junction.

Reflexively, John turned and climbed a ramp. With each step he felt stronger, and Ripman was becoming easier to hold. Ahead was a dim glow. He noticed lights hanging from the ceiling. They came to a chamber with a table, a microscope and other equipment. John slowed. Something was wrong. He was having trouble walking, misjudging each step.

"Follow the lights," Ripman ordered.

John followed the lights, all of which seemed to be burned out. Now they bounced off the walls, stumbling, but not tiring.

There was a crash behind them and a bellow, as the juvenile tyrannosaur demolished the equipment they had passed. It was gaining.

"Leave me," Ripman yelled, pushing John away.

Trying to catch his friend, John dropped his flashlight, which fell slowly, then bounced, the bulb surviving the impact. John unslung his rifle, firing into the dark passage behind, once, twice, three times.

"Now let's go!" he yelled, pulling Ripman to his feet.

"There's light," Ripman said.

John lifted Ripman with one arm. Surprised at John's strength, the friends wrapped arms around each other, then hurried toward the glow. Staggering like drunks, using the walls to keep themselves upright, they stumbled on. Then there was an opening. With powerful steps they burst into light. Falling, Ripman pushed John away.

They were in a building—a warehouse. There were three

people, strangely dressed, two in spacesuits. Their eyes were wide, mouths agape. John rolled onto his back, bringing the rifle up. He fired, hitting the tyrannosaur in the head. The beast's roar hit a new pitch.

Now hands were on John, easily lifting him and Ripman.

"John?" a voice said, incredulous.

It was Nick Paulson, the director of the Office of Strategic Science and John's boss. There was no time for explanations.

"Let me go, I can finish it," John said, pushing hands away. Blood streamed down the right side of the tyrannosaur's face. It shook its head, blood splattering everywhere, and then fixed on John, bunching its legs. Just as John raised his rifle to fire, the animal charged, but the powerful animal launched itself into the air instead, John's shot hitting the pyramid. Terrified, wounded, and confused, the juvenile tyrannosaur flew over John and the others, landing on its bloody face, and then rolled head over heels, smashing into a set of doors. Kicking and turning, the animal struggled to get to its feet.

John brought the gun around again just as the tyrannosaur rolled to its feet. Someone slapped his rifle down.

"It's too dangerous!" Nick Paulson shouted.

The tyrannosaur launched again, and again flew over their heads and bounced across the floor to slam into the wall on the far side.

"He'll crack the containment building," Nick shouted.

"Let me kill it!" John said.

"Too dangerous," Nick said. "Come with me."

Nick and the two women helped Ripman and John through a set of double doors. John recognized Reggie from the OSS, but not the one in the space suit. She was pretty, maybe Hispanic, near John's age. Behind them the juvenile tyrannosaur continued its frantic attempts at attack, crashing off walls, the pyramid, and other structures.

John and Ripman were pulled up a set of stairs and down the hall, then into an office. Emmett Puglisi was there and Phil Yamamoto. The room vibrated with the impact of the wounded juvenile tyrannosaur. Ripman and John crawled to the window, keeping their heads down. Slowly they lifted up to peek out. The tyrannosaur was using its massive jaws to crush a pallet stacked with black sheets. Blood streamed from its ruined right eye. They sank back down before they were spotted.

"John, what is it with you and tyrannosaurs? Do you have to turn them all into Cyclopses?"

John laughed, relief and exhaustion making him silly. Then he saw Emmett staring at him, his face deathly pale.

"Where is Carrollee?" Emmett demanded.

"She's not here?" John asked, unsure of where "here" was.

"She was with you. You were protecting her!"

"I don't know," John said. "I honestly don't know."

53 · INJURED MAN

Studies of the neurons of dinosauria demonstrate significant similarities in form and biochemical function, including the role of sodium and chloride ions. However, at the macro level dinosaur nervous systems are less well developed. A neural system that functions quite well in a two-meter human seems wholly inadequate in a fifteen-meter behemoth. The one advantage for these large species would be that the pain from injuries would be too diffuse to be debilitating. It would also take significant and widespread destruction to impair nervous system function.

—*Joseph Prensky,* Introduction to Dinosaur Physiology

FLAMSTEED CRATER, THE MOON

The juvenile tyrannosaur eventually settled down, cleaning its damaged eye with its tiny arms, and then licking away the blood. Moving unnerved it, so it squatted, stabilizing itself with its tail. They watched it from the window, while telling each other their stories. Emmett interrupted frequently, asking questions, demanding answers that John and Ripman didn't have. Ripman disassembled his rifle as they shared, cleaning it.

"That tyrannosaur damaged the interior airlock doors," Nick said. "I could hear them hissing."

Nick and Rosa stripped off their space suits, putting back on the clothes Phil retrieved from downstairs. Rosa was halfway through the changing process before they realized John and Ripman were paying close attention. Reggie came to her aid, blocking their view. John and Ripman did not mind, switching attention to a beautiful woman wearing men's boxers and a white tank top.

"I heard the hissing too," Rosa said. "If it won't seal, then we can't get out."

"We might be able to use it once," Nick said, "but if those inner doors are weakened, they might blow out and we would lose our atmosphere. Unfortunately, we don't have PLSS suits for John and Ripman."

"One of them can have mine," Emmett said. "I'm going into the pyramid after Carrollee."

"Give John the suit," Ripman said. "If you're going into that pyramid, you're going to need me. There's another baby rex in there."

"With Carrollee?"

"It's in there, she's in there," Ripman said coldly.

"She could be back in the Yucatan," Phil pointed out.

"Where the predators outnumber the prey," Ripman replied. "We lost three dinosaur rangers getting here."

"Stop it, Ripman," John said. "Emmett's worried enough."

"He should be. I am too. I'm just being realistic."

"You're being an asshole," Rosa pointed out.

Nick was silent, suddenly realizing they had missed the real danger.

"There may be a bigger problem," Nick said.

Everyone stopped talking.

"Emmett, can you see how much structural damage that tyrannosaur did to the building?"

Emmett crawled to the window, peeking over, studying the walls.

"It's hard to say from here. I think there are some cracks in the exterior wall but they could be superficial."

"That isn't good. I realized when we were talking about opening the exit doors that the loss of atmosphere would be temporary because the flow from the pyramid would replenish it. But what would happen if the containment building itself were breached? The Earth's atmosphere would blast through that hole into space."

"The force would tear the pyramid apart, stopping it," Emmett said.

"We don't understand the forces at work here," Nick said. "We can't risk a breach. We have to kill that dinosaur before it can do more damage."

"Killing dinosaurs is what I do best," Ripman said, slapping a clip in his freshly cleaned rifle.

The sound of breaking bones came from outside. They crept to the window, heads lined up, peeking out. The tyrannosaur was partially hidden behind the pyramid.

"He found the bone pile," Nick said.

"Bone pile?" John asked.

He was ignored.

"That won't satisfy him," Emmett said.

Now the tyrannosaur turned, head in the air sniffing. Everyone but Ripman ducked.

"He can't see ten feet in front of him," Ripman said.

The others looked again. Head held high, testing the air, the tyrannosaur was heading to the double doors.

"He may be smelling the human remains," Nick suggested

"He may smell us," Ripman said. "I can take him out in the corridor."

Ripman tried standing, and then fell back, grabbing his ankle. Reggie knelt, palpating the ankle. Ripman winced.

"Take the boot off," Reggie ordered.

"If you take it off, I may not get it back on," Ripman said.

Reggie unlaced the boot, loosening it as much as possible.

Ripman bit his lip as she eased it off. Feeling the ankle again, she frowned.

"I can't tell without an X ray, but it may be broken."

"I've had breaks before," Ripman said. "That ankle is not broken."

"Thank you for your second opinion, doctor. Broken or not, you can't put any weight on it. I'll have to splint it."

"Not until I deal with our friend down there."

"I'll kill the tyrannosaur," John said.

Ripman frowned, looking at his friend doubtfully.

"John, you're good at blinding them, but you've never killed one."

"I'll kill this one," John said.

Ripman hid his concern, nagging John like a worried mom.

"Keep the high ground if you can. Don't waste a bullet on another headshot. Hit it just under those tiny armpits if you can, but remember that heart is buried deep. The money shot will be the spinal cord. Break that and you can take your time killing it."

"Got it," John said, working a round into the chamber.

Rosa took Ripman's rifle, mimicking John.

"You need backup," Rosa said.

Nick started to reach for the weapon but stopped. Rosa probably had more training with rifles than anyone except Phil, and even Phil didn't think he should be the backup. Standing in her shortalls, weapon in hand, she looked more like a pinup girl for a B movie than a hunter, but no one argued with her.

Then John and Rosa went hunting.

54 • HUNTERS

The large carnivores are all strikingly similar with heavy skeletons, unusually large skulls, and short muscular necks. The thigh is longer than the shank, which is the opposite in most theropods. The similarity in appearance and design are dictated by size, which limits evolutionary design. Whatever the limiting factors that produced this one pattern, the hunters that come out of it are extremely efficient.

—*Joseph Prensky,* Introduction to Dinosaur Physiology

FLAMSTEED CRATER, THE MOON
PRESENT TIME

John and Rosa knelt at the top of the stairs, listening to the tyrannosaur testing the swinging doors, banging them open, over and over. They waited. Finally, it came through, head low to clear the ceiling, following its nose. They backed up out of sight—they had only one eye to worry about. The tyrannosaur paused at the stairwell, sniffing, blind eye on their side. The tyrannosaur continued down the corridor, out of sight. There was thumping, then banging, then the sound of a door being torn from its hinges. Now there was the sound of the tyrannosaur tearing up something else.

John crept down the stairs, while Rosa took a position at the top. He could hear the tyrannosaur tromping down a corridor. He hurried to the corner, peeking. The tyrannosaur nearly filled the hallway from wall to wall, giving John an unobstructed shot of its rump. It reached the end of the corridor, its head low, sniffing at a door. Then it swung its head to the side, sniffing the opposite door, its good eye toward John. Suddenly, its head snapped toward John—he had been spotted.

The juvenile tyrannosaur tried to turn and charge, its head coming up, its tail dropping. The particleboard walls collapsed, dust boiling into the corridor. Its head crushed the drop ceiling, raining down acoustic tiles. With six times too much strength, the tyrannosaur ripped out walls and aluminum ceiling supports. John aimed through the dust at the thrashing animal, and fired. The tyrannosaur erupted in new levels of destruction, managing to tear through studs and sheetrock to get around to face John. Now it charged, but erratically, crushing ceiling and walls as it came, never coming to terms with the low gravity.

John retreated, careful to control his adrenaline-powered muscles. He gently bounced around the corner. The tyrannosaur's momentum carried it past John, its head crashing into the far corner. At the same time its tail tore through the back wall as it tried to balance. John shot it in its midsection. The wound might kill it, but slowly.

The injured tyrannosaur couldn't feel more pain and didn't flinch when John's slug buried into its guts. Scrambling to its feet, tail pounding the walls, head bulldozing ceiling tiles, it attacked. Mouth dry, surprised by the punishment the half-blind animal could take, John turned and ran past the stairwell, taking his stand in front of the double doors. He could not let it damage the walls any further. John turned and fired. The bullet entered low, tearing up more of its guts. Howling, the tyrannosaur stumbled, falling on one knee, striking its head on the floor. Then there was a shot from the stairwell. The juvenile tyrannosaur started to stand and then another shot came from the stairwell. Blood erupted high on the tyrannosaur's back. It collapsed—Rosa had broken its spinal cord.

Its back legs were dead, its tiny forearms useless. Standing tall, aiming at its good eye, John shot it one last time. Keeping his rifle aimed at the tyrannosaur's head, John inched past, climbing over the legs to the stairwell. Rosa was sitting on the stairs in her shortalls, rifle in her lap.

"Nice shot," John said.

"Which one? I shot it four times," she said, smiling.

"The one that broke its spinal cord," John said, sitting next to her.

The others came up behind. Ripman was hopping easily on one foot in the light gravity. Ripman surveyed the mess and the dead tyrannosaur.

"Well, John, I'll give you an A for guts, a C for marksmanship, but an F for neatness. Rosa gets an A just for going with you."

"Let's check the airlock," Nick said.

Everyone squeezed past the tyrannosaur, John and Rosa trying to help Ripman, who kept pushing their hands away. They followed him closely but in the low gravity there was little risk of injury if he fell. The others were just passing through the double doors when Phil stopped and turned back.

"Nick, come here!" Phil shouted.

Nick, Emmett, and Reggie came back through the doors.

"Two suits are missing," Phil said, pointing to the pile of suits.

"I suppose they could be under some of that," Nick said, doubtfully, looking at the wreckage in the hallway.

"Where else could they be?" Reggie asked.

Nick decided it was best to check the exit doors before searching for the missing suits. Nick and his team studied the doors, focusing on the center seal.

"Try it," Nick said, standing and backing away.

Emmett pushed OPEN and the doors slowly slid apart, and then jammed, the motor whining.

"Stop! Stop!" Nick shouted.

Emmett hit CLOSE and the door shuddered, and then closed.

"It's bent," Phil pronounced, putting his face an inch from the joint. "You can see a crack between the doors."

"We could take turns using the suits to get everyone back to the lander," Rosa suggested. "Three of us could go back, then one return with two extra suits. We would have to think through this to make sure we got the right size suits back for the next person."

"Sounds like a math problem from algebra class," John said.

Rosa smiled and then wrinkled her brow, thinking hard.

John found her pretty no matter what emotion she was expressing.

"We may have a fuel problem," Rosa said. "These two are pretty big guys. They must add close to four hundred pounds. We computed the fuel based on returning with some samples, but not a couple of hitchhikers. If we dump the suits and strip the lander, we might be able to reach the shuttle."

"It doesn't matter. With the doors damaged I don't think we can risk opening them," Nick said.

Now Nick walked to the far wall, inspecting the damage. Like sheep, they followed. Emmett, Phil and Reggie all examined the wall, and then looked above their heads to where the juvenile tyrannosaur had made an impact during one of its overpowered leaps.

"What do you think?" Nick asked.

"It's hard to tell," Emmett said.

"They're deep and fatal," Phil declared flatly.

"I agree," Reggie said. "It's inevitable. The cracks will spread, weakening the structure. Ultimately it will fail."

Now Nick looked back to Emmett, who reluctantly nodded agreement.

"I don't see that we have any choice," John said. "We can't risk using the airlock. We have to go back the way Ripman and I came."

Now they all looked at the pyramid.

"You don't even know how you got here," Phil said.

"I'll guide us back," Ripman said.

"How will you find the way?"

"That tyrannosaur did a lot of damage on the way here. Where it didn't tear something up it scratched the surface. It will be easy to backtrack."

"Let me show you something," Emmett said angrily, pointing along the backside of the pyramid and the piles of dinosaur bones.

"That tyrannosaur isn't the only dinosaur that's come through that contraption. They could have just as easily done the damage and left the marks."

"It doesn't matter. They came from the same place," Ripman argued.

"You don't have any clue of what this thing is or does," Emmett shouted.

"It's not my job to understand it. That's your job," Ripman shot back.

"And your job was protecting my wife!" Emmett said.

Phil put a hand on Emmett's chest. Emmett and Ripman glared at each other.

"There's another option," Nick said suddenly, defusing the standoff.

"What's that?" John asked.

"We'll let the ants lead the way."

55 ▪ REUNION

Antoine Bovis . . . while walking around inside the King's Chamber, found seemingly preserved cats and other small animals, which had apparently wandered into the Pyramid and died of starvation. Bovis thought that perhaps the shape of the Pyramid might have been responsible for the . . . state of these animals, which showed no signs of decay.

—*Max Toth and Greg Nielsen,* Pyramid Power

YUCATAN PENINSULA
PRE-COLUMBIAN

With Nikki's support, Carrollee stumbled toward daylight, bursting from the pyramid into bright tropical sunlight. Squinting reflexively, Carrollee caught a glimpse of stone structures and well trod ground. The ruined structures they had explored were whole now, the pyramid-devouring vegetation still at bay. Stone walls enclosed the pyramid, the space inside essentially a meadow. Nikki helped Carrollee toward an opening in the wall and through it she could see huts and people.

"Stop, Nikki," Carrollee whispered. "Something's not right."

It was too late. A naked, brown girl had seen them and shouted an alarm. Adults pointed and jabbered, and men with spears and swords came running. Carrollee and Nikki held each other. The men wore only breechcloths, some with their bodies painted black. A few wore sleeveless shirts. Surrounding Nikki and Carrollee, they pointed spears, wooden swords, and sharp-edged clubs. Fascinated, not frightened, the warriors looked the women over, murmuring in an unintelligible tongue. Then there was commotion, and the warriors parted, letting others through. These were older men, most wearing breechcloths, but three wearing white cloth skirts. All wore shirts dyed in bright colors, and around their necks hung strings of beads, shiny metallic ornaments, or animal-shaped objects. One of the newcomers was younger and had lighter skin than the others. Nikki suddenly released Carrollee's arm.

"Kenny?" Nikki said, stepping forward.

The man smiled, spread his arms and they rushed into an embrace.

With that hug the weapons were lowered, but the men continued to stare. Occasionally a man would reach out and touch Carrollee's or Nikki's shirt or pants, or point at their boots. Nikki's blond hair was particularly fascinating and men dared to touch it, smiling, revealing teeth filed to a point or inlaid with dark materials. Carrollee avoided eye contact.

"Kenny Randall?" Carrollee asked.

The young man's face was deeply tanned, his body lean and firm.

"Yes, of course," he replied.

"Where are we?" Carrollee asked. "This doesn't look like the entrance we came through."

"You are still on the Yucatan peninsula, but many years before your time."

Carrollee was hot—feverish—her body ached and her mind was foggy. She was so sick she couldn't be sure she understood what Kenny was saying.

"We traveled back in time?"

"Yes. Quite a bit actually."

"How far back?"

"I'm not sure," Kenny said. "I haven't been able to reliably date this time period, but as far as I can tell the conquistadors have not arrived yet."

"How is that possible?" Carrollee asked, looking back at the pyramid.

"How long have you been here?" Nikki asked.

She was still pressed against Kenny, but now she was caressing his face.

"Nearly thirty years," Kenny said.

"But, you disappeared only five years ago?" Nikki said. "And you don't look that old."

Terrified shouts surrounded them as the warriors suddenly turned, weapons at the ready. Stepping from the pyramid opening was one of the juvenile tyrannosaurs that had chased them. The warriors backed away. Kenny shouted orders in their language. Nikki and Carrollee retreated toward the opening in the wall. The tyrannosaur followed, slowly, seemingly confused, wary of the numbers it was facing.

They reached the opening and wooden doors were swung closed, a thick wooden beam used to lock the door. The tyrannosaur bellowed when the doors slammed shut, then hammered the door with head and tail. The door held. Eventually, the tyrannosaur gave up, but it would try again. Unless it reentered the pyramid, it would have to get out to eat.

Carrollee and Nikki were led to a large hut at the edge of the village. Inside, the dirt floor was covered with woven mats. There was a small wooden table against one wall, with two stools. Shelves held a variety of clay pots. A shelf under the window held figurines—animals, people, and creatures with features of both. Carrollee was helped to the stool and sat, leaning on the table, exhausted. Women and children peeked in the window and door, jabbering excitedly, pointing.

"Drink this," Kenny said, handing Carrollee a cup.

Carrollee sipped the warm liquid. It was cocoa.

"Hot chocolate?" she asked, surprised.

"They invented it," Kenny said.

Kenny knelt beside her and felt her forehead.

"You have a fever," he said. "Nikki, help me take her into the next room."

A woven curtain separated the two rooms. In the second room was a hammock and they helped Carrollee into it. The hammock stretched, taking her weight, then conformed to her body as she gently rocked. Kenny brought a pillow stuffed with dried grasses, gently placing it under Carrollee's head. Her head aching, her body hot, and her head filled with worries about Emmett, Carrollee fell asleep.

She woke in the dark, confused. Trying to sit up in the hammock, a comforting hand on her forehead pushed her back. She woke again during daylight. A middle-aged woman sat on a stool next to her. The woman had long black hair, braided and tied with strips of red cloth. She wore a skirt cinched at the waist with a belt, and a necklace of fat brown beads hung from her neck. When she saw Carrollee's eyes open, she left. Carrollee was hot, but not from fever now. Pulling her legs up one at a time, she unzipped the lower half of her nylon pants' legs, then worked them off over her boots. Now wearing shorts, she felt more comfortable.

A few minutes later the woman came back with Kenny and Nikki, who were holding hands like teenage lovers. Carrollee pushed herself up, dangling her legs over the side of the hammock, careful not to rock it.

"Feeling better?" Nikki asked.

"Yes, some," Carrollee said. "I think the fever is gone."

Kenny was staring at her legs, worried. Now he took her arm and unbuttoned the sleeve of her shirt, pushing it up. Carrollee looked to see spots on her arm. They were on her legs, too.

"Measles," Carrollee realized. "My son came down with it just as we were leaving."

Cursing now, Kenny shouted orders at the woman who had nursed Carrollee. Quickly, she left.

"What's wrong?" Nikki asked.

"They have no immunity to measles," Kenny said.

Carrollee understood. It wasn't the Indian wars that killed off much of the Native American populations, it was disease, many of which were considered childhood nuisances among Europeans, but were deadly plagues to indigenous peoples from the Americas.

Carrollee and Nikki stayed inside after that, Kenny bringing food and drink. The food was surprisingly familiar. Vegetables included squash, beans, and chili peppers. There was also amaranth and manioc, which Carrollee had never tasted but found palatable. Venison and turkey were on the diet, as well as peccaries and rabbits. Carrollee sampled whatever meat was provided, except for the peca, which was essentially a large rat. The staple of the diet, however, was corn, usually in the form of tortillas. She drank copious amounts of hot chocolate, avoiding water. One night, Kenny brought a drink made of fermented honey—balche—and they got silly, forgetting where they were.

The hut had two rooms and Kenny and Nikki slept together in the hammock where they had first put Carrollee, a curtain the only privacy. Another hammock was hung in the main room for Carrollee who politely pretended not to hear the frequent lovemaking in the next room.

One day Nikki remembered the calculator and retrieved it from Carrollee's pack. Kenny was puzzled, but pleased.

"There are programs on here I don't remember," he said, exploring the files.

Kenny's explanation for how they found themselves several hundred years in the past was little more than a guess.

"What we passed through is a stable version of what created the time quilts that devastated the planet. Somehow, the pyramid shape focuses energy associated with time-space disruptions, creating a permanent time-space link."

"A stone pyramid does that?"

"No, not alone. Since at least the time of the Egyptians, there have been experiments with pyramids. Some of this was based on the computations of Zorastrus, but like da Vinci who was ahead of his time, they did not have the technology to produce an efficient collector."

"But the Maya do?" Carrollee asked.

"No, although I've been able to improve the efficiency of this one."

"Why?" Carrollee asked.

"To use it to disrupt the effect of the one on the moon."

"There's a pyramid on the moon?" Carrollee asked. "How could you know that?"

As she said it, Carrollee thought of Emmett's mission to Flamsteed Crater.

"I extrapolated from the data that something was disrupting the time-space continuum and pinpointed two locations. One on the moon, and one in the Yucatan. That led me to this pyramid and eventually to here."

"Then we can go back the same way," Carrollee said.

"It's not that simple," Kenny said, frowning. "The interior of the two pyramids are linked and changes to the interior of either can affect where and when you come out. That tyrannosaur that followed you through probably did significant damage to the interior. The pyramid will repair itself to a degree, but I can't guarantee you will return to where or when you left. You could emerge from the other pyramid."

"On the moon?" Carrollee asked, incredulous.

"Yes."

Now Kenny took Nikki's hand.

"If you decide to go back through, I can't go with you."

Nikki didn't say anything. Carrollee realized they had already talked about this.

"I have to understand what is happening," Kenny explained. "Here, in this time, I have years to theorize, and experiment. If I go back, it is a matter of days."

"Days? Another time quilt?"

"Something much worse. What happened to us was a collision between the Cretaceous period and the twenty-first century. What is coming will shred history as we know it, jumbling past and future so thoroughly that everyone in every time will be affected. Worst of all, as the past is disrupted, the future will change. Pulling a few hundred dinosaurs from our past wasn't enough to alter the evolutionary history of our planet, but what is coming will make it impossible for the present as we know it to exist."

Carrollee wanted to dismiss what he was saying, to call him crazy, but she lived in a world that had seen cities disappear and extinct animals return.

"Carrollee, I'm staying with Kenny," Nikki said.

Carrollee had expected Nikki to stay, but it left her with little hope of getting home. She would have to find her way through the pyramid not knowing what she would find at the other end.

They left Carrollee alone after that, and she thought about her options. Quickly, she realized there really wasn't any choice. She had a family somewhere on the other side of the pyramid, and she was going to find them.

Carrollee's spots faded and a few days later she had fully recovered. Kenny suggested she wait a few more days before trying to return through the pyramid, letting it repair itself. He also asked that she not leave the hut, although by now she would not be contagious. Nikki stayed with her most of the time. Kenny had to shoo the curious villagers away from the windows and doors several times a day. Once, when she was standing by the window trying to catch a breeze, Carrollee spotted Kenny coming out of the compound surrounding the pyramid, guards quickly closing and latching the gate behind him. Briefly she wondered about where the tyrannosaur had gone, but also about what Kenny was up to?

Carrollee observed as much of the village life as she could from her window. The hut Kenny lived in was wood framed and plastered with stucco and roofed with palm thatch. Other buildings were stone. Just a few huts down was a pole structure with no walls, just a thatched roof. Meals were cooked there, the cooking facilities shared, but meals taken back to individual homes. Food preparation was communal time, women gathering, laughing, gossiping, and scolding misbehaving children who ran naked in the streets.

Once Carrollee was steady on her feet again, Kenny took her and Nikki to a smaller building behind his hut. Inside was a large wooden tub filled with steaming water.

"You invented the bathtub?" Carrollee asked in surprise.

"No, the Maya bathe, although not like this. They are very clean. I built this after I had been here five years. I just wanted a good soak."

"Any soap?" Nikki asked.

"Next to the tub," Kenny said. "You'll have to share, or take turns," Kenny said, apologetically. "I made it too big and it takes a lot of work to fill the tub."

"Maybe you and Nikki should use it," Carrollee suggested.

Nikki and Kenny both blushed.

"No, this is a treat for you two," Kenny said, backing away. Then he slipped out the door, closing it behind him.

There were large windows on either side of the building, the shutters open, a breeze coming through. There would be no privacy.

"You can go first," Carrollee said, feeling it was the most magnanimous gesture of her life.

"No, together. I'll scrub your back if you'll scrub mine?"

"Deal," Carrollee said.

They stripped off their clothes, Carrollee wearing only the claw necklace that Ripman had given her. Then they eased into the tub, finding the water hot, but bearable. Carrollee immediately dunked her head, massaging her scalp. Even without soap, she felt cleaner. She came up in time to see Nikki surface, too, smiling with relief. There were three chunks of yellow lye soap, and they went to work, scrubbing their bodies, washing their hair, and scouring the grime from their fingernails—and they washed each other's backs. Then they soaked in the now milky water, letting the water cool. In the intimacy of a shared tub, Carrollee felt comfortable talking to Nikki.

"Nikki, why does Kenny look so young?" Carrollee asked, looking across the tub at her bath partner.

"I guess it's okay to tell you," Nikki said reluctantly. "It's the pyramid. He spends as much time inside as possible. He says there is a certain place you can go and it rejuvenates you."

"You don't age?" Carrollee asked, incredulous.

"You do get older, but it's slowed down. That's why he doesn't look as old as he is."

Finally the water had cooled and they reluctantly got out. Kenny had supplied cotton cloth to dry with. Once dry, they washed their clothes in the tub, and then wrapped themselves in the towels. Kenny was waiting outside. The long overdue scrubbing made them giddy and they teased him, doing the hula in their wraps. Joking and laughing, Kenny led them back to their hut and cups of balche. First, Carrollee ushered Nikki into the bedroom, sending Kenny to get new clothes.

He returned with skirts that the women of the village wore, as well as intricately woven huipils, or blouses. Woven from cotton, they had intricate diamond patterns created by expert weavers. Carrollee dressed Nikki in a huipil, with an intricate blue and yellow pattern and skirt. Then using combs Kenny borrowed from women in the village, Carrollee styled Nikki's short curls. Using the small box of makeup she carried in her backpack, she highlighted Nikki's cheekbones, and applied color to her eyelids and lips. Then, dressing herself, they joined Kenny.

Kenny was speechless. As if seeing his Nikki for the first time, he looked her over from head to toe. Embarrassed by his appreciative stare, Nikki began to strut, then twirled, showing off her new clothes.

"I've never seen anyone so beautiful," Kenny said.

Then remembering Carrollee, he gave her a quick glance. "You're beautiful too," he said hastily.

"Emmett thinks so," Carrollee said, hurting even as she said his name.

They drank balche—honeychol as Kenny called it—

laughing at silly comments, listening to Kenny tell stories of the many ways he had embarrassed himself among the Maya. It was the best time Carrollee could remember since entering the jungle, the warmest feelings, the most like being part of a family. That sobered her. Clean and healthy now, she was ready to chance her trip through the pyramid.

"It's time for me to go," Carrollee announced the next evening.

"You should stay," Nikki said, knowing the dangers.

"At least a little longer," Kenny said. "Your chances of getting back get better with each day that passes."

"I have a family, Kenny. I love them and miss them. I'll take any chance I have to, to get back to them."

Now there were voices outside, angry voices. Kenny listened, and then hurriedly left, speaking to men who gathered outside. Nikki and Carrollee stood together, listening, understanding nothing. After a minute of strident conversation, Kenny left with them. He came back twenty minutes later, grim-faced.

"The woman who nursed you and two children have fevers."

"It's too soon," Carrollee said. "Measles doesn't incubate that fast."

"They have no resistance," Kenny said. "They blame you and Nikki. They say you brought the demon to their village and now the sickness."

"They're right about both," Carrollee admitted.

"Unfortunately, they're polytheists and magical thinkers. They believe one of their gods has been angered and needs to be appeased. They want to make a sacrifice to Yum Cimil—the god of death."

"Sacrifice?" Carrollee said.

"Yes. It's to be a heart sacrifice," Kenny said.

"Us?" Nikki asked.

"They want to sacrifice the one who was sick and cheated Yum Cimil by not dying. They want to give Carrollee's heart to Yum Cimil."

56 · THROUGH THE LOOKING GLASS

I regret to report that our mission failed. Commander Baranov and five men were killed when the weapon detonated. We are returning with six injured American Deltas that we rescued when the EMP disabled their helicopter in flight. On board we also have one woman and one dog.

—*Karl Petrov, Sergeant, Spetsnaz, Weapons Recovery Unit*
(NSA Intercept/Translation/Russian/Coded)

FLAMSTEED CRATER, THE MOON
PRESENT TIME

To speed discovery, they dragged the carcass of the tyrannosaur close to the pyramid's opening. They harvested meat for themselves, although water was their biggest problem. The little they carried in their suits did not go far. They reactivated a moisture collector they found, but it only prolonged the dehydration process.

While they waited for the ants, the swelling in Ripman's ankle went down, but it remained sore. Reggie was convinced he had cracked a bone. Ripman was adamant he hadn't. Rosa and John passed much of the time together, talking and flirting. Rosa helped John choose his own outfit from the slim pickings in the building—cut-off jeans and a Hawaiian shirt. John wore the shirt open, showing off his tanned chest. Ripman snorted when he saw the outfit, rejecting Rosa's offer to put one together for him. Nick could see the jealousy in Ripman's eyes when Rosa leaned against John, hand on his chest, playing with the hair.

"I like the look," Rosa purred.

"I've got more hair on my ass," Ripman spat. "Want to run your fingers through that?"

Rosa was quick with nonverbal language.

The biggest mystery was the two missing PLSS suits. They dug through the rubble left by the tyrannosaur but did not find them. They searched the building with no better luck. Emmett wanted to search the pyramid, but Nick decided against it.

"Those suits couldn't just disappear," Emmett argued.

"I know, but until the ants show us the path, we're not going to risk wandering around in the pyramid," Nick said.

The line of ants appeared just as they did for Elizabeth and her companions years earlier. John changed back into his boots and jungle clothes the day they left. No water could be spared to clean clothes so they were as dirty as the day they arrived.

They entered the pyramid with lights ready. Two columns of ants wound their way through the pyramid, those coming empty handed, those going home carrying bits of flesh. When they reached the central chamber, Nick paused, sensing this was the point of no return. The gravity was still one sixth of Earth's, but the air had the sultry steaminess of a tropical rain forest. He led on.

At one point, the gravity and texture of the floor changed and the sudden additional weight created nausea and dizziness. Briefly disoriented, Nick followed the ants a few more yards before he noticed the walls—they were stone now. Ripman grunted from pain as he dragged his broken ankle into normal gravity. Reggie reached out for him. He took her hand gently, squeezed it, and pushed it away.

"Let's backtrack and examine the transition," Phil said.

"No!" Emmett said quickly. "We need to find Carrollee."

"Maybe one should go through the looking glass only once," Phil conceded.

Nick overruled his scientist half, deciding his first obligation was to get his crew safely home. He led off again, the ants leading them on a winding path through the interior of the stone pyramid. Coming to an intersection, Nick's flashlight illuminated bones—human bones. The collarbone was crushed and half the ribs broken. Other bones were scattered.

"It's Jose," Ripman said, pointing to remnants of cloth that still had the dinosaur ranger insignia.

"He was one of our rangers," John explained.

"These bones are too clean," Phil said. "There isn't any soft tissue left at all. And look at this," he said, running his finger across the skull wiping away a layer of dust.

"Phil, he was a friend," John said.

"He was a good hunter," Ripman said.

"Apologies," Phil said. "I only meant to show the dirt. This skeleton has been here a long time."

Nick considered the possibilities.

"I know you were running last time, but does anything seem different?" Nick asked.

"Some of those panels that slide in and out might be in different positions," Ripman said. "Back there I barely cleared one in the ceiling. That juvenile rex would have taken it out if it had been that low before."

"Now that I think of it," John said, "that juvenile tyrannosaur busted up some of those panels. It came through like a bulldozer."

"What are you thinking?" Emmett asked.

"I'm thinking someone has made adjustments in here, redirecting the energy flow," Nick said.

"To what purpose?" Emmett asked.

"Someone is playing God," Phil said.

Nick agreed with both men. But who?

Now they moved cautiously, inspecting each junction, and noting the position of each of the movable panels. The ants did not share the human concerns, rushing along in a reassuring way. Eventually, the ants led them to the exit. It was night when they emerged.

Nick found himself looking at two small stone buildings, illuminated by moonlight. His dark-adapted eyes could make out thick vegetation beyond the buildings, but no details.

"Is this where you entered?" Nick asked.

John and Ripman hesitated.

"Yes, but it's different," John said. "Those buildings were ruins and everything in here was overgrown."

Now John turned to the wall to the left of the entrance.

"There were markings carved in the stone here," John said. "Nikki said they were Akkadian."

"Akkadian writing, here?" Nick said. "That doesn't make sense."

Phil examined the stone.

"Writing disappearing from stone doesn't make sense either."

They moved out from the entrance, examining the two buildings. Both had wooden doors with simple latches. One looked like a guardhouse, with dusty bedding on the floor and a half dozen spears leaning in the corner. There was a rough-hewn table, candle stubs, and clay pots. The other building shocked them. Inside they found a half dozen computers lined up, a keyboard and a large flat screen. Phil immediately walked to the setup and examined the wiring.

"It's set up for parallel processing," Phil announced. "Someone's got a nice piece of work here."

Nick stopped Phil before he could turn it on.

"Not yet, Phil. We don't know who this belongs to."

"What's the power source?" Emmett asked, looking behind the computers and tracing a wire through the roof. "Maybe solar."

"Look here," Reggie said.

They turned to see the two PLSS suits hanging on the wall behind the door, complete with helmets and backpacks.

They left the equipment hut. Through the thick foliage to their left they could see faint flickering light. They followed a narrow well-worn trail toward the light, coming to a stone wall with a wooden gate. Nick pushed on the gate but it did not open.

"Look here," Rosa said, indicating a rope leading to a bell mounted high on the wall. "Should I?" Rosa asked, smiling mischievously.

"Might as well," Nick said.

The bell gave off a dull ring. Rosa rang it a half dozen times, then paused. The effect was immediate. Voices gathered on the far side of the gate, emoting worry, excitement, and fear. Ripman leaned close to the wall, listening.

"Can you understand them?" Nick asked.

"It's Maya," Ripman said. "I speak a little of it, but this is a dialect I've never heard. I think they sent for someone important."

The voices died to a whisper, and then grew again with excited jabbering.

"The 'Old One' is here," Ripman said.

The gate opened slowly, revealing a surprised group of men and women. Behind them they could see a village. The women were dressed in skirts, the men in loincloths or cotton shirts and pants. They carried torches or candles. In the middle of the group was an old man with a long gray beard. He came forward holding out a hand.

"Welcome, welcome, welcome," the old man said.

Nick took the old man's hand, the grip firm.

"Nick Paulson," the old man said, still holding his hand.

"Yes," Nick said, puzzled by how he knew his name.

Relief filled his face as if a great weight had been lifted from his shoulders. Now the old man tensed again, releasing Nick's hand, looking at the other faces.

"Who else is here, please?" he asked.

"This is Phil Yamamoto," Nick said, Phil shaking hands.

The old man touched his hand briefly, then looked to new faces.

"Regina Bates and Rosa Perez," Nick said.

"Yes, yes, very beautiful. Who else?"

"Robert Ripman and John Roberts," Nick said.

"And you? Who are you?" The old man demanded, ignoring Ripman and John, and stopping in front of Emmett.

"I'm Emmett Puglisi," he said.

"Thank God," the man said, briefly turning his eyes to the sky.

Now he took Emmett by the shoulders, standing face-to-face.

"There may still be time," he said.

"Time for what?" Emmett asked.

"To save Carrollee!"

57 · HUMAN SACRIFICE

The [Mayan] elite were obsessed with blood—both their own and that of their captives—and ritual bloodletting was a major part of any important calendar event. Bloodletting was also carried out to nourish and propitiate the gods . . .

—*Mystery of the Maya, www.civilization.ca*

YUCATAN PENINSULA
PRE-COLUMBIAN

'll take my chances in the pyramid," Carrollee said.

"That's not possible," Kenny replied, avoiding her eyes.

"Screw the tyrannosaur," Carrollee said, getting up. "I'll have better odds against it than being strapped down and having my heart cut out."

"I can't let you go," Kenny said.

"Please, Kenny," Nikki begged. "Give her a chance."

"I can't, Nik," Kenny said, pulling her head to his shoulder so he wouldn't have to look her in the eyes. "If they don't sacrifice her, they'll sacrifice you."

Nikki hugged Kenny tight and then pushed back, looking him in the face.

"Then she and I must both go into the pyramid," Nikki said.

"They won't let you. They're watching."

Carrollee stepped to the window. Men with spears stood

on either side. She pulled the curtain across, wishing she still had her dinosaur rifle.

"Talk to them, Kenny," Nikki said. "Make them understand."

"I tried," Kenny said. "When I first came here I brought influenza to the village. Twelve people died. They sacrificed a young girl then and the disease stopped. She died because of me."

"Not because of you," Nikki said, "because they don't understand what disease is."

"I did bring the disease," Kenny said.

"Talk to them," Nikki said again. "Try. Please!"

"All right," Kenny said.

When Kenny was gone, Nikki tried to hug Carrollee and comfort her. Carrollee politely declined, telling her she wanted to be alone. Nikki went into her room reluctantly, already experiencing survivor's guilt.

Carrollee took her pack to the table, dumping out the contents. She still had energy bars, part of a bottle of water, first-aid kit, a Swiss Army knife, ammunition for a rifle she didn't have, vitamins, water purification tablets, and a flashlight. Nikki picked up the Swiss Army knife. She folded out the blades one at a time, none of the blades a match for the weapons of the Mayan warriors. Then she came to a blade with a sawtooth edge. She paused, thinking.

Kenny was back an hour later with good news.

"I couldn't stop the heart sacrifice but the priests agreed to sacrifice someone before Carrollee. Not Nikki!" he added quickly. "They have a captive they've been saving to sacrifice to Yumil Kaxob, the god of maize. She's the niece of a noble in another city—a high quality sacrifice. They'll try to stop the disease with her first."

"Kenny, I can't let someone else die for me?" Carrollee said.

"She will die anyway. They sacrifice someone at every planting."

"Someone will have to take her place," Carrollee pointed out.

"It's their way," Kenny argued. "They do a lot of bloodletting in their ceremonies. They sacrifice iguanas, turkeys, and other animals. They spill their own blood, too. And they sacrifice people. I'm not supporting the practice, but we need to respect their culture."

"I can't respect murder and I won't let someone take my place."

"You don't have a choice, Carrollee," Kenny said.

"They should wait," Nikki said. "Give the measles a chance to run its course. Otherwise she'll die for nothing and they'll sacrifice one of us."

"They're going to do it as soon as the sun god, Kinich Ahau, is up to watch," Kenny said. "They're already preparing."

Wracked by guilt, Carrollee spent the rest of the night pacing, suggesting new arguments that Kenny could use. Even she didn't believe they would work.

"Kenny, why did they agree to try this?" Carrollee asked as dawn approached. "They think I angered their god and yet they are willing to risk more deaths by sacrificing someone else?"

"I help them now and then, and make suggestions. Like with their calendar. They're astrologers and predicting celestial events is important to them. I helped them improve their calendar and get it to three hundred and sixty-five days. Once I showed them some things about fertilizing their corn."

"Maybe you could offer them something else for sparing Carrollee?" Nikki suggested. "Maybe gunpowder."

"No!" Carrollee and Kenny said at the same time.

"I've done more than I should," Kenny said. "Everything I've showed them the Maya developed on their own anyway. But gunpowder could change history."

"It would give the Mayans a chance," Nikki said. "The Spanish are going to slaughter them."

Kenny was a peculiar man, often lost in himself like an autistic child. He was like that now, thinking.

"Kenny?" Nikki probed.

He came back slowly, not explaining where his mind had been.

"I can't interfere, Nikki. I just can't do it."

They argued some more, but Nikki's heart wasn't in it. Near dawn, there was singing, and the sound of simple musical instruments. Then men came to the hut, exchanging angry words with Kenny.

"They want us to attend the heart sacrifice," Kenny said.

"They won't . . ." Nikki said, afraid to say it.

"You're both safe. Trust me."

They followed Kenny out to the street that was filling with people dressed in finery. The sun was beginning its climb through the jungle to the sky. There was a somber mood, although the villagers were dressed in colorful clothes. The women wore ribbons or flowers in their hair, the men hats and headdresses. A procession approached, a man with an elaborate headdress at the head. He wore a loincloth and sandals, but around his neck hung an intricate necklace of hammered copper. The half dozen men behind were similarly dressed, their bodies powdered gray and wearing headdresses. One carried a stone box, another a bowl, a third a statue that was skeletal.

"The one in front is the Ah Kin Mai, the chief of all the priests," Kenny said. "Those behind are the priests and the Chacs who assist in the sacrifice."

"Kenny, you're scaring me," Carrollee said.

"Sorry."

Behind them came guards with blue loincloths, quilted body armor, bead necklaces and wooden swords, the edges sharpened with slivers of obsidian. Now came a small knot of guards. In the middle walked a young girl, wearing only a white skirt. Her long black hair was plaited and hung nearly to her waist. She was somber but not crying.

"Kenny, she couldn't be more than fourteen."

"I know it seems cruel to us," Kenny said, "but it's the side of diversity we don't like to look at."

Carrollee started forward, but Kenny blocked her with an arm across her chest.

"They'll sacrifice you both if you interfere."

As the second set of guards passed, more of the important people followed, distinguished by the quality of their jewelry. They were beckoned to join the group.

The procession entered the gate by the pyramid, and then turned along the side. Ahead Carrollee could see stairs built into the side of the pyramid, leading to the top. The leaders of the procession and a half dozen guards started up. Then two guards took the arm of the young girl and helped her up the steps. To Carrollee's surprise, she walked, the guards only steadying her.

"Why doesn't she try to get away?" Nikki asked.

"They don't believe you can get to heaven by dying a natural death. This is a sure path to heaven for her."

Kenny stopped them at the base, but one of the priests shouted orders.

"We have to go up," Kenny said.

Reluctantly, they followed the procession. The pyramid was steep, the climb long. At the top there was chanting, an unintelligible ceremony. Two of the priests alternated singing. The one Kenny had called the Ah Kin Mai took the lead, another echoing. The Chacs removed the girl's skirt and lifted her onto the altar, legs held, arms stretched above her head and held by more of the Chacs. Now a stone box was opened and a flint knife removed and held high, the black stone glinting in the rays of the early morning sun. After holding the knife above his head and chanting a prayer, the Ah Kin Mai handed the knife to another priest who took position on the opposite side of the girl. A third priest held a bowl. Then with the deliberateness of a surgeon, the knife was pressed to the girl's chest, and with a sawing motion the chest was opened. Now the girl screamed.

Tears streamed from Carrollee's eyes, yet she couldn't look away. The macabre religious practice was too distant to see details, but she saw that it took two to perform the surgery. The priest with the knife opened the chest and the Ah Kin Mai reached inside, ripping the heart from the body. The screaming stopped before the heart was removed. As the heart was pulled from the body, the third priest caught the dripping blood with the bowl. Then the heart was held high and the crowd erupted in cheers. The somber mood was now replaced by the celebration of sports fans.

The priest rubbed the heart all over his body, coating himself in blood. Other priests stepped forward, the heart passed from man to man, each smearing himself with the blood of the young girl. The crowd cheered and whistled approval. Next the Chacs lifted the body by the arms and legs, walked to the edge of the pyramid and dropped it over the side. The girl's body tumbled down the pyramid, leaving splotches of blood. The corpse landed with a thud, the crowd cheering. Carrollee turned away as priests moved in on the body, knives in hand.

"What are they doing?" Nikki said, turning away.

"I should have warned you," Kenny said. "The priests eat the corpse."

"I want to go," Nikki pleaded.

Carrollee took Nikki's hand and they brazenly pushed past the guards, heading down the steps, determined to get away from the horror and determined that it wouldn't happen to them.

58 ▪ HEART SACRIFICE

The Mayans were warlike and raided their neighbors for land, citizens, and captives. Some captives were subjected to the double sacrifice where the victim's heart was torn out for the sun and head cut off to pour blood out for the earth.

—*Mayan History, www.cyrstalinks.com*

YUCATAN PENINSULA
PRE-COLUMBIAN

They didn't speak all that day. Nikki cried in her room and Kenny spent the day comforting her. He brought tortillas and bananas for supper, but Carrollee could not eat.

"Will that satisfy them?" Carrollee heard Nikki ask Kenny late that night.

"If no one else gets sick," Kenny said. "I told them to keep everyone who was exposed, or sick, isolated. That will limit the spread. I don't know how strictly they've enforced it. They believe Kukulcan, the wind god, brings disease."

"How long will they wait to see?"

"Only a day or two."

At that Carrollee took out her Swiss Army knife, feeling the edge and cutting her finger. Getting out of her hammock, she lit a candle and then tried the knife on the table. She easily sliced off a sliver of wood. The knife was new, the blade sharper than any knife she had owned. She put the knife back in her pack. Since the bath, she and Nikki had taken to wearing native clothes and she had no pocket. The next morning she put her shirt and pants back on, dropping the knife in her pocket.

When Nikki and Kenny got up, they looked at her clothes, but said nothing. There was no sickness that day, but one of the sick children died. The next day another child was sick. That night priests came to the hut again, speaking with Kenny. He was grim when he came back.

"The priests say that the sacrifice was rejected. Even though only one more has become sick, the death of the little boy has convinced them that Yum Cimil has not been pacified."

"When are they going to do it?" Carrollee asked.

"In the morning," Kenny said, looking down.

"Talk to them again, Kenny," Nikki pleaded.

"Don't, Kenny," Carrollee said. "I already have the death of that poor girl on my conscience. I won't have another."

"They don't have another quality sacrifice, only orphans and slaves. That won't satisfy Yum Cimil. If only the conquistador horses were here. When the horses come the Mayas think they are great stags ridden by powerful warriors. They will be more impressed with the horses than by the weapons of the conquistadors. I'm just sure they would trade a horse for you."

"But there are no horses."

"No."

"Please talk to them," Nikki begged.

Sighing deeply, Kenny nodded, hugged Nikki, and then left, avoiding Carrollee's eyes. He had no hope of changing their minds.

Carrollee wasn't going to bet her life on a man she barely knew. Surreptitiously, Carrollee examined the door and the windows in both rooms. The windows were simple openings, framed with shutters to close during heavy rain. No one had bothered to close and lock them. However, guards stood at each door and window. Now Carrollee studied the walls. The hut was constructed of interlocking wooden poles and plastered with stucco.

Nikki was sitting on a stool, head in her hands. When Carrollee spoke she looked up, eyes red, face tear-stained.

"Nikki, I need to lie down. Mind if I use your and Kenny's room?"

"Yeah, sure," Nikki said, anxious to do anything she could. "I'm sure they'll listen to him, Carrollee. He's the smartest person I've ever met."

"Sure, Nikki," Carrollee said.

Carrollee took one of the candles from the room with her, pulling the curtain that separated the two rooms, and then one that covered the window. Now she knelt by the back wall, pulling out her knife and opening the saw blade. She studied the poles making up the wall, figuring the least cutting she would need to do to make an opening wide enough for her hips—unfortunately, her widest part. Then she began to saw. Sliver by sliver, she cut through a pole, trying not to disturb the stucco on the outside. With her technique refined, she attacked another pole. Her fingers blistered, then bled. Now she heard chanting.

Kenny had still not returned when she had cut through enough poles. Blowing out the candle, she lay down and tapped at the stucco, knocking away pieces until she could push her head through far enough to look around. She could see the wall around the pyramid to one side and more huts and buildings in the other direction. Directly behind was the bathhouse, and then jungle. No one was guarding the back. She pulled her head back and found Nikki in the other room. The candles had burned out, leaving Nikki asleep in the dark. Carrollee shook her shoulder, waking her.

"Nikki, come with me," Carrollee said.

"What? Where?"

"Your room."

Eyes crusted with sleep, Nikki rubbed them as Carrollee showed her the hole.

"We can escape through here and get back to the pyramid."

"What about Kenny?" Nikki said, frowning.

"They're not going to kill him, Nikki, they're going to kill me."

"I don't know," Nikki said. "We should wait and ask him what to do."

"Nikki, it's almost dawn. They're going to come for me soon. If I'm not here, they'll take you."

"You'd go without me?" she asked, surprised.

"You can yell for help if you want to stop me."

"I just found him again, Carrollee," Nikki said, crying. "I feel different when I'm with him. I feel complete, more than I am when I'm alone."

"Nikki, you are one of the bravest, most competent young women I've ever met. You survived the Yucatan wilderness on your own, helped us get back to the pyramid, fought dinosaurs, sewed up wounds and helped bury the dead. You are a complete person, and a strong, beautiful, competent woman who stole the hearts of every one of those dinosaur rangers and Ripman and John."

"But I love Kenny."

Carrollee couldn't argue her out of love.

"Nikki, cutting my heart out won't stop the measles from

spreading. When my blood doesn't stop the disease, they'll offer another sacrifice—you."

"Kenny wouldn't let them."

"Kenny won't be able to stop them! The only chance you two have to be together is to escape and then let Kenny come to you."

"Okay," Nikki said, reluctantly.

Carrollee hugged her, reassuring her it was the right thing to do.

"I should leave him a note," Nikki said.

"There's no paper," Carrollee said.

"I just can't leave without saying good-bye. At least a note."

Digging in her pack, Carrollee found her last lipstick, handing it to Nikki. Nikki removed the cap and poised over the table.

"What should I say?"

Nikki looked out the front curtain. There was a dim glow to the sky.

"Say, 'I love you. Please come for me.'"

Nikki smiled.

"Yeah," she said.

The lipstick was soft from the heat and Nikki wrote slowly and carefully. Carrollee wanted to scream at her to hurry.

"Should I say 'Please come for *us*?'" Nikki asked, pausing.

"No. Say 'come for *me*,'" Carrollee said. "This is from you to him."

"Yeah," Nikki said, smiling.

Like it was a love letter, she finished by drawing a heart. The last of the lipstick broke off when she tried to add an arrow.

"Let's go," Carrollee said, pulling Nikki to her feet.

Using the knife, Carrollee cut through the remaining plaster, large chunks falling away. Checking for guards one last time, Carrollee rolled onto her back and shimmied through the hole, then stood with her back to the wall. The sky was getting light and the chanting was louder. Nikki came through, standing next to Carrollee. Carrollee thought of racing into the jungle and then finding a way over the wall into the compound containing the pyramid, but she had no idea if there was another way over. Besides, once their escape was discovered, the hunters would easily track them down. The gate was their best chance.

Carrollee led Nikki straight to the bathhouse, and then circled it. Then they got down on their hands and knees, crawling slowly, keeping their heads low. There was ample growth at the edge of the village where no one trampled the sprouts. They used it for cover, getting to the wall and then crawling along the wall toward the gate. The guards by Kenny's hut were standing, but heads angled toward the chanting, listening. Keeping tight against the wall, they crawled over broken building stones, trimmed during the construction process. They reached the gate undetected. Now, there was no way to hide as they opened it.

"Nikki, we have to lift the bar together," Carrollee said.

"Okay. On the count of three?"

"One, two, three," Carrollee whispered.

They stood, ran the few steps to the gate, and then lifted the bar. They were spotted immediately, the guards by their hut alerting the village. Adrenaline pumping, they lifted the bar out of its brackets and then dropped it, pulling on the gate. The bar blocked it from opening wide enough to get through. They both furiously kicked at the beam, moving it inches, and then pulled the gate open. Carrollee held the gate while Nikki squeezed through. Then it was her turn, Nikki holding it from the inside. Carrollee was almost through when her shoulder was grabbed. Painted skin and pointed teeth were inches from Carrollee's face. Reaching back with her free arm, she clawed at his eyes and wrenched herself free.

They ran for the pyramid, watching for the tyrannosaur. Nikki was ahead of her, rounding the first stone building near the entrance. With shorter legs, Carrollee had lost a few steps but was nearly there when she was tackled from behind. Then there were other hands holding her down, men cursing her unintelligibly. Nikki came back, cautiously peeking around the corner of the building by the entrance.

"Run, Nikki! Run!" Carrollee shouted

She did not listen. Instead, she came forward, timidly. Warriors took her by the arms. She didn't resist. Carrollee understood. They had their sacrifice. They did not need two.

Kenny appeared, talking to the men holding Nikki. They let Nikki go, Kenny taking her by the arm. Carrollee was trussed, her wrists and ankles tied with rope. They carried her from the compound, Kenny and Nikki hanging back. It was Kenny who closed the gate.

They deposited her in a different hut, with two guards standing over her. She worked at the bonds, but every time they noticed they would whack her with the end of a spear. She would not give up on seeing Emma, Lee, and Emmett again, so she was bruised from head to toe when they came to get her.

She had expected to be anointed or dressed in ceremonial clothes, but they did neither. Instead, they untied her feet and forced her to walk in the procession. Men, women, and children lined the route, falling in behind as before. There was a festive mood among the onlookers, who sincerely believed that cutting out a living human heart would cure disease. There was also curiosity, since they had never seen a woman that looked quite like Carrollee.

They reentered the compound, warriors spreading out, watching for the tyrannosaur. The procession continued to the steps that led to the top of the pyramid. Carrollee refused to take the first step, so she was lifted by the armpits and dragged up.

To the east, the sun was just clearing the horizon, the sky the orange of dawn. Below the spectators gathered, in a festive mood. Warriors with spears were spaced along the stone steps. There were six priests and four guards with Carrollee at the top. The chief priest gave orders, and the guards pulled knives, grabbed her and began cutting away her clothing. She struggled, but was punched and cuffed into submission. When they tore her blouse off the chief priest suddenly shouted orders that stopped them. Stepping forward, he slowly reached out. Carrollee cringed. Gingerly, he picked up the claw that hung between her breasts on the rawhide shoelace. The other priests leaned forward, mumbling with wonder. Now the stripping stopped, the priests conferring. Tenderly, the chief priest put the claw down. They stepped back, talking in nervous whispers.

Carrollee had hope again. Her shirt and nylon pants were gone, she was bruised from head to toe, and she had many small cuts from the crude knives used to cut her clothes away. Only her boots and underpants remained, but she still had hope. Ripman's gift frightened them. If only she could speak to them, she could build on their fears.

A heated argument erupted between underlings, while the chief priest stood apart, listening, eyes flicking to the claw hanging from her neck. Virtually naked, and held by strong men, she tried to look confident, even defiant.

With sharp barking commands, the chief priest ended the argument. Now giving orders, a wooden bowl was produced and a piece of parchment. Then the Ah Kin Mai loosened his loincloth, pulling out his penis. Carrollee tried to back away but was held firmly. Next, the Ah Kin Mai took a flint knife from his belt, stretched out his foreskin and then pierced it. A second priest held the bowl beneath his bleeding penis, the blood dripping onto the parchment. Then the knife was removed, the penis continuing to bleed onto the parchment and into the bowl. Finally, the Ah Kin Mai wrapped his penis in a cloth, and then tucked it back in his loincloth, cinching it at his waist. Next he took the bowl and lifted the parchment. Two other priests looked over his shoulder. Now they conferred, talking in whispers, all in agreement.

Shocked by the bizarre ritual, Carrollee waited for the answer. It came swiftly. With a sharp command, they cut away the rest of Carrollee's clothes, leaving only her boots. Then hands were all over her, lifting her, laying her on the stone table stained black from dozens of bloody sacrifices. Chacs held her feet, and then her hands were stretched above her head and held by more Chacs. She struggled now, but they were too strong. The Ah Kin Mai finished his prayer and handed the blade to the priest that would actually do the cutting. The priest brought the knife down toward her heaving chest. Terrified, helpless, she wet herself.

"Help me, someone help me," she shouted.

No help came.

"God help me!" she prayed, the knife nearly to her chest. She screamed when the priest started the incision.

59 • MISSION

When Adam had lived 130 years, he had a son in his own likeness, in his own image; and he named him Seth. After Seth was born, Adam lived 800 years and had other sons and daughters. Altogether, Adam lived 930 years, and then he died. . . . Seth lived 912 years. . . . Methuselah lived 969 years.

—*Genesis 5:3-27*

YUCATAN PENINSULA
POST CONQUEST

Where is Carrollee?" Emmett demanded of the old man.

"The Maya are going to sacrifice her to Yum Cimil, the god of death," he explained. "She brought measles to the village and two people died."

"Where? Where is this going to happen?" Emmett demanded.

"On the top of the pyramid," the old man said.

Emmett looked at the pyramid, but it was too dark to see anything. Nick knew something was wrong. There were no torches to light such a ceremony.

"Give me a rifle!" Emmett said, reaching for Ripman's.

Ripman held him back with a hand on his chest.

"The sacrifice isn't in this time," the old man said.

Emmett was confused, anxious, near panic.

"Calm down," Nick shouted, taking control. "First, who are you?"

"Kenny Randall," the old man said.

Nick had seen too many bizarre things to be surprised.

"Carrollee ended up here? Nikki too?"

"Yes, many years ago."

"And Carrollee brought measles to the village?" Nick said.

"I'm afraid that's true," Kenny said.

"She was sick," John confirmed.

"Our little boy was sick when we left," Emmett said.

"And she is going to be sacrificed because of it?"

"Not in this time period," Kenny said, now looking at the sky. "It's starting to get light. If Emmett doesn't go now, he may not make it in time."

"Where do I go? What do I do?" Emmett demanded frantically.

Kenny spoke to two young men painted black. They ran into the village.

"Come," Kenny said, leading them to the stone building with the computer equipment, coming out a few seconds later with a calculator.

"These graphs will act as a map. When you come to the end of one, go to the next screen. It is three-dimensional. Can you follow it?"

"Yes," Emmett said, taking the calculator.

"Put the calculator here when you are done," Kenny said, indicating a ledge in the hut.

Kenny nodded.

"You must leave the calculator when you arrive!" Kenny repeated firmly.

"I will," Emmett said, surprised by Kenny's tone.

"I'll go with Emmett," Nick volunteered.

"No! You must stay here," Kenny said, but did not explain.

"Give me a gun," Emmett said.

"We have only two," Ripman pointed out, hanging tightly on to his.

Then the young men came back carrying two M-16s.

The presence of the rifles puzzled Nick, but he knew Elizabeth and the Russians had preceded them through the pyramid.

"Who else will go?" Kenny asked, handing a rifle to Emmett.

"Me," Ripman said.

"You can hardly walk," John said. "I'll go with Emmett."

"Me, too," Rosa said, stepping forward, smiling at John.

Phil hung his head, hating the fact that he was old and slow. Ripman was frustrated by his injury, and embarrassed by his helplessness. Kenny handed Rosa the rifle, and then gave Emmett and Rosa spare clips.

"Try not to kill anyone," Kenny said. "Remember they are basically good people with a different belief system than yours."

"I'll do what I have to, to protect Carrollee," Emmett said.

"Your guns will not be enough," Kenny warned. "The Maya are fierce warriors and not afraid of death. They will willingly die to protect the priests."

"We can't just let them kill her!" Emmett said.

"We'll find a way," John said.

"Let's do it," Rosa said.

With Emmett in the lead, calculator in hand, he led them back into the pyramid. Nick watched them go reluctantly. He didn't like making a decision without fully understanding the situation. Their team had just been cut in half and separated, and he didn't fully understand why.

Now Kenny came toward Nick. He walked with effort, but without a cane. His hair and beard were gray, his eyes baggy, his face a competition of wrinkles.

"We need to talk," Kenny said, looping his arm around Nick's. "Let's have a cup of cocoa."

60 · FUTURES

Within the multiverse there are endless alternate realities in which, supposedly, a huge army of mutant copies of everyone on this and other planets plays out an almost limitless variety of dramas. According to this worldview, each time we make the smallest decision the entire assemblage divides along different evolutionary paths like some vast ant colony splitting off in divergent directions.

—*Julian Brown,* Minds, Machines, and the Multiverse

YUCATAN PENINSULA
POST CONQUEST

'm three hundred and forty two," Kenny said, sitting in a rocker.

Too many surprises in the last few weeks left Nick numb. Nick and Kenny were alone in Kenny's stone house. The others were being entertained in another building so Kenny could talk with Nick. Candles with polished copper reflectors lighted the room. There was a table, three chairs, and wall to ceiling shelves filled with manuscripts. A magnifying glass lay on the table.

"It's the pyramid, isn't it?" Nick said.

"Yes. It stretched out my life, but now it only stretches out my agony. Every one of my joints aches. It takes me ten minutes to pee. I throw up half of what I eat. I am ready to die. Past ready."

"Then why do you keep going?"

"I've been waiting for you," Kenny said. "There are decisions to be made about the future and I won't make them. That is your job."

"I don't know what you are talking about," Nick said.

"I doubt that is true."

They each held a ceramic mug of hot cocoa. The urgency with which the old man had sought out Emmett had passed; now Kenny was relaxed.

"Will Emmett save Carrollee?" Nick asked.

Kenny's face darkened, the corners of his mouth sagging.

"That's the test," Kenny said. "I was there when it happened. They held her across the altar and cut her heart out. Then they smeared their bodies with her blood and threw her body off the pyramid. The priests dismembered her, skinned her, and ate her flesh. She died a horrible death and I couldn't do anything about it. At least until now."

"But if Emmett and the others save her, then you should remember it that way," Nick said, puzzled.

"Should I?"

Nick thought about how little they knew about time-space phenomena. While he wanted to think of time as a unified thing, there were theorists who believed that different time-lines could coexist. Carrollee could be saved in one timeline, but die in another.

"You called it a test," Nick said. "But if they save her and your memories change, you won't know that there had ever been any other outcome."

"True. It's a unidirectional test. If they save her and I don't remember it, then that tells us something very important."

"Do you have any memory of Emmett and the others being there?"

"No, but they would not have time to arrive yet. The time elapsed in our present corresponds with the time elapsed in the past. The pyramids are crude devices at best, and I could not tune them to do more than open windows. Once this window is closed, we cannot send anyone back until the next window, which will not occur until after it is too late."

"Too late?" Nick probed.

"Until civilization ends."

"When does that happen?"

"We have two days to choose our future."

"But we are several hundred years in the past."

"We have two days in this window that is connected to your present. It's still two days."

Nick understood. The combination of the time waves and the drain of orgonic energy had created a tunnel through space and time with outlets in the pyramids. Kenny had manipulated these in some way.

"What happens in two days?" Nick asked.

"That depends on you," Kenny said, sipping his cocoa. "I have done what I can to delay the effect, but in two days the time waves will collide on the moon. I'm afraid the result will be catastrophic."

"More time quilting?"

"Much worse," Kenny said. "Do you remember the story of the Dutch physicist, Christian Huygens and his clocks?"

"Vaguely. He invented the pendulum clock."

"Very good. Once, he fell ill and was confined to his bed for several days. With little to do, he eventually noticed that the pendulums of the two clocks in his bedroom oscillated together. These clocks were heavy things, close to one hundred pounds each. When he moved them to opposite ends of the room, the clocks no longer synchronized the swing of their pendulums. Huygens began to experiment. First, he eliminated the possibility that air vibrations were synchronizing the motions. Next, he mounted the clocks on a plank and rested the plank on the top of two chairs. Just like on his wall, the pendulums swung together—one would tick as the other tocked. Perfect sympathy. That's what our universe is under normal conditions.

"Then Huygens did something that shocked even him. Huygens put the pendulums in opposite motions. Now the chairs began to shake and rattle, bouncing around, and the boards almost rattled off the backs of the chairs. Eventually, the clocks reestablished synchrony and settled down."

"The vibrations from the clocks were transmitted through the boards—or the wall—influencing both pendulums," Nick said.

"Correct. Each clock acted to keep the other clock in synchrony. When that synchrony was disrupted by Huygens, the result was violent."

"The time quilting was certainly destructive," Nick said.

"From our perspective, yes," but that disruption was mitigated by the orgonic energy in the system, which worked to minimize asynchrony. We've been draining the orgonic energy."

"Surely one or two pyramids can't affect the universe so drastically."

"It isn't drastic as far as the larger universe is concerned, just a local, insignificant blip. However, from our perspective, the effect is going to be catastrophic. The asynchrony will shred the timeline, scrambling past and future, eliminating the possibility that civilization as we know it can exist."

"I've come face-to-face with the impossible so many times it would be foolish not to believe you," Nick said, "but I can't help being skeptical."

Kenny got up from his rocker slowly, walking to the shelves, opening a small wooden box and taking out a pair of glasses. Perching them on his nose, he selected a thick manuscript. He motioned Nick close and then unfolded it. It was filled with equations.

"Let's begin here," Kenny said.

For the next two hours Kenny walked Nick through his calculations. Nick spent three more hours doing his own calculations while Kenny napped. A young woman with brown skin and blue eyes brought lunch—tortillas, bananas, and meat he could not identify. Nick ate little. By mid-afternoon he conceded he couldn't find any obvious flaw, but he would need a year, a team of mathematicians, and a supercomputer to be sure.

"There is little time," Kenny reminded him.

"Can we stop it?" Nick asked.

"Yes, if that is the choice we make. But if we do we must choose which future we want to live in."

"Meaning what?

"We live in a multiverse and the time-space hole we have opened allows us to glimpse our possible futures. Before our choice is made, you must see the possibilities."

Only Nick was to see the futures, leaving the others to rest and relax in the village. The villagers were curious, cordial, and hospitable. Nick noticed there were more buildings than people, and many buildings were in disrepair or abandoned. The wall around the pyramid was also in need of repair, and sections were overgrown. On the far side of the compound, invading roots had broken out large sections of stone. Guards accompanied them into the compound, young men painted black, wearing loincloths and bead-and-feather necklaces. Many had body tattoos.

Kenny stopped by the stone building with the electronic equipment, taking a calculator from the same spot he took the one he gave to Emmett.

"That's not the same calculator, is it?" Kenny asked.

"If it is, then we know that Emmett made it somewhere back in time."

"But you still don't remember him or John? Rosa?"

"I still remember Carrollee dying," Kenny said sadly.

Kenny pulled out a rifle hidden behind the computer equipment and then directed Nick to bring the PLSS suits. They were heavy and Nick dragged them to the pyramid. The guards took positions by the smaller stone buildings.

"The first passage will be the most difficult," Kenny explained. "We will visit this future first when I am strongest. Wait here."

Kenny entered the pyramid by himself. While he waited, Nick noticed writing chiseled into the stone by the entrance. He had seen enough copies of Zorastrus's prophecies to recognize the characters. Twenty minutes later Kenny was back.

"All is ready," he said cryptically.

"Where did this come from?" Nick asked, indicating the writing.

"It's a message and clue. I wrote it in Akkadian to draw attention to the pyramid and to Zorastrus's prophecies."

"Won't this alter the future?"

"Apparently not," Kenny said. "The message isn't discovered because this pyramid is not discovered until I find it and then your people. Outside this valley the conquistadors have conquered most of the Mayan empire. I knew what was coming and began preparing. I isolated this village to protect it and the pyramid. Apparently I was too successful. The village and the pyramid were forgotten and lost. The message is not discovered in time."

With Nick dragging the suits, and Kenny carrying the rifle, Kenny led the way into the pyramid. Using a candle lamp, the old man's pace was about as much as Nick could manage with the suits. Nick found the grades difficult, sweating up and down. Finally, they reached the central chamber that Nick remembered. There was the table and the stereoscope.

"Wait here," Kenny said, leaving the rifle.

Again he disappeared for twenty minutes.

"Now we must have the suits," Kenny said.

Kenny began to put the suit on, showing some familiarity with how it was done. Without the sensor-laden underwear, most of the physiological displays were useless. When Nick lifted the pack onto Kenny's back, the old man sagged.

"Are you sure you can do this?" Nick asked, genuinely concerned.

"It will be my last trip. I will make it."

They helped each other seal their suits. Surprisingly, the suit's batteries were charged, and the indicators lit up showing the air supply half full, cooling and scrubbing functions working. Soon, Nick felt the temperature dropping.

"You took these on the moon," Nick said, testing the radio.

"Many years ago. I knew you would not use them again."

Leaving the rifle, Kenny led the way, calculator in hand. A short distance later, Kenny suddenly turned around, pushing Nick down a side corridor.

"Turn off your light. Something's coming," Kenny said.

In the suits, Nick could not hear anything but felt the vibrations of something large passing.

"The dinosaurs are attracted to the pyramid," Kenny explained.

After that, they came to a sliding panel.

"Push that panel in," Kenny ordered.

As soon as he did, he felt dizzy. They started off again, stopping at a junction. Three panels hung over the connecting passages.

"Push these two up," Kenny said.

Nick did as he was told, and now felt he was being pushed from behind.

"What is that force?" Nick asked.

"Wind," Kenny said.

Two corridors later, Kenny had Nick adjust two more panels. A few steps later and the gravity shifted. After adjusting two more panels, they exited the pyramid on the moon—but not the moon Nick had left a short time ago.

The containment structure had failed, part of the building exploding outward, leaving a large gap in the wall. Portions of the rest of the ceiling had collapsed on the pyramid, rubble sliding down to the bottom. Looking through the gap, Nick could see wispy clouds against a blue-black sky.

"The moon has atmosphere," Nick said, amazed.

"Yes, it came through the pyramid from Earth."

"It's what we feared," Nick said. "How much came through?"

"It never really stopped, although once the pressure difference was reduced, the hurricane force winds diminished to what you felt."

"But the moon has too little mass."

"Yes, it cannot hold the atmosphere. It continues to dissipate into space."

"What about Earth?"

"We will see," Kenny said.

Kenny picked a path through the rubble, and then led Nick out through the break in the wall. The scene was bizarre. The pockmarked surface of the moon was gone, now covered with gray lichen. The atmosphere was so thin the stars could be seen even though it was daylight. When Nick turned toward the sun it was so bright, two sun shields slid into place.

"Over here," Kenny said, pointing.

Following the point, Nick could see the Earth, even

through wispy clouds. The Earth had sharp contrasts of blue and brown, with little green.

"It doesn't look right," Nick said.

"The Earth's atmosphere is depleted. Surface pressure is ten millibars. Just a little above Mars."

"Nothing could live in that," Nick said.

"Cockroaches," Kenny said.

"Why didn't they stop it?" Nick asked, looking up at the planet. "Hit it with a nuclear bomb. They've used that solution before."

"You'll understand soon," Kenny said.

Nick wanted to explore the new moon. It was horrifying and fascinating at the same time, but Kenny moved back through the rubble to the pyramid. He left Nick at the entrance and entered by himself again. Nick understood that the secret to determining where and when you came out in time depended on the adjustments that Kenny made. When he came back he had the rifle.

They repeated their wanderings through the pyramid, Kenny consulting his calculator as they went. Along the journey, Kenny felt the gravitational change that indicated they were back on Earth. Kenny did not stop to remove their PLSS suits. When they reached the outlet of the pyramid, Kenny understood why.

The sun was so intense, the screen slid into place again. Nick assumed they were back in the Yucatan Peninsula but there was little resemblance to the Yucatan he had left. The two stone huts in front of the pyramid were virtually unidentifiable, with no more than two stones remaining stacked on one another. The landscape beyond was a junk heap of human history. Nick recognized the desiccated carcass of a triceratops next to part of a burned 767. Next to that was a section of cemetery, then a large open space that connected to a patch of dead redwood trees. None of these patches of human history were larger than a suburban neighborhood lot. Following Kenny, Nick wandered through the jumble, finding a chariot, Model A Ford, and dugout canoe, all within the length of a football field of one another. There were large tracks of dead jungle and leafless trees suddenly interrupted by concrete, portions of buildings, and in one heart-wrenching scene, a swing set.

"There are bodies if you want to see them," Kenny said, pointing to a three-story apartment building in the distance.

"No. I think I understand."

"The scrambling of our history destroyed civilization. People of all eras, all cultures, all languages, were suddenly mixed. There were floods, of course—the planet is two-thirds water—fires, and airplane crashes. Parents watching their children at play in the yard saw them disappear right before their eyes."

"Or did the parents disappear? How do you know this is the future and not the past?"

"The pyramid is our anchor, an island in the time stream."

Nick looked back at the stone structure that was weathered but relatively unchanged. Looking at the simple structure it was hard to remember that by itself it had only the smallest power, but connected to the high-tech version built in Alaska and powered by the confluence of time waves created by the nuclear age, it was one end of a time-space tunnel.

"Is there no one left?" Nick asked.

"The atmosphere can't support higher life-forms. There may be life in the oceans yet, but eventually it will die, too. If you travel east for a few miles there are the remains of a village. I learned there, that after the disaster civilization broke down. Few civil authorities survived and those that did ended up fighting civil wars. Several regional nuclear wars finished off what little was left of the technological age. By then the structure on the moon ruptured and the atmosphere drain began. Because this pyramid was so remote it was little more than a rumor. There was a permanent hurricane around the site and no one could venture near. Temperatures rose, radiation levels crept up, disease and starvation swept the planet. I couldn't find any evidence that anyone on Earth ever figured out what the problem was and where."

"But you could stop this," Nick said. "You could leave a message in the past. Warn us in the future of what is coming."

"Zorastrus did try to warn us, but over the centuries his

writings were lost or corrupted. By the time we understood, it was too late."

"You could leave it in English," Nick said.

"An ancient message in modern English? It would be dismissed as a fraud. Besides, you're forgetting that we already know that I didn't leave such a message."

Nick's mind reeled, trying to understand the implications of time travel.

"So if Emmett saves Carrollee, and your memories change, then you can change the future, but we won't know it because we won't have this conversation."

"Exactly. But because we are here, the future has not changed, and we are having this conversation, then we can conclude—"

"That we can't do anything to save the planet."

"Not in this future," Kenny said. "Come with me."

"Back over the rainbow?"

"It gets stranger."

They continued to wear their PLSS suits even though they no longer needed them except for cooling. They exited the pyramid to find the buildings out front intact—Kenny checked and the calculator was on the stone shelf—and in his hand. There was a village outside the fence, but no gate. There were people in the village, but unlike Kenny's village, which was peopled by Mayans with brown skin and dark eyes, this was a rainbow village with people of different shades of skin color and hair, including blond and red. Kenny held Nick back, keeping out of sight, watching the village from inside the wall. After a few minutes, a triceratops came into view. It was wearing a harness and pulling a train of carts with large wooden wheels.

"Domesticated dinosaurs?" Nick exclaimed, his voice broadcast to Kenny's suit.

"Yes. They use them like horses and cows. They farm this land and at the seacoast there's a thriving trading economy. They ship cocoa, bananas, maize, mahogany logs, and cotton. They mostly import metal goods—plows, pots, utensils, knives, axes, and jewelry. The cargo ships are all sailing ships and not windjammers either, simply coastal trawlers. There is no sign of anything more sophisticated than a compass."

"When is this? Why is there atmosphere?"

"It's the future but somehow the destruction of the atmosphere is avoided," Kenny said. "But not the time disruption. Look over here."

Kenny led Nick along the wall to an overgrown mound.

"Dig in there," Kenny said.

Nick did as he was told, tearing out vines and uncovering a rusty mound. He recognized the engine from the 767.

"So if the atmosphere can be saved, then civilization begins again."

"Yes, but there is a price. The reason I didn't want them to see us is because of our suits. They abhor technology and destroy it when they find it. As near as I can tell, this is nearly a millennium after the disaster and there hasn't been any progress, even in medicine. They live like the Amish, locked in one time."

"Surely they can't maintain the status quo. If not among these people, somewhere on the planet civilization must be advancing."

"I can't know for sure but there are no radio or television broadcasts, no shortwave radio, no orbiting satellites, no engines, not even steam."

"I still can't believe they can sustain it."

"I disagree. They practice population control through infanticide in order to keep the number of mouths to feed at or below agricultural production. Old people aren't revered, they are euthanized. On rare occasions they will practice warfare to reduce the population by wiping out a neighboring village. They've created a stable system with checks and balances. Only another catastrophe could break them out of their equilibrium. It may be different somewhere else on the planet, but a thousand years is long enough for a culture to develop technology and spread it."

"Eden always comes at a price," Nick said, disappointed.

"Let's get back before we get discovered," Kenny said.

This time they left the PLSS suits in the central chamber but kept the rifle. Kenny had Nick carry it. Kenny was a lot spryer without the suit weight and now moved like a younger man—a two hundred-year-old. Again, they emerged from the stone pyramid. This time there was no sign of the village.

"Careful," Kenny said. "I've never found any sign of people in this age, but plenty of dinosaurs."

The pyramid was surrounded by a Yucatan that must have existed before humans ever set foot there. The trees touched the sky, vines draped limbs, monkeys and birds populated the canopy. The forest had reclaimed much of the pyramid, creepers slithering to the top, small trees rooted in its sides. The pyramid would be virtually invisible to anyone a hundred yards away. The stone fence surrounding the pyramid was distinguishable only as a linear mound visible here and there.

Kenny led the way through waist-high growth, scattering blue butterflies from his path. It was warm, over eighty, and insects began tasting Nick's exposed legs. There was a depression where the opening to the village had once been. They passed through to find a meadow where the village had stood. At the far end, a herd of stegosaurs grazed, indifferent to Kenny and Nick.

"How far have you traveled in this age?" Nick asked.

"As far as the coast. It took me weeks. It is wild, like no place I've ever been. The coastal cities are gone; nothing left but artifacts and remnants of piers. No radio signals, no television, and no satellites. Just like before, but without people."

"But how could this happen? Why don't people survive in this future?"

"I visited several times before I thought to check the radiation levels—don't worry, they are safe now. There was a nuclear war in this timeline."

"But there was in the last timeline, too," Nick said.

"What happened in this timeline was a full ballistic exchange. The remnants of humanity either died of radiation poisoning or fed the growing population of superpredators. Mammals were decimated, but many survived."

"But that would mean that the nuclear exchange would have had to take place before history is scrambled. There wouldn't have been enough coordination left to launch more than regional strikes afterward."

"That is what I concluded. Irradiated pieces of this time period were sprinkled through history, poisoning everyone, killing off whole family trees until there were too few human lines to support human culture."

Nick thought back to what was happening in the world when he left. The Israelis and Palestinians were fighting over a thirty-kilometer hole in their security wall. Israel was insisting on encompassing all of the time quilt section and the Palestinians wanted the same. That conflict had set off another round of terrorism, Muslim fundamentalists using homicide bombers to attack Western interests around the world, including two attacks in the U.S. Nick also knew the Russians were supposedly currying favor with the oil-rich Arab countries, by offering to supply them with nuclear weapons. Then he remembered Elizabeth's letter about the Russian nuclear weapons in Alaska.

"Oh no," Nick said suddenly. "I might have triggered the war."

Nick explained what he had done, while Kenny listened attentively.

"Governments can be sensitive about foreign military and nuclear weapons on their soil," Kenny said. "However, it is just as likely that one of my actions triggered the war in this timeline."

"What do you mean?"

"You are not the first people to emerge from the pyramid," Kenny said. "You know about Carrollee and Nikki, but there was another group. They came like you did, following army ants."

"Elizabeth? Was Elizabeth Hawthorne with them?"

"I remember Elizabeth well. I remember all of them."

"What happened to them?"

"I sent them to change the future, but they failed."

"What do you mean?"

Kenny frowned, then turned back toward the pyramid. "You must see the last future first. Then I will explain." Kenny stopped Nick at the entrance. "This may be the most dangerous of the futures, Nick," Kenny said. "Because it is the future we lived the least."

Kenny didn't explain his cryptic comment, leading Nick through the pyramids again. This time there was no gravity change. After winding through, and adjusting panels, they came to the central chamber, which had changed. There was equipment like Kenny had never seen before, including three softly glowing flat panels lying on a table, and what Nick guessed was a central control unit. Its display was blank and there were no wires connecting the panels. Kenny paused, letting Nick look closer. There was no power cord.

"Watch this," Kenny said, and then said "Display."

Three holographic images appeared over the panels. Two were graphs, the axes labeled in units Nick could not identify. The third was a three-dimensional model of the pyramid they were in. Now for the first time Nick could see the interior passages. The pyramid was structured like a pyramid inside a pyramid inside a pyramid inside a pyramid. Nick studied the passages.

"These don't seem right."

"Very good," Kenny said. "It took me many passages before I noticed. Now follow me and you'll understand why it is different."

As they approached the exit of the pyramid, Kenny pulled him down a side passage and then reached above one of the retractable panels and pulled out two jumpsuits.

"Put this on," Kenny said.

The suits were blue with plastic strips where the zipper should be. Nick studied the strips, puzzled.

"Like this," Kenny said, touching the strips together, and running his thumb up the length.

Now Kenny led Nick back to the exit, peeking outside. Nick leaned out next to him. The pyramid was sitting in the open on what looked like rubberized asphalt. A sphere of about the same mass as the pyramid sat a hundred yards away. Three low buildings sat to one side. The sun hung low over the buildings. Behind the buildings were low hills, covered with sagebrush.

"This isn't Alaska and it sure isn't the moon."

"It's Idaho. A private research facility near Twin Falls."

"How far in the future?"

"One hundred and eighty years. But this future has a different past than ours. There was no time quilt in this timeline. The modern and Cretaceous periods never collided. We didn't lose New York, Atlanta, Portland, and all those other cities. Those millions of people lived out their lives."

"But how is that possible?"

"You asked me about Elizabeth and the others. I sent them to try and stop the catastrophic time quilting. Ten years after they left, I discovered that the routes to the future and past had changed and a new future was opened to me—this future. I did nothing to open this passage and yet it appeared."

Nick looked around the compound. There were no wires connecting the buildings. The windows were seamless with the walls, the roofs domed and copper colored. There were no vehicles.

"You said this was a research facility. Do you think they created this pyramid and used it to alter their timeline?"

"I believe so, but there is no record of it."

"But there wouldn't be if they succeeded."

"That is the most likely outcome. However, anyone in the pyramid at the time of the alteration might retain a memory of the previous timeline."

"You still remember Carrollee dying, don't you?"

"Yes. It's possible I left that timeline before Emmett arrived, but if he took that long I'm afraid he was too late. Besides, I have no memory of Emmett arriving at all. A predator might have gotten him in the pyramid, or he might have lost his way. There is no way to know."

"Do you know the history of this world? How did they avoid the time quilt?"

"Their past and ours are the same until 1952 when there

was a nuclear accident. Our first hydrogen weapon destroyed San Diego. It was a horrific tragedy. That tragedy built on the residual horror of Hiroshima and Nagasaki. The U.S. shut down its fusion-bomb program for two decades so there were no secrets to leak to the Soviet Union. There were still fission weapons of course, but the world never subscribed to the defense madness of mutually assured destruction. When the economic gulf between east and west began to widen, the Soviet Union responded by decentralizing production planning rather than arming client states and building walls along its borders. Communism died a decade earlier in this timeline and because there were very few tests of fusion weapons, the planet never suffered the time quilt."

Nick looked at the low buildings in the distance, longing to explore them, to see the technological marvels that must be inside. This world seemed like a paradise to Nick.

"You said this timeline appeared? Are you sure you just hadn't discovered it?"

"I've had centuries to map the passages. I did not miss it."

"Did Elizabeth or the others do something to create this timeline?"

"I don't believe so. There would be no way for them to reach 1952."

"Then whoever built this pyramid, must have effected the change."

"Yes," Kenny said. "However, there is currently no passage to that era. Also, there is no record in this facility's computers of such a passage or such a plan to go into the past. As far as these researchers are concerned, this is a low priority project exploring the relationship of mass, form, and orgonic energy."

"Without the disruption of time-space caused by the micro black holes at the center of fusion detonations, the fabric of time-space wasn't weakened," Nick said.

"Exactly. In this future they are unaware of what has happened in our timeline so they don't know the potential of this pyramid to give passage through time-space. I believe that in their original timeline they suffered like we did, but found the resources to build a pyramid with enough power to punch through to 1952 and change their future. Whether it was government or private enterprise, someone made the decision to alter their future. They paid for this future with the lives of a million people."

"San Diego?"

"After the accident, two congressional committees concluded it was an accident. Three decades later, declassified military documents revealed that the bomb code named "Mike" wasn't armed when it passed through San Diego."

"Someone from this future detonated the bomb?"

"No. Someone from this future took a fusion weapon to the past, got it close to Mike, and detonated it. If you dig into the report, you find that the military investigators discovered that the yield far exceeded predictions."

"They murdered a million people to create a new future," Nick said, shocked.

"They spent those lives to save many more."

"To save their own lives," Nick said, disgusted.

"That, too. But unless someone was in transit at the time, no one in this timeline will have to live with the knowledge that their happiness is built on the graves of a million innocent Americans."

"I couldn't live with that."

Now Kenny stepped out of the pyramid, looking at the sky. It was clear, blue, no clouds in sight.

"It's safe," Kenny said. "This facility is little used."

"Nick stepped out on the strange surface. It was firm but porous. Nick knelt, touching the black material. It was warmer than the air temperature."

"It absorbs orgonic energy and feeds it back into the pyramid," Kenny said.

"I'd love to have a sample."

"You can have more than that, Nick. You said a minute ago that you couldn't live with the knowledge that this future was purchased with human life. But all futures are purchased at that price. It was either the residents of San Diego or the residents of New York and Portland."

"We don't know what happened to those people," Nick said. "Or do you?"

"Not exactly. But they will appear in different timelines at different points in history. Most will survive the transit."

"The people in those cities were lost by accident, not design."

"But both were the result of human action. Is it really less moral to think through the consequences and make an informed decision than to stumble uncontrollably into disaster?"

"It's a matter of conscience," Nick said. "If I shoot at a deer and accidentally kill a man, I can reconcile the conflict between my actions and my belief that murder is wrong. If I deliberately shoot an innocent man, there is no moral reconciliation."

Kenny pointed up to the sky. There was nothing there.

"I wish you could see the moon. It has no atmosphere of course. Flamsteed Crater is just a crater, but there is a base on the moon, and on Mars. There are six Mars transport vehicles in constant transit from Earth to Mars, flying in an endless loop. There are plans to build a ship to fly to another star and thousands of people have volunteered to go even though they know it will be their children who actually visit the system they will travel to. They have mastered nuclear fusion for power generation. Cancer is controllable. World populations have stabilized and food production exceeds demand. There are border skirmishes here and there, but there hasn't been a major conflict in five decades. It's a paradise, Nick."

"Have they cured the common cold?"

"No, but it's still a better future than the one coming at you, Nick. You could come here, and bring your people with you. They would be welcome here. They could have happy fulfilled lives."

"But aren't we here already?"

"Not all of you. You're not here. Emmett is not here."

"We died?" Nick asked, uncomfortable hearing of his own death.

"You just disappeared," Kenny said. "There are newspaper reports about you and Emmett. You simply don't show up for work one day."

"That makes no sense," Nick said.

Now Kenny frowned, his textured face seemed to age as he spoke.

"Someone had to take the bomb in to the past," Kenny said.

Nick literally staggered as it sank in.

"No. It's not possible. I couldn't do it! I wouldn't do it."

"To save billions, you might. But you never came back, Nick. Emmett either."

"Why tell me this? If you want me to live here, then why tell me?"

"You would find out sooner or later. Would you come to this future and then not try to find yourself? You needed to know now, before you make your decision about which future to live with."

"I won't come here. The others can, but I won't."

"There are costs for the other futures, too," Kenny said.

"They can't be as terrible as this," Nick said.

"Can't they?" Kenny said. "Time to get back and choose your future."

61 ▪ DEMON

Casa de Montejo, built in 1549 by one of Cortés' soldiers who founded the city, Francisco de Montejo. . . . on its fortress-like walls are busts of family and carvings of armed warriors standing on the heads of vanquished demons.

—*Huw Hennessy,* Guatemala, Belize, and the Yucatan

YUCATAN PENINSULA
PRE-COLUMBIAN

With Emmett in the lead, they hurried through the pyramid they had just left. At one point, Emmett paused, listening. John heard it, too—something was moving through the pyramid. Emmett was an automaton, intently focused on the calculator, rarely hesitating at junctions, moving confidently. Up and down, around and around they went, and then there was a glow. They emerged from the pyramid, but the thick vegetation was gone, the ground nothing but grasses and ferns clear to a surrounding wall. A crowd of people filled the space along one side of the pyramid; others sat on the compound wall. The men wore breechcloths, the women skirts and blouses. Most wore hats or feathers in their hair. Emmett paused only long enough to go into one of the stone buildings and leave the calculator as Kenny Randall insisted.

Now marching forcefully up to the back of the crowd, he fired his rifle into the air. Women and children screamed, and cowered in fright. Recklessly, Emmett walked into the parting crowd. John and Rosa followed, rifles ready. Immediately, warriors with wooden swords confronted them. Again, Emmett fired his gun. The men cringed, giving way reluctantly.

The crowd continued to part, staring in shock at the strangers. When they reached the bottom of the stairs leading to the top, men wearing elaborate headdresses confronted them. Emmett stopped, looking up the pyramid. A naked body lay across a stone table.

"Carrollee?" Emmett screamed. "Carrollee?"

Now the men blocking their way began to speak, forcefully, demanding something. Emmett lifted the rifle and fired again. The crowd shrank back, but the warriors around them merely cringed.

"They're beginning to think it's a noisemaker," John said.

Emmett aimed the rifle at the chest of the man blocking his way.

"Don't shoot a priest," Rosa said.

"Then who?" Emmett demanded. "I can see Carrollee up there."

Carrollee hadn't moved since they had arrived.

"Shoot a warrior," John suggested.

"No, a woman," Rosa said. "A woman would have less value."

The warriors were getting their courage back, inching forward.

"We have to do something," Rosa said. "If they rush us we're done for."

John looked around, noticing a young man cowering behind the priest. He wore a ragged loincloth and carried a large gourd. John pointed at him, the man's eyes going wide, dropping the gourd, and spilling water.

"Him," John said coldly. "He's a slave."

Emmett did not hesitate and shot the man in the chest. After the initial shock of the rifle report, the priest looked at the dead man, surprised. When Emmett aimed the rifle at him, he stepped aside. When they started up the steps, six warriors with spears and body armor, converged on the stairs. A thousand people were gathered below, spread out along the edge of the pyramid, engrossed in the drama. More warriors gathered at the bottom of the steps, trapping them between two forces.

Emmett marched toward the warriors on the stairs, who stood ready with wooden swords. Then there was shouting from above, one of the priests giving orders. The warriors parted, letting them through. With Emmett in the lead, John and Rosa backed up the rest of the pyramid steps.

"Carrollee?" Emmett shouted, as they neared the top.

The priests on top looked from Emmett to the still form of his wife, puzzled. Emmett rushed to Carrollee, putting his weapon down. She was lying naked across a stone slab, her arms above her head. Her chest was bloody. Crying, Emmett wrapped his arms around her, pulling her close, smearing the blood on his shirt. The priests watched, curious.

"She's alive," Emmett said, relieved. "She's alive."

Carrollee woke in Emmett's arms.

"Em?" she said, and then she pushed away, pressing a hand to the wound on her chest. "They were going to cut my heart out, Em."

"Which sonofabitch cut you?" Emmett asked, murder in his eyes.

"No, Em. Let's just go."

Conscious of her nakedness, Carrollee folded her arms across her chest, now looking at Emmett's shirt.

"Em, what are you wearing?" Carrollee asked, seeing the half-naked women and demonic symbols on his T-shirt.

Emmett started to pull off his shirt.

"Take mine," John said, unbuttoning his long sleeve shirt.

John knew his shirt would cover more of Carrollee's body. While Rosa held her gun on the priests, John took off his shirt and then stepped next to Rosa while Emmett helped Carrollee put it on. The priests looked puzzled by the whole procedure, but didn't move to interfere.

"Now what?" Rosa asked.

"Now we get out of here," John said.

Emmett helped Carrollee walk up next to them. Her hand now pressed John's shirt to her chest. John waved his gun, indicating the priests to move away. They did not move.

"Shoot one of the bastards!" Emmett said, but held his own fire.

Sensing danger, warriors came running up the stairs.

"This could get bloody," John said. "Anyone see any choices?"

"Call for Kenny!" Carrollee said.

"What?" Emmett said. "Kenny Randall is here?"

"Call for him!" Carrollee insisted.

Emmett shouted down at the crowd below, calling Kenny's name. He shouted several times before there was motion at the edge of the crowd, a man passing through. He was dressed like the Maya, although slightly lighter in skin color. When he got to the base of the pyramid the warriors stopped him until the priest at the top called down permission. Kenny came up the stairs reluctantly. When he saw Carrollee dressed in John's shirt, he came faster.

"Carrollee, you're alive," Kenny said.

She took her hand from her chest, revealing a bloody patch.

"Just barely," she said.

"We're trying to leave, Kenny, but they won't let us," Carrollee said. "We don't want to have to shoot our way out."

"I don't think that would work," Kenny said, looking at Emmett, John, and Rosa, but not asking the obvious. "For them a violent death is the quickest way into heaven."

John studied Kenny Randall. He was the same man who had sent them to rescue Carrollee, but much younger.

"Let's take a couple of the priests hostage," John suggested.

"I wouldn't touch the Ah Kin Mai," Kenny said. "It would be like spitting on the pope."

"Then the others," John said.

"The Chacs? They aren't that revered and the other priests would gladly give up their lives."

"They were afraid of this," Carrollee said, holding up a claw necklace hanging around her neck.

"Where did you get that?" Emmett asked.

Carrollee ignored her husband as Kenny came over to look at it.

"It might work," Kenny said.

Now he lifted the cord over her head, holding it out toward the priest, speaking rapidly. They listened intently. Then the head priest exchanged words with the others. The discussion was animated and intense. Now the priests shouted orders down the pyramid and a wooden bowl and a piece of paper were brought up.

"What's your name?" Carrollee asked, turning to Rosa.

"Rosa."

"You may not want to watch this," Carrollee said as the Ah Kin Mai loosened his loincloth.

Carrollee turned her head, but Rosa could not, mesmerized by the bizarre divination. John squirmed through the procedure.

"That's something I wish I'd never seen," John said.

"Well, we know one thing for sure," Rosa said.

"What's that?" John asked.

"They're not Jews."

John fought to keep from laughing.

The head priest was examining the bloody paper now, talking with the others. Now he turned back to Kenny and they exchanged words.

"They're going for it," Kenny said.

"For what?" Emmett demanded.

"They'll exchange the heart of a demon for Carrollee's. They considered it a more attractive sacrifice."

"Where are we supposed to get a demon?" John asked.

"A juvenile tyrannosaur followed Carrollee out of the pyramid," Kenny said. "It's been spotted since then, coming and going from the pyramid."

John and Rosa looked at each other. They had managed to kill a partially blinded tyrannosaur hindered by a narrow corridor and a low ceiling. Could they do it again?

"My claw is from a small velociraptor," Carrollee said, "not a tyrannosaur."

"Either will do."

"We know where there's a dead tyrannosaur, maybe we can find our way back and get the heart," John said.

"It has to be beating when they pull it from the body," Kenny said. "You need to bring the animal to them alive."

"Are you nuts?" John said, shaking his head in disbelief.

"We have to," Emmett said. "For Carrollee."

"No," Carrollee said. "One person already died for me, I don't want anyone else to die."

Rosa stepped to Carrollee's side, putting her arm around her shoulders.

"Don't worry about us. John and I have experience hunting dinosaurs."

Carrollee looked them over doubtfully. John was shirtless, Rosa wearing shortalls and deck shoes.

"Really, no problem," John said, trying to convince her.

"Promise me you'll come back alive?" Carrollee said.

"Damn right," John said, "You've got my shirt."

Carrollee tried to hug John, but winced when she tried to spread her arms, then pressed a hand to her chest again. Reluctantly, Emmett agreed to stay with Carrollee, keeping his weapon in case John and Rosa failed. Then they talked about weapons, worrying that John's dinosaur gun would be too powerful to bring one back alive. He ended up switching with Emmett. The priests allowed Carrollee to return to her hut where Nikki greeted John with a tight hug. Rosa was distant, until it became clear Nikki and Kenny were a couple.

John asked for bait, and the locals provided them with two monkeys, crushing their skulls and then slitting their throats so that the blood dribbled from the bodies. Each with a flashlight, dragging monkey carcasses, Rosa and John reentered the pyramid.

Using the blood like chum, they carried balls of twine, unwinding it as they went, marking their way through the pyramid. Once they had laid a blood trail deep into the pyramid, they backtracked. If they kept going, they ran the risk of laying a blood trail to the moon or back where they came from.

When they were done, there was blood on Rosa's legs and John's trousers, making them part of the bait. Squatting, ready to run, they turned off their lights and waited. They waited for hours. Their legs cramped and they took turns sitting. They rubbed each other's numb limbs. They sang whispered songs. They thumb-wrestled. They dragged the carcasses through the corridors again. They took turns sleeping. They talked.

"John, how could you just pick out some guy to die?" Rosa asked.

It was an honest question, not a judgment.

"It was reflexive. I knew someone was going to die, probably a lot of people. Emmett was ready to kill everyone between him and the top of that pyramid. Once he started shooting we would, too, and innocents would die. It was a cold-blooded choice, but only one man has died and maybe only one will have to. But don't think it's been easy on my conscience. I'll always remember the look on that slave's face when I pointed him out."

Now she came up behind John and leaned against him, slipping her free arm around his waist, her rifle in her other.

"It took courage to do what you did," Rosa whispered.

They stood together like that for a while. Then they sat. Then they held hands. Then they made out. It was during the kissing that they heard the thud of an approaching bipedal dinosaur.

"Now the damn dinosaur comes?" John said, breaking from a deep kiss.

"It's bigger than a raptor," Rosa said.

John covered the lens of his flashlight and turned it on, gradually uncovering the lens until they could see. The tyrannosaur was coming with its head low, sniffing and licking the floor. Barely fitting into the corridor, it was bigger than the first one they had killed. With the olfactory sensitivity of a shark, it came on, tongue flicking in and out, tasting monkey blood.

Covering the lens again, they backed away, feeling the twine, leaving the monkey carcasses. They hid at the next junction where John let out enough light to see again. The tyrannosaur reached the carcasses, sniffed the first, and then delicately bit into it. Satisfied by the taste, it bit the carcass in half, then ate both halves in two gulps. It finished the second carcass just as quickly.

"Now comes the fun part," Rosa said.

"Ready?" John asked.

"Ready."

They turned their lights on, pointing them at each other. Immediately, the tyrannosaur saw them glowing in the corridor, cocking its head sideways, studying the unexpected apparitions. It didn't attack.

"I guess we better move," Rosa said.

Waving his arms, John shouted at the tyrannosaur.

"Suppertime!"

The tyrannosaur charged. Shoving Rosa ahead, they ran, lights on the twine, following it up and down and around corners through the pyramid.

The tyrannosaur was fast, but not built for maneuverability. While the tyrannosaur gained on the straightaways, they would make up the distance as they rounded corners. Soon they were tiring. The tyrannosaur wasn't. Then John saw light ahead and he slowed just long enough to get his finger on the trigger and fire a shot, announcing their return. Thinking the rifle report a battle cry, the tyrannosaur responded with a bellow that sounded inches from John's back.

They broke in two directions when they burst from the pyramid. The tyrannosaur followed John. The hunters were waiting.

Using spear throwers, they launched their weapons. Only three spears in the first volley struck deep enough to hold, the rest glanced off, or missed. The tyrannosaur spun when hit, facing the warriors who had attacked it. Charging, it was among them before they could launch another volley. The tyrannosaur tore through them, its weapons the massive jaws and flailing tail. Biting, then tossing, the tyrannosaur scattered the warriors, keeping those behind it at bay with vicious swipes of its tail. Warriors came running from the other side. John ran for position, taking aim, but the tyrannosaur was moving fast and the Mayan warriors were swarming the beast, attacking and retreating. The tyrannosaur turned at each attack, leaving an opportunity on the other side. A half dozen warriors were down, either dead or suffering with fatal wounds. Two snuck in from the back, but were sent tumbling by a powerful tail swipe.

Now Rosa was at John's side, rifle at her shoulder, as frustrated as John.

"Do they want us to help?" Rosa asked.

"I don't know," John said, as another warrior lost an arm to the tyrannosaur. "I can't stand this any longer."

Rushing forward, John ran between two warriors just launching their spears. They ran as soon as they struck. The tyrannosaur was a pincushion now, but with no fatal wounds. Turning at that attack, the tyrannosaur faced John, who held his ground. More spears struck from the other side, confusing the tyrannosaur, freezing it in profile. John raced forward, put the muzzle of his gun inches from the tyrannosaur's knee, clicked the M-16 on full auto, and fired. The knee blew apart, the tyrannosaur screaming and twisting. John backed away, now facing jaws. Leg collapsing, the tyrannosaur lunged, mouth wide enough to swallow John whole. John fell back, the jaws snapping at his face.

Victory screams erupted from the Mayans and the attack increased in frenzy. The head and jaws were lassoed. First the good leg and then the bad were snared, warriors dashing in, tossing loops around the legs, then running back out. Four more warriors were injured before the tyrannosaur was hogtied. The tail was still loose, sweeping back and forth, but the warriors kept their distance, letting their demon exhaust itself.

The Maya were experts in bloodletting, and now they bled the tyrannosaur, cutting its neck, collecting its blood in bowls and jugs, distributing it among the people. They kept it alive, however, weakening it, preparing it for the heart sacrifice. Finally, they were able to lash and stake the tail, the beast now immobile.

The priests from the top of the pyramid came in procession. Emmett, Carrollee, Nikki, and Kenny trailed.

Carrollee hugged John and then Rosa. "Thank you," she said.

The crowds surged forward, mesmerized by the demon that lay in the meadow, black eyes, heaving chest, bloody jaws. The dead and dying testified to the high price the village paid for this heart, and that meant it would be highly prized by the gods. Only Carrollee could not watch the ceremony. Emmett helped her push through the crowd. After singing, ritual, and prayers, the villagers went to work on the tyrannosaur. As they cut into its chest, a dozen men helped hold the weakened beast down. They worked quickly, two of them opening the chest, the chief priest reaching in arm's length, then sawing away, finally wrenching the heart free, holding the still-beating heart in both hands. The size of the heart sent gasps through the crowd. After displaying the heart for the gods, the priest rubbed himself with the warm organ, smearing blood all over his body. Other priests did the same, and then the tyrannosaur was butchered, the priests distributing meat and body parts. Rosa and John had seen enough.

Kenny and Nikki escorted John and Rosa into the village. "Would you two like a nice cup of cocoa?" Kenny asked.

"Or you can share a bath," Nikki said, eyes twinkling.

John looked at Rosa, letting her decide.

"We'll take the bath," she said, slipping her arm around John.

62 · WELCOME

The discovery of the bones of fifty "giants" in the spring of 1969 baffled archaeologists. The tiled coffins holding the remains were unmarked, and the coffins dated from the time of the Roman Empire. Each man measured six to seven feet tall, which was very tall by Roman standards. In a post time quilt world, one wonders if these so-called "giants" weren't a group of modern men transported to the ancient world where they would indeed appear to be giants.

—*Nick Paulson, keynote address,*
National Association of Temporal Research

YUCATAN PENINSULA
PRE-CONQUISTADORS

Everyone was a little drunk. Never more than a social drinker, Elizabeth had stepped a little over her usual line. She nearly spit out her first taste of balche, but after her second cup, it went down much easier. The Russians took to it immediately. Andy and Leo toasted everything and everyone, from their host Kenny Randall, to continued peace between America and Russia, to the beautiful women they were spending the evening with. Jennifer and Valerie giggled appreciatively while Elizabeth feigned indignation.

"We are not sex objects," she objected. "We are professional women."

"Apologies," Andy said. "In Russia women can be both."

"I'm okay with the whole sex-object thing," Jennifer piped up.

"Me, too," Valerie added, smiling at Leo.

The Russians toasted them again.

Kenny Randall kept in the background, drinking, laughing, but watching more than participating. Kawabata was like that too, sitting next to Kenny's rocker, exchanging whispers now and then. Phat was part of the fun but refused the balche, drinking hot cocoa instead. Even sober, he was having a good time.

Kenny had come hurrying from the village when the ant trail led Elizabeth and the others to an exit back on Earth. Phat had recognized his old friend immediately, despite the fact that Kenny was now well into middle age. Surrounded by half-naked villagers, jabbering and pointing, Phat and Kenny had hugged and slapped each others' backs. Kawabata was reserved and showed no surprise when Kenny appeared. Rescuing them from the curious, Kenny led them to his house, which was a three-room stone building with a thatched roof. After hearing their story, Kenny turned one of the rooms into a jail with armed guards at the window. Now Walters, Whitey, Marissa, and the others listened to the party through the curtain that separated the rooms.

The shock over finding out they were now even further into the past quickly wore off when Kenny assured them he could send them home. The party started with Phat and Kenny sharing stories of their pre-quilt experiences as protégés of Dr. Chester Pilcher and George Coombs, the leaders of the group that originally predicted the time disaster. The stories were tinged with sadness, since both leaders were killed after the time quilt, but the stories of their eccentricities kept everyone laughing and smiling. The arrival of balche helped, and more stories and eventually silliness began, Kenny fading into the background, then disappearing with Kawabata for a while as the party carried on into the night. Now, with the party winding down, Kenny got their attention again.

"Your future is not set," Kenny began. "It may be possible to change the course of history by disrupting the timeline that brought you here."

The usual questions erupted.

"But if we alter the timeline, then we wouldn't end up here and we couldn't be sent back," Phat pointed out.

"Or, what if what we end up doing in the past creates the situation that brings us here in the first place. Then nothing changes," Jennifer asked.

"Not necessarily," Phat interjected. "If the universe exists as a multiverse, then it may be possible to change antecedent events to track us onto another possible timeline."

"Very good," Kenny said, smiling appreciatively.

Drunk or not, everyone listened intently, especially Leo and Andy who were as suspicious as interested.

"Through the pyramids there are three possible futures."

Elizabeth and the others were quickly engrossed, listening to their possible futures, struggling at the same time to understand how there could be more than one. One found the Earth as a permanently primitive culture, violently opposed to technology, a second a future with no atmosphere and no human life and the third a future where animals ruled a human-free world. None of them appealed to Elizabeth.

"Why not return us to Fox Valley and let us stop the detonations?" Elizabeth asked when Kenny was done.

"If the pyramid is not sent a decade into the past to the moon, then the timeline since the time quilting is altered so significantly we cannot see the possible outcomes. It may save the Earth from the shredding of history, or those behind it may accomplish their goal in some other way."

"Those are the ones responsible," Andy said, pointing at the curtain.

"With our unwitting help," Kawabata said, hanging his head in shame.

"They would be free to act in the new timeline," Kenny said.

"Sir, what can we do?" Phat asked.

"We must destroy the pyramid on the moon in your present," Kenny said. "Destruction of the pyramid will release the stored orgonic energy, which will mitigate the asynchrony, restoring sympathy to space-time."

"We will need explosives," Andy said. "Perhaps a hundred kilos. That material is like flexible steel."

"You will need more than that. The destruction must take place in multiple timelines distributed between two astral bodies, one surrounded by vacuum. The energy dissipation will be significant."

"How many kilos?" Andy asked. "And where will we get it?"

"Not kilos, kilotons," Kenny said. "You must return to Fox Valley and take one of the nuclear bombs in place around the valley. Reenter the pyramid, and take the bomb to the moon."

Now everyone was confused.

"But if we remove one of the bombs, there will not be enough kilotonnage to displace the pyramid," Phat pointed out.

"True," Kenny said.

"So, to save the Earth we must kill ourselves?" Elizabeth asked.

"Exactly," Kenny said.

63 · EAVESDROPPER

The Industrial Revolution and its consequences have been a disaster for the human race. Industrialization and technological advancements have destabilized society, turned life into a mad pursuit of material wealth, inflicted inhuman suffering on the Third World and caused nearly irreparable harm to nature. The only salvation for the human race is to humble itself before Mother Nature and beg forgiveness.

—Vince Walters, Ph.D., Earth Day Address, San Francisco

YUCATAN PENINSULA
POST CONQUEST

Whitey and Marissa were asleep, Marissa's head in Whitey's lap. Vince was jealous. Marissa was not one of his favorite lovers, but she belonged to him until he decided to give her away. Vince fumed, wondering what Marissa saw in Whitey. He was a stocky man, with beefy arms and chest, and more hair on his arms than on his head. His nose was flat, his forehead overhanging like a Neanderthal, yet she was sleeping in his lap. Whitey wouldn't ever have had a lover if Vince hadn't assigned one of his own to sleep with him. Now the feelings Marissa was showing for Whitey threatened both his ego and his authority. Cut off from the colony he had planned to establish in the new world, the only women available to him were now locked in this room—three, but that was only if you counted Marissa. Latoya and Wings were prettier than Marissa, and even prettier than Star, but his real prizes were hiding in his underground bunker in California, waiting for him. Selecting, cultivating, educating, he had nurtured his garden of followers, weighting it toward women, making sure the men wouldn't challenge him for leadership. All of the women were to be his, unless he chose to share and that would be on his terms. All of that was out of reach now and what was left was less than he was used to, and less than he had planned. There were too few to share as it was. Whitey would have to be dealt with, but first Vince saw a chance to salvage what he had started.

While the others fell asleep, Vince had remained by the door, listening, learning. He was the only one still awake when the party in the next room settled down and Kenny Randall described the mess space-time had become. It was an education for Vince. As he listened, he was amazed at what he had accomplished. He was succeeding beyond his wildest expectations. He also realized there was a better future out there than the one he had intended to create. One of the futures described was a virtual Garden of Eden, with no Adam or Eve. That was the world he wanted for himself. A world where he could start from scratch, building a new civilization where people and nature lived in harmony.

When Kenny laid out the plan for the others, Vince listened intently, making his own plans.

64 · KENNY'S PLAN

Karl Drbal . . . made a cardboard model of the Great Pyramid about 6 inches high and placed within it an ordinary razor blade. The blade was supported at a point that marked one third of the distance between the base and the apex of the pyramid, at the same level as the King's Chamber in the Great Pyramid, and both blade and pyramid were oriented north-south. Karl Drbal shaved more than a hundred times with that single blade.

—*Marshall Cavendish*, The Unexplained

YUCATAN PENINSULA
PRE-CONQUISTADORS

Follow the directions exactly," Kenny said, handing Baranov the calculator. "When you leave the pyramid put the calculator on the ledge here," Kenny said, pointing.

The sun was up but still fighting through the trees, barely illuminating the shelf Kenny indicated.

"You must remember to put it here," Kenny said firmly.

"Seven times you have told me this, thank you very much," Baranov protested, releasing the clip in the M-16 and checking the number of rounds. "Why is this so important?"

Kenny smiled.

"It is the map and you are not the only one to use it."

That made no sense to the Russian, but it was no odder than being several hundred years in the past.

Elizabeth held her rifle awkwardly. She and Phat had fifteen minutes of instruction and ten minutes of practice just after dawn. At first she tried to refuse the weapon, but Baranov insisted. "There are some nasty beasts in that pyramid," he reminded her. She remembered the carnage. She took the weapon.

Elizabeth hugged Jennifer and Valerie, saying good-bye. They would stay behind with Kenny and Kawabata.

Kenny was still repeating the instructions, a routine he had started last night and continued until well into the morning. Baranov nodded and grunted regularly, feigning attention as he practiced with the calculator.

"Everything is set up for you to make the trip to Fox Valley, but you must make adjustments to get to the moon and then back."

"I understand," Baranov said.

"That is the only way home for you."

"Yes. You have explained it well."

"You have only a fifteen-minute window once you have the bomb."

"Fifteen minutes. I remember."

They were at the entrance. Now Baranov turned to Kenny, offering his hand.

"Trust me. This is what Leo and I do for a living."

They shook hands, and then each person shook Kenny's hand as they passed and entered the pyramid.

Kenny sent the others back to the village, waiting in one of the small stone houses by the entrance. Uncovering a hidden computer he called up the Randall-Puglisi model, studying it. An hour later hands rested on his shoulders, massaging. Then there was a light kiss on the nape of his neck. Kenny turned, and Nikki sat in his lap. They kissed deep and long, then Nikki rested her head against his.

"How did it go?" Kenny asked.

"It's all set," Nikki said.

"Did you . . . ?" Kenny started to ask.

"Yes, dear, I put the calculator back."

"Then we've done all we can," Kenny said. "Now we have the long wait."

"Will you sleep with me tonight?"

"Yes. I'll meet you there when I'm finished."

Getting up, she walked to the door and then paused.

"I wish they could all end up as happy as we are."

"They'll have to find what happiness they can in whatever future is ahead of them."

65 · ESCAPE

Over increasingly large areas of the United States, spring now comes unheralded by the return of the birds, and the early mornings are strangely silent where once they were filled with the beauty of bird song.

—*Rachel Carson*, Silent Spring

YUCATAN PENINSULA
POST CONQUEST

Their only weapon was Vince's pocketknife, which the Russians had overlooked or dismissed. He held that knife now, and walked back to the door, testing his wounded leg. The wound had healed surprisingly fast. He listened, hearing nothing from the two guards outside the door. Jennifer and Valerie were off taking a bath, Kawabata was walking through the village, and Kenny had taken the others to the pyramid to start them on their mission. Now was the time.

Whitey, Latoya, and Wings were on the opposite side and signaled ready. Vince peeked through a space in the curtain, making sure the guard was still on his side. A sword hung from the guard's belt, but his arms were folded, and his head sagged.

Shoving the curtain aside with his left hand, he swung his knife hand at the man's chin. The sound and movement shocked the guard awake, his head snapping up, allowing the knife to catch him under his chin. The blade buried deep in the guard's throat. The others tackled the other guard before he could pull his sword. Marissa's hands clamped over the guard's mouth, and they held him down. As one guard struggled to pull the knife from his throat, Vince took his sword, stepped to the other, and buried it in his stomach. It was a mistake. The man bucked violently. The women and Whitey struggled to hold him. Now Vince pulled the sword free, and then plunged it into his chest. Next, Vince stepped back to the first guard and brought the sword down on his neck, nearly severing it.

The others stopped now, horrified by their handiwork. Two of the women wept and Whitey was white now, staring at the bloody mess that had been two human beings.

"This is not our fault," Vince said quickly. "We were forced to come here and be held prisoners. We have a right to take our freedom back."

Whitey continued to stare at the bodies.

"Isn't that right, Whitey? We had a right to take back our freedom!"

Slowly Whitey broke his stare.

"Yes," he said.

"Drag the bodies into the back," Vince ordered.

They complied. Then they gathered up the bloody floor mats and switched them with mats from the back room. In another room they found three rifles and a small amount of ammunition. There were also four packs, trail food, and water bottles. They loaded the packs, and then they waited. Vince wanted Kawabata to return, but Kenny came back first. Waiting inside the door, his back to the wall, Vince stepped behind Kenny, putting his knife to his neck.

"Make a sound and I'll kill you."

Kenny said nothing.

"Where is Kawabata?" Vince demanded.

"He's not here?" Kenny said, puzzled.

"He went for a walk," Vince snarled.

"Oh. Then you know more than I do," Kenny said.

Vince pushed the point into Kenny's neck, drawing a drop of blood.

"Please, Vince," Marissa pleaded.

"Where are Jennifer and Valerie?" Vince demanded.

"I suppose they are still in the bathhouse," Kenny said. "Leave them be."

"Take us there," Vince said fiercely, shoving Kenny.

"What for, Vince?" Whitey asked. "We need to go!"

"Not without them, Whitey," Vince said, not wanting to tell more.

Whitey struggled with compliance. Rifle in hand, he had the power to take the leadership. Vince knew he couldn't do it.

With an occasional jab from a rifle, Kenny was compliant, leading them through the village toward the pyramid, then between two huts to one in the back. Villagers studied them, children skipped alongside until Kenny shooed them away. The former prisoners carried their rifles casually, and no villagers interfered. Splashing and giggling could be heard inside. Kenny paused at the door.

"Open it," Vince whispered.

"We should knock," Kenny said.

Reaching past Kenny, Vince lifted the latch and kicked the door open, shoving Kenny inside. Jennifer and Valerie were in the tub and now gasped, ducking into the water of the huge tub. Vince held his rifle on the young women.

"Get out and get dressed!" he ordered.

They hesitated, looking past him to Kenny. Infuriated, Vince hissed at them.

"Get out now, or I'll kill you!"

Kenny nodded, then turned away, giving them privacy. Whitey did the same. Latoya kept her rifle trained on the pair and Wings looked on, embarrassed and afraid at the same time. Vince watched the two women dress, appraising them.

Jennifer was skinnier than he preferred, Valerie's breasts a bit too large. It didn't matter. He had no choice. They would have to do.

"All right, take us to the pyramid," Vince ordered Kenny. "If anyone calls for help I'll kill all of you."

They complied, Kenny in the front, Vince a half step behind him, rifle aimed at Kenny's side. Valerie and Jennifer came next, Whitey, Marissa, Latoya, and Wings behind. Again, the villagers gawked, and whispered, but did not interfere. They reached the pyramid, pausing by the first stone hut.

"Get the map," Vince ordered.

"I sent it with the others," Kenny said.

Vince jammed the rifle into his side and Kenny winced. Then he stepped into the hut and came out with a calculator, handing it to Vince. Vince turned it on, checked the power, and then scrolled through the menu, remembering what he had overheard the night before.

"Okay, let's go," Vince said, motioning Kenny forward.

"You don't need me. Leave me, and Jennifer and Valerie."

"No. Go."

"Why take them?" Whitey said. "They'll just slow us down."

Vince paused, thinking.

"He can stay. They go," he said, pointing at the women.

"They're not part of our group," Latoya argued.

"They go!" Vince said forcefully.

Vince saw the skepticism in their eyes.

"If we can't reach the others, we'll need them to help with the work," Vince lied.

"Can't we go home?" Wings asked.

Vince scowled. His followers were losing their commitment.

"Not after what we did in Fox Valley," Vince said. Now in honey sweet tones he said, "I listened last night and heard him describe an Earth that is a literal Garden of Eden. It's a world where animals have been freed from bondage. We can live with them, not as masters, but as equals. The trees will provide us food and shelter, and we can live in harmony with our animal brothers and sisters. One species won't exploit another. It's what we dreamed of. It will be our home and with this," Vince said, holding up the calculator, "we can get there. We can find that future and then bring our human brothers and sisters to our own world. *Our own world!*"

They didn't fully understand, but he had seduced them back under his spell.

"Can it still be the way you promised, Vince?" Wings asked.

"Even better," Vince said.

Now they were anxious to go. Confident again, he pointed the gun at Kenny's head.

"If you follow us, I'll kill you and as many of your people as I can."

"I won't follow you, but please leave Jennifer and Valerie," Kenny begged.

Vince realized he had stepped on his own story, promising the others they would bring their own followers to the new Garden of Eden. If so, then why take Jennifer and Valerie?

"We'll let them go once we get safely to where we're going."

That satisfied his followers for now. Now they plunged into the pyramid, following the maps displayed on the screen, one after another. Vince had two objectives: To find the route to the Garden of Eden and to stop Elizabeth Hawthorne and the others from destroying the passages in space-time.

66 · EDUCATED GUESS

The central recognition of the theory of relativity is that geometry is a construct of the intellect. Only when this discovery is accepted can the mind feel free to tamper with the time-honored notions of space and time.

—*Henry Margenau, physicist*

YUCATAN PENINSULA
POST CONQUEST

Kenny walked slowly through the village to a hut several down from his own stone house. He was thinking about Vince Walters, his followers, and especially Valerie and Jennifer. He thought through his actions and decisions over and over, looking for a way to mitigate the harm he had done. When he got to the hut, Kawabata was sitting at a small table, sipping tea.

"Things went as expected?" Kawabata asked.

"Not exactly. They killed two guards—I knew that was a risk. I know the families of both men. Good people."

"That is truly regrettable," Kawabata said. "Perhaps we can compensate them."

"Yes, of course. I will take care of it. Something else happened that you should know about. They took Valerie and Jennifer."

"Ms. DeWitt and Ms. Conroy? But why? They are outsiders. They would introduce disharmony into Dr. Walters's Eden."

Kenny fixed himself a cup of tea, sitting next to his new friend.

"I think I underestimated the size of Dr. Walters's ego," Kenny said.

"Not possible," Kawabata said.

Kenny smiled.

"Perhaps I should say I underestimated the breadth of his ego. He sees himself as the father of a new nation, both figuratively and literally."

"I see," Kawabata said.

They sipped tea in silence for a few minutes.

"Is there hope for them?" Kawabata asked.

"Perhaps," Kenny said. "Let us think of what can be done."

67 ▪ DOPPELGANGERS

Now that superstring theory has opened up a portal into an indescribable world of multiple dimensions . . . experimenters have been turning away from the more mundane tasks of precision measurement to search for traces of other dimensions in the gravitational field. They expect to fail. But if they succeed, we are in for some dramatic intellectual surprises on a par with the discovery of life elsewhere in the universe.

—*Sten F. Odenwald,* Patterns in the Void

FOX VALLEY, ALASKA
PRE-DETONATION

Kenny was an extraordinary planner. The calculator map led them directly through the pyramid mazes, to the familiar territory of the pyramid back in Fox Valley. The timing was amazing, arriving during the day, before Elizabeth had been dragged inside. The passages were lit with electric lights, the central chamber had its table and stereoscope.

"We must hurry," Phat whispered. "Marissa and I came to check the experiment every two hours."

True to his word, they found coveralls and parkas stuffed

behind a panel near the exit. Putting on the coveralls, they draped the parkas over their rifles, then strolled toward the exit. Elizabeth saw Jennifer sitting on a stool, leaning over a workbench, wearing a clean suit.

"Oh no!" Phat gasped, stepping next to Elizabeth, keeping her between him and Jennifer.

"Phat?" Jennifer called.

They kept walking.

"Phat? Is that you?" she repeated.

Just then the double doors opened and Phat and Marissa came out, heading toward the pyramid. Jennifer did a double take.

"Oh, there you are," Jennifer said.

Phat smiled, then walked over, talking to her.

They reached the exit, pushing the open button. As soon as it was shoulder wide, Phat jumped in, sliding into a corner, trying to hide. The others filed in after him, then the door closed.

"Isn't this dangerous?" Phat asked. "What if I meet myself?"

Everyone shrugged.

"Let's not find out," Baranov said.

Once outside, they left the snow machines where they were parked, then hurried around the building and through deep snow. They were barely in the tree line when they heard the sounds of the snow machines firing up. Elizabeth looked at the sky.

"They might be moving the bomb. We timed that well."

"Someone timed it well," Baranov said.

Leo and Baranov took turns in the lead, breaking trail. Elizabeth began wishing she had snowshoes and then suddenly remembered Eilene. She stopped, looking across the valley to where she and Eilene would be hiding. Taking his turn in the rear, Baranov came up behind her.

"What's wrong?"

"I was thinking of a friend," Elizabeth said. "Before I was captured I was with a woman. She was my guide and brought me here in a dogsled. I think Walters shot her. If I left now I might save her."

Baranov pushed his parka back, letting excess heat radiate from his head.

"I have no official knowledge of whom you speak. However, I have heard rumors that a woman named Eilene was rescued by heroic Russian soldiers."

Elizabeth smiled, walked back to Baranov and hugged him. Now she kissed him on the cheek and whispered in his ear.

"Thank the heroic Russians for me."

They had only vague directions to one of the other bunkers. After an hour of climbing through thick snow, Baranov and Leo left Phat and Elizabeth resting under a tree and split up, searching. Thirty minutes later they were back. Baranov had found it. They were getting underway when they heard shots in the distance. Elizabeth shivered from dread, turning to Baranov. He winked.

The bunker looked like the one Elizabeth and Eilene had visited. Leo managed to open the lock without tearing off the hasp. Inside was an identical device to the one Elizabeth had found. Leo and Baranov stood on either side of it, studying the wiring.

"Can you do it?" Baranov asked.

Leo shrugged his shoulders.

"Perhaps. Build something to move it with, just in case."

Phat and Elizabeth helped Baranov cut wood and fashion a litter for the bomb. When they got back Leo was outside, leaning against the wall.

"Well?" Baranov asked.

"We can separate it from the timing circuit at any time. I can stop the countdown but without the codes I cannot reset the clock."

"Can you start the clock again?" Baranov asked.

"Dah."

"Good enough," Baranov said.

After cutting the bomb loose, they waited inside to conserve heat. As the hours passed, Elizabeth pictured what was happening below. Baranov, Leo, and their men would arrive.

The raptors would attack. Many people would die horribly. She wanted to stop it all, but knew she could not, not if there was to be any hope for the future. Everyone was morose, thinking similar thoughts. They could change what was happening now, or they could save the Earth. It was the kind of choice Elizabeth had been involved with when she worked at the White House. She had made those decisions rationally then, but she never saw the consequences up close. This was different.

They slept. They ate. They talked about everything, passing the time. Leo regularly scouted the area, coming back to report that he could see people working on the building, installing something on the roof. Finally, it was time.

They loaded the bomb onto the litter Baranov had fashioned, then carried it down the hill toward the building. Walters's people should have finished modifying the building by now, and been torn to pieces by the velociraptors. They left the bomb's timing circuits open so it could receive signals broadcast from the control computer. Disconnecting it would not stop the countdown but might alert those inside. Besides, the bomb was the best timer for what they needed to do. They paused behind the building, waiting.

"We go at fifteen minutes," Baranov reminded them, sounding like Kenny Randall.

Huddled around the bomb, they watched the countdown. Inside their doppelgangers were gathering, huddling, afraid. Soon Elizabeth would write her name on the wall. None of that would matter now because that Elizabeth—she—would be vaporized when the remaining bombs went off. Elizabeth's mind reeled trying to understand. She was the Elizabeth inside the building, yet she was also here, outside. How could she kill herself and still exist?

"It's time," Baranov announced.

Leo reached into the guts of the bomb, cutting two wires. The timer stopped at 15:03. Now Baranov started the timer on his watch.

"Let's go."

Baranov and Leo picked up the litter with the bomb then

hurried along the outside of the building. The controls to the exit had been replaced with the simple OPEN button. Leo reached for it but Baranov grabbed his hand.

"Be prepared," Baranov said. "Remember what is inside."

Elizabeth did remember. She had helped collect body parts and clean blood from the floor. Even so, when the door opened it was a shock. There were two bodies in the entrance lying in crimson pools. They tried to avoid stepping in the blood, but it was impossible to maneuver the bomb inside as well as everyone else and not step in it. Like strangers in an elevator, they stood in the blood, staring at the inner doors, waiting for the air pressure to adjust and the doors to open. When they did, there was no relief. Between them and the pyramid was carnage. Watching where they stepped, they worked their way through the bodies. Elizabeth glanced up at the window into the office where she was sitting right now, waiting, praying.

"Phat, Elizabeth," Baranov whispered. "Get your rifles ready. One of those raptors escaped into the pyramid."

Awkwardly, Elizabeth and Phat raised their rifles, leading the way into the pyramid. The lights were on in the pyramid and there was no velociraptor in sight. Phat led the way through the pyramid to the central chamber where they put the bomb down and checked the time.

"Seven minutes," Baranov said, looking at his watch.

Now Phat slung his rifle over his shoulder, taking Andy's place with the litter. They moved deeper into the pyramid, Baranov consulting the calculator map, stopping periodically, adjusting movable panels in or out according to instructions. It slowed them down, eating up precious time. Even with the threat of a velociraptor somewhere inside, they had to move fast. Even Kenny wasn't sure what would happen inside one of the space-time corridors when the two remaining fusion bombs detonated.

"Two minutes," Baranov announced.

The interior changed to stone.

"Are you sure this is right?" Elizabeth asked, breathless.

"Yes," Baranov said, not slowing down.

They were using flashlights now, moving at a reckless pace. Phat stumbled, almost falling, the litter tilting. Elizabeth jumped between the bomb and the wall, helping steady the bomb while Phat got back to his feet.

"One minute," Baranov said, pulling a panel down, then hurrying on.

They were deep into a stone pyramid now.

"Better hang on to something," Baranov said.

The bomb was dropped on the floor, Elizabeth sat next to it, back against the wall. Phat sat next to her, his breaths coming twice as fast as hers. Elizabeth took his hand and squeezed it.

"You'll be back with your family before you know it," Elizabeth said.

"You mean after I die?"

"After we both die."

68 · BLOOD SCENT

We need another and a wiser and perhaps more mystical concept of animals. . . . In a world older and more complete than ours they move finished and complete, gifted with extensions of the senses we have lost or never attained, living by voices we shall never hear. They are not brethren, they are not underlings; they are other nations, caught with ourselves in the net of life and time, fellow prisoners of the splendor and travail of the earth.

—*Henry Beston,* The Outermost House

INSIDE THE PYRAMID CORRIDORS

The velociraptor licked its wounds, the taste of its own blood washing away the taste of its prey. As dinosaurs went, raptors were at the genius end of the scale. Even though it had well below human cognitive abilities, the velociraptor had a sense of self, a form of loyalty to its own kind, and a level of free will that allowed it to overrule hunting instincts, thus making it even more dangerous. Now wounded, grieving the loss of its mates, it fought back the urge to lash out blindly, destroying anything and everything in reach.

Distant vibrations caught the raptor's attention and it stopped licking, nose in the air. With a highly evolved olfactory sense, it picked the smell of prey out of the air—the prey that had killed its mates. Smelling, listening, feeling, the velociraptor took a bearing. Moving slowly now, head low, it moved through the corridors, pausing regularly to smell for its prey. The prey were moving rapidly away. The velociraptor moved faster, confused in the dark passages. Suddenly, there was the smell of fresh blood.

Its nose an inch from the floor, it sniffed, walking slowly—there was a blood trail. Smelling deeply, the velociraptor picked out the blood of one of its mates. Now the anger swelled in his chest, a deep rumble escaping its throat. It sniffed again, following the trail a short distance in both directions. The blood scent was stronger one way. Turning, it followed the blood scent the other direction, knowing from experience, somewhere ahead were the prey.

69 · WALKING DEAD

"But, Lord," said Martha, the sister of the dead man, "by this time there is a bad odor, for he has been there four days." Then Jesus . . . called in a loud voice, "Lazarus, come out!" The dead man came out, his hands and feet wrapped with strips of linen, and a cloth around his face.

—*John 11:39–44*

FLAMSTEED CRATER, THE MOON
PRESENT TIME

The pyramid shook violently when two bombs went off in Fox Valley, but they felt no heat and no blast. That exit, and that future, were cut off from them forever. So Elizabeth was dead there, but alive here.

"Phat, what does this say about our souls?" Elizabeth asked.

"God is omnipotent and omnipresent," Phat said. "Our souls are the part of us closest in substance to God's being, so our souls are with us and they are not. We died and we did not. Jesus died for our sins and yet he lived again. Why is it when we are most like God we believe in Him the least?"

Phat was a thoughtful man and a committed Christian, and his answer insightful and contradictory at the same time.

"We have two hours to position the bomb," Baranov said.

Kenny had given them a small window of time when the bomb had to be set off. Once past the window, the shredding of Earth's history could not be stopped. They set off again, Elizabeth trailing, Baranov leading, Phat and Leo carrying the bomb. She was about to offer to take a turn with the litter when they made the stomach churning transition to lunar gravity. Phat sighed audibly, the bomb and his own body weight now one sixth of normal. Eventually, they came to the central chamber of the moon pyramid, moving the table with the stereoscope and setting the bomb down in the middle. Leo took his knife and bent over the bomb.

"Wait," Baranov said. "Once you trigger it we have only fifteen minutes."

Baranov studied the maps on the calculator.

"I will reset the panels on the first map and then return for you. That should speed our escape."

Baranov left them resting with the bomb, walking back down the corridor, his light bobbing, then disappearing around a corner. Elizabeth closed her eyes, resting, exhausted enough to sleep, and a little hungover. Why did Kenny let them drink the balche knowing what he was going to send them to do? Maybe he knew they needed to be drunk to accept killing themselves. Elizabeth opened her eyes to see Andy's light bobbing back. Had she slept? The light was bright now, shining in their eyes.

"Turn your light," Phat complained.

The light came on, still in their eyes. Suddenly, Leo reached for his rifle. The light swung toward him and a rifle sputtered, the energy absorbing walls softening the report like a silencer. Leo took two of the rounds in the chest, dead before his body hit the floor. Elizabeth flicked on her light, pointing it at the gunman. It was Vince Walters.

"Move, and I'll kill you. Please move. Please."

Phat and Elizabeth sat still. Marissa squeezed past Walters, gathering their rifles. Then Whitey came in dragging Baranov's unconscious body under one arm, Valerie and Jennifer helping on the other side. Latoya and Wings came up behind. Marissa handed them rifles. They dropped Baranov's body at Elizabeth's feet. Elizabeth got to her knees, leaning forward to check Baranov's condition.

"I said don't move," Walters repeated.

Elizabeth ignored him. Baranov had a scalp wound, his hair matted with blood. Elizabeth dabbed at the blood with her sleeve. The wound was an inch long and should be stitched. She didn't know if the blow had been hard enough to crack his skull or cause intracranial bleeding. Phat moved to help her.

"Don't think the slack I cut her extends to you," Walters said.

Phat froze, then inched back to his place. Now Elizabeth crawled to Leo who had slumped onto his side. She felt for a pulse on his neck and then wrist. None.

"They could have killed you and they didn't," Elizabeth said.

"A mistake I didn't make," Walters retorted, then turned to Whitey. "Check the bomb," Walters said.

Whitey got down and looked into the bomb, poking at the severed wires.

"They cut the timing circuit but left the power. The detonation countdown is stopped."

"Can you fix it?"

"Easily," Whitey said, leaning inside and stripping insulation off of wires with his teeth. "Then I'll fix it so only we can use it."

When Whitey finished fixing the circuit the countdown started up again. Then he entered an access code, cleared the countdown clock, and entered commands. When he finished, the display had a single line of random digits.

"Let them get through that," Whitey said.

Walters pulled a calculator from his pocket, like the one Baranov had been using. Elizabeth pretended to check Andy's vital signs, feeling his pockets for the calculator. It wasn't there. She looked back down the corridor but in the dim light she could not see far. No calculator.

"You and you, carry the bomb," Walters ordered Phat and Elizabeth.

Now he pointed his rifle at the back of Baranov's head.

"No, Vince," Whitey pleaded. "You don't need to do that."

"Who's going to carry him? You?"

"Yes," Whitey said, stepping forward.

As Whitey lifted Baranov, Jennifer and Valerie helped. Even in the light gravity a limp human body is awkward to maneuver. Then Jennifer slipped her shoulder under Baranov's arm, Whitey on the other side. Walters shook his head, disgusted.

"I'm not taking him with us," Walters said. "Him neither," he said, now indicating Phat.

"Can we stash them somewhere, just till we get away?"

Vince's eyes flicked from his followers to his captives, carefully considering his options. Now he studied his calculator.

"Okay, that way," he indicated.

Elizabeth and Phat carried the bomb, walking ahead of Walters; the others followed, Marissa taking up the rear. Elizabeth thought she spotted a long black line on the ground, and she felt crunching as they were pushed along

with jabs from Vince's rifle. They emerged on the moon, but
not the moon they had left. The remains of a small tyrannosaur now sat right outside the exit. Ants swarmed it, the
carcass almost stripped clean. Elizabeth and Phat skirted the
carcass, leaving Walters puzzled. The others came out, all
just as curious.

"Something must have dragged the carcass here," Walters said.

"This isn't a velociraptor, Vince," Whitey said. "Look at
those jaws. It's a tyrannosaur, but I never saw one this small
before."

"It doesn't matter," Walters declared. "Take the bomb into
the back. We can stash it there until we need it."

Elizabeth and Phat complied, carrying the bomb to the
double doors, then pushing them open. They froze. The corridor was filled with debris, the walls and ceiling destroyed.

"What happened here, Vince?" Marissa asked, dismayed.

"It doesn't matter. We're not staying anyway."

Walters ordered them to sit on the floor in front of the
stairs while he talked with his people. Baranov was still unconscious and they carried him down the corridor, gently
laying him on the floor.

"They don't know what to do with us," Elizabeth said,
watching the animated discussion.

"They know what to do with me," Phat said. "I'm a dead
man—again—so is Baranov. It's you Dr. Walters isn't sure
about."

"I'm no different than you," Elizabeth protested.

"He's right," Jennifer said. "He's gathering women. He's
always been like that. When we worked for him he made
passes at both Valerie and me. He's slept with half the
women at the facility."

"I always thought he was creepy, but a lot of the girls
thought he was sexy and insightful, kind of a secular mystic," Valerie said. "He took us but left Kenny because he
wants us to be part of his harem. You too, Elizabeth."

Elizabeth understood. Vince had been working to destroy

the planet, and to gather a group of followers he could use to reestablish society and repopulate the Earth, and he planned on doing most of the fathering.

"I'm awake," Baranov whispered. "Don't let them know."

All started to turn toward Baranov, then stopped, looking away.

"When they come back tell them I'm dead. When they get close to check, I'll wrestle a gun away from one of them."

"That's not a plan, that's suicide," Elizabeth said.

"Russians do this all the time, thank you very much," Baranov said.

"Listen, comrade, we're all in this together," Elizabeth said. "We all jump them, or no one jumps them."

"You are not a soldier," Baranov said.

"Be quiet, please," Phat said. "They will hear."

"We'll grab them," Valerie suggested, volunteering her and Jennifer. "He wants us alive. He won't shoot us."

"He will if you are winning," Baranov whispered.

"Then you and Phat better hit them from behind before he does," Elizabeth said.

"Look!" Phat suddenly said in a near shout.

Walters and his people turned at Phat's voice. Elizabeth saw one of the double doors was swinging in and out in increasing arcs. Now it stopped and then the other door began the same odd behavior. Finally, there was a loud thump and the door swung wide enough for them to see a velociraptor on the other side.

"Hide," Elizabeth said.

They reached for Baranov just as the velociraptor crashed through the doors, then with a hop it launched itself, clawed feet first, at the knot of people in front of him. His overpowered leap put his head into the ceiling, catching aluminum ceiling brackets, jerking its head back, throwing off its balance. Jumping aside, Vince and his people got out of the way, and the velociraptor tumbled down the hall. Elizabeth and the others dodged, and the velociraptor continued down the hall and into the wreckage.

Helping Baranov up the stairs, Elizabeth looked back to see Vince dragging Jennifer by the hair, and kicking Valerie to her feet. Whitey was next to him, rifle ready. The velociraptor was tangled in the wreckage, making a terrific racket as it tried to pull itself free. Elizabeth started down the stairs.

"No," Baranov said weakly, holding her back.

"But Valerie and Jennifer?"

"They're safer with them than with us."

They retreated up the stairs. Now there was gunfire, the velociraptor screaming defiantly.

"Fools," Baranov said. "Wasting ammunition."

They headed for Kawabata's office, closing the door, then dragging the desk to block it. Baranov sagged to the floor, back to the wall, gingerly touching his scalp. Phat crawled to the window, peeking over the edge.

"What of Leo?" Andy asked.

"I'm sorry," Elizabeth said. "Walters killed him."

"He was young and didn't know any better. But I was the fool that got himself clubbed."

"They made it to the pyramid," Phat whispered, still watching through the window. "They're leaving us here and taking the bomb."

"What of the velociraptor?" Baranov asked.

"It didn't follow them," Phat said.

A few seconds later they heard the *click, click, click* of a six-inch claw on the linoleum.

70 · FUTURE HISTORY

Mr. President, the oscillation in atmospheric radiation is continuing to accelerate and each cycle has been reliably linked to another time displacement. The most recent deposited a small herd of wooly mammoths near Cannes.

—*Caroline Mauck, Director of the CIA*

YUCATAN PENINSULA
POST CONQUEST

Elizabeth and the others only partially succeeded," Kenny explained to Nick. "They managed to steal the bomb, but it was never detonated at the nexus of the space-time channels. In that timeline, the Fox Valley pyramid was destroyed and the action blamed on Russia. Ultimately it led to a full nuclear exchange. China attempted to take advantage of the subsequent power vacuum but underestimated the remaining Russian and American nuclear arsenals. The briefest alliance in history was formed and America and Russia used their remaining warheads to destroy China and its allies. The resulting radiation levels were lethal and surely would have killed everyone but before it could, the asynchrony of the time waves reached its peak, and history as we know it—a linear phenomenon—ceased to exist. Radiation was spread through Earth's history, killing off human civilization."

"So the timeline devoid of humans might not have existed if you hadn't sent them," Nick said.

"That's a reasonable conclusion," Kenny said. "I'm responsible for the destruction of human life on Earth—in that future."

"Send me back, I'll get the bomb to the right time and place," Ripman said, sipping balche.

"With a broken ankle?" Reggie asked.

"It's not broken," Ripman snarled.

"I'll take Emmett and John when they get back," Nick said.

"There's no time," Kenny said. "Besides, we don't know for sure they will ever get back."

"What about me?" Phil asked, obviously hurt by being overlooked.

"I was already counting on you, Phil," Nick lied.

Phil was a computer genius but an old man. Nick could have used Ripman; he was the fittest and had the right skills, but not with a broken ankle.

"I'll go too?" Reggie volunteered.

"I'll be more useful with a broken ankle than she would be with two healthy ones," Ripman said, pushing himself to his feet, grimacing.

"At least now you admit it's broken," Reggie said.

"Kenny, how do you know that by taking this action we don't create another timeline. Maybe nothing can ever be changed."

"Nothing can be worse than the complete destruction of humanity," Kenny said.

"Okay, tell me what we need to do," Nick said.

Kenny smiled with relief, and put his hand on Nick's shoulder.

"You must rescue the girl, find the bomb, and save the world. All in a matter of hours."

"It's about damn time," Phil said.

71 ▪ ROBERT RIPMAN

When trouble comes, the weak always run to the hills and there they'll find me waiting.

—*Robert Ripman*

YUCATAN PENINSULA
POST CONQUEST

Ripman watched as Kenny gave Nick a calculator, instructing him on how to read the graphs as maps and to interpret the instructions that went with them. Nick had Ripman's dinosaur gun, Reggie and Phil M-16's. Giving up his dinosaur gun was the only useful role left to him. Now, watching them get final instructions, Ripman felt wretched. All his life he had struggled to find a place to fit in. He was a misfit in high school, preferring time alone to the terrors of his home life and the awkward questions his only two friends asked about his many bruises and split lips.

His affinity for the solitary life led him to develop hunting skills that saved his, John's, and for a time, Cubby's life when they were caught up in the first time quilt. Later it had given him a semi-legal career as a hunter and guide. But not since he helped John find his way through a dinosaur-infested forest while looking for his family, had he felt really needed. He had acquaintances, not friends, and the women he attracted were too civilized, and civilization was something he was never comfortable with. During the time spent with Carrollee, Nikki, Reggie, John, and the dinosaur rangers, Ripman had bonded, genuinely coming to like and admire Marion, Jose, and Mitch. He had especially been attracted to Nikki, who was a survivor, like him. Now she was lost somewhere, John was on a rescue mission, and Nick was off to save the world.

Ripman hung back when the others shook hands with Kenny and then entered the pyramid. Then Ripman hobbled back toward the hut.

"Robert Ripman, why so sad?" Kenny asked, catching up to him.

"They could use me, that's all," Ripman said.

"Have you thought of your future?" Kenny asked.

"Yes, getting home alive."

"To your wife?"

"No wife."

"Girlfriend?"

"I travel a lot."

"I understand you have unique skills," Kenny said.

"I'm a hunter. I like the wilderness. To tell you the truth, the time quilt created the kind of world I was made to live in."

"The challenge of survival helps you forget?"

"Forget what? There's nothing I need to forget!"

Angry now, Ripman limped faster.

"I have a mission for you, Robert," Kenny said. "If you choose to take it."

"What kind of mission?" Ripman asked suspiciously.

"The kind you won't come back from," Kenny said honestly.

"Why should I?"

"You have a unique set of skills that are rare in the modern age. Perhaps no one else could do what I'm going to ask you to do. Why should you do what I ask? Well, that's up to you to decide after you hear what it is."

"It doesn't matter, not with this ankle."

"Come, let's take care of that ankle while I explain," Kenny said, leading him back toward the pyramid.

72 · CLASH

When we start considering this possibility, we come upon a contention which is so astonishing that we must dwell upon it. This contention holds that what we call our civilization is largely responsible for our misery, and that we should be much happier if we gave it up and returned to primitive conditions.

—*Sigmund Freud*, Civilization and Its Discontents

FLAMSTEED CRATER, THE MOON
PRESENT TIME

The velociraptor had their scent and was testing the door. Phat and Baranov were holding the desk that blocked it, while Elizabeth sat on the desk to add weight. Phat and Baranov pushed with all their might. The blood from Andy's scalp wound trickled down his neck. Between pushes by the velociraptor, Baranov wiped away fresh blood.

"It can smell this," Baranov said.

Now the velociraptor hit the door harder—the door held. There was a pause, then *click, click, click.*

"What's it doing?" Phat asked.

"Thinking," Baranov said.

Suddenly the door was slammed hard, over and over, but the velociraptor was hitting the door low, the desk absorbing much of the energy. Just as suddenly, the pounding stopped.

"If he hits that door high," Phat whispered.

"I know," Baranov said.

Now they could hear the velociraptor sniffing the crack at the bottom of the door. Then the sound of retreating *clicks.* They held their position.

"They can't be that smart," Phat said. "That door was ready to split in half."

"Shhhh!" Baranov said, head cocked.

After a few minutes Baranov released the desk and tiptoed to the door, lying down with his head toward the crack at the bottom.

"No breath sounds," Baranov said. "No footfalls."

Now Phat crawled to the window, peeking over the edge.

"I don't see it—wait. Here it comes. I think it's following Dr. Walters and the others."

Elizabeth felt guilt and relief all at the same time. Relief that the velociraptor was hunting someone else, and guilt that two of the hunted were friends.

"It's going toward the pyramid," Phat said, his head rising a little higher.

Baranov sat up, back against the desk, feeling his wound. Elizabeth crawled across the room to an old easy chair, taking the doilies off the arms. She took the doilies to Baranov, folding them to make bandages.

"Thank you very much," he said, pressing the doilies to his wound.

"You should see what it is doing," Phat said from the window. "It is hopping and bouncing around. Wow, it can really get some air. Look out NBA!"

"It is testing the gravity," Baranov said. "Tell me when it has gone."

"You're going after the bomb?" Elizabeth asked.

"Yes."

"I'll go with you."

"Thank you, very much," Baranov said.

"He's at the entrance," Phat said. "He's sniffing the air again. Looking around—Oh-oh! He spotted me."

"Get down," Baranov shouted too late.

Phat turned, pale, his back to the window.

"I'm sorry," he said.

Then the window behind him darkened as a large hurtling body crashed through the window. Phat went down in an explosion of glass shards. The velociraptor hooked Phat as he tried to get out of the way, wounding him. Still uncoordinated in the low gravity, the velociraptor scrambled awkwardly to its feet, sending glass shards in all directions with the speed of bullets. Then it leaped on Phat, pinning him to the ground with a powerful leg.

Baranov was up, shoving the desk aside. Then he threw open the damaged door, and pulled Elizabeth after him.

"Phat!" Elizabeth had time to shout.

Her last view of Phat was when the velociraptor snapped his neck. Terrified, now she raced Baranov for the stairs. She passed him on the way down and without being told, ran down the corridor and through the double doors. She didn't look back, beating Baranov to the pyramid and plunging inside. Somewhere behind her she could hear a rapid *click, click, click.*

73 • STRANGERS

Scientists had ridiculed the concept of time travel for centuries. Even after the return of dinosaurs to the modern world, naysayers have argued that the forces that created the time quilt are uncontrollable. One must admire the gall of someone who can stick to an erroneous position even in the face of overwhelming evidence.

—*Emmett Puglisi, quoted in* Newsweek

FLAMSTEED CRATER, THE MOON
PRESENT TIME

In the light gravity Elizabeth and Baranov bounded like superheroes across the surface of the floor and into the pyramid. Now they struggled for control, hopping down the narrow corridors, hands outstretched, bouncing off of walls and ceiling. Suddenly Baranov shouted for her to stop.

"Why?" Elizabeth shouted, struggling to arrest her momentum.

Baranov pushed her aside, got onto his knees and came up with the calculator.

"Got it!" he said.

Baranov turned the calculator on, searching through the graph maps. Elizabeth heard a commotion behind them.

"This way," Baranov said.

"It's coming," Elizabeth said.

"Good! It is our only weapon."

Now they ran, skipping several yards at a time. They passed the central chamber where the bomb was to be set. It was not there. Barely pausing, they kept up a quick pace. Occasionally, Baranov would stop, listening.

"It is falling behind," Baranov said after one stop.

"That's good, right?"

"No!" Baranov said, then he struck his injured head against the wall, leaving a bloody patch.

"Let's go," Baranov said.

Elizabeth followed the crazy Russian, a trickle of blood running down his neck. Now at every junction he rubbed his head against the wall. Suddenly they transitioned from Moon to Earth gravity and soon they were in the stone pyramid. Baranov continued the routine, pausing, listening, and leaving a blood trail. They couldn't hear the velociraptor now but they didn't doubt it was coming.

Suddenly, Baranov turned out his light. In the gloom Elizabeth could see a light ahead, bobbing down the corridor. They had almost caught Walters and his people. Baranov didn't move to catch them.

"What's the plan?" Elizabeth asked.

"Something's not right," Baranov said.

Elizabeth could make out three figures. There was no bomb litter and only one of the figures was female.

"Who is that?" Elizabeth whispered.

"I don't know," Baranov said, consulting his watch. "But the Earth is just about out of time."

74 ▪ SECRET WEAPON

One theory is that the pyramid focuses and intensifies unidentifiable energies to the extent that healing is possible. Another theory is that the atmosphere inside the pyramid stimulates an acceleration of enzyme action which accounts for the effects of mummification, preservation and possibly even the intensity of meditation.

—*Max Toth and Greg Nielsen,* Pyramid Power

INSIDE THE YUCATAN PYRAMID

Nick could see lights ahead, moving rapidly. With Phil right behind him and Reggie in the rear, they picked up the pace, closing the distance.

"Put out the lights," Nick said.

Now they closed on the group in front. Two of them carried a litter. When they came to the central chamber, Nick ran forward, shouting.

"Everyone freeze," Nick said.

The lights from the group turned toward him, partially blinding him. Phil came into the chamber, moving away from Nick, setting up crossfire. Reggie hung back. There were two men and five women in the chamber. Two of the women had been carrying the bomb.

"Who the hell are you?" one of the men demanded.

The man was missing a pant leg and had a scar along the outside of his leg. Now his eyes went to Phil and then to Reggie.

"Nick Paulson, I presume?" he said, smiling.

"Drop your weapons," Nick ordered.

Guns hung from their shoulders, but no one moved to put them down.

"We've never met, Dr. Paulson. I'm Dr. Walters."

"I know who you are. You're the madman behind the time asynchrony."

"Madman? I'm a dreamer and a doer. In the future historians will write about my life as a profile in courage. I'm Columbus without the genocide, Henry Ford without environmental rape, I'm Adam without God to punish me for thinking for myself."

"Put the gun down, Adam," Phil mocked.

"I don't like you," Walters said, pointing a finger at Phil. "Reggie, shoot him."

Reggie did as she was told, shooting Phil. Phil collapsed.

"Excellent shot," Walters said, now unslinging his rifle.

Shocked, Nick turned to face Reggie, aiming his rifle at her. Now they each stared down a barrel. Reggie was crying.

"I liked him," Reggie said. "I didn't want to kill him."

"Put it down, Reggie," Nick said. "You know what is at stake. We have to stop it from happening. Billions of people depend on us."

"It's for the best, Nick. It really is. Tell him, Vince."

The barrel of Walters's rifle touched the side of Nick's head.

"The world is a cesspool," Walters said. "We're living in our own filth, apart from nature, not part of nature. We were killing our future anyway and our animal brothers and sisters, too. This way the world gets a fresh start. Order is restored to the animal kingdom and we resume our rightful place as equals, not rulers."

"Reggie, you can't want this," Nick said. "What about your friends, your family?

"These are my friends and family," Reggie said, sobbing.

"Put the gun down," Walters said firmly.

Nick dropped the dinosaur gun.

"Now get over with the others," Walters ordered.

"Stop right where you are," a voice called.

Walters swung his rifle, aiming behind Nick. Nick turned. A man dressed in cotton pants and a green T-shirt was illuminated in the corridor. There was blood on his shirt and the hair on the right side of his head was matted. Behind him was Elizabeth.

"Elizabeth!" Nick shouted.

Elizabeth started to run forward and then stopped.

"Do come forward," Walters said. "You, too, Comrade Baranov."

"Put your gun down, or else," Baranov said.

Nick couldn't see any weapons on the man, only a flashlight.

"Or what?" Walters asked. "You are unarmed."

"Not quite," Baranov said. "I have a secret weapon."

Walters laughed.

"You better believe him," Elizabeth said emphatically, quickly coming forward and stopping next to Baranov.

"Then show me your secret weapon, before I kill you," Walters said.

"It's right there," Baranov said, and then shone his flashlight back down the corridor.

There, frozen like a deer in headlights, was a velociraptor. Walters gasped. The velociraptor charged. Lights bobbed as people panicked, creating a strobe effect. Nick dove for his rifle just as shots were fired, muzzle flashes lighting the interior. The velociraptor leaped into the chamber, snapping and snarling, confused by the lights, the gunfire, and the panicked people. It spun, striking out at running figures. Nick found the gun, worked the bolt, got to his knees and looked for the velociraptor. He couldn't make it out in the confusion.

"Hit it with lights," Nick shouted.

Suddenly two lights searched for it and then found it. The velociraptor turned toward the lights—Baranov and Elizabeth. With a defiant screech, the velociraptor squatted, then leaped. Nick fired. The beast screamed but its momentum carried it. Nick worked another round into the chamber while the velociraptor was thrashing and screeching. Terrified of hitting Elizabeth by mistake, Nick hurried to the animal, shooting it three times at point-blank range.

"Elizabeth?" he called.

"Here," she answered.

They found lights, then each other, embracing, kissing, swearing to never be apart again. Then they remembered the others. Baranov was looking at the bomb when Nick and Elizabeth came over, lending their light. Baranov paused, examining Nick's dinosaur rifle.

"American secret weapon," he said. "It will be in production in Russia by spring."

"What about the bomb?" Nick asked.

"No good news. They have entered a security code. The bomb is still armed but I can't trigger a detonation."

"Code?" a voice called. "Did someone say code?"

Phil staggered out of the darkness, the left side of his chest soaked in blood.

"Oh, Phil," Elizabeth said, reaching out, supporting him.

"Hello, Elizabeth," Phil said, puzzled at seeing her. "What code?"

There was no time to try and stem the bleeding. If the code was not broken, they would all die anyway, along with every friend and relative. Phil studied the digits displayed across the screen and then called up another screen that requested his password. Phil typed in a series of digits and letters. When the screen returned to the first line of digits, some had changed.

"Very clever," Phil said, Elizabeth still holding his arm.

Now Phil worked back and forth between the two screens, the digits changing every time he entered a different password. The blood continued to spread across his chest, and down his side.

"Now I've got you," Phil muttered.

He typed in a new password and suddenly they had access. Phil called up a menu. DETONATION COUNTDOWN, was on the list of options.

"Sounds right," Baranov said.

Phil selected it.

"How long?" Phil asked.

Baranov and Nick both looked at their watches.

"I have fifty-five minutes left," Nick said.

"Good enough," Baranov said. "Twenty-five, maybe thirty minutes to return the bomb to the right chamber and set it up."

"About," Nick agreed.

"Might as well set it for one minute then," Baranov said.

"What?" Elizabeth asked. "That's not enough time."

Nick's joy at finding Elizabeth made the pain of knowing he was going to lose her again even worse.

"There's not enough time to get back to the Yucatan," Nick said.

"We can try," Elizabeth said.

"It is best to embrace death," Baranov said.

"Leave me," Phil said, now slipping to the ground, lying on his back.

"We won't," Elizabeth said.

"No one gets left behind," Nick said, then leaned over and kissed Elizabeth. "Let's do it."

Baranov shook his head and then smiled.

"You Americans want all the credit for saving the world. World War I, you take credit for victory even though you showed up late for the party. World War II, same thing. Not this time, thank you very much. Not without Russia. Not without me! Now take hold of the litter, thank you very much."

Nick and Baranov carried the litter while Elizabeth supported Phil. The bullet had passed through Phil's chest and out the other side, missing heart and lung but breaking a rib. Breathing hurt more than walking, but walking soon had Phil gasping for breath. Nick marveled at the man's toughness. Relief came when they transitioned to moon gravity, Phil sighing. Now Elizabeth could practically carry him and they made good progress, finally reaching the spot Kenny had selected for detonation. Nick trusted Kenny's description of the spot as the "nexus" of the time passages.

"How much time?" Nick asked.

"Twenty-two minutes," Baranov said.

"We can get a long way away in that much time," Elizabeth said.

"Sure," Nick said. "We'll get as far away as we can."

Baranov said nothing.

"Phil, set the timer for twenty minutes. Our timing might be off by a minute or two."

"Nineteen," Baranov said.

"Okay, nineteen," Nick said, knowing it would not make any difference.

Elizabeth helped Phil kneel by the bomb, letting him punch in the command. Then he hit enter. The countdown clock showed 19:00. A second later it read 18:59.

"Let's go," Elizabeth said, starting to help Phil up.

"Wait," Phil said, taking short quick breaths.

Phil called up another screen and typed in a series of commands and then hit enter. Now the screen went blank. As before, a line of digits stretched across the screen. Unlike before, the digits were now in color, a dozen different hues randomly distributed. A second later some of the digits changed to new colors.

"Walters may still be lurking around here somewhere. Let's see him break that code!"

Now they helped Phil up, Baranov and Nick both consulting their calculators.

"This way," Baranov said, going back the direction they came.

Nick took Phil from Elizabeth. Phil's breathing was so shallow Nick could hardly hear it. Nick was thinking about how hard the transition to heavy gravity was going to be for Phil when a solution hit him.

"We're going the wrong way!" Nick shouted.

Baranov stopped, looking at the calculator.

"I think not," Baranov said.

"Trust me, it's the wrong way."

Nick turned Phil around and then picked the man up piggyback and ran, Elizabeth and Baranov following, shouting questions. He ignored them, racing on, estimating how much time they had left. They would need every second of it.

75 · MESSAGE

In a display case in Cairo's Museum of Antiquities is a wooden model. It is clearly an airplane including wings, fins, and tail. When you throw it the model will glide a few feet. This model airplane is dated to 200 B.C. This find was inexplicable until we came to understand that many of our missing aircraft had been displaced in time.

—Nick Paulson, interviewed on
Fox News Special Report

John and Rosa's bath took three hours, the two of them returning clean, flushed from head to toe, and inseparable. Carrollee was resting in a hammock, Emmett next to her, holding her hand. She wore a skirt now and a light cotton top that was thin enough to see through. John could see a bandage covering the wound on her chest. She wore the claw that Ripman had given her outside the shirt. Nikki and Kenny were at the table, talking. John and Rosa were instantly the center of attention when they came in.

"Well, you two should be clean," Carrollee said mischievously. "Did you scrub every part?"

"Every part," Rosa said.

John blushed.

The village was celebrating, everyone dressed in their best clothes: cotton skirts and tops dyed bright colors on the women, men in loincloths, some with colorful shirts, others with necklaces of beads and hammered metals. Headdresses decorated with feathers, beads, and clay figures were everywhere. Kenny allowed them to watch from a distance, but did not take them close.

"Some of it you don't want to see," Kenny explained.

They held their own party, eating tortillas, bananas, corn, and they drank balche. When evening came, the village was still partying, but they retired early. Emmett and Carrollee sharing one hammock, Rosa and John sharing the other. Kenny and Nikki left to sleep somewhere else.

In the morning Kenny came back with a calculator, scrolling through screens, studying some of them intensely.

"Something wrong?" John asked.

"No," Kenny said quickly.

Kenny didn't volunteer any more, but he was quiet and continued to work with the calculator. Carrollee was feeling better now, joking with Emmett, and refusing to let him put the black T-shirt back on.

"Do you want your children to see you in that?" she said.

"We get MTV," Emmett said.

"Not after I get back," Carrollee said.

Kenny rounded up sleeveless cotton shirts for Emmett and John. The weaving was fine, the shirt light and comfortable in the humidity. They ate breakfast, the horrors of the day before forgotten, the strangeness of their setting accepted. The morning went by quickly and Kenny joined them late for lunch. As they finished, he asked them to leave.

"I have enjoyed your company," Kenny said, "but it is time for you to go."

"Is there something you are not telling us?" John asked.

Kenny had been missing most of the morning. When he returned he did not have the calculator.

"There's something I don't quite understand," he said honestly. "It's best if you get out of this time period as soon as possible. Besides, we can't risk contaminating this culture any more than we have."

No one objected to leaving, all anxious to find Nick and the others and compare stories, trying to make sense of it all. Selfishly, John wanted to find Ripman and brag about bagging another tyrannosaur.

"The model doesn't predict these time passages," Emmett said. "I need to get back and find a way to measure the impact of the pyramids and orgone energy on the time waves. I can't do that here."

Wearing a mix of Mayan and modern clothes, they packed up gear, taking gourds of water and packets of dried corn and fruit. They were standing in front of the pyramid, villagers watching from a distance, when John realized Nikki wasn't carrying any supplies.

"Nik, what's going on?" John asked.

"I'm not going, John," Nikki said, stepping toward Kenny, putting her arm around his waist.

"Kenny, you should come, too," Carrollee said. "You don't need to stay here."

"I think I do. I think I have to. More importantly, I think I did stay here."

John thought of the old Kenny who had sent them back to

save Carrollee. How far into the future was that? John was sure Nick Paulson would know by now.

Now Carrollee stepped to Nikki and gently hugged her. That set off a round of hugs and handshakes. Then Kenny handed Emmett his calculator.

"Just like before. Follow the maps and the instructions and—"

"I know, I know," Emmett said. "Put the calculator on the ledge."

Then it was time to go, Kenny and Nikki waving good-bye, arms around each other.

The trip back seemed to take longer than the trip to save Carrollee. Emmett was careful now, not reckless. They wound through the pyramid, passing through the modern version they had encountered on the moon. Then they were back in stone passages, working in dim light. Finally, there was daylight ahead. They stepped out of the pyramid expecting to find Nick, Phil, Ripman, and the old Kenny. They weren't there and there were no discernible walls, no thriving village. They were back in the Yucatan in their present.

"We did something wrong," John said. "We should be with Nick and the others."

"I followed it exactly," Emmett said, turning the calculator back on and searching the menu. "There's nothing in here but that one map."

"Then let's go back," John said. "Find out how to get to the others."

Emmett hesitated, looking at Carrollee. John saw the bandage showing through her thin top.

"We should get Carrollee to a doctor, John," Rosa said.

She was right, John knew, but his best friend was still somewhere through that pyramid and he was injured.

"I'm okay," Carrollee said, touching her chest.

"Maybe we could split up," John suggested, knowing it was a bad idea.

"We only have three rifles," Carrollee said. "Remember where we are and the hell we went through to get here."

Emmett and Rosa had heard the stories, knew the lives

that had been lost. It would be just as big a battle to get home and they would do it without the rangers and without Ripman's expertise. All their choices were bad.

John looked at the sky. There was a lot of daylight left, but John wasn't comfortable leaving until he was sure it was the right thing to do.

"Let's wait until morning," John said.

They all agreed, and Emmett took the calculator to the ruined hut to leave it. John, Carrollee, and Rosa stepped back into the pyramid opening, out of the sun. Emmett came hurrying back.

"There's a note," Emmett said.

He was holding a piece of crude paper. Emmett read them the note.

"Dear Emmett, Carrollee, John, and Rosa, I trust you all found your way safely back to your place in time. It is important for you to get as far away from the pyramid as you can, as quickly as you can. For your own good, be miles away before sunset. If Dr. Paulson and the others succeed, the time passages will be destroyed. Nikki sends her best. Kenny Randall."

There was no indecision now. They grabbed their gear and searched for a way out. Ripman found the pyramid by falling through the canopy. They couldn't get back the way they came, but on Nikki's first trip she and Kenny had come from a different direction. John in the lead, they entered enemy territory again.

76 · ERUPTION

If concentrated orgone were allowed to escape as an expansive force, it would spread that concentrated energy out over a wide area. Given the nature of orgone, the effect of such a release would be unlike the release of any other pent up energies.

—*Rex Bard, Ph.D., private communication with Toru Kawabata*

Phil was still conscious when they emerged from the pyramid, back on the moon. While Elizabeth helped Phil get to the exit, Nick led Baranov to the PLSS suits. As Nick expected, there were four. Nick helped Phil into his suit while Elizabeth and Baranov mimicked each move. Then Nick climbed into his suit.

"How much time?" Nick asked.

"It's either enough, or not," Elizabeth said, struggling with her second glove.

Nick picked up Phil's helmet, pausing. Phil's eyes were closed.

"Phil?" Nick said.

Phil gave him a gloved thumbs-up sign. One by one Nick helped the others into their helmets, then put his on, relieved when the heads-up display lit.

"Can you hear me?" Nick asked.

A jumble of voices replied. Nick lifted Phil and then let go. Phil swayed, but did not fall. Now Nick pushed the OPEN button, the doors sliding apart and then jamming.

"Get in, quickly!"

Awkwardly, Carrollee and Baranov maneuvered through

the partially opened doors. Picking up Phil, Baranov pulled him through then took him and stood him in a corner like a stuffed animal. Nick squeezed through, then hit close. The motors were smoking but managed to reverse, the doors sliding closed.

When the doors closed, Nick pushed the EQUALIZE PRESSURE button. Nick could feel the vibration of the pumps. The wait seemed eternal. Finally, he was sure it was taking too long. Squatting, he put his helmet against the seal of the door. Now he could hear the leak. Turning, he pushed his bottom against the door and pressed with all his might. The pumps droned on. Nick was about to give up when the OPEN light on the opposite door lit up.

"Push it, quick," Nick said.

Elizabeth slapped the button and the doors slid apart. Nick waited while Elizabeth and Baranov helped Phil out. Now he relaxed, standing. It felt like there was a drill in his back. Nick looked at the seal. The gap was getting wider.

"Get away!" he shouted. "Get away."

They turned, saw what was happening, and then angled away. Nick stopped outside, next to the wall. The leak was now a vapor jet visible in the vacuum. Nick hit the CLOSE button, but it was too late. As the exterior doors started to slide shut, the interior doors buckled, then blew out. The blast took out the exterior doors as well and now there was a horizontal geyser of material. Dinosaur bones, sheet rock, aluminum struts, a refrigerator, human bodies, clothes, tools, all shot from the pyramid, the force of the blowout sending the debris far across Flamsteed Crater.

Avoiding the stream, Nick bounded after the others. Unfamiliar with walking in the suit, Elizabeth and Baranov were using regular walking motions, making slow progress. Nick caught them, taking Phil.

"Like this," Nick said, bunny hopping.

They copied his motion.

Nick looked at the clock in his display, estimating how much time was left—not much.

"Those rocks," Nick said, pointing to three large boulders sitting a couple of hundred yards away.

Even with Phil, Nick made better time, getting there first, setting Phil on the far side and then grabbing Elizabeth as she bounced near. The debris continued to vomit from the pyramid. A crumpled vending machine was spit out like a watermelon seed, tumbling across the plain.

"It's going to suck that bomb out of its gut," Baranov said.

Nick worried about the same thing. The bomb was deep in the pyramid and would have to negotiate many twists and turns, but it could be done. Then there was a flash of brilliant light, their sunscreens protecting their eyes. A split second later the moon began to quake violently. Huge chunks of the containment building flew over their heads, arcing into the distance, disappearing over the horizon. Some chunks shot toward space with enough velocity to reach orbit. Smaller particles peppered their protecting boulders. Then the shower of debris stopped. Leaning back, Nick could see a pillar of light shooting toward the stars. The moon shook more violently now, the boulders that protected them rocking, threatening to fall over.

"Back away," Nick shouted.

They did, carrying Phil with them. The tower of light was spectacular and they couldn't look away, a silent sword of light cutting into the heavens. Then suddenly it was cut off at its base, winking out, leaving them blinking away spots.

Cautiously, Nick hopped out from behind the boulders. The containment building was destroyed, only the corners distinguishable. There was no sign of the pyramid and no sign of atmosphere leakage.

"This part of the plan worked out," Elizabeth said. "Please tell me there's a part two."

"Trust me," Nick said.

"Trusting you is what got me into this mess," Elizabeth said.

"Be nice or I won't let you ride in my lunar lander," Nick said.

"You can fly a spaceship?" Elizabeth asked, surprised.

"The computer flies it," Nick said. "We just need Phil to push the up button for us."

Phil said nothing.

Baranov pressed his helmet against Phil's.

"I can't hear anything," Baranov said.

Now they all called Phil's name, the suit speaker cutting in and out as they spoke over one another.

"Knock it off," Phil said suddenly. "I'm not dead yet."

Relieved, they began the trek to the lander with Phil supported between Nick and Baranov.

"Nick, you owe me," Elizabeth said.

"And I'll be happy to pay," Nick said.

77 · PUZZLE MAN

How sublime is the silence of nature's ever-active energies! There is something in the very name of wilderness, which charms the ear, and soothes the spirit of man. There is religion in it.

—*Estwick Evans, in Roderick Nash's*
Wilderness and the American Mind

YUCATAN PENINSULA
PRESENT TIME

They were two valleys away when the pyramid blew. The sun was just down when the sky lit up like day, and then came the distant rumble. A tower of fire rose a thousand feet into the sky. It was unlike any explosion John had ever seen. The birds took to flight, and the monkeys panicked, leaping from tree to tree. A minute later the pillar winked out as quickly as it appeared.

They slept in trees that night, John now the expert on survival. He remembered some of the tricks they had learned on the way in, and planned on finding a herd to mingle with, gambling there wouldn't be another coordinated tyrannosaur attack.

Rosa was in good shape, and, despite the deep cut on her chest, Carrollee managed a good pace. Emmett was overattentive and Carrollee scolded him.

"Em, you're making it harder, not easier!"

"Sorry, I thought you were dead when I saw you on that altar. It scared the hell out of me."

"It wasn't any fun being on the altar, either."

"I can imagine. I don't want anything to happen to you."

"That's sweet," Carrollee said, hugging him. "If something did happen to me you would have reason to be afraid. You would have to face my mother."

They made good progress, John wondering about their luck. He remembered that the pyramid attracted dinosaurs because of the magnetic field that surrounded it. Was the field gone? If so, the concentration of dinosaurs might be dissipating.

They climbed another hill, John wishing he had thought to bring one of the swords used by the Maya. Without a machete, he had to find a path, not make one, and he didn't want to use paths traveled by dinosaurs. They crested the hill, finding a meadow. It had been recently grazed and there were huge piles of feces. He led them around the perimeter, finding where the herd had exited. They were traveling east, not the direction they needed to go.

Now John led them across the clearing, everyone relieved to find the going easier. They were nearly across when birds erupted from the trees ahead.

"What is it?" Rosa whispered.

"Trouble," Carrollee said, already backing away.

Suddenly a flock of hypsilophodon broke from cover, the small green bipeds flowing from the undergrowth and around the humans. Startled, they let the little squealing beasts rush on to wherever they were going.

"That wasn't so bad," Rosa said.

"It's what they're running from that we need to worry about," John said, getting his dinosaur gun ready.

When it came it was nothing they had encountered before. Ten feet high, thirty feet long, it was a carnivore with a thick neck, but smaller head and jaws than a tyrannosaur and more functional front arms, but the same powerful back legs. It easily weighed three tons, as the ground vibrated with each step.

"What is that?"

"Allosaurus," John said.

"We need to run, don't we, John?" Rosa said.

"Any second now," John said, raising his rifle.

The allosaur spotted them, head lowered, tail stretching out.

"It's going to charge," John said. "Get ready to shoot and run."

John cocked his rifle. The allosaur crouched lower, emitting a deep rumble. Suddenly a helicopter shot overhead. The allosaur cringed, like it had been attacked. The helicopter circled, the roar of the twin turbines deafening, the backwash blowing up a dust cloud. A man in the door threw objects and gas grenades blew in front of the allosaur.

Shocked, the allosaur bellowed defiance. The gas cloud spread, and the allosaur backed away, tears running from its eyes. The helicopter landed behind them and they ran to the open hatch. A soldier in the door manned a machine gun, ignoring them and keeping his eyes on the allosaur. John and Emmett helped Rosa and Carrollee inside, then were pulled up themselves. They scooted deeper into the helicopter's hot interior. The helicopter lifted off, taking them to safety.

"Nachos!" Carrollee cried, excited.

"Nice to see you Doctor Chen-Puglisi," one of the crewmen said.

John recognized the crewman from their trip to the village where they had started their mission.

"Now I expected to find you, but not Dr. Puglisi."

"It's a long story," Carrollee said.

"Have anything to do with that explosion?"

"I think so."

"How is it you can fly?" John asked.

"After the explosion the magnetic interference dropped to near zero. We started searching for you immediately."

Nachos let them alone, and they settled in, trying to get comfortable.

"We've got to get to a telescope," Emmett said. "And find out what happened on the moon."

"First, we're going to see Lee and Emma," Carrollee said.

"Of course," Emmett said, embarrassed.

"By the way, Em, I had a few unexpected charges on the Visa."

"Charges?" Emmett started to ask.

"Hey, doctors," Nachos interrupted. "What's a five-letter word for lethargic?"

"Inert," Carrollee and Emmett said at the same time.

Now Carrollee and Emmett wrapped their arms around each other, holding each other close, the Visa charges forgotten.

"That looks good to me," Rosa said, and then pushed her way under John's arm.

It was hot, and they quickly stuck together, but neither minded. Soon Rosa was sleeping, lulled by the constant drone of the helicopter blades. Carrollee and Emmett were asleep, too, and John felt exhaustion creeping through his body. Nachos studied his passengers, then duck-walked close to John, speaking loud enough for John to hear.

"I need a word that means 'take out of circulation.'"

"Me," John said, closing his eyes and running his hand across Rosa's back.

She snuggled closer, pressing her breasts tight against him.

"Not enough letters, sir, it has to be six."

"Retire," John managed to say just before he fell asleep.

78 · PARADISE

... civilization is the villain in environmental thought, which is why the radical Earth First! battle cry is "Back to the Pleistocene," that is, back to a time before agriculture and cities—in short, before Iron Age civilization began ...

—*Bruce S. Thornton,* Plagues of the Mind

YUCATAN PENINSULA
FUTURE TIME

It was approaching sundown when they emerged from the pyramid into paradise.

"It's perfect," Vince said, spreading his arms, walking into the meadow that was the front porch of the pyramid.

Marissa, Reggie, Latoya, and Wings ran deep into the meadow, chasing butterflies, picking flowers. Whitey followed Marissa around, interested in whatever pleased her. Jennifer and Valerie stood by the entrance, ready to dart to freedom, until Vince waved them away with his rifle.

"Hey, there's a note," Reggie said, pointing at the wall next to the exit.

The note did not belong in Vince's new world and he tore it off the wall. It read:

GET AWAY FROM THE PYRAMID BEFORE SUN-DOWN BECAUSE IT IS GOING TO GO KABOOM. BIG KABOOM!

"Everybody, this way," Whitey shouted.

The women complied, following Whitey to where the village had been. Flustered, Vince hurried after them, fuming because his place was in front. There was no discernible village, just occasional stones still showing the marks of tools. Vince shouted for Whitey to stop.

"This is far enough," Vince said.

"Not for me," Whitey said, starting off again.

"I'm in charge," Vince said.

"Yes," Whitey said. "And as leader you should understand the kill radius of a twenty-megaton bomb."

"That bomb is on the moon," Vince argued.

"I'm not taking any chances," Whitey said, jogging away.

Only Reggie hesitated, hanging back as the others raced into the forest.

"We better make sure they don't get into any trouble," Vince said.

Nettles tore new wounds in Vince's leg as they ran. They climbed down into a gulley, Whitey helping others in treacherous places. When it was Vince's turn, Vince slapped away Whitey's proffered hand. At the bottom Vince ran past the milling women, starting up the other side.

"Wait," Whitey shouted, studying the sky. "It's safer down here."

"It's a nuclear weapon, Whitey," Vince said, trying to regain dominance.

"Yes, but there's no time to get anyplace safer."

Vince never got a chance to argue. A bright flash startled everyone to silence, followed by the loudest sound any of them had heard. Now chunks of stone rained down, taking out limbs and pulverizing trunks, setting off chain reactions of falling trees. One-ton stones were buried in the soft ground, creating impact craters, ejecta spraying in all directions. Three large stones landed in their gulley in quick succession. Reggie jumped up to run, but Whitey tackled her, wrestled her down and then covered her with his body.

There was a bright shimmering light shooting toward the heavens. Vince cowered in the gulley, awestruck at what he had unleashed. A minute later the light disappeared like the beam of a flashlight switched off.

Reggie was crying, Whitey comforting her. Now Valerie

and Jennifer joined them, then Marissa. Soon his whole community was in a group hug.

"Let's go," Vince said. "We need to find shelter before dark."

"But Vince," Marissa said. "Don't you know what this means? Without the pyramid we can't get the others here. We can't even get supplies."

In his anger over the usurper, Whitey, Vince had forgotten his plan to bring others to this future. Worse, he had planned on using the pyramid as a continuing source of supplies. Still, he had the future he wanted and enough women to keep him happy.

It was getting dark, so they climbed up out of the gulley, and then looked for a place to sleep the night. Whitey talked the others into climbing into trees; Vince finally copied the others, spending an uncomfortable night wedged in the fork of a tree limb.

Vince regained some control the next day, taking the lead. They wandered east, Vince projecting confidence he didn't feel. The terrain was rugged, but sloping down gradually, the downhill walk Vince's primary reason for heading in that direction. There were monkeys in the trees. Many birds and occasionally larger animals could be heard crashing through the forest. Eventually, they came to a meadow with a stream along one side that emptied into a small lake. By now everyone was exhausted, hungry, and covered with insect bites, the natural life losing some of its appeal.

Vince declared the meadow their new home, directing the building of a shelter. They had few tools to work with, making do with two knives. It took them two days to erect a lean-to with a palm frond roof. They set it up against a rock wall, and then drove pointed stakes into the ground all around to keep predators away. There was barely enough room for all of them to get under the shelter that night when they were hit by a downpour. The roof leaked so badly, they were soon as wet as if there had been no roof. Come morning, everyone was shivering.

Vince sat under the still-dripping roof, watching the others work. The women had fanned out in pairs, looking for food. Whitey was on his knees with Marissa, trying to start a fire. Whitey had carved a groove in a chunk of wood, and was rubbing a smaller stick in the groove. Marissa started chanting.

"Go, Whitey, go! Go, Whitey, go! Go, Whitey, go!"

Whitey was red-faced from the exertion.

"Go, Whitey, go! Go, Whitey, go! Go, Whitey, go!"

"Everything's too wet," Vince said.

Whitey kept up his exertions.

"We gathered twigs and moss from under the trees," Marissa said. "It's really dry."

"Stop wasting your energy," Vince said, irritated by the defiance.

"It's smoking! It's smoking!" Marissa suddenly squealed.

"Put moss in!" Whitey shouted, keeping up the pace.

Marissa dropped a small piece of moss at the end of the groove. It began to smoke, then there was a tiny flame. Marissa squealed with delight, feeding the tiny fire, building it slowly.

"Man creates fire!" Marissa said, watching her little fire grow. "My hero!"

Now she fell on top of Whitey, kissing him deeply. Vince fumed.

"Hey, a fire!" Latoya shouted.

The others all came running, gathering, holding hands over the tiny fire. Valerie, Jennifer, and Reggie ran to find more wood and soon the fire was big enough to warm everyone.

"What the hell is the point of a fire?" Vince argued irrationally. "There's nothing to cook over it."

"I found corn!" Latoya said. "Can we roast it?"

Everyone thought that was a good idea and half of them ran off, coming back a few minutes later with a dozen ears. Now they didn't know what to do.

"It will just burn if we put it in the fire?" Reggie said.

"I know!" Wings said. "I saw it done at a party in Ohio once. You bury them in the coals."

"You'll have to wait for it to burn down," Vince said, stating the obvious.

"Maybe not," Wings said, using a piece of wood to dig into the ground next to the fire. Then she laid out six ears, covering them with green leaves and then a layer of dirt. Now she criss-crossed dry wood on top, then set it on fire with a branch from Marissa's fire.

"Very clever," Whitey said.

There was a good feeling now, everyone joking and talking about who looked the worst. Reggie, who cared the most about her appearance, complained the most, but everyone else thought she looked the best. Desperate to return the pecking order to normal, Vince squeezed in between Reggie and Latoya, putting his arm around Reggie's waist. She didn't respond, just letting his hand rest there. Then he slid it down to her bottom. She pushed his hand away.

"I'm going to wash up," Reggie said, leaving the circle.

Everyone had seen Vince's move, and now all of the women decided it was time to wash their hands. They hurried after Reggie, whispering with her all the way to the pond. Only Whitey was left to manage the fire.

"We're going to need more than corn to survive," Vince said, covering his embarrassment.

"We can do a lot with corn," Whitey said. "We can grind it to get corn meal, press it to get corn oil, make tortillas out of the flour, use the fibers in the husks for twine and rope."

"Don't be stupid, Whitey," Vince grumbled. "That's not a balanced diet."

Whitey reddened but kept his eyes on the fire. Vince studied Whitey. He was an engineer; bookish, a nerd, not an athlete, but he was built like a wrestler, with thick arms and a barrel chest. Vince was taller, muscular, but not a fighter—a thinker, a persuader, a Pied Piper with a silver tongue. Could he take Whitey if he had to? If he wanted to? The man needed to know his place.

"I'll show you an easier way to start a fire later," Vince said.

"I'll look forward to that," Whitey said sarcastically.

"We better find some fruit," Vince said.

"Jennifer found some bananas, but she couldn't reach them," Whitey said in a more civil tone. "There should be nuts, too. We can gather seedlings and start our own orchards. Plant some corn, too."

"That's the plan," Vince said, trying to take credit.

Now Whitey looked uncomfortable, scuffing his feet.

"There are fish in that pond," Whitey said.

"What are you suggesting?" Vince asked angrily.

"I'm just saying we could use the protein," Whitey said.

"No. We won't resort to murder. Not as long as I'm the leader."

The others were coming back now, smiling, laughing. Seeing the beautiful women he had gathered together walking through the deep green meadow, picking flowers for their hair, Vince knew he had made the right decision. This was his paradise.

Wings remained in charge of the corn roast, the others falling into a silly routine. "Is it done yet?" one would ask. "No, not yet," Wings would reply. A second later another would ask, "Is it done yet?" the others giggling like it was the funniest joke they had ever heard.

The fire over the corn had burned down to coals and now Wings cleared the glowing embers, and then scraped away the layer of dirt. The leaves underneath were soggy. Carefully, she picked up the leaves, tossing them aside, revealing steaming ears of corn. Using green leaves, Wings picked up an ear by the stem, then stripped down the husk. This wasn't the corn sold in supermarkets, the kernels uneven in size and color, but everyone "oohed" approval. Wings held out the ear but no one took it.

"You're the cook," Valerie said. "You get the first taste."

Wings smiled, then gingerly took a bite of the warm corn, scraping kernels from the small end. She munched the small mouthful, then smiled.

"It's good!" she declared.

Everyone but Vince cheered. The corn was passed around

and everyone ate, declaring it was the best meal ever.

"What's for lunch?" Whitey asked as he finished his ear.

"Wings's corn!" Marissa said.

Everyone cheered.

"What's for dinner?" Whitey asked.

"Wings's corn!" they all responded.

"Hey, who made me the cook?" Wings asked, in mock indignation.

"You did," Whitey said, holding up his cleaned cob.

They scattered out after breakfast, searching for food. A couple of hours later they had gathered some overripe bananas, squash, and chili peppers. Valerie and Jennifer came back excited, carrying handfuls of white fluff.

"Look at what we found," Valerie said.

"It's cotton," Whitey said.

Vince slapped the cotton out of their hands. The two captives cringed, shrinking out of the group.

"I told you to get food. We can't eat cotton."

"But we can wear it," Whitey said, pointing to the ragged condition of his shirt.

"I set the priorities," Vince said. "I'm the one that led us here. I'm in charge, not you, Whitey!"

Now there was uncomfortable silence.

"Well, let's eat what we do have," Vince said.

Silently, Wings cut up the fruits and vegetables, dividing them into equal proportions. The fire had died down, everyone hot now, but they fed it enough to keep it burning. After lunch, everyone but Whitey and Marissa rested, the heat of the day sapping their strength. The "couple" wandered off, holding hands. Vince pictured them in the bushes somewhere making love. It angered him and aroused him. Surveying his many attractive women, Vince decided it was time to assert his sexual rights. A few minutes later Reggie roused, heading toward the pond. Vince gave her a few minutes lead, then followed.

He found Reggie, naked, squatting waist deep in the pond, clothes neatly folded on the bank. She was washing the sweat from her body. Vince studied her profile, aroused, convinced he had created his own personal heaven. Reggie's short red hair was limp in the high humidity, but she was the most beautiful redhead on the planet—Vince silently laughing at his own joke. She was also the oldest woman on the planet, but her breasts were still firm, her form athletic. She was an energetic lover, although controlling—he would fix that.

"Great idea," Vince said, now coming to the bank. "I'll join you."

Startled, Reggie covered her breasts with her arms, then turned away. Vince unbuttoned his shirt, irritated by her re-action, but aroused by her modesty.

"You can have the pond," Reggie said, starting to stand, then, embarrassed by her nakedness, sank back down, her eyes flicking to her clothes.

Vince sat, taking off his shoes and socks, and then his pants and underwear. Reggie looked away. Now Vince waded out toward her. Suddenly she got up and hurried toward shore.

"Where are you going?"

"I'm done," she said. "It's too cold."

"Come here, I'll warm you up," he said.

"No thanks."

Reggie got to shore and, not bothering to dry, stepped into her underwear, her back to Vince. Vince stormed out of the pond as she hurriedly put her bra on. Vince grabbed her and spun her around, holding her by the shoulders, squeezing so tight she winced. When he leaned down to kiss her, Reggie turned her head.

"What's going on?" Vince demanded.

"Nothing. I'm just not in the mood."

"I'll get you in the mood," Vince said, trying to kiss her again.

"Stop, Vince. I don't want to. I feel bad about what I did. I shot a friend."

"You did what I asked you to do. You should always do what I tell you to do, Reggie. I got us here, didn't I? To this paradise?"

"Do you think I killed him?"

"I hope you did kill him. He was an animal-murdering bastard."

Again she tried to struggle free, pushing on his chest. Now he grabbed her hair, pulled her head back and kissed her on the lips. She didn't respond and when he broke off she was crying.

"Stop," she said.

"No," Vince said, now pushing down on her shoulders, trying to get her to the ground.

"Stop it, Vince," Whitey suddenly called.

"Get back to camp!" Vince ordered, not turning around.

"Let her go!" Whitey said, clamping a meaty hand on Vince's shoulder.

Vince released Reggie, spun and hit Whitey in the face. The big man staggered back, his nose bleeding. Now Vince could see Wings, Latoya, and Marissa behind Whitey. The others were coming across the meadow.

"This is between me and Reggie!" he shouted.

Whitey wiped blood from his nose. Vince looked at the size of the man. He had never seen him angry, but an angry Whitey could be too much for him. He kicked Whitey in the groin and when he sagged, Vince punched him in the face again. It was a mistake. He could see pity for Whitey in the eyes of the women. Suddenly Reggie rushed past him, clothes in her arms. Jennifer and Valerie took her under their care, shielding her from Vince while she got into the rest of her clothes.

"It wasn't supposed to be like this," he said softly.

He was losing their admiration. Now he watched as Marissa and Wings helped Whitey to his feet, then slowly walked back to camp. Vince stayed by the pond, thinking, plotting. Whitey had to go. That night he found out that they had been plotting, too.

After a dinner of Wings's corn and fruit, they built the fire up, both to light the camp and to keep predators away.

"Vince, we need to talk about leadership," Marissa said suddenly.

Vince looked around. In the flickering firelight, he could see everyone but Whitey and Marissa avoiding his eyes.

"There's nothing to talk about."

"Yes there is," Marissa insisted.

Vince fixed her with a stare. Whitey put his hand on her knee, patting it. The man had been limping all afternoon and was not in shape to fight again.

"You're giving all the orders, but we're doing all the work," Marissa said.

"I do my share," Vince said, stung.

"No, you don't," Wings said. "And you complain about everything."

Now half the group was looking him in the eye.

"Who did the work to get us here?" Vince asked.

"We weren't supposed to be here at all," Latoya said. "We were supposed to be at the refuge. The one we stocked and where our friends are. Besides, Marissa was the one who made the discovery."

Now everyone in the group was staring him in the eye. Vince stood, using his size to intimidate. Marissa stood, too, pushing Whitey back down when he tried to stand.

"We want to elect a leader," Marissa said.

"The only vote that counts is mine," Vince said.

Control was slipping from his grasp.

"We've decided, Vince," Marissa said. "We want more say—"

Vince hit Marissa in the face, sending her staggering back. Whitey caught her, lowering her to the ground, then started to get up. Vince kicked him under the jaw, snapping his head back, and then ran for the rifles, coming back armed.

"Get over there," he ordered, keeping his back to the fire.

The others helped Marissa and Whitey to their feet, both wobbly. Marissa's nose was bleeding.

"We're going to settle this here and now," Vince said, making up his plan as he went along. "From now on I'm keeping all of the rifles and the ammunition. Tomorrow, you will begin to build a bigger building, with walls and a proper roof. That will be for me. Then you can build yourselves shelter. I'll expect one of you to sleep with me every night— a different one per night."

He noticed Whitey. "Except for you, Whitey," he said, and then laughed.

"I won't sleep with you," Reggie said.

Vince swung the rifle toward her. "What did you say?"

Reggie cowered briefly, and then stiffened. "I said, I won't sleep with you."

"Me neither," Wings said.

Then one by one, each of the women rejected him. Infuriated, Vince turned the gun back on Marissa.

"You started this! You're responsible."

Vince's finger tightened on the trigger. He was thinking through the pros and cons of killing her—they were all pros. Then he realized everyone was staring past him toward the fire. Before he could turn around he felt something hard press against the back of his neck.

"Put the rifle down!"

Vince didn't recognize the voice. He hesitated. They were supposed to be alone here. Now he heard a rifle bolt pulled back, a live round ejected onto the ground next to him and then the sound of a new round sliding into the chamber.

"Put the rifle down!"

Vince lowered his rifle, set the butt on the ground, and then felt it pulled away.

"You—I think your name is Marissa? Come get the rifles."

Marissa did as she was told, walking behind Vince. Then Vince felt the pressure removed from the back of his head and Marissa reappeared with two rifles. Vince realized the man behind him was now unarmed and turned. The man was about Vince's age, the same height, but a little thinner. He was tanned, wearing a camouflage patterned baseball cap, and camouflage clothes.

"Ripman, is that you?" Reggie exclaimed.

"Hello, Reggie," Ripman said.

"Who the hell are you?" Vince asked, worried by the man's military look.

The man ignored Vince.

"My father used to beat me," Ripman said. "Until I got big enough to fight back. Now I can't tolerate a bully."

"This isn't any of your business!" Vince said, sizing up Ripman.

"Let's take a vote," Ripman said. "How many here want me to beat the hell out of this man?"

Everyone's hand except Whitey's went up.

"Well it's not unanimous, but it's a majority."

Vince swung at Ripman's face. He was ready for it, deflecting it with his right arm, then punching Vince in the rib cage with his left. It staggered Vince, but didn't knock the wind out of him. Vince had hope now. If that was the newcomer's best punch, Vince would kill him. Vince kicked out, Ripman jumping back. Vince charged, launching punches with both hands. Both landed, but on Ripman's shoulders and he ducked, and lunged, head-butting Vince in the solar plexus. Now gasping for breath, he discovered Ripman had better punches in him; many better punches. Raining blows on him, Ripman beat him from head to waist, driving Vince to his knees. Then the beating stopped. There were cheers and the others came forward, shaking his hand, kissing him on the cheek, hugging him.

Vince stayed where he was, forgotten, watching in the orange firelight as his tribe adopted a new member. Now they led Ripman under the shelter, asking him where he came from. Even though they were disappointed when they learned there was no way home, they brightened again. Soon it was a party mood when Ripman ran off into the dark and came back with a jug.

"Balche," he said.

They passed the jug around, sipping, gasping as the burning liquid trickled down their throats. Whitey and Marissa sat next to each other, holding hands. The other women arrayed around Ripman, laughing and smiling, as obsequious as if he were a god.

"That should be me," Vince hissed, sitting in the dark.

Now plotting, he thought of the rifles. They were stacked near the new man. He couldn't get to them now, but he would, sooner or later.

"Tomorrow I'll patch up this roof for you," Ripman was

saying. "Then we better get started on a stockade."

Ripman looked over the sharpened stakes they had set around their camp.

"These stakes are a good idea, but they won't stop the top predators."

He was taking charge. Where was the discussion of an election now?

"That corn roast was pretty clever," he said. "Who thought that up?"

"Wings!" they all said at once.

Wings got up and bowed.

"You know, I spotted some wild goats. We might be able to catch a few and start a herd. We can make butter from their milk."

"Buttered corn! Wonderful!" Marissa said.

Vince spat blood from his mouth, cursed them all, and then got to his feet, swaying, grimacing. He moved gingerly. Nothing was broken, but tomorrow his body would be bruised from head to waist. Laughter behind him—he ignored it, walking toward the pond, plotting. The new man would have to sleep. He would be cautious at first, probably have one of the others stand guard, but eventually he would make a mistake. Then Vince would strike. He would kill Ripman and Whitey. There could be only one rooster in the barnyard.

Vince sat on the marshy shore, scooped up water, washing his face. Already he was feeling better. While he waited for a careless moment, he would pretend to be a new man. He would do extra work, and laugh at their juvenile jokes. He would use his charm to win them back, one by one. He could do that. He had done it all his life.

A fish broke the water, the ripples reflecting the firelight at oblique angles, creating an orange kaleidoscope. Mesmerized, he lost himself in the flickering surface. Now he kneeled, putting his face in the water and holding it there, the cool water clearing the residual fuzziness. Now he sat up, sputtering, wiping the water from his eyes. Then he relaxed back on to his bottom. He felt something hot on his neck—breathing.

Slowly he turned. The bright fire created a silhouette out of the jaguar behind him. The jaguar lunged, taking him by the neck, crushing his windpipe. It dragged him still alive from the shore. People came running from the camp, Ripman in the lead, rifle in hand, aiming it. Silently, Vince begged him to hurry, to save his life. Now Vince reached up, pushing on the jaws. The jaguar crunched down, snapping Vince's neck. Still conscious, but unable to move or feel, he saw Ripman fire three quick rounds, the jaguar dropping in its tracks.

Vince was still conscious when they pried the jaws open and pulled him free.

"Is he dead?" Wings asked.

Reggie knelt, touching his neck.

"Yes," Reggie said.

Vince wanted to scream at her, to call her a quack, to tell them that he was alive, but he realized she was right. He was dead. Then everything that he was, everything that he had dreamed, was taken from him.

79 ▪ SECOND STRIKE

Only within the moment of time represented by the present century has one species—man—acquired significant power to alter the nature of his world.

—*Rachel Carson*, Silent Spring

NEAR WHEELER RIDGE, CALIFORNIA

Two years ago, Winifred (Winny) Johnson had run over a chipmunk with her car, crushing it flat. At the moment of its death she felt its spirit enter her body. Since then the chipmunk's soul had melded with hers. In recognition of this spirit bonding, Winny had changed her name to Chipmunk. Now as she prepared to detonate the bomb, she worried, wondering whether the Chipmunk spirit would remain with her as she entered her next incarnation. She hoped so, since she hadn't been lonely since the bonding.

Before becoming Chipmunk, she had been in a downward spiral, driving friends away, alternating between angry and sullen. Most of the anger was directed at the boyfriend who had given her AIDS, the disease that was slowly killing her, but enough spilled over to her friends that they began to ostracize her. It was in her darkest hours that the Chipmunk spirit came, and then Vince.

The Chipmunk had given her a bond with nature and Vince had brought her into his circle and given her friendship and hope. Through him she learned not to fear leaving this world because she would return in a new body, a healthy body. The same would be true for her Chipmunk spirit. No spirit could ever die so there was no need to suffer through the horror of AIDS when a new body awaited her. That is, no reason except to make the world a better place before she moved on. She believed that. She believed everything Vince told her.

So it was with righteous anger that she shot one of the men responsible for the destruction of Earth's habitat. As he was an arms broker and environmental rapist, she found it easy to shoot him and even her Chipmunk soul did not judge her for her actions. Now Vince had given her a way to get to her new body and strike a blow for Gaea.

They called the bomb a backpack bomb, but it was much too heavy for her to carry, especially in her weakened condition. The last doctor she saw wanted to hospitalize her, pump her full of chemicals—fight poison with poison. She refused, preferring to get through to her new life as soon as possible. Instead of carrying the bomb, she pulled it with a two-wheeled cart resembling a rickshaw. The oversized wheels with balloon tires rolled easily, although she was still laboring as she pulled her cart. It was midafternoon, worst heat of the day, as she rolled along the highway berm toward the popular truck and auto stop. They had picked the location for dramatic purposes. It was one of the gateways to Los Angeles, where Interstate 5 fed into the environmental abscess that was Los Angeles. This target would minimize the loss of animal life, yet have a lasting impact on Los Angeles. Cutting one of the major arteries wouldn't kill the city, but it would sicken it.

They had dropped her a mile from the target with her cart, then drove north on the interstate to be well away when she detonated the bomb. The people in the cars that passed her stared, but none offered to help. No one would stop to help her. Her eyes were dark hollows, her clothes ragged, her arms and legs a spiderweb of veins. Near exhaustion now, she stopped at the corner of the truck stop just as another diesel-guzzling monster pulled in, this one a gasoline tanker. On the other side of the building were the gasoline pumps where families stopped to fill up and then step inside for a bathroom break or snack. She avoided looking at the children, instead picturing in her mind a seed. That's what Vince had called this act, a seed that would grow into a beautiful garden.

Chipmunk sat now, resting, visualizing the garden and meeting Vince there with her new healthy body. He promised he would make love to her in that garden, when she was healthy again. Opening the large duffel bag strapped to the cart, she studied the display. Entering the access code, the display lit up showing only one second on the screen. She told Whitey to set it up that way. Now visualizing the garden, imagining herself in Vince's arms, Chipmunk pushed the enter button.

80 · RESPONSE

Be sure to carry your credit cards, cash, checks, stocks, insurance policies, and will. Every effort will be made to clear trans-nuclear attack checks, including those drawn on destroyed banks. You will be encouraged to buy U.S. Savings Bonds.

—*Federal Emergency Management Agency, Executive Order*

WASHINGTON, D.C.

This time Willa heard about the explosion on the news. Her administrative assistant burst in, shouting for her to turn on the television. Every channel carried the same images, showing a towering plume with the San Bernadino Mountains in the background. The reporter was babbling, describing what every viewer could see for himself.

"There are conflicting reports coming from witnesses. Many report seeing a blinding flash and a mushroom cloud that could indicate a nuclear device. However, our sources tell us that the size of the explosion was too small to be from a thermonuclear bomb. Since we know that the explosion took place at or near a truck stop, some authorities believe this may have been a massive truck bomb headed for Los Angeles that detonated prematurely."

Willa knew from experience that "some authorities" meant the reporter's own speculation. Willa turned off the audio. The news anchor was mistaken. A suitcase bomb would have a yield small enough to be confused with a very large truck bomb. DOD would know as soon as they overflew the site with radiation detectors.

Willa headed for the situation room without being called. The president and Clark were there already, an officer carrying the nuclear football was standing by. The president had a report in his hand and he looked grim.

"The sonofabitch didn't believe me," President Pearl said. "I warned Petrov about what would happen if he didn't cooperate with us in tracking down these weapons."

The wall monitor crackled to life and General Flannery came on the screen.

"Mr. President, I can confirm it was a low-yield nuclear weapon of Russian design. I have the plutonium signature. What do you want to do, sir?"

Carolyn Mauck arrived, grim faced, her black hair pulled into a tight bun.

"Do you have a casualty estimate?" the president asked.

"Rough estimates only, sir. Perhaps a few hundred. I'll have fallout pattern predictions in a few hours. Ground zero was a popular travel center. There were a number of restaurants in the area, some light industry. We're lucky they didn't make it into Los Angeles before detonation."

"Carol, how many more of these bombs are out there?" the president asked.

"A minimum of a dozen are unaccounted for, Mr. President."

Now the president sighed, drummed his fingers, looking from face-to-face.

"I'm going to take us to DEFCON 1 and demand President Petrov come clean on these weapons. If not, I want response options. Something less than a preemptive strike. Select a target with similar numbers of casualties and economic impact. If they don't come clean, we'll hit them once just to get their attention."

"Sir, a limited strike will only serve to tip our hand," General Flannery said. "I recommend a full strike or no strike at all."

"I know the risks, General, but I'm not prepared to launch a full strike."

"After two nuclear attacks on our own soil?"

"Get me a target list, general!"

"Sir," Willa cut in. "It won't matter. President Petrov and his ministers know they can't go toe to toe with us in a nuclear exchange. When we go to DEFCON 1, they will launch a preemptive strike themselves, forcing us to retaliate. We can't risk it. Sir, they may be telling the truth. They may not be responsible."

"Both of these weapons have been confirmed as Russian. There's no mistake."

"I agree with the vice president," Mauk said. "Russian armed forces are on alert. With inferior weapons the military will be telling President Petrov that their only hope would be to strike first."

The president studied his cabinet, thinking, drumming his fingers.

"The risk is acceptable," he said finally. "Take us to DEF-CON 1, General. I'm going to give the missile commanders their launch codes in case the vice president is right and the Russians move to launch their missiles. If they fuel their birds, we launch."

Now the president called for the officer with the briefcase carrying the nuclear launch codes. Both the officer and the president carried keys, and both were needed to unlock the briefcase. The president removed the sealed envelopes with the launch codes. Then there was a rap at the door and a communications officer from the situation room came in.

"What is it?" the president asked.

"Sir, I have an urgent call for you."

The president looked puzzled.

"It's from the moon," he said. "It's Nick Paulson."

"It can't be," the president said. "They lost contact with him."

The president took the call over a speakerphone, the delay from the moon noticeable.

"Mr. President, I understand there have been nuclear detonations in the United States. These are not, I repeat, not, attacks by Russia. If you haven't already, you will detect explosions in the Yucatan at the site we were exploring there, and on the moon. The structure in Flamsteed Crater has been destroyed. I can explain more fully but the story is going to take some time."

"How do you know this? You've been in space or on the moon through all of this."

"I met someone here who can explain."

"You met someone on the moon? How could they get there?"

"It's hard to explain, but he is with me. Elizabeth Hawthorne is also here. He is Russian and a member of their special forces. He was sent to Alaska to retrieve a stolen weapon. Instead, he stumbled onto something much more complex."

Willa watched the president's face. Bewildered, doubtful, questioning; all of these emotions were there.

"His name is Anatole Baranov."

A few seconds later Baranov spoke.

"This is Anatole Baranov, I am speaking to you from the moon and I assure you that the Russian government had nothing whatsoever to do with the attacks on your great country. Thank you very much."

Now Willa relaxed. The president was too shocked to do anything but listen.

81 · HINDSIGHT

Peace is the skillful management of conflict.

—*Kenneth Boulding, "A National Peace Academy,"*
Beasts, Ballads, and Bouldingisms

TWIN FALLS, IDAHO

Kenny, looking thirty years old, emerged from the pyramid to a warm hug from Nikki, as young and pretty as the day she checked out of the hospital. Kawabata was there, too, looking twenty years younger than the day he first met Kenny Randall.

"What did you find?" he asked as Nikki and Kenny separated.

"There are no time passages left. Either the other timelines ceased to exist, or they are sealed off from us."

They were at the Idaho facility, funded by a foundation they had set up a century earlier.

"I'm sure it worked," Nikki said hopefully.

"There was sufficient stored orgonic energy," Kawabata said.

"Yes, history was protected, but the price, Toru, the price."

"It was the only way to give them back their future."

"They could have had ours," Nikki said.

"They didn't want it," Kenny said. "But now we'll never know what happens to them."

"That's the way the future should be," Nikki said. "Just like ours."

82 ▪ HONEYMOON

Finally, I must reluctantly recommend that all data, results, analysis, and even proposals associated with the research into orgone energy be classified and that no further funding be provided for such research. The disruption of space-time will take a century to repair. If other governments, or anarchists, were to discover the potential harm they can inflict by using orgone to manipulate time waves, they would surely use it.

—*Nick Paulson, classified report to President Pearl*

HONOLULU, HAWAII

Elizabeth and Nick sunbathed on the deck of the sailboat while Emmett relaxed in the stern. They had struck the sails, floating while Carrollee, Emma, and Lee were below deck, fixing sandwiches for lunch. The sun was warm but not hot, the gentle breeze keeping them comfortable. Oahu was on the horizon.

Elizabeth stirred, sitting up.

"Isn't it a little weird to take a honeymoon with another couple?" she asked.

Nick rolled onto his side.

"No, but asking them to share the honeymoon suite would have been."

Elizabeth looked over the rail, sunglasses hiding her eyes but not her feelings.

"You're still bothered by what happened, aren't you?" Nick asked.

"I try not to think about it but I can't help it. I should be dead—I am dead in Fox Valley."

"You don't know that, Elizabeth. There's nothing left in Fox Valley."

"But we know what happened."

"No, we don't. That timeline ceased to exist once we altered it. You are here, so you did not die."

"But that other timeline does exist, parallel to ours. That's the theory and there I died and so did everyone in that building."

"It's theory," Nick said.

He took off his sunglasses so she could see his eyes.

"Whatever happened, it's not your fault. Kenny Randall manipulated all of us. He was controlling the energy baffles in the pyramid. He was directing us to different points in time for his purposes. He had an outcome in mind that he was working toward. Maybe this is it! Maybe not! But it's all we have."

"So you don't believe the world was going to end?"

"I believe we were going to go through another time quilting much worse than the one a decade ago. It would have been disastrous and civilization as we know it would have been devastated. He helped us avoid that. For that I'm grateful. The rest of it? The futures he showed me? I think there are an infinite number of possible outcomes at any moment in time. The pyramids allowed us to see some of those. Who knows whether there was ever any real choice. Maybe all of his manipulations were part of this future that we're living right now."

"This future worked out for us," Elizabeth said, smiling sadly. "But it cost so many lives."

"And saved so many," Nick said.

Carrollee, Emma, and Lee came back on deck, the children carrying plastic bags of sandwiches to Nick and Elizabeth.

"Thank you," Elizabeth said.

The children walked carefully back to their mother and father. Carrollee wore a one-piece white swimsuit that showed off her tanned skin. A white scar was clearly visible on her chest.

"What kind did you get?" Elizabeth asked.

Nick peeled back one of the slices of bread.

"Butter and turkey," Nick said.

"Peanut butter and grape jelly," Elizabeth said.

"Trade?" Nick offered.

"No chance."

They sat on the deck, feet hanging over the side. Occasionally, waves slapped the hull, the spray cooling their feet. They ate in silence, tossing big chunks of the sandwiches to fish.

"Hey, looky!" Emma shouted.

The Puglisis were standing, looking off the port side. There was an animal a dozen yards from the boat, with a large body just under the surface and a long thin neck stretching twenty feet into the air. The head was only a little larger than the neck.

"What is it?" Emma asked.

"Pleisiosaur?" Elizabeth suggested.

"No!" Carrollee and Emmett said together.

"We've seen one of those up close," Carrollee explained.

"It's a relative, though," Emmett said. "Elasmosaurus, I think."

Suddenly the head stabbed into the water, coming up with a fish, then, straightening its neck, it swallowed the fish whole.

Emma and Lee squealed with delight.

"If that's a new arrival, please let it be from the Cretaceous," Elizabeth said.

"It's from the Cretaceous," Emmett confirmed. "When it got here is another question."

"The unusual electromagnetic radiation subsided immediately after the pyramids were destroyed," Nick said. "And Emmett's model shows no significant confluences among the time waves."

"Then this is the world we're stuck with," Elizabeth said.

The elasmosaurus was fishing again, neck stretched high, head pointed at the water, flippers and body still. Nick turned, leaned against the rail and looked across the blue sea at the emerald island in the distance. Elizabeth leaned against him, wrapping an arm around his waist.

"As futures go, this isn't a bad one to be stuck with," Nick said.

"And we can always make it a little better," Elizabeth said.

TOR

Award-winning authors
Compelling stories

Please join us at the website
below for more information
about this author and other great
Tor selections, and to sign up for
our monthly newsletter!